Praise for BRENDA NOVAK's
Every Waking Moment

"A page-turner... A darn good read."
—*All About Romance*

"Novak knows how to relate a suspenseful tale.
[The heroine's] almost palpable fear fuels
this gripping tale."
—*Publishers Weekly*

"A brave but very human heroine and a grieving hero
obsessed with vengeance manage to find both healing and
love as they deal with the past—and the violent present—
in this fast-paced romantic thriller. Exceptionally vivid
descriptions and realistic but not overwhelming details
of the day-to-day aspects of raising a child with diabetes
add depth to a story more complex than most."
—*Library Journal*

"This story's strong, edge-of-your-seat suspense
starts on the first page and doesn't let up until the end....
Novak's book is an extremely tense and emotional story
with a satisfying conclusion."
—*RT Book Reviews*

"Brenda Novak's gift lies in grabbing the reader mercilessly
by the throat and not letting go until the very end...
Fast-paced scenes filled with sparkling dialogue,
romantic tension, and a series of pulse-racing twists
bring the story to a heart-stopping climax.
An exciting, compelling, entertaining read."
—*Mayra Calvani, Midwest Book Reviews*

"Strongly defined characters, sizzling sexual tension,
and a tautly constructed plot steeped in danger
blend brilliantly together in Novak's
exceptionally intense, powerfully emotional novel."
—*Booklist*

"*Every Waking Moment* is an absolute must-read."
—*Dawn Myers, Writers Unlimited*

BRENDA NOVAK

DEAD

GIVEAWAY

MIRA®

ISBN-13: 978-0-7783-2886-5

DEAD GIVEAWAY

For questions and comments about the quality of this book please contact us at Customer_eCare@Harlequin.ca.

www.MIRABooks.com

Printed in U.S.A.

To Kendra DeSantolo,
who supports me in everything I do.
She reads my work and holds my feet to the fire
until I get each story just right. She donates
and shops at my annual online auction for
diabetes research. She delivers food
when I shut myself up in my house for days
to finish a book (and my family is gone and I
have nothing but a bag of almonds in my desk).
She offers sage advice when I need input on
various life subjects. She notifies me of any
bake sales in the area (I love bake sales).
And she listens when I need to complain.

I'm glad she's part of my life. She's a true friend.

Dear Reader,

Is it ever okay to do the wrong thing for the right reason? That's one of the themes I wanted to explore when I wrote this story. Clay Montgomery has certainly walked on the wrong side of the law—is *still* walking on the wrong side of the law. Which makes it pretty tough to get together with a police officer. But faced with the same set of circumstances in which he found himself nineteen years ago, he'd do it all again. That's what I love about him. He's uncompromising in his determination to protect those he loves, regardless of the personal sacrifice. I don't think I've ever created a character with such a strong sense of responsibility, or so much courage.

Please visit my Web site at www.brendanovak.com. There you can read various excerpts and reviews of this book and all my others, or sign up for my monthly contests. And don't forget my online auction to benefit diabetes research. My youngest son has this disease, so my auctions are held on my Web site every May, in honor of Mother's Day.

I love to hear from readers. If you don't have Internet service, please feel free to write me at P.O. Box 3781, Citrus Heights, CA 95611.

Here's hoping you enjoy your visit to Stillwater, Mississippi!

Brenda Novak

"Any coward can fight a battle when he's sure of winning; but give me the man who has pluck to fight when he's sure of losing."
—George Eliot (Mary Ann Evans)
English novelist, 1819–1880

1

Any coward can fight a battle when he's sure of winning; but give me the man who has pluck to fight when he's sure of losing.

—George Eliot (Mary Ann Evans)
English novelist 1819–80

They hadn't meant to kill him. That should've mattered. It probably would have—in a different time, a different place. But this was Stillwater, Mississippi, and the only thing smaller than the town itself was the minds of the people living in it. They never forgot and they never forgave. Nineteen years had passed since Reverend Barker disappeared, but they wanted someone to pay for the loss of their beloved preacher.

And they'd had their eye on Clay Montgomery from the beginning.

The only bit of luck that had gone his way was that, without a body, the police couldn't prove Clay had done anything. But that didn't stop them—and others—from constantly poking around his farm, asking questions, suggesting scenarios, attempting to piece together the past in hopes of solving the biggest mystery Stillwater had ever known.

"Do you think someday he'll come back? Your step-daddy, I mean?" Beth Ann Cole plumped her pillow and arranged one arm above her head.

Annoyance ripped through Clay despite the beautiful eyes that regarded him from beneath thick golden lashes. Beth Ann hardly ever pressed him about his missing stepfather. She knew he'd show her the door. But he'd let her come over too much lately and she was beginning to overrate her value to him.

Without answering, he kicked off the blankets and began to get out of bed, only to have her grab hold of his arm. "Wait, that's it? Wham, bam, thank you, ma'am? You're not usually so selfish."

"You didn't have any complaints a minute ago," he drawled, glancing pointedly over his shoulder at the claw marks she'd left on his back.

Her bottom lip jutted out. "I want more."

"You always want more. Of everything. More than I'm willing to give." He stared at the delicate white fingers clutching his darker forearm. Normally, she would've recognized the warning in his expression and let him go. Tonight, however, she went straight into her "how can you use me like this" mode, an act she put on whenever her impatience overcame her good sense.

The cloying sound of Beth Ann's voice bothered Clay more than usual. Probably because he'd so recently had bad news. The police chief's daughter, Allie McCormick—a police officer herself—had returned to town. And she was asking questions.

Swallowing a curse, he rubbed his temples, trying to alleviate the beginnings of a headache.

The pounding only grew worse when Beth Ann's voice rose. "Clay, are we ever gonna move beyond a physical relationship? Is sex all you're interested in from me?"

Beth Ann had a gorgeous body and occasionally used it to get what *she* wanted—and he knew what she wanted right now was him. She often wheedled or pouted, trying to coax him into a marriage proposal. But he didn't love her, and she understood that, even if she liked to pretend otherwise. He rarely made the first move, hardly ever asked her out, never made any promises. He paid her way if they went anywhere, but that was a matter of courtesy, not a declaration of undying devotion. She initiated most of their contact.

He remembered the first time she'd come to his door. From the day she'd moved to town nearly two years ago, she'd flirted with him whenever possible. She worked in the bakery of the local supermarket and did her damnedest to corner him the moment he crossed the threshold. But when he didn't immediately fall and worship at her feet, like all the other single men in Stillwater, she'd decided he was a challenge worthy of her best efforts. One night, after a brief encounter at the store, during which she'd made some innuendo he'd purposely ignored, she'd appeared on his doorstep wearing a trench coat—and not a stitch of clothing underneath.

She knew he couldn't ignore that. And he hadn't. But at least he didn't feel guilty about his involvement in her life. Maybe she liked to act as though he was the sex fiend and she the benevolent provider, but after experiencing her voracious appetite over the past several months he had his own opinions about who'd become the provider.

"Let go of my arm," he said.

Obviously uncertain, she blinked at the edge in his voice and released him. "I thought you were starting to care about me."

Presenting his back to her, he pulled on his jeans. Sex

relaxed him, helped him sleep. Which was why he'd let his relationship with Beth Ann continue for so long. But they'd just made love twice, and he felt more wound up than ever. He couldn't stop thinking about Officer Allie McCormick. His sister Grace had told him she'd been a cold case detective in Chicago—a damn good one. Would she finally bring an end to it all?

"Clay?"

Beth Ann was getting on his last nerve. "I think maybe it's time we quit seeing each other," he said as he yanked on a clean T-shirt.

When she didn't answer, he turned to see her gaping at him.

"How can you say that?" she cried. "I asked one question. One!" She laughed in a manner meant to suggest that he'd completely overreacted. "You're so jumpy."

"My stepfather is not a subject I'm prepared to discuss."

She opened her mouth, then seemed to reconsider what she was about to say. "Okay, I get it. I was tired and didn't realize how much the subject would upset you. I'm sorry."

She should've told him to go to hell and walked out.

He scowled. Although he'd tried to make it clear that he was the most emotionally unavailable man she'd probably ever meet, she was becoming attached. He didn't understand how, but there it was, written all over her face.

He had to make a change. He wasn't even willing to admit he had a heart, let alone open it to anyone. "Get dressed, okay?" he said.

"Clay, you don't really want me to leave, do you?"

He used to send her home as soon as they were finished, so there could be no confusion about the nature of their relationship. But the past few times they'd been together, she'd faked sleep and he'd let her stay the night.

Softening his stance had been a mistake. "I've got work to do, Beth Ann."

"At one in the morning?"

"Always."

"Come on, Clay. Stop being a grump. Get back into bed, and I'll give you a massage. I owe you for that dress you bought me."

She grinned enticingly but with enough desperation to make his neck prickle. He should've said goodbye a month ago. "You don't owe me anything. Forget me and be happy."

Her eyebrows shot up. "If you want me to be happy, that means I matter to you."

Determined to be completely honest—or at least retain his hard-ass image—he shook his head. "No one matters to me."

As tears slipped down her cheeks, he silently cursed himself for not seeing this coming. Perhaps he'd relied too heavily on the fact that Beth Ann wasn't a particularly deep person. Anyway, she'd get over him as soon as some other man strolled through the Piggly Wiggly.

"What about your sisters? You love them," she said. "You'd take a bullet for Grace or Molly, even Madeline."

What he'd done for his sisters was a case of too little, too late. But Beth Ann wouldn't understand that. She didn't know what had happened that long-ago night. No one did, besides him, his mother and his two natural sisters. Even his stepsister Madeline, Reverend Barker's only natural child, had no clue. She'd been living with them at the time, but as fate would have it, she'd spent that night at a girl-friend's.

"That's different," he said.

Silence. Hurt. Then, "You're an asshole, you know that?"

"Better than you do, I'm sure."

When he wouldn't give her a target, she drew herself up onto her knees. "You've been using me all along, haven't you!"

"No more than you've been using me," he replied calmly, and pulled on his boots.

"I *haven't* been using you! I want to marry you!"

"You only want what you can't have."

"That's not true!"

"You knew what you were getting into from the start. I warned you before you ever peeled off that trench coat."

She glanced wildly around the room as though stunned to recognize he was really through with her. "But I thought…I thought that for me you might—"

"Stop it," he said.

"No. Clay." Climbing out of bed, she came toward him as if she'd wrap her arms around his neck and cling for dear life.

He put up a hand to stop her before she could reach him. Not even the sight of her full breasts, swinging above her flat stomach and toned legs, could change his mind. Part of him wanted to live and love like any other man. To have a family. But he felt empty inside. Dead. As dead as the man buried in his cellar. "I'm sorry," he said.

When she saw how little her pleading affected him, her top lip curled and her eyes hardened into shiny emeralds. "You son of a bitch! You…you're not going to get away with this. I…I'm going to…" She gave a desperate sob and lunged toward the nightstand, grabbing for the phone.

Because Beth Ann was so prone to histrionics, Clay guessed she was playing some kind of dramatic game, possibly hoping to get one of her many male admirers to drive over and pick her up, even though she had a car parked outside. He watched dispassionately. He didn't care if she used the phone, as long as she left right afterward. This was a blow to her pride, not her heart, and it couldn't have come as a surprise.

But she pressed only three buttons and, in the next second, screamed into the receiver: "Help! Police! Clay Montgomery's trying to k-kill me! I know what he did to the rev—"

Crossing the room in three long strides, Clay wrenched the phone from her and slammed down the receiver. "Have you lost your mind?" he growled.

She was breathing hard. With her gleaming, frantic eyes and curly blond hair falling in tangles about her shoulders, she looked like an evil witch. No longer pretty.

"I hope they put you in prison," she said, her voice a low, hateful murmur. "I hope they put you away for life!"

Scooping her clothes off the floor, she hurried into the hall, leaving Clay shaking his head. Evidently she didn't grasp that she already had her wish. Maybe he wasn't in a physical prison, but he was paying the price for what had happened nineteen years ago—and would be for the rest of his life.

Officer Allie McCormick couldn't believe what came through her police radio. Pulling onto the shoulder of the empty country road she'd been patrolling since midnight, she put her cruiser in Park. "What did you say?"

The county dispatcher finally swallowed whatever she had in her mouth. "I said I just got a call from 10682 Old Barn Road."

Allie recognized the address. She'd seen it all over the case files she'd been studying since she and her six-year-old daughter had moved back to Stillwater and in with her parents several weeks ago. "That's the Montgomery farm."

"There's a possible 10–31 C in progress."

"A homicide?"

"That's what the caller said."

Allie thought there might have been one murder committed on that property years ago—if the Reverend Barker hadn't disappeared of his own volition. But there'd never been any proof.

This was probably a prank. Kids screwing around because of all the rumors that had circulated about Clay and his missing stepfather.

"Was it a man or woman you spoke to?"

"A woman. And she seemed damn convincing. She was so panicked I could barely understand her. Then the call was disconnected."

Shit. Skeptical or not, Allie figured that couldn't be good. "I'm not far. I can be there in less than five minutes." Peeling out, she raced down the road.

"You want me to rouse Hendricks for backup?" the dispatcher asked, still on the line.

The other officer on graveyard wasn't the best Allie had ever worked with, but if there was trouble, he'd be better than nothing. "Might as well try. I'll bet he's sleeping at the station again, though. I caught him with his chin on his chest an hour ago, and once he's out, an earthquake won't raise him."

"I could call your dad at home."

"No. Don't bother him. If you can't get Hendricks, I'll handle this on my own." Hanging up, she flipped on her strobe lights to warn any vehicles she might encounter that she was in a hurry, but didn't bother with the siren. Once she got near the farmhouse, she'd turn it on to let the panicking victim know that help had arrived. Until then, the noise would only rattle her nerves. She wasn't completely comfortable being a street cop again. She was too rusty at the job. As a detective in Chicago, she'd spent the last seven years working mostly in an office, the past five in the cold case unit. But her divorce, and coming home so that she and her daughter would be closer to family, meant she'd had to make some sacrifices. Hitting the streets was one of them.

Rain began to plink against her windshield as she drove down Pine Road and hung a skidding left at the highway. It had been a wet spring, but she preferred it to the terrible humidity they were facing as June approached.

Staring intently at the shiny pavement ahead of her, she ignored the rapid *swish, swish, swish* of her windshield wipers, which were on high but beating only half as fast as her heart. "What're you up to, Mr. Montgomery?" she muttered. She couldn't imagine he was really trying to kill anyone. Other than an occasional fistfight in the bar, Stillwater had next to no violent crime. And Clay was a real loner. But, like everyone else in Stillwater, she felt a little nervous around him. The Reverend Barker's disappearance—an incident she clearly remembered—was highly suspicious. She didn't believe such a well-respected man, the community's spiritual leader, would drive off without saying a word to anyone and without packing or withdrawing any money from his bank account. No one would do that without good reason. And what reason, good or otherwise, could Barker have had to abandon his farm?

If he was alive, someone would've heard from him by now. He still had plenty of family in town: a wife, a daughter, two stepdaughters, a stepson, a sister, a brother-in-law and two nephews.

His daughter Madeline—who, like Clay, was thirty-four, a year older than she was—was certain he'd met with foul play. But Madeline was equally certain that her step-mother, stepsisters and stepbrother had nothing to do with it.

It made for an interesting mystery. One Allie was determined to solve. For her own peace of mind. For Madeline, whom she'd known her whole life. For Barker's nephew, Joe, who was pressing her to solve the case almost as hard as Madeline was. For the whole town.

Gravel spun as she arrived at the farm and whipped into the long driveway. She realized that the property looked far better than it had when Reverend Barker lived there. The junk he'd stacked all around—the rusty old appliances, flat tires, bits of scrap metal and other odds and ends—was gone. The house and buildings seemed to be in good repair. But she didn't have time to look the place over very carefully. She was too busy flipping her siren on and off before coming to a halt.

Leaving her lights flashing, she jumped out of the car and hurried toward the front door, only to be intercepted by a woman wearing a pair of slacks unbuttoned at the waist and holding a shirt and purse to her bare chest. "There you are," she cried, stumbling toward Allie from the direction of the carport.

The woman appeared to be alone, so Allie relaxed the hand she'd put on her gun and reached out to steady her. It was Beth Ann Cole, who worked in the bakery at the Piggly Wiggly. Allie had seen her several times. Beth Ann wasn't someone she—or anyone else—was likely to forget. Mostly because she had the kind of face and body people admired. Tall, elegant and model pretty, she had healthy, glowing skin, long blond hair and slanted, cat-green eyes.

"Tell me what's going on," she said.

Suddenly, the other woman was crying so hard she couldn't speak.

"Try to get hold of yourself, okay?" Allie used her "cop" voice, hoping to cut through Beth Ann's near hysteria, and it seemed to work.

"I—I'm cold," she managed to say, glancing toward the house as if she was afraid Clay might come charging out after her. "C-can we sit in your car?"

"Of course." Allie didn't hear or see anything that made her feel threatened, but until she knew exactly what had happened, she didn't want to approach Clay. She'd never met a more difficult man to read. She'd gone to junior high and high school with him and had certainly noticed his swarthy good looks. But she'd never gotten close to him. No one had. Even back then, he'd made it abundantly clear that he wasn't interested in making friends.

If she waited, maybe her backup would arrive.

She helped Beth Ann to the passenger side. Then, once again checking to make sure Clay wasn't about to spring out of the azalea bushes near the house, she slid behind the wheel.

After locking the doors and turning off her flashers, she twisted in her seat and studied the other woman as well as she could in the dark. A floodlight attached to the barn had come on when she pulled in, revealing Beth Ann's smudged mascara. But it had been activated by a motion sensor and chose that moment to go off, and Allie didn't want to turn on the car's interior light until Beth Ann was fully dressed.

"Take a deep breath," she said.

Beth Ann sniffed and dashed a hand across her face, but more tears followed, so Allie started with a simple question, trying to relax her. "How'd you get out here?"

"I drove." She pointed to a green Toyota Avalon not far from where Allie had parked. "That's my car right there."

"Do you have the keys?"

She nodded and sniffed again. "In my purse."

Despite her desperation to escape, she'd been able to grab her purse? "What time was it when you got here?"

"About ten."

"Are you the one who called in the complaint?"

"Yes, he's an…animal," Beth Ann responded. She broke into sobs again but spoke disjointedly through them. "He—he killed that reverend…guy everyone's always talking about. The man…who's been missing for…for so long."

The hair rose on the back of Allie's arms. Beth Ann had stated it so matter-of-factly, as though she had no doubt. And her words definitely supported the majority opinion. "How do you know?"

She rocked back and forth, still covering herself with her shirt but making no attempt to put it on. "He told me. He s-said if I d-didn't shut up, he'd b-beat me to a bloody pulp, like he did his s-stepfather."

Physically at least, Clay was capable of beating just about anyone. Nearly six-four, he had a well-defined body with shoulders broader than any Allie had ever seen. The long grueling hours he worked maintaining a farm that should have taken two or more people to run kept him in shape.

But he hadn't been very big at sixteen. He'd been a tall, lanky kid with a shock of shiny black hair and cobalt-blue eyes. When he wasn't aware of being watched, he occasionally looked lost, even weary, yet he consistently resisted any and all kindness. He hadn't filled out until after she'd gone to college—presumably in his early twenties.

"Did he explain *how* he killed his stepfather?" she asked.

"I told you. He—he beat him." Much to Allie's relief, Beth Ann finally put on her shirt. Allie had seen a lot in her days working for the law—more dead bodies than she cared to count—but having the very busty Beth Ann sitting next to her half-naked, and knowing she'd probably just left Clay's bed, was a little too up-close and personal. There was no cushion of anonymity in Stillwater.

"You're telling me he killed Reverend Barker with his bare hands? At sixteen?" Now that Beth Ann was dressed, Allie snapped on the interior light so she could read the nuances of the other woman's expressions. But storm clouds covered the pale, waning moon outside, and the cabin light was too dim to banish all the shadows.

"He's strong. You have no idea how strong he is."

Allie was familiar with Clay's reputation. He'd broken a number of weight-lifting records in high school. But that was as a senior, when he'd had more meat on him, not as a skinny sophomore. "He might've weighed a hundred and sixty pounds at the time," she pointed out.

Silence met the skepticism in her voice, then Beth Ann said, "Oh, I think he used a bat. Yeah, he used a bat."

Something about this interview wasn't right, but in an effort to avoid the kind of snap judgments that could sabotage a case, Allie tried to go with it a little longer. *If* Beth Ann was telling the truth—and by now, she thought that was a pretty big if—what could Reverend Barker have done to cause Clay to take a bat to him? Had he grown too strict? Was his discipline too severe?

That was possible. Allie remembered Barker as a particularly zealous preacher, and Clay had never been puritanical. He'd always liked women—there'd never been any shortage of females eager and willing to do whatever he wanted—and he'd been involved in a few fights. But he was kind to his mother and sisters. And, as far as she knew, he had no problems with drugs or alcohol.

"The police never found a murder weapon," she said, hoping to draw more information out of Beth Ann.

"He must've gotten rid of it."

"Did he *tell* you he used a bat?"

She glanced outside at the house. "No, but he must have."

He must have… Allie allowed herself a sigh. "When did Clay make this confession to you?"

"A…a few weeks ago."

"Did you tell anyone?"

"No."

The rain began to fall harder, drumming against the hood of the car and making the air smell of wet vegetation. "What about your mother or father? A friend?"

"I didn't talk about it. I—I was too afraid of him."

"I see," Allie said. But she didn't see at all. Beth Ann had shown no fear of Clay when Allie had seen them together at church last Sunday. On the contrary, Beth Ann had touched him at every opportunity, clung to him like lint, even though he'd continually brushed her off. "And you came out here tonight, although you're afraid of him, because…" She let the sentence dangle.

"I'm in love with him."

"But…"

"He attacked me!"

"What precipitated the attack?"

"We…had an argument."

Allie said nothing, merely waited for Beth Ann to continue. Generally, people kept talking when the silence in a conversation stretched, often revealing more than they intended to. Sometimes it was the best way to reach the truth.

"I—I told him I was pregnant." She wiped at a tear. "He…insisted I get an abortion. When I refused, he started slapping me around."

It was difficult to tell in the eerie glow of the interior light, but Allie couldn't see anything more than smeared makeup on Beth Ann's face. There was certainly no blood. And she was calmer relating this part of the story, which should have evoked more emotion, not less. "Where?"

"In the house."

"No, I mean, where did he hit you?"

Beth Ann made a vague motion with her hands. "Everywhere. He wanted to kill me!"

Allie cleared her throat. She wasn't sure how she felt about Clay Montgomery, but he'd been pretty tight-lipped over the past two decades. She doubted he'd suddenly divulge his culpability in a capital crime to someone like Beth Ann, and then let her run straight to the police. Besides, if he'd really wanted to hurt her, she wouldn't be sitting here safe and sound—in his driveway, no less. By her own admission, Beth Ann had her car and her keys. Yet she'd chosen to wait for Allie instead of speeding away from danger. "How did you manage to escape him?"

"I—I don't know," she said. "It's all a blur."

Allie pursed her lips. Apparently only Clay's confession was crystal clear.

Grabbing the notepad she kept in her car, she scribbled down Beth Ann's exact words. Then she peered thoughtfully outside. "Stay here. I'd like to hear what Mr. Montgomery has to say. Afterward, you can follow me downtown and give me a sworn statement. Unless you feel you need to go to the hospital first," she added, her hand on the door latch.

Beth Ann ignored the hospital suggestion. "A sworn statement?"

"Attempted murder is no small crime, Ms. Cole. You want the D.A. to press charges, don't you?"

Beth Ann tucked her hair behind her ears. "I—I think so."

"You told me he assaulted you. That he tried to kill you."

"He did. See this?" Beth Ann shoved out her arm.

Allie saw a superficial wound that resembled claw marks. Hardly the type of damage she would've expected Clay to inflict. In a fight, a man typically aimed for the face or midsection. But it was her job to document the injury, just in case. "We'll get pictures of that. Do you have any other scrapes, cuts or bruises?"

"No."

"And yet he hit you how many times?"

"I guess he didn't hit me that hard," she replied, retracting what she'd said earlier. "He grazed me with his nails when I was trying to get away. It frightened me more than it hurt me."

An accidental scratch was a far cry from attempted murder. "What about his confession? Did you remember *that* correctly?"

"Yes. Of course."

Allie had her doubts there, too. "You'll swear to it?"

Beth Ann stared at the house. "Will he go to jail if I do?"

"Would it make you happy if he did?"

"Me and almost everyone else in this town."

Allie hesitated before answering. "If what you say is

true, prison is a possibility. But your story would require corroboration. Can you offer any supporting evidence?"

"Like what?"

"The location of Reverend Barker's body? The location of Reverend Barker's car? The murder weapon? A taped or signed confession?"

"No, but Clay *told* me he killed him. I heard it with my own ears."

Allie didn't believe a word of it. She didn't even believe Beth Ann had been attacked. But, because it was still smart to be cautious, she radioed dispatch to see if her backup was en route.

"I couldn't reach Hendricks," the dispatcher told her. "Are you sure you don't want me to wake your father?"

Allie flipped off the interior light and considered the quiet farm. Getting soaked seemed to be the only threat she faced. "No, I'll take care of it. If you don't hear from me in fifteen minutes or so, go ahead and rouse someone."

"You got it."

Adjusting the gun on her belt, Allie hung up and stepped out of the car. "Sit tight and lock the doors."

"What will you tell Clay?" Beth Ann asked.

"Exactly what you told me."

Beth Ann stopped her from closing the door. "Why? He'll just deny it. And you can't trust someone with his reputation."

Allie didn't respond. She knew there'd be plenty of people willing and eager to put Clay away based on such flimsy testimony. But she wasn't one of them. She wanted the truth. And she was going to use everything she'd ever learned about solving cold cases to find it.

2

Clay took his time answering her knock. Allie knew he must have heard the siren when she pulled up, must have known that she and Beth Ann had been sitting in his driveway. And yet the only clue that he'd paid them any mind at all was the subtle movement of a curtain in the bedroom overlooking the front yard as she'd approached the house.

When he finally opened the door, he was dressed in a clean T-shirt, a pair of faded jeans that molded comfortably to his long legs, and work boots. If he was concerned or upset, he didn't give himself away. But then, Clay Montgomery rarely revealed his emotions. He came across as brooding and uncommunicative, just like always.

Or maybe not always. According to the files, which included statements from everyone even remotely connected to Reverend Barker, Clay had once been a popular and fun-loving kid. Although Allie hadn't become fully aware of his existence until the scandal broke, there were plenty of folks who remembered him from when he'd first come to town, right after the widowed reverend married Irene and moved her little family from neighboring Booneville to the farm. Those statements also said that Clay hadn't changed into the very guarded person he was now until after his stepfather disappeared.

Which definitely left room for conjecture.

"What do you want?" he asked without preamble.

Allie had seen Clay around town once or twice since she'd been back, but he'd acted as if she didn't exist. Not that she'd expected him to take special notice of her. Only five foot three and barely a hundred and five pounds, she had a small, compact body—a tomboy's body—with dark hair that she'd recently cut into a very short style and brown eyes. Being athletic was a plus. But she had rather small breasts and wore a badge. She couldn't imagine that was a lot to recommend her to a man like Clay Montgomery, who socialized with bombshells like Beth Ann and hated the police with a passion. Even minus the uniform, she doubted she'd ever turn his head. Despite his dubious past, he could have almost any woman he wanted. He possessed more sex appeal than a man had a right to. And he had a reputation for remaining just a hairbreadth out of reach.

For many, the challenge proved irresistible. But Allie knew better than to let anything about him appeal to her. Maybe other women liked moody men, but she'd already made the mistake of getting involved with one.

Still, she couldn't help admiring the thick black hair that fell across Clay's forehead, the nose that was, perhaps, a touch too wide, the prominent jaw. Every feature was intensely masculine, except his eyes. Fringed with the longest lashes she'd ever seen, they held a world of secrets. And, possibly, pain.

"I have a woman in the car who claims you assaulted her," she said.

His gaze slid to the cruiser but he said nothing.

"You don't have a response to that?"

The forbidding expression on his face made Allie realize

why most people chose to leave him alone. Beyond his impressive height and massive shoulders, he could shrivel a person with one glance. "Does she look like I assaulted her?"

"Tough to tell in the dark."

"Then let me help you out—she's lying."

"So what are you saying? You didn't touch her?"

Although she knew he wasn't doing it on purpose, his muscles bulged conspicuously as he folded his arms and leaned against the doorjamb. "Is that a trick question, Officer?"

"Excuse me?"

He lifted one shoulder in a careless motion. "Sure, I touched her—in all the places she wanted me to touch her. We weren't playing checkers. But I didn't hurt her."

Normally when a suspect made that kind of statement, it registered only in the cognitive part of Allie's brain. She was good at gathering facts, reconstructing the circumstances surrounding a crime, solving puzzles. But working in her hometown where she knew almost everyone made police work so much more personal. Clay's comment evoked images she'd rather not see.

Wetting her lips, she quickly steered her focus back where she needed it to be. Because of who Clay was, and the number of people in Stillwater who'd love to see him behind bars, this was a more sensitive situation than it would've been otherwise. She didn't want to screw up—for his sake, more than anyone else's, although she doubted he'd believe she had his best interests at heart.

"Is it true that you and Beth Ann argued about the baby?" she asked.

"What baby?"

Confederate jasimine scaled the lattice on both ends of

his porch. Allie could smell its sweet scent despite the rain. "She didn't tell you she's pregnant?"

The word made him rock back as if she'd just landed a solid right hook. Even Clay had his limits, because he wasn't able to prevent the abject terror that flooded his face. *"What?"*

"She said you demanded she get an abortion."

"That's bullshit!" he shouted, and if Allie hadn't stepped in front of him, he probably would've charged out to the cruiser. "Bring her back here. She can't be pregnant."

Allie arched her eyebrows. "You weren't playing checkers…."

"We might've had…but we never—" He raked his fingers through his hair. "Hell, what we did or didn't do is none of your damn business. I'll handle this."

"I'm afraid it is my business," she said, refusing to back down. "Beth Ann said—"

"She's making it up!"

"Perhaps. But I have to investigate her story all the same."

His nostrils flared, but he seemed to rethink his belligerent attitude. "Okay, how specific do you want me to get?" he asked. "She was on the Pill, and I'm religious about using a condom. But we didn't always do it the conventional way. She liked it best when I used my mouth. Or sometimes I'd get her off by—"

"That's enough," Allie said, hating the blush she could feel creeping up her neck. She knew he'd been trying to singe her ears, to punish her for treading where she didn't belong, and hated giving him visual proof that he'd succeeded. But she was human and not completely at ease discussing the sex habits of such a private—and virile—man.

"Would you say it's possible she hasn't been taking her pills?" Somehow Allie managed to maintain eye contact despite the extremely personal nature of her question.

"Maybe. But not likely. She wouldn't get pregnant on purpose."

He said that with absolute certainty, but Allie could tell his mind was frantically racing through possibilities. He seemed so panicked, she almost felt sorry for him. "Because…"

"Because she wouldn't want to be saddled with a baby and no husband to take care of her. She knows I don't love her. I've never led her to believe otherwise."

"Maybe she thought a baby would make you change your mind."

"God." He pinched the bridge of his nose.

"Mr. Montgomery?"

Dropping his hand, he sighed as he met her eyes. "I want a pregnancy test. Tonight."

"I can't force her to take one."

"Of course not," he said dryly. "You wouldn't want to invade anyone else's privacy. Why break with tradition?"

Allie let the verbal jab go because he had a point. The police and others had sometimes pressed him too hard. "I can't force her," she explained, "but I will tell you that if her other claims serve as any indication of her truthfulness in general, I don't think she's pregnant."

At this, his eyebrows drew together, and he studied her more closely. Allie got the impression he was so used to being bullied by police that he couldn't believe she'd offer even this small amount of comfort. He seemed to suspect her of laying a trap for him, of trying to gain his trust so she could stab him in the back. "We didn't argue over anything like that," he insisted.

"But you did argue."

"I asked her to leave. It's my house. I should have that prerogative."

"Would you do me a favor, Mr. Montgomery?"

"What's that?" he asked, continuing to search her face.

"Will you show me your hands?"

His expression darkened as if he'd finally guessed her motive. "No."

"Mr. Montgomery—"

"I grow cotton, Officer McCormick. I rebuild antique cars. I fix my own tractors and repair my own house, barn and outbuildings. In other words, I use my hands. A lot. They're not going to look like some pencil-pusher's from the big city. I won't let you use a knick here or a cut there as proof that I struck her."

The fact that he'd called her Officer McCormick without even glancing at her badge told Allie he'd known all along who she was. They hadn't exchanged a word since she'd been back, but his familiarity with her didn't come as any big surprise. Word traveled fast in Stillwater.

"I'm not unrealistic, Mr. Montgomery," she assured him. "Beth Ann has accused you of a very serious crime, and it's my job to see if that accusation has any basis."

"And if I refuse to cooperate?"

"It might raise my suspicions."

"Which would affect the situation in what way, exactly?"

She lifted her chin at the challenge in his voice. It wasn't much, but it was all she could do to overcome his tremendous height advantage. "I might have to arrest you and take you down to the station."

"You and what army?" he asked, his eyes narrowing at the threat.

She smiled sweetly. "Trust me. I could arrange it."

"I'd get an attorney," he countered. "I happen to know a good one."

He was referring to his sister Grace, of course, who'd worked as an assistant district attorney in Jackson before moving back to Stillwater nine months ago. "That's your choice," Allie said as amiably as possible. "Grace can join us. But if I remember right, she's about to deliver a baby. Do you really want to wake her in the middle of the night and ask her to come out in the rain? It won't make any difference in the end, you know. I'll see what I want to see. It'll just take longer."

The muscle that flexed in his cheek told her what he thought of her response. He didn't like being cornered. He reminded her of a lion trapped inside a small cage, a lion that paced back and forth, resenting his captivity.

After another long, defiant stare, Clay shrugged and thrust his hands at her. "I have nothing to hide."

Allie checked his palms, then turned his hands over and examined the backs.

"So, did I beat a defenseless woman?" he asked sarcastically. "A woman who has no injuries?"

Allie noticed a few calluses and cuts, but no more than she'd expect to find on a man who worked outdoors. "I want pictures."

"For what?"

"Proof."

"I didn't hit her!"

"A picture would show that your knuckles aren't swollen and that your nails are too short to have made the gouges on her arm."

He hesitated, obviously still skeptical that she was on his side. "There aren't any gouges on her arm."

"There are now," she said. Even if Beth Ann's injuries were self-inflicted, as Allie suspected, there were other people who might try to use those marks to pressure the D.A. into building a case against Clay. Reverend Barker's nephew was one of them. Joe Vincelli hated the Montgomerys—and he had powerful friends. "Beth Ann's a bit…undecided about what really happened. But that doesn't mean Mr. Harris can't press charges if he chooses to. Now…" Allie was reluctant to move any closer to Clay but she inched forward to avoid the rain dripping down her collar. "Would you please remove your shirt?"

"What?" he said as though she was out of her mind.

Where was Hendricks? she wondered. This would be easier if she had a male officer with her. "I think you heard me."

"Why?"

"For the same reason I wanted to see your hands."

She expected him to refuse her again. Allowing her to be in charge ran contrary to his nature. But he didn't. Instead, he riveted his blue eyes on hers, and his sensuous lips curved in a devilish grin. "After you," he said.

Obviously, he was changing tactics. The best defense was a good offense and all that. But she refused to let him rattle her. "I'm convinced you've seen much more than I have to offer," she said. "I'm hardly centerfold material."

"Maybe I like my women small."

She conjured up a prudish expression. "If you don't mind, I'm in a bit of a hurry."

He glanced in the direction of her cruiser, and she knew he'd probably find it demeaning to be examined in front of his accuser.

Damn Hendricks.

"We could go inside, if you prefer," she said politely.

"Shouldn't you get rid of her first? In case you decide to stay?" His suggestive smile indicated that he was still trying to make her as uncomfortable as possible.

"She's fine where she is. I'm pretty sure I'll be able to control myself."

Chuckling, he sauntered into the house as if he didn't care, but she knew he did. The way he sobered the moment they were safe from Beth Ann's prying eyes told her that much.

"Is this really necessary?" he asked softly and there was a hint of desperation in his voice.

After all the police interest he'd endured, Allie had little doubt he wanted to be left alone. But, for some reason, getting visual proof of his innocence was important to her. Word of what had happened tonight could provoke some strong reactions, and she'd always been a sucker when it came to the underdog.

Why she thought of Clay as the underdog she had no idea. Except that public opinion was already stacked against him, and he never tried to change it. He was his own worst enemy.

"If I specify in my report that your hands and body show no signs of an altercation, the district attorney will be much less likely to take action."

"There wasn't an altercation! All I did was end the relationship."

It was the past that made the situation volatile. But Allie didn't want to tell Clay that Beth Ann had claimed he'd confessed to Reverend Barker's murder. If he wasn't angry enough already that could do the trick. Why provoke a confrontation between them while they were in such proximity? She'd simply add Beth Ann's statement to the file, where it'd join the plethora of other unsubstantiated claims Allie planned to investigate—slowly and methodically. "It's for your own protection, Mr. Montgomery."

She wasn't sure he really believed her but, with a nod that seemed incongruously boyish for such a strong man, he pulled off his shirt.

Allie had never seen a more beautiful example of the male body. A gold medallion hung around his neck, fitting nicely in the groove between his pectoral muscles. It appeared to be a tribute to a Catholic saint, which surprised her. She didn't think of him as particularly religious.

Their eyes met and, for a moment, she was afraid he could read her grudging appreciation of his looks.

"For a cop, you don't seem very comfortable with some of the stuff you have to do," he murmured, and this time all the bullshit was gone from his voice. The "I don't give a damn what you do to me" and the "I'm too tough to care." He'd ditched the whole "screw the world" routine.

"My forte is dead bodies, not live ones," she said.

"Surely live ones are more fun."

He was flirting again, but she could tell he didn't mean anything by it. He was probably searching for a way to keep his mind off the indignity of being inspected like an animal.

"Maybe," she said. "But they're also a lot more threatening."

His good humor slipped away. "I didn't hurt her."

"I'm not talking about that kind of threat." She touched his arm to get him to turn around, but he wouldn't budge.

"If I was beating a woman, and she was fending me off, the marks would be on my face, neck and chest," he said.

She saw no evidence of a struggle. But his reluctance

to show her his back made her curious to know the reason. "There are a few exceptions." She gave his arm another tug.

"I've shown you enough," he argued. But she insisted he turn around and when he complied, she saw what he hadn't wanted her to see: several scratches, all of them fresh.

"I take it you got these tonight?" she asked.

He shot her a sullen glance over his shoulder. "Not from fighting."

Right. Judging by the direction and angle of the scratches, Allie could easily guess what he and Beth Ann had been doing at the time. He'd already painted her a very vivid picture.

Relieved to be finished, she stepped away from him. "Thank you. If you'd like to meet me down at the station after I'm done with Beth Ann, I can take a few photographs, to show that you're in great shape." She blushed when she realized how her words could be interpreted, and hurried to clarify. "I mean, free from any injury that would show you've been in a fight."

He didn't acknowledge her slip. "Do you believe me?" he asked.

"It doesn't matter what I believe. I'm just going to document the facts. The district attorney will draw his own conclusions. If you're willing to play the odds that my notes will be enough of a defense if Beth Ann doesn't back down from her story, there's no need to come to the station. Otherwise—"

"Allie."

She blinked. She'd had no idea he knew her first name. "What?"

"I've *never* struck a woman. Do you believe me when I say I didn't hit her?"

She stared up at him, weighing her instincts. She'd

been trying not to make any judgments one way or the other, to simply do her job. But it was Beth Ann's words that had rung false, not Clay's. She thought maybe he needed to hear that from someone in uniform.

"I do," she admitted. Then she walked out.

Clay sat at his kitchen table, listening to the clock tick above the stove while telling himself that he didn't need to go down to the police station. Beth Ann's charges were completely unfounded. Allie McCormick had said she believed him. But he had little faith that she'd stick by her words if her father or anyone else read the facts differently. Why would she? Clay knew the night's events couldn't have reflected well on him. The hysterical woman calling from his house. The marks on his back. Beth Ann's assertion that she was pregnant and that he'd demanded she get an abortion.

It was humiliating. He was almost positive Beth Ann wasn't pregnant, or she would've told him—to stop him from breaking off the relationship. She was manipulative enough to use that bargaining chip if she possessed it. But this scare convinced him that he wanted no more women in his life. He couldn't even have casual relationships without regretting it.

"Shit," he muttered and stood to collect his keys. He'd go down and let Officer McCormick take her damn photos. Stripping off his shirt and revealing Beth Ann's nail marks couldn't be any more demeaning the second time around. He owed it to his sisters and mother to clean up the mess he'd made.

Anything to deflect interest. Anything to make Beth Ann's accusations fade away so he wouldn't draw any more unwanted attention.

Anything to make up for the past.

* * *

Allie hadn't expected Clay to show up, so she was more than a little surprised when he strode into the police station at nearly three o'clock in the morning. Beth Ann had left a few minutes earlier, and Hendricks had finally dragged his lazy butt out on patrol.

Which meant that, once again, she was alone with Clay.

"Mr. Montgomery." She assumed he'd tell her to call him by his first name. They were nearly the same age, had gone to school together. But he didn't.

"Officer McCormick."

She'd been about to pour herself a cup of coffee, but set the pot aside instead. "I'm glad you're here."

"You got your camera ready?" he asked.

"I do," she said and retrieved it from her desk.

"Then let's get this over with."

She snapped photographs of his hands. Then he stripped off his T-shirt and she took several pictures of his face, chest and arms. When she purposely neglected to take pictures of his back, he raised an eyebrow. "That's it?"

"That's it."

"So…is this going to blow over?" he asked hopefully, pulling his T-shirt on over his head.

Even with Beth Ann no longer on-site, Allie felt reluctant to discuss his alleged murder confession with him. Mostly because, regardless of what Beth Ann had said, she wasn't prepared to point a finger at Clay or anyone else. She needed proof, forensic proof, not circumstances and hearsay. And she was good enough to find it. Eventually.

But eventually wasn't now, and it was only a matter of hours before he heard what Beth Ann had told her. Especially since Hendricks knew. The other officer had listened avidly to every word Beth Ann had said. If Allie didn't tell Clay herself, he'd probably feel as if she'd duped him in some way, and she saw no reason to alienate anyone involved in the case. She'd learned long ago that help often came from unexpected places. "I don't think there are grounds for an attempted murder charge, if that's what you mean."

She let him know by the tone of her voice that there was more, and he didn't miss the inflection.

Standing with his legs spread a shoulder width apart, he folded his arms. "Somehow I'm getting the impression I'm not completely off the hook."

Allie sat on the edge of her desk. "Not quite."

The shuttered look returned to his face but not before Allie saw a hint of the underlying weariness she'd occasionally noticed before. "Feel free to explain anytime," he said.

"She says you killed your stepfather."

He seemed unaffected. "A lot of people say that."

"She's claiming you admitted it to her." Allie clasped her hands together, knowing, if he was innocent, how terrible Beth Ann's words must feel. "She just signed a statement to that effect," she added gently.

Allie had thought he'd get angry and holler, as he had about the pregnancy that might or might not be real. But he just stared at her—or, more accurately, stared through her.

"I didn't confess anything," he told her at last.

"That doesn't mean you're innocent of the murder," she said, to gauge his reaction.

His chest lifted and fell again. "It doesn't prove the opposite, either."

Allie's question hadn't rattled him into revealing more

than he wanted to. She could tell by his response that he already knew Beth Ann's statement wasn't as incriminating as his enemies would like to think. So she played it straight. "What's really going on? Is she out to get you?"

"Of course. And she's not the only one."

"That's the problem, isn't it?" she said. "Fortunately, I intend to discover the truth."

He picked up the picture of Whitney, which she kept on her desk. "What I've heard is true, then?"

"What have you heard?"

"That you're determined to find out what happened to my missing stepfather."

She waited until he looked back at her to answer. "Madeline has requested my help. We've known each other since high school, socialized a bit in the past. I'd like to bring her some closure, if I can."

He returned the photograph to her desk. "Madeline still believes her father is alive."

"What do you believe?" she asked.

"I believe nineteen years is a long time. It won't be easy to find anything."

Was that wishful thinking on his part? Or was he merely stating a fact? "I've solved older cases."

"I'm guessing those cases had some forensic evidence. There is no evidence here. Plenty of other people have tried to find it and failed, including your father."

"I have tools the police didn't possess back then."

"That's hopeful," he said, but the slight twist to his mouth made Allie wonder if he was being sarcastic.

"If your stepfather's dead, wouldn't you like to see his killer brought to justice?" she asked.

The expression on his face gave nothing away. "I'm all for justice," he said, his voice completely deadpan.

* * *

"What are you doing, waking me up so early? It's barely seven!"

Only five foot two—but with a bustline to rival Dolly Parton's—Clay's mother hid behind the door of her little duplex, which she'd recently begun to redecorate. It was becoming so cluttered with new rugs and furniture, paintings and knickknacks, Clay couldn't help worrying that others would soon suspect what he already knew. Irene obviously wasn't buying such expensive items with the money she made working at the dress shop. She told everyone she'd gotten a raise, but even an idiot would guess she couldn't be making that much.

"Considering I get up at four most mornings—" and that he hadn't slept at all last night "—I don't feel too sorry for you," he said. Especially because he knew she wasn't really grumbling about being dragged out of bed. She hated anyone to catch her before she could "get her face on," as she put it. Even him. He could count on one hand the number of times he'd seen his mother without the thick mascara she wore on her lashes and the deep red lipstick she put on her lips. "Are you going to let me in or not?"

"Of course." She tightened her bathrobe, then patted her dark hair, which she usually backcombed, before stepping to the side. "What's gotten into you, anyway? What's wrong?"

He barely fit inside the cluttered room. Since he'd last been over a month ago, his mother had acquired a new leather couch, two lamps, a big-screen TV and some sort of fancy tea cart.

"Tell me you quit seeing him," he said the moment she closed the door.

"I don't know what you're talking about," she responded, but she wouldn't look him in the eye.

The gardenia scent of her perfume lingered as she headed straight to the kitchen, which had been remodeled so that it opened directly into the living room. "Would you like some coffee? I have the most delicious blend."

Gourmet coffee. Allie's father was sure taking care of her. "Do you realize what you're doing?" he asked in amazement, following her. "Do you know what you're risking?"

"Stop it," she replied. "I'm living, like everyone else."

She was living, all right—in denial. Most of the time, her unwillingness to acknowledge what had happened to Barker was harmless enough. As long as Clay was around to take care of her and his sisters, he figured everything would be okay. He wanted them to be happy…and to forget. That was why he stayed on the farm. That was why he diligently guarded any evidence to be found there. So they could have the kind of life he wanted for them. But if Irene refused to listen, all his efforts could soon be for nothing. "Allie McCormick is working on Lee's disappearance," he told her.

She revealed no visible sign of distress. "Not officially."

"That doesn't matter. She used to be a cold case detective. She's trained in forensics."

"I know." She continued to make coffee. "She's an excellent police officer, just like her father."

The proud note in his mother's voice made Clay's jaw drop. *"What?"*

"Grace told me all about her," she said. "But don't worry. Allie's been through a painful divorce. She's lonely and bored, so it's natural that she'd want to poke around a bit. What else is there for a crack detective to do in a one-horse town like this? She'll grow bored with it eventually."

"Bored," he repeated, unbelieving.

"It's Madeline who's egging her on, you know."

"Allie's not just toying with this case, Mother. Unless I completely misread her, and I don't think I did, she's serious about locating your husband—or what's left of him. That doesn't concern you?"

He knew he should add that Beth Ann's accusations wouldn't help matters. After last night, Allie had to be more curious about him and the case than ever. But he'd been stupid to allow himself to fall into the mess his relationship with Beth Ann had become, and he was ashamed to have put his mother and sisters at risk.

Irene turned her back to him while she sealed the small package of gourmet coffee. "Why should anything Allie does concern me?" she asked. "What happened was in another lifetime. Like I've told Grace over and over, that's all behind us now. Why won't anyone let me forget and enjoy what's left of my life?"

"You're happy settling for a married man?" he asked. "A man who can only see you on the sly? Who can't acknowledge you in public?"

"He treats me better than any man ever has!" she spat, her eyes sparking in a rare display of temper. "Look at this lovely robe he gave me. Look at this place. Finally, I'm in love with someone who loves me back, someone who knows how to treat a woman."

Clay hated the guilt that welled up inside him when he thought of his mother being satisfied with so little. It was largely his fault she'd gone through what she had during the past two decades. If only he'd done as she'd told him that night and stayed home with Grace and Molly. But he'd been sixteen years old—too innocent to conceive of the possibilities, too young to understand the threat his mother had begun to sense. "Mom, it'd ruin him if anyone found out about the two of you. He's the chief of police, for God's sake!"

"No one's going to find out."

"You don't know that. How long do you think you can sneak around before someone begins to suspect? To watch you more closely? Grace and I guessed the truth, didn't we?"

"Did you tell Molly?"

"No." Fortunately, his youngest sister had moved away when she went to college and never returned to Stillwater. They heard from her often—she also came to visit two or three times a year—but more than any of them, she'd managed to put the past behind her.

"Well, even if you didn't tell her, I bet Grace did," she said.

Clay knew that was true. Somehow, though, they'd been able to keep it from Madeline. "You have to give him up. We have enough to hide already."

"I'm not seeing him anymore," she said in a sulky voice.

He wanted to let it go at that and hope for the best. But with Allie nosing around, he needed more of a commitment. "If you haven't left him yet, make sure you do."

"Easy for you to say," she grumbled.

"Not as easy as you think. Anyway, consider the people who'll be hurt if you don't. I know you care about that."

Irene slammed the cupboard shut. "It's okay if *I'm* the one who's hurt?"

"He's married! You don't have any real claim on him!"

"It's not as if I planned for this. It just…happened. Sometimes marriages fall apart."

"As far as we know, his marriage is fine. It's his libido that's leading him into trouble."

"Stop it!" she cried. "Stop treating me like I'm a tramp!"

He wanted to tell her to quit acting like one. But he couldn't be that disrespectful. Besides, he could almost understand why she'd fallen for Chief McCormick. Both the men she'd married had mistreated her. But Dale was a kind man who lavished her with gifts and attention.

"Mom, if Allie finds out, she'll be determined to prove that we're responsible for Reverend Barker's murder. What better revenge would there be?"

The scent of coffee filled the room. "Dale and I haven't been together since Allie came back," she grumbled.

Clay studied her, wondering if that was true. Judging from her expression, he decided it probably was. "That's good. But you're planning to be with him as soon as you get the chance, right?"

"No."

He didn't believe her. Without a definite breakup, he knew a relationship like theirs could go on for years. "You've got to tell him you can't see him anymore."

Tears welled up in Irene's eyes as she came toward him. Seeing her cry made Clay wish he could tell her everything would be okay. But he couldn't. If Chief McCormick left his wife for Irene, the whole town would be out to get her. They'd never liked her much to begin with—thanks to Reverend Barker. He'd isolated her right from the start by refusing to let her go anywhere except church events. He'd also taken every opportunity to imply that he'd made a mistake when he married her, that he was now saddled with a wife who was too flighty, lazy, vain—a cross for him to bear. Occasionally, he'd even criticized her in subtle, demeaning ways from the pulpit. And his parishioners had bought every word. After all, he'd had a history in this place—land, family, friends and the illusion of purity. Irene had had nothing, except the hope of a better life.

A hope the man behind the pious mask had quickly dashed.

But no one else knew that man. Not like the Montgomerys did.

"I'm sorry," Clay said softly. "You don't have a choice. Not really. You know that, don't you?"

She swiped at the tears spilling down her cheeks. "Yes."

3

"Mommy…Mommy…"

Her daughter's voice and small hand, jiggling her shoulder, came to Allie as if through a fog, waking her that afternoon. She was still tired—she'd gone to bed only five hours earlier, after getting Whitney off to school—but she struggled to open her eyes. She wanted to be available to her child as much as possible. That was why she'd moved back to Stillwater, taken a cut in pay and accepted the night shift.

"Who's this?" Whitney asked.

Squinting to see clearly in the light filtering through a crack in the blinds, Allie focused on the object her daughter was trying to show her. "What do you have there, sweetheart?"

"It's a picture," she said, confusion etching a frown on her soft, round face.

"Of who?"

"A man."

The sleepiness Allie had felt a moment ago fell away as she realized her daughter was holding a photo of Clay Montgomery. Allie had brought his file home, hoping to finish her report on last night's events. Whitney must have been going through the box she used to transfer work back and forth.

"No one you know," she said in a careless tone.

Her daughter wrinkled up her nose. "Why isn't he wearing any clothes?"

Allie might've smiled at Whitney's distaste—if she hadn't been so aware of Clay when she was taking that picture. "He's wearing pants," she said.

Whitney still seemed skeptical. "I can't see them."

Allie searched the bottom of the photograph for any hint of a denim waistband. "I guess they don't show up, but they're there."

Her daughter continued to stare at Clay. "Why isn't he smiling?"

"He's not the type to smile." Allie remembered the sexy grin he'd given her when she'd asked him to remove his shirt. *After you.* "At least not very often." Which was probably a good thing, she added silently. It was almost intoxicating when he did.

"Are you going to put this on the fridge, beside my picture?"

Allie could imagine what her parents would think of having a bare-chested Clay Montgomery facing them every time they reached for a gallon of milk. "No, honey. I only have that because I need it for work."

Hoping to divert her daughter's attention from Clay's photo, Allie asked, "Where's your grandma?"

"In the kitchen. She's getting me a snack. She said I shouldn't bother you, but I wanted to say hi."

She gave her daughter a big hug. "You can say hello to me anytime."

As always, Whitney returned the embrace with plenty of enthusiasm. She was so loving that Allie couldn't believe her ex-husband could feel such animosity for their child, that he could hate being a father. His attitude toward

Whitney was completely inexplicable to her. "You're getting big, aren't you?"

"I'm not in kindergarten anymore," she said proudly.

But the distraction didn't last. As soon as Allie released her, Whitney bent her blond head over Clay's picture again. "Is this a bad guy?"

Allie didn't think Clay was a bad guy in the sense that Whitney meant it. But his reputation suggested he wasn't an innocent, either. There were a lot of questions when it came to the Barker case, questions he hadn't gone out of his way to answer. "No. I took this picture to show that he doesn't have any marks on him that would indicate he'd been in a fight."

"Oh," she said, as though that cleared up all the confusion.

Fortunately, before Whitney could ask another question about Clay, Allie's mother's footsteps sounded in the hall.

When Whitney glanced expectantly toward the door, Allie shoved Clay's picture between her mattress and box spring. She'd taken that photo and the others to establish the truth, but she knew protecting Clay, even in the interests of truth, wouldn't be applauded in Stillwater, even in her parents' home.

"How are you feeling?" Evelyn asked as she stepped into the room.

"Boppo, I asked for cookies," Whitney complained when she saw that her grandmother carried a plate laden with a sandwich and chips. "I already ate lunch."

"This is for your mother. Your cookies are out on the counter."

"Oh!"

Evelyn grinned as Whitney hurried past her, then handed the plate to Allie.

Allie had never dreamed she'd move back in with her parents. Not at thirty-three and with a child of her own. It was humbling, maybe even a little humiliating, to find herself right back where she'd started. No one liked to feel like a failure. But Dale and Evelyn owned a three-thousand-square-foot single-story rambler on four and a half acres. It didn't make sense to pay for two households when they had so much room. Especially when living with Grandma and Grandpa meant Whitney could sleep in her own bed while Allie worked. Dale and Evelyn had a guesthouse down the hill, closer to the pond. Allie could've taken that—and would if it became necessary—but so far she liked being close to her parents more than she didn't like it. The last six years of her ten-year marriage had been particularly rough. Living in her own personal hell had made her grateful for their love. "Thanks, Mom."

"It was no trouble. How was work last night?"

"Interesting." She kicked off the covers. It was only mid-May, but she could already feel the humidity of summer creeping up on them.

Her mother smiled. "Interesting?" she asked in apparent surprise. "What, did you give out a speeding ticket? Pick up someone for expired tags?"

Evidently her father hadn't learned about the excitement last night. He hadn't called Evelyn about it, anyway. Regardless, Allie preferred not to discuss it. She'd heard her mother talk about Clay Montgomery before, knew Evelyn would believe Beth Ann before she'd ever believe Clay, and didn't want to feel defensive.

"I drove a few folks home from Let the Good Times Roll," she said—which was true, an hour or so before the call came in from the county dispatcher.

"That's it?" Evelyn asked.

"Pretty much." Allie knew she could convince her mother that Clay hadn't really attacked Beth Ann, that the evidence didn't support it. But she was uncomfortable with the fact that she'd felt slightly attracted to him and was afraid that, in the process of explaining, she might somehow give that away.

Ironically enough, in a roundabout way, Evelyn brought up the subject of Clay herself. "Are you making any progress on the Barker case?" she asked, sitting on the edge of the bed. Because she was so thin, she had more wrinkles on her face than Dale, Allie's father, who was ruddy and barrel-chested and looked about ten years younger than his real age. But her mother was still attractive, in a faded-rose sort of way.

"A little." Just reading all the reports and statements in the boxes that were stacked in the small locked storage room at the station had been a chore. Allie had one more box to go; she hadn't had time to wade through its contents yet. Her father kept giving her other assignments. And she was the only one really working the night shift. It wasn't as if Hendricks was any help.

"From what I've seen so far, there're a lot of contradictions," she said. "Deirdre Hunt claims she saw Reverend Barker heading out of town at eight-thirty. Bonnie Ray Simpson says she saw him pull into the farm at about the same time. And you know Jed Fowler was there that night, fixing the tractor in the barn. He says he never heard or saw anything."

"He also confessed to murder when he thought your father had found the reverend's remains."

"Those remains turned out to be a dog."

"So? The point is, Jed tried to protect the Montgomerys, which means he might know more than he's saying."

"True. Rachelle Cook and Nora Young's statements certainly suggest he's lying. They claim Reverend Barker was going home when they said goodbye to him in the church parking lot just before he disappeared."

Allie knew her mother had heard all of this before. Everyone in Stillwater had. She would've been more familiar with it herself, had she not moved away as soon as she graduated from high school. After that, she had college, marriage and her own work to keep her busy. She'd thought about the missing reverend only when her father mentioned some facet of the case.

"You have to decide who's got a reason to lie," her mother said.

The way her mother loved mysteries and true-crime books, it was too bad *she* hadn't gone into law enforcement. Especially since she was surrounded by a family of cops. Besides her husband being chief of police, and her daughter serving on the same force, her oldest child, Daniel, was a sheriff in Arizona. When Allie's brother called to discuss his various cases, it was often Evelyn who offered the best advice.

"Is Dad over at the station?" Allie asked.

"If he's not out on a call. Or at the doughnut shop," she added wryly. A year ago, the doctor had warned Dale that his cholesterol was too high. So Evelyn had put him on a diet. But they both knew he thwarted her attempts to curtail his calorie consumption. He'd sneak off to Two Sisters, a local café, for homemade pie, the Piggly Wiggly for chips and soda, or Lula Jane's Coffee and Cake, for a gigantic apple fritter.

"He's not very cooperative," Allie mused.

Evelyn shook her head. "He never has been. Not when it comes to food."

Only five-ten and nearly two hundred and fifty pounds, Dale could stand to lose some weight. But he'd always been stocky. Allie hated to see him denied what he loved most. "Maybe you should ease up on the diet restrictions."

Her mother shook her head adamantly. "I can't. The doctor said he could have a heart attack. Or a stroke."

"It's a good thing he's got you," Allie said.

"We could lose him if we're not careful." Evelyn reached out to tuck Allie's hair behind one ear, the way she used to when Allie was little. "Your dad and I have been together forty years. Hard to believe, isn't it? Where has all the time gone?"

Allie pressed her cheek into her mother's palm. "Thanks for letting me come home."

Evelyn lowered her voice because they could hear Whitney skipping down the hall, singing. "You should've told us what you were dealing with a lot sooner."

"I thought the medication would help his mood swings. And it did, to some extent. I could've lived with his ups and downs if only he'd cared about Whitney."

"He was just too—" Whitney entered the room, and Evelyn finished with a simple "—selfish."

Allie's daughter had chocolate smeared on her face and was grinning from ear to ear. "Boppo makes the best cookies. I'm glad we live here!"

Whitney didn't seem to miss her father. Considering the way Sam had treated her, Allie wasn't particularly surprised. "I'm glad, too, honey."

"That makes three of us." Evelyn collected Allie's empty plate. "Come on, Whitney. We'll let your mother grab a quick nap."

Whitney didn't answer. She was too busy searching the

bed and the floor. "Where is it?" she asked in obvious disappointment. "Where did it go?"

Allie had slumped back onto the pillows. She planned
to get up and help her daughter with homework. But she
craved fifteen more minutes before she had to roll out of
bed. "Where did what go?" she asked, her mind having
shifted to the poster board Whitney needed for a project at
school.

"The picture," Whitney replied.

"What picture?" Evelyn asked.

"Of the naked man. The one Mommy took at work."

Allie could feel her mother's gaze, but pretended not
to be paying attention.

"Allie?" her mother said.

"Give me a few minutes," Allie mumbled, feigning sleep.

"Mommy," Whitney started but, much to Allie's relief,
Evelyn managed to coax her from the room with the
promise of calling Uncle Daniel in Arizona to say hello.

"Will Aunt Jamie be there, too?" Whitney asked.

"Maybe," Evelyn said. "We'll see."

As soon as they were gone, Allie pulled Clay's photograph from under her mattress, intending to return it to the
file. She had no reason to feel embarrassed that she had
it. It was work, that was all. And yet his fathomless blue
eyes held her spellbound.

Was he a murderer? An accomplice? Or a convenient
target?

At this point, she had no idea. She only knew he was
the handsomest man she'd ever met.

With a curse, she shoved the photograph back between
the mattresses—she didn't want her mother and Whitney to
catch her leaving the room with it—and forced herself to
get up.

* * *

It rained again that night, and steam rose from the warm earth. Clay stood at his bedroom window, watching it, listening to the wind whip the trees against the house. The ferocity of the storm made him feel more isolated than usual, and yet it reminded him that seasons changed and life went on—even though he felt like he was trapped in the past.

The phone rang. After a long day of plowing, he'd replaced the roof on one of the sheds behind the barn. His back ached from hauling the heavy roofing material up the ladder and from bending over to attach each shingle. He wanted to go to bed. But, tired as he was, he strode to the nightstand and reached for the handset. It had to be Beth Ann. He'd tried calling her twice earlier.

"Hello?"

"Clay?"

It was her, all right. Stretching out on the bed, he gazed up at the ceiling, wondering why he wasn't angry. She'd done her best to land him in prison, which was still a possibility. But he blamed himself more than he blamed her. At least she was willing to make a commitment. He couldn't even offer her friendship.

"What's up?" he said.

There was a moment's hesitation, during which he felt her surprise at receiving his typical greeting. "You're not mad?" she asked.

"That depends on what you mean by mad."

Her voice dropped. "I'm sorry, if that helps."

She sounded contrite, which made it even more difficult to hold what she'd done against her. Maybe she wasn't the finest person in the world. But she wasn't the worst, either. And Clay didn't think he'd be nominated for sainthood anytime in the near future. "It happened. It's over. I think we should both forget it and move on."

"I agree," she said eagerly.

Did that mean they *could* move on? He squeezed his forehead, anxious about what he might learn in the next few minutes. It was unlikely that Beth Ann was pregnant—but *unlikely* wasn't *impossible*. "Just tell me one thing."

"What's that?"

Thunder boomed in the distance and rolled across the sky, loud enough to rattle the windows. "Is it true, what you said?"

He thought she'd immediately know what he meant. But he realized that wasn't the case when she answered.

"No. Whatever Allie told you, she must've made it up. I was upset and I mouthed off. But she's the one who wouldn't let me go until I'd signed that silly statement."

At this point, the damage from last night had already been done. All that mattered to Clay was whether or not there was a baby. But Beth Ann's words were so unexpected they managed to distract him. "Are you trying to tell me it was Allie's fault you said I confessed to murder?"

"Yes! She took advantage of me. Maybe you haven't heard, but she's planning to solve your stepfather's case. I guess she wants to show all us country bumpkins what a detective from the big city can do."

Allie's image appeared in Clay's mind. She wasn't a beauty like Beth Ann, but she had a unique face. Short dark hair framed large brown eyes, a handful of freckles dotted her small nose, and her chin was, perhaps, too sharp. Because of her diminutive size, the freckles made her look almost childlike. But she had a beauty mark on her right cheek that added a degree of sophistication. And there was nothing childlike about her mouth. Full and soft-looking, it seemed a little misplaced juxtaposed against that nose and those freckles, but it was a very womanly feature and somehow pulled all the disparate parts of her face together.

"Stop blaming Allie," he said, growing irritated. Allie was honest. He could tell. But that didn't make him trust her. Because it was the truth that posed the biggest threat to him.

"It was her."

"Bullshit. Allie's not that kind of person."

"Since when do you know her so well?"

He could read the jealousy in Beth Ann's voice. But he had no patience for that, either. "You don't have to know her. All you have to do is meet her. She takes that badge seriously."

"She's a chip off the old block, Clay. And the police have been out to get you for a long time."

"Allie's not out to get me, Beth Ann." At least not yet. But that could change once she discovered that her father was having an affair with his mother. Or when she dug a bit deeper into the disappearance of Lee Barker.

"I wouldn't have signed that statement without her, Clay. I promise."

Beth Ann obviously thought it'd make a difference if she passed the blame. Clay understood that, but he couldn't admire it. "I don't care about the statement you gave Allie. If that was enough to put me in prison, I'd be there already. I just want to know about…"

"What?"

"The baby."

"What baby?"

"You told her you were pregnant, remember?"

"Oh, well—" she laughed uncomfortably "—like I told

you, I was upset and said some things I shouldn't have. But I retracted them right away."

Closing his eyes, he let his breath seep slowly between his lips. "So it's not true?" he asked. He needed to be sure.

"No, but—" her voice fell to a hopeful whisper "—would you have married me if it was?"

Although he hadn't wanted to acknowledge it, the answer to that question had been lurking in his heart and mind for twenty-four hours—ever since he'd first learned of the possibility. Which was why he'd been so frightened. After what he'd experienced growing up, he wanted to raise any child of his on a full-time basis and, if he could, he'd ensure that child received the support of both mother and father. Even if it meant marrying a woman he didn't love. "Probably," he admitted.

When his answer met with complete silence, he knew he'd shocked her.

"I'll let you go," he said.

"Wait…Clay, if it's a baby you want, I'll give you one. We could make it work."

He imagined hearing a little girl's laughter in the house, or taking his son out on the farm. Since Grace's marriage, he had two nephews. Teddy and Heath belonged to Kennedy, her husband, but Clay loved them as much as if they were blood relatives. He wanted a couple of boys just like them, or maybe a little girl like Grace. Strained though their relationship had been since Barker, they were getting along much better these days. She'd always been his favorite, not only because they were closer in age, but because she was so fragile and lovely.

Thinking of his nephews made Beth Ann's suggestion more tempting than he'd ever imagined it would be— almost worth the trade-off. He was thirty-four years old.

Had his situation been different, he would've been married by now.

But what kind of life could he offer a wife and child when he was harboring such a dark secret? What if Allie McCormick, or someone else, managed to reveal the truth?

He'd have to take full responsibility. And then he'd go to prison.

Beth Ann didn't realize it, but he was doing her a favor. "No," he said, "it's over."

"Don't say that," she cried. "Let me see you again."

She didn't know when to back off. "I'm tired, Beth Ann."

"This weekend, then. Or next weekend. One last night together. For old times' sake."

"Don't," he said and hung up.

When Allie went to work, she found her father sitting at his desk with a stack of paperwork. He usually kept regular office hours, but he hadn't been home since leaving for the station at eight that morning. He hadn't even joined them for dinner. Evelyn had mentioned that he'd called to say he was busy, but Allie was surprised that he hadn't asked to talk to her. Surely by now he'd heard about the call she'd handled at the Montgomery farm—from Hendricks or someone he'd told, from the rumors Beth Ann had probably started, from the dispatcher. From someone.

"It's been a long day for you," she said, setting the sack lunch she'd packed for later on her own small desk in the corner. "What's going on?"

He grunted in annoyance but kept typing on his computer, using only his index fingers. Her father didn't welcome technical advancements with any enthusiasm. He preferred to work the old-fashioned way. "Everyone's up in arms about Clay Montgomery's confession," he muttered.

So he did know. Allie slid her report in front of him, then scooted a chair closer to his desk. "Word's out already, huh?"

"Thanks largely to your fellow officer."

"Hendricks?"

"Who else? He's done everything but call the damn paper, claiming we finally have our man."

She expected Dale to pick up her report, glance through it for the real story. But he didn't. "What do you think?" she asked.

"Hendricks is an idiot."

She checked the window for headlights, knowing Hendricks could arrive at any moment. "I agree. But his father is on the board of supervisors. And I was talking about the case. From what you've heard, do you think Beth Ann's statement will have any impact?"

"It could."

Allie had anticipated a different answer, a confirmation of her own opinion. "What about my report?"

"What about it?"

"Aren't you going to read it?"

"I don't need to."

"What?"

He didn't answer.

"Dad, if you're not going to read the report, I'll tell you. We don't have much more than we had yesterday. Beth Ann is merely claiming Clay told her something he swears he didn't. That's not physical evidence."

"It all adds up," he said indifferently.

"Last I heard, we needed more than 'he said, she said'

to charge someone with murder. At the very least, a body would be nice."

"Try telling that to all the people who've been calling here, demanding Clay's arrest," he snapped. "I swear they'd lynch him if they could, without proof that he's guilty of anything—except, perhaps, refusing to kiss the right asses."

Allie had never heard her father be so supportive of Clay. "You once told me you thought he was guilty, and that his mother and sisters were covering for him," she said. "Have you changed your mind?"

His two fingers continued to pluck at the keys. "What I think doesn't matter." He angled his head toward her report. "What *you* think doesn't matter, either. Only what we can prove."

"But we can't prove he killed Barker. So how can the D.A. run with this?"

"He can and he might. It's a political hornet's nest right now."

"That's crazy," she said. "We need to find the real culprit."

"You don't think it's Clay?" He looked up at her.

"It could be him or one of several other people," she hedged.

He went back to typing. "Don't waste any effort on Barker's disappearance."

Allie sat straighter. Her father had acted as if the Barker case wasn't a high priority to him, but this was the first time he'd actually stated it. "What did you say?"

"Whatever physical evidence there once was is long gone."

"Not necessarily," she argued. "The files themselves could contain the key to the whole mystery."

"Maybe, but what's to be gained for all the hours you'd have to spend doing the research and interviewing everyone who ever gave a statement? The offender's never acted again. It's not an issue of public safety."

"It can stop the D.A. from going after the wrong guy. Although I doubt they'd get a conviction against Clay, even if they tried him."

"They could if they tried him around here."

Allie didn't like that answer. "It's a matter of justice," she said. "Of giving Reverend Barker's relatives the answers they crave. A man has gone missing, Dad. As far as I'm concerned, it's our job to find out what happened to him."

"He went missing a long time ago," he said. "As far as I'm concerned, we've got more pressing problems."

Allie gaped at him. "Why the change of heart?"

"Solving a cold case takes months and months of hard work. You've told me that yourself."

"It does, but—"

"I don't see any point in chasing this one," he interrupted. "On or off the job. I need you to take care of the problems that are cropping up today, not two decades ago. And you're a single mom, Allie. You don't want to be spending all your off-hours working on Barker's disappearance."

After hitting a final key, he pushed away from his desk, and the printer whirred into action. As it pumped out the document he'd just created, Allie could see that it was a letter to the mayor; she hoped it explained the lack of evidence against Clay Montgomery. But she didn't retrieve it for her father. "I don't understand," she said.

He met her gaze. "What's not to understand?"

"You used to be as interested in this as I am."

Scowling, he yanked on his coat. "I've put the past behind me. The rest of this town should do the same."

"Dad, they've lost a friend, a family member, a neighbor. And they don't know why."

"They're out to pin it on someone whether he's guilty or not."

Allie felt her irritation increase. "If we solve the case, we solve the problem."

"Maybe some cases are better left unsolved," he grumbled.

"What?"

He didn't answer. "I'm beat. I'm heading home."

Allie watched him sign the mayor's letter, put it in the out-box and cross to the door. For a moment, she thought he was going to leave without saying goodbye. But then he turned back. "How about keeping things quiet tonight?" he said and tossed her a tired grin.

Allie forced a smile. "Be careful, Dad. It's ugly outside."

He paused to shake out his umbrella. "Where's that damn Hendricks?" he asked, consulting his watch.

Allie shrugged. "Late, as usual."

"Worthless," he muttered. Then he opened the door and the wind blew into the room, smelling of rain.

Allie used the coffee cup he'd been drinking from to keep his papers from scattering to the floor. At first she was so preoccupied with trying to make sense of her father's uncharacteristic responses—*some cases are better left unsolved?*—that she wasn't really seeing what was in front of her. But a moment later, her eyes focused on the cup she'd just moved. It had a teddy bear on it and said, "Life would be un-bear-able without you."

Life would be un-bear-able without you? Frowning, she

picked it up to take a closer look. Where had her father gotten this? Her mother always chose plain, masculine items for Dale, and elegant, classy things for herself. Allie couldn't remember ever seeing cutesy objects like this in her parents' house. And it wasn't the type of cup a man, especially Dale, would purchase for himself....

She glanced over at the coffeemaker and the odd assortment of cups that accumulated there. Who knew where any of them came from? she thought, and carried the cup to the sink.

4

"There you are."

Allie twisted to see Officer Hendricks standing in the doorway of the storage closet, rubbing his giant belly as if he had indigestion. It wouldn't have surprised Allie if he did. He ate more than anyone she'd ever known; he had a grease stain on his collar right now.

"What ya workin' on?" he asked, hooking his thumbs into his belt and leaning against the doorjamb.

That was rather obvious since she was sitting on the floor with the Barker files spread out in front of her. But, contrary to what a police uniform generally signified, Hendricks wasn't known for his deductive reasoning. "I'm searching for leads on the Barker case," she replied.

"Leads?" He scowled. "Why? We already know the devil who did it."

"We do?" She arched a sardonic eyebrow at him.

He reacted by scratching the top of his head, where his thinning blond hair had been reduced to a mere three or four strands. "Shoot, you're the one who took Beth Ann's statement."

"And you can prove what she's saying is true?"

"Just because we can't prove Clay's the one, doesn't mean he ain't," he countered.

She'd heard that line from almost everyone in town. But

she wouldn't accept it from a fellow cop. "You can suspect all you want. But it doesn't mean anything until you collect the proper evidence. Without it, we don't have a case."

"The evidence is there somewhere," he said. "We just haven't found the thread that'll unravel it all."

"That's why I'm combing through the files, trying to figure out what's been overlooked."

He took a handkerchief from his pocket and dabbed at his forehead. It was cold outside—cool in the station, too—but he always sweated profusely. "Last I heard, your daddy didn't want us messin' with the Barker case no more."

She retrieved another stack of files from the box in front of her. "He doesn't want me wasting a lot of time on it, and I'm not." When he left, her father had been too pre-occupied to give her any new assignments. And it was a quiet night. She didn't see any problem with pushing forward. She'd promised Madeline Barker some answers, and knew Clay's stepsister would be calling any day to check on her progress. Madeline touched base with her once a week, sometimes more often.

Besides, Allie knew if she wasn't intent on some goal, she'd nod off the way Hendricks usually did. She'd been up since Whitney woke her at two-thirty this afternoon, doing homework with her daughter, taking Whitney to her piano lesson, helping her mother with dinner, and then going through Whitney's bedtime routine. She was exhausted, but felt she owed the taxpayers. She believed pursuing the Barker case was the highest and best use of her skills. Maybe it was nineteen years old, but it was still very present in the minds of so many—Reverend Barker's daughter and extended family, the Montgomerys, Jed

Fowler, who'd fixed the tractor at the farm the night it all happened, Reverend Portenski, who'd taken over for Barker at the church, and Reverend Barker's whole congregation. Even the Archers had a stake in it now that their son had married Grace—and they were a very prominent family.

Allie couldn't imagine why her father would make this case such a low priority, especially when he used to be so determined to solve it. He'd often berated his predecessor for bungling the original investigation and swore if it had been handled correctly they would've had the answers ages ago.

So why not handle it correctly now?

"What are you findin' that we don't already know?" Hendricks asked.

"Not much," she said. But she was actually quite intrigued by the report she held in her hand. According to Officer Farlow, the officer whose position she took when he moved to Tennessee, Reverend Barker's nephew had found the pocket Bible Reverend Barker had carried with him everywhere. This was last July, and it had since been released into Madeline's care, but Joe claimed he'd discovered it at a campground on Pickwick Lake and insisted that Grace Montgomery had buried it there.

Records confirmed that Kennedy Archer had rented a spot at the campground during the month in question. Kennedy readily admitted Grace had been there with him, along with his two boys. But both he and Grace denied knowing anything about the Bible. Interestingly enough, Joe had camped with them one night, and although he and Kennedy had once been good friends, they were now pointing fingers at each other. Joe said it was Grace who'd stashed Barker's Bible; Kennedy suggested Joe had buried it there in an attempt to frame Grace.

Allie could see how Kennedy might be tempted to lie in order to protect the woman he loved. But she could also understand why Joe might resort to providing the police with "proof" against the Montgomerys. He was positive they were responsible for the death of his uncle and wanted to see them punished. He figured he'd waited too long. But, prior to last July, the Bible hadn't been seen since the reverend went missing. If Joe had planted it, where did he get it in the first place?

She made a note to ask Madeline if she could take a look at it.

Hendricks gathered phlegm in his mouth and spat into the wastebasket behind her, jerking her out of her concentration.

"Do you mind?" she asked, disgusted by the crude noise.

"Mind what?" he replied and pointed at her notepad. "What's that you're writing?"

If she ignored him, would he leave? she wondered hopefully. But she wasn't that lucky. Her silence only encouraged him to hunch down and peer over her shoulder. "If…Joe…found…the…Bible…at…the…campsite…as…he…claims…how…did…he…know…where…to…look?" He read slowly, trying to decipher her handwriting. "Where…else…could…he…have…gotten…it? Who…has…it…now?"

"Hendricks, don't you have—" Allie started, but he interrupted her.

"Heck, I can answer those questions for you." He used the door frame to straighten because his knees struggled beneath his weight. "Grace took the Bible off Reverend Barker when Clay killed him, just like Joe says."

"Then why would she keep it for so long before trying

to dispose of it? She was an assistant district attorney, for crying out loud, and very successful at her job. Don't you think she'd know better than to hang on to something that would raise so much suspicion if she was caught with it?"

"Maybe she was moving it to another hiding place," he said. "Like she tried moving Reverend Barker's body."

"There's no proof that she was moving anyone's body," Allie reminded him.

"What do you suppose she was doing at the farm in the middle of the night with a flashlight and a shovel?"

"According to her—" Allie thumbed through some sheets of paper, came up with the statement she'd read only a few minutes earlier and quoted Grace. "'After hearing so many people accuse my mother and brother of killing my stepfather, I was finally ready to see for myself if he was buried out behind the barn.'"

"Yeah, right," Hendricks said.

"She wouldn't want to do it in the middle of the day— let anyone else know she'd begun to doubt her family. Besides, if they knew what she had planned, they might've tried to stop her. Makes sense."

"I don't care. I don't believe her."

Allie wasn't sure she believed Grace, either. But she wasn't going to jump to the same conclusions as everyone else. When she operated from a preconceived notion, she often missed the most salient clues in a case. She'd learned that the hard way. While tracking down a serial rapist in Chicago, she'd been so sure it was one man when it was really another that she'd misled the whole task force and the real culprit had slipped away. It had taken them an additional two years to find him. "We can't prove she's lying," she said. "As a matter of fact, right now we can't prove anything. Joe marked the spot where Grace was digging, then we took a backhoe to Clay's farm. And what did we get for our trouble? The remains of the family dog, which died of old age before Barker ever went missing. That's it."

"We?" he challenged.

"The police," she clarified.

"I was there, and I'm telling you, as soon as we struck bone Grace was sure we'd found Barker. You should've seen her. She nearly fainted when we pulled that skull from the ground."

"She might've thought it proved someone in her family had killed her stepfather. She actually *says* that's what she thought in here." Allie slapped the report on the concrete floor. "Finding out that you're so closely related to a murderer would be shocking for most people."

"I think she already knew her brother had done the evil deed and she was scared he'd get caught."

Allie stretched her legs in front of her because they were getting cramped from being crossed for so long. "Then why didn't we find any human remains?"

"Because Clay moved the body before we could get there, that's why."

"Was Clay watching you dig?" she asked.

"Yes sirree. No one steps onto his property without him knowing it. And it's best to get permission—with or without a search warrant. It could be dangerous to startle him."

She set aside the report she'd been reading, interested at last. "Did he seem nervous? Frightened? Like Grace?"

"How could you ever tell? That man's made of stone."

Allie remembered the subtle evidence of vulnerability she'd witnessed in Clay last night, the embarrassment and humiliation, the anger and simmering resentment. He'd tried to flirt with her to ease the discomfort they were both feeling, so he wasn't without sensitivity.

"He's as human as the rest of us," she said.

"No, he's not. I could put a gun right between his eyes and cock the damn trigger—and he'd dare me to fire. I've never seen a tougher sumbitch."

Clay was tough, all right. Allie suspected that life had made him that way. How else would he have survived the constant doubt, the suspicion, anger and animosity he'd battled for so many years? Allie could only wonder why he hadn't moved as far away from Stillwater as possible. What kept him around? The farm? As Barker's wife, Irene had inherited it when he disappeared. Then once Clay had graduated from college, she'd passed it on to him. Allie wasn't sure what kind of an agreement he had with his mother and sisters as far as the property was concerned, but surely he could sell out, pay them off if he owed them money, and buy another piece of land where no one had ever heard of the missing reverend.

"Why do you think he stays put?" she asked. If he'd killed Barker and buried him at the farm, that would explain it. But if he was innocent…

"Where else would he go?" Hendricks asked.

"There must be towns where he'd be welcomed. He's young, strong, handsome. Without Reverend Barker's disappearance hanging over his head, he'd be like anyone else."

Hendricks wiped the perspiration beading on his forehead. "Guess he stays 'cause he's got family in the area."

Why didn't they *all* find a new home? Allie wondered. Molly, the youngest of Irene's children at thirty, had left as soon as she graduated from high school. According to Madeline, she was currently designing clothes in New York. Grace had left, too, but she'd come back, and now that she was married to Kennedy Archer, Allie didn't think she'd leave again. Kennedy, along with his father, owned the bank. He wouldn't want to uproot his boys, abandon the family business and leave his parents. His father had just survived a bout with cancer. But Clay and Irene had never even attempted to get away. When he returned from college, she'd moved into town and let him take over at the farm. And that was that.

"Do you know much about Clay's background?" she asked, adjusting her position so she could see Hendricks without putting a crick in her neck.

"Aren't the details all there, in the files?" he asked.

Some of them were. But the Stillwater police force hadn't investigated many missing persons—or murders, for that matter—and the files weren't as detailed as they should be. She was looking for the word-of-mouth snippets her father and his predecessors had deemed unrelated or unimportant. If Hendricks was going to impose his presence on her, she figured she might as well learn what he knew. He loved gossip and generally picked up on whatever was being said around town. "There're a few bare facts. Where he was born, that sort of thing."

"He was born in Booneville, wasn't he?"

She nodded.

"My little sister was in his class when he moved here. Said he made good marks in school. Until he was older."

"Did his grades start to fall before or after Reverend Barker went missing?"

"Mary Lee told me it happened about the same time, but I've never checked his transcripts."

"What about his natural father?" she asked.

"Ran off is all I heard."

Clay's file indicated that much, but no more. "Has anyone ever tried to locate Mr. Montgomery?"

"Not that I recall. Why?"

She shrugged, but to her surprise, Hendricks caught on, anyway.

"You don't think Clay might've killed him, too?"

She rolled her eyes. "I'm no genius, but my guess is Clay would've been too young."

He didn't respond to the sarcasm in her voice. "So you were thinking of Irene? Of course!" He clapped his hands as if they'd just solved the case. "*Now* I know why they paid you the big bucks in Chicago. I doubt anyone else has even thought of that."

Probably because Allie was the only person in Stillwater jaded enough to consider it. The cops on her father's force had never come up against the kind of heinous criminals she'd dealt with. "It's worth checking," she said slowly.

"Sure. Makes sense." Hendricks's head bobbed like the bobble-headed puppy Allie's grandmother used to display in the rear window of her giant Oldsmobile. "If Clay's father was alive, he would've come around at *some* point. The Montgomerys have lived in Stillwater for…what, twenty-three years? But no one's seen hide nor hair of him. Curious, ain't it?"

If Clay's father was dead, and the circumstances surrounding his death were at all suspicious, Allie needed to examine that coincidence. But Hendricks was getting more excited than such a slim possibility warranted. "Not necessarily. There could be lots of reasons we've never seen him. So don't get carried away," she cautioned. "Chances are, Mr. Montgomery's alive and well and living in some other state."

"Right," he said, but she could tell he wasn't really listening. He was too busy jumping ahead. "If we got Irene for one murder, we'd get her for the other. It's brilliant."

"Hendricks." She stood and grabbed hold of his arm to make sure he understood that she was serious. "It's a real long shot, so don't go spreading it around."

"Who me?" He waved a dismissive hand. "I won't breathe a word," he said. But it wasn't a day later that someone approached her at the Piggly Wiggly to ask if Irene Montgomery was a serial killer.

Reverend Portenski's hand shook as he removed the floorboard in the far corner of the old church and reached into the dark hole beneath. He had stumbled upon this small recess quite by accident a decade ago, when he was moving furniture and doing some repairs to the building— and had rued the day ever since.

If only God would let him know what he should do with what he'd found. While trying to decide, he'd replaced the heavy table that had hidden the loose floorboard and tried to forget its existence, to forget what was beneath. But during the dark quiet hours of the night, when the pressures of the day began to dissipate, he remembered the contents of this hiding place, which conjured up images he wished he'd never seen.

After ten years, he was tired of the guilt, the nagging worry, the indecision. It was time to put the matter to rest. He pulled the paper sack from the hole and walked as quickly as his arthritic joints would allow to the small study at the back of the church.

A fire burned in the sparsely furnished room. He

wasn't as poverty-stricken as such a study might indicate. He could've afforded more elegant appointments. But he had no wife or children to make comfortable and eschewed all but the most necessary physical possessions. He craved knowledge and enlightenment, and believed that intelligence was the true glory of God. So he spent every dime he possessed, above what he devoted to the church and his flock, on books. They lined the room on three sides, residing on makeshift shelves he'd built himself, using unfinished wooden planks and cinder blocks.

It was a sacrilege to bring what he carried into this room. The words of some of the greatest men who'd ever lived—renowned philosophers and theologians—resided here. But the devouring heat and glimmering flames of the fire beckoned.

Portenski pressed closer. He felt as if the hounds of hell were nipping at his heels as he drew his hand back to toss the sack into the fire.

Do it! Throw it! his mind screamed. *And never think of it again.*

But he couldn't. As much as he wanted to protect the church and the faith of his parishioners, he couldn't in all conscience destroy what he'd found. Neither could he take it to the police. He'd waited too long. Besides, doing that wouldn't change anything; it was too late.

Which brought him right back where he'd been for the past ten years: he was the guardian of a secret he could neither tell nor keep.

Slumping into his seat, he slowly opened the sack and spread several Polaroid pictures on the desk.

As penance, he forced himself to focus on each one— and then he threw up.

* * *

His mother was calling him.

Clay shaded his face with his arm and gazed toward the driveway that circled around to the chicken coop, barn and outbuildings. Sure enough, there she was, hurrying toward him in a red dress, a flamboyant hat and high heels.

"Stay there, I'm coming," he called and dropped his shovel before she could break an ankle in the loose gravel. He'd been cleaning out irrigation ditches all morning. The exertion made his long-sleeved T-shirt stick to him, but it was actually a mild, overcast day.

"Have you heard?" his mother cried before he could reach her.

He didn't know what she was talking about. If the shrillness of her voice was any indication, he didn't *want* to know. But she wouldn't have left the boutique where she worked unless it was important.

He braced himself for the worst. "What's wrong?"

"Allie McCormick is searching for Lucas."

He'd expected to hear Barker's name. "Lucas?"

"Your father, Clay! Don't you remember the name of your own father?"

With one sleeve, he wiped the perspiration rolling from his temple. Of course he remembered his father's name. It was just that he didn't think about Lucas anymore. He had more pressing concerns. But there'd been a time when he'd longed for his father on a daily basis—to the point of nearly making himself ill.

"Why is she looking for him?" he asked.

"Folks are saying I killed him! Can you *believe* it? He's probably as alive as you and me, and a darn sight richer."

He raised a hand. "Whoa, slow down. Why would Allie be interested in Lucas? He's got nothing to do with

Reverend Barker or Stillwater or anything else. He's never even been here."

"She thinks I'm some sort of black widow. Mrs. Little just told me."

Mrs. Little owned the dress store where Irene worked five days a week. Although the Littles had been grudging with their friendship at first, and still kept the relationship mostly on a professional level, they were kinder to Irene than anyone else in town.

"So she's searching for him," Clay said with a shrug. "Let her. The more time she spends on Lucas, the less she can spend on Barker."

"But what if she finds him?"

"Maybe she can collect the back child support he owes you."

She made a face. "Stop being facetious. I'll never see a dime from him, and you know it. Not at this late date. I don't even want his money."

Clay didn't understand why she was so worked up. "What exactly are you worried about?"

"If she contacts him, it might bring him here. I don't want that."

"He won't bother us, not after so many years."

"He could see it as an opportunity to make amends," she said. "Especially with you. You were the oldest. He knew you best."

Clay brushed some of the dirt from his pants. His father had never come back. Not even for him. It was a wound that would likely never heal. But he refused to indulge in self-pity.

Anyway, something else was going on. He could feel it. "You think I'd welcome him back?"

"You used to worship the ground he walked on," she said.

She was right. Lucas Montgomery had once been Clay's hero. He was the man who showed up on payday and took them to town for an ice-cream cone. The man who waltzed Irene around the kitchen, or pretended her spatula was a microphone, making them all laugh. The man who held Molly on his lap until she fell asleep, then tucked her safely in bed. Clay's life—and he assumed it was the same for the rest of his family—had been better, more complete whenever Lucas was around. He couldn't lie about that.

But even when Clay was only five or six, Lucas had stopped coming home on a regular basis. And when he began staying away two and three days at a time, the fighting started. Clay could still hear his mother pleading with his father. "Lucas, you've gotta stop drinkin' and carousin', do ya hear? The water bill's due. What we gonna do if we can't pay the water?" and "You've got children to take care of now, Lucas. How's Clay gonna learn to be a man if you don't stick around and teach him?" His father always said, "It has nothin' to do with drinkin', Irene. I'm still a young man. I've got a lot of life to live, a lot of places to see. And I can't do that strapped down to a wife and three kids."

Clay had initially sympathized with his father. It was his mother who was wrong, who tried to tell his daddy that he couldn't have any fun. She was the reason he didn't stick around like he used to. Then Lucas abandoned them altogether, and Clay was forced to grow up almost overnight. As he worked for the local feed store, making less than half of what he would've been paid as an adult, Clay had realized which parent really loved him.

Occasionally, he still felt guilty for the way he'd blamed his mother during those years. But, as a child, he'd found it was difficult to fault the parent who was always smiling and saying, "I'm just funnin', Irene, don't get yourself in a state."

"There's no reason to worry," he told his mother. "I don't want anything to do with him."

"It's his fault, you know. We'd still be living in Booneville if it wasn't for him."

"I know," Clay said. When his father walked out, he'd left Irene so destitute she'd almost lost her children. Without an education, she couldn't make enough to feed them. Clay remembered eating nothing but oatmeal for one entire summer. So when Reverend Barker had asked Irene to marry him, she'd agreed mostly out of desperation. They all knew that. Clay suspected even Barker understood. How else could he have gotten a woman so much younger and so much more attractive than he was?

At least Irene had gone into the relationship determined to be a good wife, to make the best of what she considered a second chance. Clay remembered her treating Reverend Barker's daughter, Madeline, the same as Grace and Molly, remembered her pulling him aside to say that the reverend might not be a handsome scoundrel, or make them laugh, but he had his priorities straight. He was a man of God, and they were finally going to be a complete and happy family.

Little did she know life would only get worse from then on….

"Talk to Allie, convince her to stop what she's doing," Irene said.

Clay blew out a long breath. "Why? Let her do what she wants and ignore it. If you react, she'll know she's struck a nerve and she'll keep after it."

"But she has struck a nerve! You need to explain how

it was for us after Lucas left. Tell her not to bother with him."

"Mom, you're not making any sense. If Dad hasn't looked back before now, what makes you think he's going to? And even if he does, I've just told you it won't make any difference to me. I'm sure Grace and Molly feel the same. You have nothing to lose."

She clasped her hands tightly. "That's not true," she said, her gaze intense.

Clay narrowed his eyes. "What are you talking about?"

"He called me once," she admitted.

"When?"

"Not long after Lee died."

"How'd he find you?"

"Everyone in Booneville, including his own cousin, knows I married a reverend and moved to Stillwater. I'm sure it wasn't hard."

Clay jammed a hand through his hair. "Okay, he called once. Why is that so significant?"

"I was at my lowest, Clay. I—I was inches away from a nervous breakdown. Grace was…you know what Grace was like after what that bastard did to her. She'd walled herself off from both of us. And Molly was just a little girl, confused but mostly oblivious. You were all I had, and you were only sixteen."

Adrenaline began to pound through Clay's veins. "Tell me you didn't," he said.

"Clay, I needed him. I—I'm ashamed to admit it, but I was so desperate that I pleaded with him to come back."

His chest constricted. "How much did you tell him?"

"All of it," she said. "I had to talk to someone, let the pain out. My head was going to explode if I didn't. And I thought if he knew what we were facing and how unfair it all was, he'd stand by me and be the man I'd always wanted him to be. How could any man hear how his daughter had been abused, defiled by her own stepfather, and not support her?"

Anxiety made it difficult to speak. "What did he say?"

"He promised to come. He was living in Alaska, said it was beautiful and that he'd move us up there with him."

Clay dropped his head in his hands. "Even if he'd kept that promise, we couldn't have left," he said. "You knew that. We still can't. The moment we sell the farm, the police will get the new owner's permission to search, and they'll go over every inch."

"Maybe he realized that," she said softly.

"Because…"

Her gaze fell to the ground. "I never heard from him again."

"God." Clay squinted into the distance, out across the cotton fields. What was he going to do? If Allie tracked down his father and started questioning him, there was no telling what Lucas might say. And once the details of Barker's death were revealed, they wouldn't be hard to prove. The police would find Barker's car in the quarry, where Clay had driven it. They'd get another warrant to search for Barker's remains, and this time they wouldn't walk away empty-handed. Clay had poured cement over the earthen floor of the cellar, but that wouldn't stop them. "What if he's told someone? What if he tells Allie?"

"He swore he wouldn't."

As if that counted for anything. "Can't you get Chief McCormick to call off his daughter?" he asked.

"Are you kidding? He won't even mention my name in front of her."

"What the hell does he think happened to Barker? Has he ever asked you about it?"

"No. We've never discussed it. I don't think he wants to know."

Clay clenched his jaw. "You've heard from Dale recently, then?"

"He called me yesterday."

"What did he say?"

"He misses me."

Clay knew from the way she'd spoken that she missed him, too. "Did you tell him it was over?"

She cringed visibly.

"Mom!"

"I couldn't," she said. "It was the first time we've been able to talk in over a week. But I will. I promise," she added quickly. "Just get Allie to quit searching for Lucas, okay? You have to stop her before she contacts him."

Clay rubbed the whiskers on his chin. He had no leverage with Officer McCormick. She wouldn't back off because he asked her to. Especially after the other night. "What can *I* do?" he asked.

"She's lonely," his mother volunteered.

He rocked back. "I hope that doesn't mean what I think it means."

She straightened her hat, as if she needed to keep her hands busy. "Women like you, Clay. You can make Allie like you, too. You could even make her fall in love, if you wanted. A woman will do anything for love."

"No," he said. "Absolutely not. I won't play with her heart."

"But she's attractive and—"

"No!"

"Okay, don't go that far. Just…be nice to her, take her

out a few times. Maybe you'll enjoy her company. You never know. You could do worse than end up with a woman like Allie."

Clay couldn't believe it. "Are you insane?" he asked. "How long do you think it would be before she figured out the whole scenario?"

"It's better to make her your friend than your enemy," she replied. "You're not opposed to having another female friend, are you?"

He said nothing.

"Come on," she continued. "Madeline says she's very nice."

His mother didn't need to convince him of that. He could already tell Allie was a good person. She'd certainly been fair with him the other night, despite the prejudice he faced from the rest of the community.

"I don't know," he said. He couldn't imagine befriending a cop under any circumstances. He'd spent too many years avoiding them. But there was wisdom in the old adage "Hold your friends close and your enemies closer." The more information he gleaned about her investigation—what she was finding and which direction she was going—the more he'd be able to protect himself and his family.

"I don't like it," he said. Her suggestion made some sense, but he'd be using Allie, and he didn't feel right about that. He preferred to keep his distance.

"Can we really afford to hunker down and just hope for the best?"

No. He knew they couldn't.

"Clay." His mother touched his arm.

"What?"

"We have to do whatever we can."

She was right. He couldn't pretend Allie didn't have the skills and determination to reveal what—so far—he'd managed to hide. Maybe he *should* spend some time with her, try to neutralize the threat. What better choice did he have? He could be careful, maintain just enough distance.

He wondered if he'd ever be able to throw off the yoke of the past. "Fine," he said with a sigh.

His mother smiled in apparent relief, as if she thought he'd crook his finger and Allie would forget all about Lucas and Barker. Problem solved.

If only it was that simple.

5

That evening, after Clay stepped out of the shower and finished toweling his hair, he called his stepsister, Madeline, on the cordless phone he'd taken into the bathroom. He loved Maddy, talked to her often. Irene, Grace and Molly did, too. After her father "went missing," she'd chosen to stay with them instead of going to live with Barker's extended relatives and was as much a part of the family as any one of them. They shared everything with her—except the secret destined to make her hate them if she ever found out.

"Hey, I ran into Beth Ann when I was getting gas today," she said the moment she heard his voice.

He hung the towel on the rack behind him. "Am I supposed to be excited about that?"

"I thought you might want to know that I already heard what happened at the farm night before last."

"Somehow that doesn't surprise me," he said, leaving the steamy bathroom and heading into his bedroom.

"Well, maybe this will. The version she gave me is quite different from the rumors going around town."

He twisted in front of the mirror to see how the scratches on his back were healing. "Is this good or bad news?"

"Good news."

The scratches were almost gone. That was good news, too. "Then she didn't tell you I tried to kill her?"

"She just said you broke up with her."

"Even that isn't true," he muttered as he delved into his underwear drawer.

"How's that?"

"There wasn't any commitment between us to begin with."

"She was hoping for one. She feels terrible about calling the cops on you, by the way. She claims she's in love with you."

He pulled on his boxer briefs. "Don't worry. She'll be in love with someone else next week."

"You're so cynical," she said, laughing. "But maybe you're right. She had John Keller in the car while she was crying over you, and he seemed more than willing to comfort her."

"John Keller?" he repeated, not immediately recognizing the name.

"The guy who manages Stillwater Sand and Gravel for Joe Vincelli's parents. Why? Jealous?"

"No." He selected a pair of jeans. "I thought Joe managed the gravel pit."

"He has the title. But he doesn't do much other than chase women and drink beer. At least since he divorced Cindy. John's the one who keeps the business afloat."

If Madeline said it, it was probably true. No one knew Stillwater and the people living in it better than she did. It was her job to know. She owned the *Stillwater Independent,* a weekly paper she'd bought two years ago from the old couple who'd published it before.

"Good old Joe," he said, putting on his pants.

"I know. Not your favorite person."

"An understatement if I've ever heard one." Joe had instigated the last search of the farm. And Joe had mistreated Grace. Clay knew he didn't have the whole story and doubted Grace would ever tell him, but he'd gathered enough to suspect that the hatred between his sister and Joe stemmed from high school. Clay also guessed the contact between them had been sexual in nature. But after what his sister had been through, he didn't judge her. Barker had nearly destroyed her. After what had happened when she was only thirteen, she'd acted out in various ways, no doubt hoping to finish the job—and Joe had been there, ready and eager to take advantage, to inflict even more damage.

Clay had done what he could, but Grace had thwarted his attempts to protect her, and he couldn't help her if she wouldn't confide in him. So, he'd watch helplessly as she searched for the attention she needed, the love and support she'd rejected from her family.

Until recently. Somehow, she'd managed to survive even her own self-loathing and Joe's opportunistic abuse. And now she was happy, and Clay was going to make damn sure she stayed that way, if he had to sit at the farm and guard whatever forensic evidence remained until he rotted right along with Barker.

Which reminded him of the purpose behind his call.

"What are you doing tonight?" he asked, holding the phone with his shoulder so he could button his fly.

"Kirk said he'd like to shoot some pool. Why? Want to come?"

Kirk Vantassel, a roofing contractor, was Madeline's longtime boyfriend. Clay kept expecting them to marry but, so far, they weren't even engaged. In some ways, they acted more like brother and sister than boyfriend and girlfriend.

"I know you don't like crowds, and Good Times is busy on Friday night," she said. "But it'd be fun for you to get out. You don't do it often enough."

"I'll meet you over there." He held the phone out as he pulled on a T-shirt. "Any chance you could convince Allie McCormick to come?" he asked when he had his head through.

"You mean with us? You want me to set you up with Allie?"

"Nothing like that," he replied. "I was just hoping to get to know her a little."

"I see," she said, drawing the word out as though she saw far more than he intended.

"Stop it." He shrugged into a button-down shirt and splashed on some cologne. "She's investigating Dad's case, isn't she? I figure I might as well talk to her, see if there's anything I can do to help." Clay hated making such statements, hated being the hypocrite he was when it came to Maddy but, once again, past actions propelled current ones.

"Considering how you feel about the police, that's generous of you. I'll call her," she said. "I've been meaning to, anyway. She left a message on my answering machine, asking about Dad's Bible."

"Why? Does she want to look at it?"

"Yeah."

Clay felt another trickle of unease. Would Allie see the demented man behind the notes the reverend had made in the front and back pages of that Bible? Or, like Madeline, would she see a pious man who loved his new family—and was particularly impressed with his oldest stepdaughter?

At times like this, Clay felt almost justified in keeping

the truth from Madeline. Wondering where her father had gone was hard. Especially because she had to deal with the fear that he'd abandoned her. But learning that her father wasn't fit to breathe the same air as other human beings would be much harder. Of course, that was assuming she'd believe the truth if she heard it. Certainly no one else would.

"I'm going to grab some dinner," he said. "I'll see you at Good Times."

"Are you eating at home or in town?"

"I'm on my way to Two Sisters. Why? Would you like to join me?"

"I'm tempted, but I should finish the article I'm working on. Besides, Kirk's still out, patching a leaky roof. I'll eat with him, then catch up with you later."

"What article are you writing?" he asked. Whatever it was, Clay hoped it wasn't about him. One week, his stepsister had published a piece on the cars he restored in his barn and the fact that he'd recently sold a 1957 Chevrolet Bel Air for $52,000 and had a client waiting for his 1960 Jaguar XJ6 at a much higher price. Another week she'd written about the way he managed "a large, successful farm" all on his own, as if there'd never been a better farmer. But the worst was when she'd put him in her Singles section and referred to him as "appealing to women" and possessing an "elusive, mysterious allure." Suspicions being what they were, he already drew enough attention when he walked into a room. He didn't need her training the spotlight on him.

But, according to Madeline, she sold more papers when she included an article about him, so he didn't complain. He figured it wouldn't kill him to occasionally boost her circulation.

Still, he cringed at her next words.

"After the thing with Beth Ann, I'd like to do one on what causes a woman to make false claims against the man she loves."

"When?"

"In a few weeks."

Hoping she'd forget by then, he picked up his wallet and keys. "What are you working on now?"

"A series of articles on Allie."

"Will they run in the Singles section?"

"No, this is front page stuff. I'm writing about some of the murders she solved while she was working in Chicago."

"Sounds interesting."

"It is. In one case, she found the guilty party because of the stitching on the bedsheet that was wrapped around the victim's body."

"The stitching?" he repeated.

"Yeah. I guess she could tell that the sheet wasn't the type typically purchased for home use. So she contacted the big commercial cleaners who wash linens for hotel chains in the area and, sure enough, each hotel has different-colored stitching to designate which sheets belong where."

"How did that lead her to the killer?" he asked.

"You can read the details when the article comes out. It was pretty darn smart of her. But, basically, she traced the sheet to a major downtown hotel and one of their employees."

"Great," Clay said. But he wasn't sure he wanted to read the article. He was worried enough already.

"Allie?"

Her father's voice intruded on the Disney movie she was watching with Whitney. Picking up the remote, she muted the sound so Dale wouldn't have to yell quite as loudly. "What?" she called back.

"Telephone!"

Allie hadn't heard it ring. She'd been dozing. She was off work for the weekend, which meant she could sleep through the night. But she was having trouble staying awake until bedtime. "Coming!"

She turned up the volume again, leaving Belle singing to the Beast as she walked into the adjoining room—her father's den. It took a moment to find the phone amid the clutter on his desk. "Hello?"

"Allie?"

"Yes?"

"It's Madeline."

Allie sank into her father's leather chair. She'd been expecting this call. "How are you?"

"Good. And you?"

"Hanging in there."

"Glad to hear it. I have the Bible you were asking about. I've pored over every single word and I can't find anything that could be called a clue. But I'd be happy to let you see it."

"A fresh pair of eyes might help. I'm not making quick progress on your father's case, but I am working on it. It takes a while to go through so much material, especially when I'm trying to note every detail."

"I understand. I'm grateful you're being so thorough. You'll uncover the missing piece. I'm sure of it."

Allie pitied the hope in Madeline's voice. Maddy had waited nineteen years to find out what had happened to her father and was still waiting. Allie couldn't imagine how difficult that must be. "I can't make any promises, but I'll try."

"If anyone can help me, you can."

Allie prayed that Madeline's confidence wasn't misplaced. For every case she'd solved, there were at least five she'd been unable to break. That was the nature of the business. She'd mentioned those statistics when she'd granted Madeline the interview for the paper, had talked about evidence that was often too degraded to use and key witnesses who'd died or could no longer remember what they'd seen or heard. But Madeline had focused on Allie's successes. Apparently Madeline's five-part series would summarize some of her toughest cases, but only those that had a happy ending.

Maybe Madeline needed to tell those stories to bolster her faith that she'd eventually find the resolution she sought.

"I'll do my best," she said again.

"I know you will. Anyway, I have another question for you."

Allie rolled closer to her father's desk and glanced idly through his Rolodex. "What's up?"

"Are you working tonight?"

"No, why?" She stopped at the number for a Corinth florist written in her father's hand. She'd never known him to order flowers. He was too practical. Had someone died? No one close to them. And if it was a professional acquaintance, her father would've handled it at the station….

"I was hoping you might be interested in going out dancing or playing pool tonight."

As she considered Madeline's invitation, Allie continued to flip through the small cards. She liked Madeline a lot and ordinarily would've jumped at the chance to go out with her. They'd sometimes hung out when they were kids. And although her two best friends from high school had married and moved away shortly after she did, there were other people she remembered and wanted to see. So far, though, she'd been too busy moving, getting Whitney started in a new school and becoming familiar with her job.

But she was *so* tired. "I would if I could keep my eyes open," she said, covering a yawn. "I'm still getting used to working graveyard."

"Really?" Madeline seemed genuinely disappointed. "Clay was hoping you could make it."

"Clay?" she repeated, nearly choking on the name.

"He called me a few minutes ago and asked me to invite you."

Allie's jaw dropped as she immediately conjured up an image of Clay—the image in the picture beneath her mattress. "Why would your brother want me there?"

"He said he'd like to get to know you, and maybe talk about Dad."

Dad... Madeline had said that as if Clay called Barker "Dad," but he didn't. At least not in front of Allie. Did he play it differently when he was with Madeline?

It'd be interesting to watch the two of them together, Allie thought, when they were relaxed and didn't feel they were under scrutiny. The way they interacted might tell her something about the case, certainly more than Clay intended to divulge.

"If he's ready to share, I guess I'd better not miss out," she said, reversing her earlier decision. "He's not usually so open."

"Not to police officers in general, but that's because they're almost always prejudiced against him," Madeline said, a defensive note creeping into her voice. "He's not the one responsible for whatever happened to my father."

"You've told me that before. But I can't rule him out, Maddy." Especially since Joe Vincelli and others claimed exactly the opposite. "I can't rule anybody out. I have to keep an open mind. Otherwise, I won't be any good to you."

Madeline seemed to struggle between loyalty and common sense.

"Tell me this," Allie said softly.

"What?"

"If it was Clay—"

"It's *not*," she insisted. "Don't listen to what people around here say. They don't know him the way I do."

"I'm just asking—*if it was*—would you want to know?" To Allie, justice was justice. The case needed to be solved, regardless. But did Madeline really understand what she was asking? She craved answers, but what if those answers only caused her fresh pain?

"I don't have to worry," Madeline said. "It's not him."

For Madeline's sake—and Clay's, too, because he was so young when it'd all happened—Allie hoped not. "I'll take your word for it," she said. "For now. But I definitely don't want to miss out on the opportunity to talk to Clay while he's willing to speak with me."

"There'll be other chances."

Allie wasn't willing to risk it. "No, I'll tank up on coffee and go out with you. Just let me get Whitney to bed."

"Okay. But don't press my brother too hard. He doesn't socialize much, and I want him to have a nice time tonight."

"I'll be on my best behavior," Allie said. But she couldn't imagine anyone pressing Clay further than he wanted to go.

* * *

Clay spotted Allie the moment she opened the door of the crowded pool hall. She was wearing a black miniskirt and a hot-pink, long-sleeved stretchy top. The skirt could've been a lot shorter, but it was short enough to be surprising on someone so conservative. And while the top wasn't low-cut, it clung to her in all the right places. Maybe she wasn't soft and voluptuous, but she looked… trim, fit and well proportioned, especially for her size. She'd also put some gel in her hair and styled it in a shaggy, fashionable way. The short length emphasized her eyes—and her slightly oversize mouth. That mouth had been sexy even when she wore that off-putting uniform.

Clay saw more than a few male heads turn as Allie spotted him, Madeline and Kirk and began to stride toward their table in the back corner. Evidently, he wasn't the only man in the place impressed with her transformation.

"Hi," she said, giving Clay a no-holds-barred smile as she slid into the one empty chair, which happened to be right next to him.

He refused to let his gaze linger on her mouth. "Hello," he responded. Then he drained his beer. He had a feeling that it was going to be a long night. He didn't like what he was doing or why he was doing it. But that didn't matter. He had to do what he could. It always came down to necessity.

"You look great," Madeline said. "I hope you've found your second wind."

"I took some No-Doz. It was quicker and easier than drinking a gallon of coffee," she said.

Clay knew his stepsister was very attractive, with her long, thick auburn hair, dramatic cheekbones and large hazel eyes. But Allie didn't look drab by comparison. It was her mouth…. And that beauty mark. Heck, Clay was even beginning to like her freckles. She was different, unusual…and seemed unaware of the effect she was having on the men around her.

"Coffee makes me jittery if I drink too much," Allie was saying. "It's the curse that goes along with having a high metabolism. I'm usually hyper until I can't go anymore, and then—" she snapped her fingers "—I'm out. So, if this affects me the same way and I go to sleep—" she smiled at Clay again "—wake me up."

"We'll take care of you," he said.

Her eyes met his, and he read frank curiosity in them.

"Would you like a drink?" he asked.

"I'll have a beer."

At his wave, the waitress hurried over, and he ordered two beers. "Anyone else?"

"I'm all set," Madeline said.

Kirk lifted his half-filled glass. "Me, too. I don't know about you, but I'm ready for a game of pool."

Kirk was as easygoing and affable as he looked. Until he was confronted by a threat to someone he loved. Then he was a force to be reckoned with. Clay liked him, thought he'd make Madeline a fine husband.

"A table's opening up," Madeline said, calling out to a friend to hold it for them. "We gonna bet on the game?"

"Hell, yeah," Kirk replied. "I came to win big." Shoving his dark hair out of his eyes, he turned to Allie. "Fifty bucks says Maddy and I can take you and Clay."

"I'll bet fifty, too," Madeline said.

"You?" Clay asked, obviously taken aback.

"I'm expecting a sizable tax refund."

"So what do you say?" Kirk's focus was still on Allie.

Allie's eyebrows slid up. "You two aren't confident or anything, are you?"

"We might be confident, but are we any good? That's what you have to ask yourself," he replied with a teasing wink.

"That's not the only factor in the equation." Allie winked right back. "Maybe you two *are* good, but maybe Clay and I are better."

Madeline made a taunting sound and spoke over Kirk. "Ooh, I love it. She's not going to let you intimidate her."

"We won't know until we play," he said.

Allie leaned closer to Clay, thoughtfully tugging on her bottom lip. "You've seen what these two can do. What do you think? Will I have to carry you?"

Clay coughed in surprise. Women generally assumed he'd be the better player.

"I might be a burden," he replied dryly, "but I'll try to hold my own."

She studied him a little longer, then flashed him a grin. "Let's do it."

As Allie, Kirk and Madeline headed over to the pool table, Clay intercepted the waitress who was bringing their drinks and carried them into the back room, where Kirk was already racking balls.

Allie accepted her beer with a nod of thanks, took a sip, then set it on the edge of the table. "Who breaks?" she asked above the babble of voices around them.

"You can," Kirk said, but Allie didn't respond. She was too busy staring across the room.

Clay followed her gaze to see Joe Vincelli coming toward them, a smirk on his face.

"Out on the town tonight, Officer McCormick?" he asked.

Allie's spine visibly straightened. "Something wrong with that, Mr. Vincelli?"

"No, of course not. It's just that when you said you were going to find the man responsible for my uncle's murder, I didn't expect you to go out drinking with him. That's a hell of a way to investigate."

Instinctively, Clay stepped in front of her. He wouldn't allow Joe to bully a woman in his presence. But, even at barely over five feet tall, Allie didn't seem to feel she needed his protection. She put a hand on his arm and gently but firmly pushed him out of the way. "I'll drink with whoever I want," she stated flatly.

Joe's jaw tightened as his eyes sought Clay, but Clay could sense that he was weighing his response. Obviously not wanting to get his ass kicked, Joe reined himself in, which came as a bit of a disappointment to Clay. He'd long been eager for the opportunity to rearrange Joe's weasel-like features.

"What's your problem?" Clay asked. "Why are you always harassing women? First Cindy, then Grace and now Allie. I'm right here, Joe. If you want a piece of me, let's take it outside."

He thought Allie might interfere—maybe assume her role as cop—but she didn't. She stood where she was and didn't speak, but he could feel the tension in her as Joe considered his options.

Finally, Joe backed away. "He's a cold-blooded killer, Allie. Don't let him fool you."

"He doesn't frighten me," Allie said. "Nor will he or anyone else interfere with the integrity of my investigation."

Joe risked throwing one more glance at Clay. "If that's the truth, I wouldn't go anywhere alone with him. Maybe if you learn too much, you'll go missing next."

6

Cursing Joe Vincelli, Allie bent over to take her first shot. Just when Clay seemed to be relaxing, Joe had to come up and cause trouble. Now Clay was wearing a closed, rather grim expression and had fallen silent. Why couldn't the people in this town trust her to do her job?

Setting the cue ball on the dot, she sent it flying into the triangle of solids and stripes, which scattered across the table. Two solids dropped with a double thunk into opposite corner pockets. The others rolled to a stop. She didn't do as well on her second shot, but she didn't leave her opponents with anything they could capitalize on, either.

"Not bad, eh?" she said, teasing Madeline and Kirk.

"I haven't lost any money yet," Kirk said and motioned for Madeline to take her turn.

When nothing fell for Madeline, Kirk put his arm around her and, kissing her temple, joked none too quietly that she'd better come up big next time or he was going to dump her.

Clay chuckled as he chalked his cue. "Watch it," he said. "That's my sister you're talking to."

Secretly admiring his fluid movements, Allie watched Madeline's stepbrother circle the table. When he paused at the end, as though he'd found an angle he liked, he looked up at her.

"Do you really want to take the toughest shot available?" she asked in amazement.

"Yes, he does," Kirk said, laughing. "This game's no fun for him unless he tries fancy shit like that. That's how I knew we were going to win."

Allie arched an eyebrow at Clay. "You try that, and you're the one who'll have to pony up the cash when we lose."

Clay's teeth flashed as he grinned at her, and she knew she'd said just the thing to make him relish the challenge. Bending over the cue ball, he tried to bank the three twice before sending it into the side pocket.

The move didn't work.

"Nice," she said sarcastically.

He came around the table and clicked his beer bottle against hers. "I'm depending on you to pull us out."

Allie wished she didn't like the smell of his cologne, or the way his jeans fit his body. But she did. For the duration of the game, she almost forgot she'd come to the pool hall with a goal in mind. Especially when they lost. Because Clay had actually sunk as many balls as she had, he made her split their losses with him.

"At least I took reasonable shots," she complained. "The shots you attempted were crazy."

"I made a few," he said.

And he had. Which was pretty impressive. He was obviously a much better player than the rest of them, but he hadn't exploited his advantage.

"Let's get another drink," Madeline said. "Then we'll play again."

"Okay, but I'm not betting any more money," Allie said, sulking. "Cops don't make enough to get taken at pool, especially by their own partners."

In the crush near the bar, she and Clay got separated from Kirk and Madeline. Allie almost lost Clay, too—but then his fingers curled around her hand and he guided her through the people between them. "So why'd you become a cop?" he asked as the press of bodies jostled them closer.

"I guess I like the chase," she said.

She hadn't realized how flirtatious that would sound until the words were out of her mouth.

Clay pivoted to face her, his expression conveying surprise and predatory interest. She'd definitely caught his attention. Deep down, she knew she was too fresh from her divorce, that she was letting the excitement of this night go to her head. But she felt young and free, as if she'd managed to turn back the clock ten years, and it was an exhilarating experience. Especially after she'd put in so much work and time and effort to get through college, get a job, improve her marriage, survive her divorce, raise her daughter....

"The chase, huh?" he murmured, his gaze riveted on her lips. "What's it like when you get your man?"

Her heart began to pound. She'd started this, so she wasn't about to reveal that she was already in over her head. "Last time I'm afraid the chase was the best part," she admitted. "But I'm not sure that was entirely my fault."

"Last *time?*"

"I've only been with my ex."

"Sounds as if it was disappointing."

"Very."

"It's not always like that."

She gave him a weak grin. "I'll take your word for it."

"Not interested in a walk on the wild side, eh?"

"I'm the daughter of a cop, remember?"

"And a cop yourself. How could I forget?" He averted

his eyes, but she could feel his hand at her back, steering her through the crowd. The warmth of his touch seemed to burn right through her shirt, but she was glad he was there when someone in front of her threw a playful punch and the person who dodged to get out of the way stumbled and nearly fell into her.

Clay pulled her out of danger, against his chest. "Did he step on your toes?" he murmured in her ear.

His breath tickled. Suppressing a shiver, she said, "No. Thanks to you," and purposely avoided his touch as they continued to the bar.

They each got another beer, then went to play a second game of pool. This time she and Clay won back their money. But the No-Doz she'd taken before she'd come wasn't mixing well with the alcohol. She was beginning to feel as if she were floating above everyone else.

She needed to find a ride home, she decided. She'd lost all focus on the reason she'd come; she'd have to talk to Clay later, when her mind was clear.

But Madeline wouldn't hear of letting her leave so early. Clay's sister announced that they should all dance and, a few seconds later, Allie found herself in Clay's arms, swaying to Rascal Flats singing "Bless the Broken Road."

"Are your parents amenable to watching your daughter when you go out?" he asked, his voice a deep rumble.

"It hasn't been an issue so far," she said. "This is the first time I've gone out at night, other than to work."

"In *six weeks?*" he said.

"Is that how long I've been back?" She couldn't remember clearly. In any case, she didn't really want to talk. She wanted to listen to the music and press closer to the hard body that was moving against hers, making her breasts tingle. It felt like forever since she'd been with a man, especially a man who smelled as good as Clay—

Suddenly, he shifted to hold her away from him.

She looked up and would have released him, except that he kept his hands on her waist.

Was she the one who'd snuggled so close? She must've been. Otherwise, he wouldn't have reacted like that. "I'm sorry," she said, embarrassed. "I'm not thinking straight."

"I know."

"I've gotta go."

He didn't answer immediately, but when he did, he said, "That's probably a good idea. I'll take you home."

"No, you've got your stepsister and Kirk here. I'll call my father."

"There's no need. I'm leaving anyway. Meet me outside in five minutes," he said as if it had all been decided.

"*Meet* you?" she repeated. "Are you going somewhere else before we leave?"

He subtly indicated one side of the room. When she glanced over, she saw that Joe was watching them again.

"You don't want to start any rumors, do you?" he said, putting his back to Barker's nephew and effectively shielding her from his view.

Her thoughts were a little fuzzy, but she was fairly sure any rumors that might get started wouldn't bother Clay in the least. Folks had whispered about him for most of his life. And having people believe he'd bagged the cop who was supposed to convict him of Barker's murder would be a feather in his cap. Wouldn't it?

Which meant…he was protecting her. He'd been protecting her when he put some space between them while they were dancing, too, she belatedly realized. But he was supposed to be the bad guy. So why wasn't he taking advantage of the situation?

She thought of the pool they'd played. He could easily have stoked his own ego by dominating the game and walking away with all the winnings. But he hadn't. He'd kept each game close, even lost the first one. And now, instead of slinging an arm around her and taking her outside as if he'd just claimed some kind of trophy, he was thinking of her—and how any affiliation with him would affect her.

She liked Clay. A lot.

But she was light-headed, she reminded herself. For the sake of remaining objective in her investigation, and preserving her peace of mind, she hoped she'd like him a great deal less when she sobered up.

Clay could tell Allie was tipsy but, except for those few minutes on the dance floor when she'd melted into him, she was trying hard to compensate. She sat in his truck as he drove, holding herself rigid and staring out at the landscape as if she was afraid she might say or do something she'd regret if she wasn't careful.

"Do you plan on living with your parents for very long?" he asked.

"I never planned on moving back home in the first place."

"You seem to be making it work."

"It's better than farming my daughter out to day care."

"That was your other choice?"

"If I'd stayed in Chicago and kept my old job."

"What about your ex-husband? He couldn't help?"

"When you have a man who never wanted a child in the first place, you don't get a lot of support."

Clay knew what that was like. His father had never wanted him or his sisters or things would've turned out differently. "At least in this day and age he has to provide some financial support."

"No, he doesn't."

Clay turned on the car radio. "How's that?"

"I made him a trade. He signed papers relinquishing his rights to Whitney, and I gave up child support."

Clay wished he could ask why she'd done that. Regardless of whether or not her ex had wanted the child, he *was* her father. But those questions were far too personal.

"Take this street," she said.

"I know where you live." He could tell she wasn't interested in conversation. Even though she hadn't drunk all that much, she was too busy fighting the effects of the alcohol combined with the No-Doz she'd taken earlier. But he figured this might be his only chance to talk to her about Lucas, to—hopefully—dissuade her from contacting him.

"Word has it you're interested in finding my father," he said as they came to a stop at the intersection of Fourth and McDonald.

She looked over at him, seeming puzzled. "You knew that."

He lowered the volume on the radio, which, oddly enough, was playing the same song they'd just danced to. "I'm talking about my real father."

"Oh."

He drove down McDonald, then took Response Road. "Why Lucas?" he prompted.

"It's not because I think your mother's a serial killer, if that's what you've heard." She scowled and, talking mostly to the window, she muttered, "I hate the gossip in this town."

Clay opened the vents to stop the windows from steaming up. "What are you after, then?"

She tucked a few strands of her short hair behind a small, perfectly shaped ear. "General information. I always do a thorough background search on everyone involved in my investigations. I'd be stupid not to. People don't exist as separate entities. We're all part of a network, a number of networks. I can't get a clear picture of who I'm dealing with if I don't also examine the networks."

"But Lucas isn't part of my family's 'network.' He left long before Lee Barker went missing."

"Lucas? You don't call him Dad?"

Clay passed a slower moving truck as he headed away from town. Maybe Allie was slightly drunk but she was perceptive enough to capitalize on what he'd said instead of letting him guide the conversation. "He walked out when I was only ten years old. What else would you expect?"

"That must've been rough," she said.

"We survived." Not easily, but he didn't add that. "And I don't want him coming back."

She closed her eyes and leaned her head against the seat. "You think he might?"

"I'd rather not take the chance."

She regarded him from beneath her lashes. "Then I should probably tell you not to worry. He's remarried and living in Alaska."

Her words provided a one-two punch that made Clay ease off on the gas. She'd already spoken to Lucas? Had he kept his mouth shut? Or had he let some detail slip that would eventually expose them?

And, on a deeper level, how come Lucas had finally settled down? He hadn't loved his first family enough to stick by them, hadn't loved Clay enough. But he could do it for someone else?

"Are you okay?" she asked.

They were still decelerating. Clay brought the truck up to normal speed. "Of course."

"Maybe we should talk about this tomorrow. Your father's got to be a difficult subject for you, and right now I'm not capable of being as sensitive as I should be."

"I don't need you to protect my feelings," he said irritably. "Just tell me how you found him."

She shrugged. "It wasn't hard. I got his social security number from the trucking company where he worked when you were a boy and performed some databank magic."

It was too late. Now Clay's hands were tied.

"What did he have to say?" he asked, fearing the worst.

"I haven't talked to him yet. He wasn't home when I called, so I left a message with his wife."

His wife… Clay wished those two words didn't turn his stomach. He told himself they shouldn't. He wasn't a needy little boy anymore; he was thirty-four years old. But the pain was still there. "Do you know if he has other children?"

"No. But I can tell you what he does for a living."

Clay hesitated, but curiosity ended up getting the better of him. "What?"

"He's a pilot. Flies fishermen to remote lakes and streams."

I've got a lot of life yet to live, a lot of places to see….

"Makes sense, I guess," he muttered.

"What makes sense?"

"Nothing."

She put a comforting hand on his arm. "I'm sorry."

Embarrassed that he'd given away his true feelings, he shook her off. "My father doesn't matter to me."

The moon lit one side of her face as she studied him. "You expect me to believe that?"

He slung an arm over the steering wheel in the most careless pose he could summon. "You don't?"

"Not for a minute."

Clay wasn't sure how to respond. Most people took him at his word. But he was quickly finding that Allie wasn't like most people. She knew he might be involved in a murder, was moving forward with an investigation that would include him at some point, and yet she treated him fairly. Innocent until proven guilty. She hadn't automatically assumed the worst the other night, although the situation couldn't have reflected favorably on him—or Beth Ann, either. And, earlier at the pool hall, she hadn't let Joe intimidate her into avoiding him.

She was trying to give him the benefit of every doubt, reserving judgment, relying on facts instead of prejudice.

In a way, he appreciated her generosity; in another way, he resented it. Because now he had something to lose.

"It's been a long time since he was part of my life," he said, trying to suggest that what he felt about Lucas was unimportant.

"I can get a few more details about him when he calls me, if you want," she offered. "I could even give you his number."

"No." He pulled to the side of the road in front of her house. The porch light on Chief McCormick's long brick rambler glowed yellow across the sloping lawn, but the rest of the house was dark. The cars in the driveway, and the knowledge that Allie's parents were asleep inside, made him feel sixteen again, as if he were dropping off a date.

"Maybe he misses you, too, Clay," she said.

"He couldn't miss me too badly, could he?"

She didn't respond, so he continued, "Anyway, as far as I'm concerned, he's no longer my father. I certainly don't want anyone to engineer some sort of reunion."

She nodded. "Okay. Let me know if you change your mind."

Clay almost asked her not to talk to Lucas if he called. But now that she'd already left a message, he feared that pressing the issue would only raise Allie's suspicions. Why had his mother given the man who'd triggered all the terrible events of the past a chance to destroy their future, as well?

Clay wanted to be angry with Irene, but if Lucas had called *him,* he might've been tempted to reveal just as much. Lucas could win anyone's confidence. His problem was that he couldn't live up to the promises he made.

And that might prove true once again.

"Good night," Clay said as Allie opened the door to climb out.

Her lips curved in a sympathetic smile. "It's his loss, Clay."

"Don't."

Her eyes widened. "Don't what?"

"Pity me." He turned to look at her. "Love me or hate me. But don't pity me."

She rubbed her arms. She hadn't brought a coat. "Interesting choice," she said and shut the door.

"How'd it go last night?"

Allie's mother sat beside her father at the breakfast

table, drinking a cup of coffee. Evelyn was wearing a bathrobe and slippers, but Dale was dressed in the clothes he wore to mow the lawn. His reading glasses were perched on the end of his nose and he was skimming the newspaper while doing his best to ignore Whitney, who kept yelling, "Jump in!" and tossing her Barbies into the kitchen sink.

"Aren't you going to answer your mother?" he asked when Allie didn't say anything.

"It was fine," she said. She hoped to minimize the fact that she'd even gone out. She'd asked her mother to babysit so she could do some investigative work. Instead, she'd let loose and simply had fun. She'd rather not analyze why, but she knew it had a lot to do with how she felt when she was around Clay.

"That's it?" Evelyn said. "Just *fine?*"

Allie shrugged, feeling uncomfortable beneath the pointed stare of her father. "Pretty much."

"Where's your car?" he asked solemnly, angling his head to see her more clearly over his glasses.

Her parents had always watched her closely. It came with being the daughter of a cop. But she hadn't expected her father to resume the old watch now that she was thirty-three. "I see you're still on your toes," she said wryly.

"I had some caulking to do in the shed earlier."

"Right." She drummed her fingers on the table. "What time did I get in?"

"Two."

"Two what?"

"Two-thirteen."

She chuckled. "Some things never change."

"But I don't want to go swimming," Whitney said in a high-pitched voice, posing a Barbie on the edge of the sink.

Dale leaned forward. *"Where's your car?"*

"It's at the pool hall," she said as indifferently as possible.

"What's it doing there?"

She lowered her voice. "I didn't want to drive."

This explanation met with a moment's silence, enough to tell Allie her parents didn't approve.

"You weren't drunk!" her mother whispered, sounding horrified.

"*Buzzed* would be a better word. But before you start to panic, let me assure you that one night does not constitute a problem."

Evelyn's forehead wrinkled in concern. "I don't understand why you'd drink so much. Ever."

"I was tired so I took some No-Doz to help me stay awake. It didn't mix well with beer. That's all."

"And you thought it would?" she asked as if such a flimsy excuse made it even worse.

"At least I didn't try to drive," Allie said, hoping they'd see that as something positive. But they weren't so easy to console.

"Who were you drinking with?" her father asked.

They'd finally arrived at the inevitable question. Allie took a deep breath, because she knew her parents wouldn't like this answer any more than they had the others. "Madeline Barker. Kirk Vantassel. And Clay."

"Montgomery?" her father bellowed.

Whitney dropped her Barbies and turned to watch the drama unfolding at the table. Allie wanted to tell Dale to calm down, but she had her mouth full and couldn't speak. She'd taken a big spoonful of cereal in an attempt to act nonchalant, as if she expected Evelyn and Dale to react no differently to Clay's name than to the others. But her ploy hadn't worked.

"Tell me it's not true," her mother said.

Allie managed to swallow "It's true."

"I've never known you to be a drinker."

"I'm not."

"Yet the first time you go out with Clay, you come home after two in the morning, drunk."

"Stop it! You—it's not how you're making it sound. I was tired, but Madeline said Clay would be at the pool hall, and I wanted to ask him a few questions about Barker's disappearance. That's why I took the No-Doz."

"And then you drank on top of it."

"I didn't think a few beers would make any difference. And then…" She stopped because she couldn't explain, at least to their satisfaction, how her interview intentions had so easily turned into pool and dancing. Especially dancing. When she closed her eyes, she could still smell the scent of Clay's cologne and feel the strength of his arms around her, guiding her body in perfect rhythm with his.

Dale set the newspaper aside. "And then?" he encouraged when her words dwindled away.

She figured the less she said, the better. "When I needed a ride home, Clay was kind enough to offer."

"You think he was being *nice?*" Dale said.

"Yes."

"Shows how naive you are!"

"How do you know he *wasn't* simply being nice?" she challenged, irritated by the whole Inquisition routine.

"Because I'm familiar with his reputation."

"So am I. Most people in Stillwater keep a list of every mistake he's ever made!"

"Yet you got into his car, knowing he could be dangerous."

Clenching her jaw, Allie began to tap her spoon against

the side of her bowl. "If you think he's dangerous, why won't you support me in my investigation? Officially reopen the case? Don't you want to know if he's really the one who murdered Lee Barker?"

Her father rattled his paper as if he had a lot to say but was deliberately holding back.

"Dad?"

"I told you, we have more important issues to worry about," he snapped. "You should spend your time on something that matters."

"Why don't we ask Madeline if this matters?"

"You have no business with Clay Montgomery." His face turned even redder than when he'd caught her necking on the porch after her junior prom. "You've chosen poorly once. I'm not going to stand by while you do it again."

"Dale," her mother warned, but it was too late. Allie shoved her cereal bowl aside and got up.

"How dare you!"

Gripping the table, he pulled himself to his feet and loomed over her. "I dare because I'm your father!"

Allie refused to let him intimidate her the way he used to. "You wouldn't be treating Danny like this."

"He's a man."

"So? We're all adults, and you're being ridiculous." She glanced between her parents. "You're making a big deal out of nothing."

"Just stay away from Clay, from all the Montgomerys," he said.

"Mommy? Are you in trouble?" Whitney asked, her eyes round.

Allie glared at her parents. "No. I'm old enough to make my own decisions," she said and stalked out of the room.

7

Clay reserved most weekends and weeknights for working on the vintage cars he restored in his barn. It was a solitary occupation, but most of his activities were. He didn't mind being alone. He took his time with each car and generally enjoyed the change of pace.

Today, however, he hadn't been himself. He felt listless, bored, preoccupied. Again and again, his thoughts drifted to Allie. At first, he tried to convince himself that he was merely searching for the best way to neutralize the threat she posed. Holding his enemy close and all that. But by midafternoon he was ready to admit that his desires didn't stem from a motivation nearly that subversive. He wasn't strategizing about how to protect himself or his family. For once in his life, he wasn't even thinking about the past.

He wanted to take her to dinner. To go out as though he wasn't harboring any dark secrets, as though he was just like any other man.

After wiping his greasy hands on a towel, he began putting away his tools. There was no point in working on the Jag today; he wasn't making any real progress. He kept staring off into space, remembering the expressions that had flitted across Allie's face the night before, and repeating the same thing: *Forget it. Why would she ever go out with you?*

He could think of one very obvious reason: she still wanted to talk about Barker. She'd go if she believed he'd provide her with some detail she didn't already know. But he was reluctant to entice her with such an irresistible hook. He wanted her to go because she wanted to be with him. It was that simple—and that complicated.

"Clay? Where are you?"

Recognizing his sister's voice, he poked his head out of the barn to find Grace standing on the steps of his back porch, her extended stomach clearly defined by her dress. New life. He was fascinated by her pregnancy, loved hearing her talk with so much enthusiasm about the coming baby. Her husband's gaze trailed after her wherever she moved; Heath and Teddy cuddled up to her at every opportunity.

A yearning for the things that really mattered in life grew so strong in Clay that it momentarily stole his breath, and he halted in mid-stride. In the glare of the afternoon sun, which was unseasonably hot for mid-May, he could easily imagine another woman standing where Grace stood now. A woman waiting for him, big with *his* child.

"What's wrong?" she called.

Shaking his head to clear away the silly daydream, he started forward again. He couldn't bring a woman—a wife—to the farm and expect her to fight the same negative sentiments he did, couldn't claim her heart and then leave her husbandless if the truth ever came out.

"Nothing." He shaded his eyes with his hand as he approached. "How's the baby?"

"Fine. Getting big, as you can see. I feel like a moose."

"Don't," he said. "You've never been prettier."

She smiled when she reached her. "You're sincere about that?"

"Would I lie to you?" He offered her a lopsided grin. "Besides, how can I not think you're beautiful? You look just like me."

She gave him a playful slug, then settled into the porch swing.

"Would you like a cold drink?" he asked.

She'd pulled her thick black hair into a ponytail, but several strands fell loose around her face, framing eyes the same blue as his own. "No, thanks. I had a late lunch."

He needed to wash up, but ridding himself of the grease on his hands required heavy-duty soap, a stiff-bristled brush and ten full minutes of scrubbing. Because Grace never stayed at the farm very long, he decided he'd get to see more of her if he waited until she left to start that routine.

He sat next to her. "Where're the boys?"

"Fishing with their father one last time before the baby gets here."

"What if you go into labor while they're gone?"

"They're not far, just down at the old Hatfield pond. And Kennedy's got his pager with him." Kicking off her sandals, Grace tucked her feet beneath her and leaned her head on his shoulder.

"I'll get you dirty," he warned.

"I don't care." She seemed so peaceful and content as she closed her eyes and let him swing her that he began to feel guilty about the dissatisfaction he felt with his own life. At least his sister was happy. How many years had she suffered because he hadn't looked out for her the way he should have? "I didn't know Kennedy had a pager," he said.

"He didn't until last week. He went out and bought one because he doesn't trust his cell phone. I'm supposed to call both the minute I go into labor."

Clay chuckled and continued to move the swing. "You'll remember to call me as soon as Junior arrives, won't you?"

"Of course."

"Have you decided on a name?"

"If it's a girl, she'll be Lauren Elizabeth."

"Nice. But I'm predicting a boy."

Her smile grew shy as she sat up. "Then he'll be Isaiah Clayton."

He studied her in surprise. "After me?"

She slipped her hand into the crook of his arm. "If you don't mind."

"Why?"

"Because you're such a good brother."

A lump swelled in his throat, making it difficult to talk.

They rocked in silence for a moment. Then she nudged him. "I hear Allie McCormick is searching for Dad."

He nodded.

"What a relief he doesn't know anything that can hurt us."

Clay glanced at her but kept his mouth shut. Irene hadn't told Grace? Considering Grace's situation, he was glad. She didn't need the worry. She'd been through enough, and none of it had been her fault. "Yeah, what a relief," he echoed.

"Do you think she'll find him?"

He stared at his greasy hands. "She already has."

She put her feet down to stop the swaying motion. "Where is he?"

"Alaska."

"What's he doing all the way up there?"

"He's remarried."

The expression on her face momentarily revealed the

old fragility. The mention of Lucas had obviously brought back bad memories.

Reaching out, Clay squeezed her hand despite the grease on his own. "He's not worth the pain," he said softly.

Her smile appeared forced, but she nodded. "Has Allie come snooping around here yet?"

"She's been by, but not because of Barker."

"You're talking about what happened with Beth Ann."

He scowled. "God, is there anyone who *hasn't* heard?"

She laughed and, relieved to see her smile again, he relaxed in the seat.

"She's telling everyone you want a baby, you know," she said, wiping the grease he'd transferred to her on his dirty T-shirt.

"I didn't know. But that's crazy."

She angled her head to size him up. "Is it?"

"Of course. I'm not even married."

"You've been almost as interested in this baby as Kennedy."

"Why wouldn't I be? I'm the kid's uncle."

"Maybe it's time you started thinking about settling down and having some children of your own."

They both knew a man didn't get more settled than he was. Unless he wanted to wind up in prison, he couldn't go anywhere. And he'd be stupid to marry. But he knew it hurt Grace to acknowledge the limitations of his situation, so he played along. "I'm sure I'll know when I meet the right woman."

"Don't let what happened stop you," she said, suddenly fierce.

How could he not let it stop him? He couldn't pretend he *didn't* have the remains of his stepfather buried in the cellar. "Don't worry," he said. "I'm fine as I am."

She stared off into space, toward the barn. He'd torn down the horse stalls to make room for his car shop, but he knew that, for Grace, the barn held the worst memories of all. At one end was the reverend's office, where Barker used to prepare his sermons. It was also where he'd tie Grace up and—

Clay winced, unable to think about it. They'd left that office completely intact for nineteen years, as if they believed he might one day return, until last summer when Grace had finally snapped and torn the place apart. Clay had since boxed up the reverend's belongings and passed them on to Madeline, but that two-hundred square feet of space still felt evil. Clay never went in there.

"What is it?" he asked. Once the memories crowded this close, Grace never lingered—unless she had a good reason.

When she reached for his hand, her fingers were cold, despite the warmth of the sun. "I ran into Reverend Portenski at the drugstore."

"I didn't realize you knew Reverend Portenski." Grace never went to church anymore. Of Irene's three children, she'd once been the most receptive to spiritual guidance. But that was before Barker.

"We've seen each other around town, of course. Usually he won't even look at me, and I ignore him. I guess he hasn't seen my soul as worth saving. Or he knew he'd be wasting his breath, even if he tried. But this last encounter…"

"What?" Clay prompted.

"He approached me with the oddest expression on his face."

"What kind of expression?"

"Sort of pained or filled with regret or…I'm not sure."

"What'd he say?"

"That God knows all things and that his wrath will destroy the wicked."

Clay felt instantly defensive. He was always defensive of Grace. But judging by his own experience with Portenski, what she'd just told him didn't make any sense. "That doesn't sound like him," he said. "When I first started going back to church several months ago, he made sure everyone knew he was fine with having me there. I think some people, like Joe, were trying to convince him I shouldn't be allowed to participate, because he delivered a rather passionate sermon saying it wasn't his place to judge. 'God is the only one who knows the thoughts and intents of each man's heart and reserves judgment for himself,' he said."

"But I didn't get the impression that he was blaming me, Clay. It was almost as if he was trying to tell me that *Barker* will be punished for his sins."

Clay's muscles tensed. "Do you think he knows?"

"I do."

"But how could he? We searched the entire church and personally boxed up everything in Barker's private rooms. The pictures weren't there. What we burned must've been all of them."

"No." They'd had this discussion before. Although it was difficult for Grace to talk about, she always maintained that there had to be more. Barker's fetish included the camera. She claimed he'd taken hundreds of Polaroids.

"Then, where did he hide them?"

"I don't know. But I believe Portenski's found them."

"If that's true, why hasn't he come forward? Used them to put one of us on trial? They certainly establish a strong enough motive."

"They also reveal what a monster Barker was. Maybe Portenski has sympathy for the thirteen-year-old child in those pictures."

She'd spoken as if that thirteen-year-old child was a stranger to her. Clay wondered if that was how she coped, by divorcing herself from the little girl she used to be.

"He said if I ever decide to come back to church, he'd love to see me in his congregation," she murmured. "That God can heal all wounds."

"What'd you say?"

"I told him I'll never set foot inside a church again, particularly that one."

"How'd he respond?"

"He nodded, as if he understood, and shuffled away."

Like Grace, Clay had stopped attending church after what had happened with Barker. He'd tried to pretend he didn't need religion in his life, but the beliefs and rituals were too big a part of his upbringing, and he couldn't deny himself indefinitely. Intellectually, he recognized that a preacher could be bad without making the doctrine he taught bad. This understanding was what had led him back. But Clay's emotions sometimes got the better of him and he occasionally walked out in the middle of the sermon, if a word or phrase or even a look reminded him of Barker. The kind of hypocrisy he and his mother and sisters had witnessed changed a person, and once that innocence was lost, there was no reclaiming it.

Grace touched her stomach, and a hint of a smile instantly replaced the haunted expression of a moment earlier.

"The baby's kicking?" Clay asked.

"More like he's rolling over. If your hands were clean I'd let you see for yourself. I know how much you like it."

"Who says I like it?" he teased.

"You might fool other people, but you don't fool me." She laughed. "Are you sure Beth Ann isn't the woman for you?"

"Absolutely." His life seemed to exist in shades of gray, but at least here he was speaking God's honest truth.

"I want you to find someone to love, Clay. I want you to find someone and be as happy as I am."

Her earnest words tugged at his heart. "Quit worrying about me," he said gruffly.

"I can't help it," she said. "I worry about you, Molly, Madeline, Mom." She rolled her eyes. "Especially Mom."

"I've got Mom covered."

Her eyebrows shot up. "You do? Then why did she just tell me she's going out of town for the weekend?"

He blinked at her. "You're kidding, right?"

"I wish I was."

"With Chief McCormick?" He kept his voice low, in case someone was coming down the driveway.

"She *says* she's going alone, but you and I know that's highly unlikely."

"This wouldn't be happening if she lived here with me."

"She couldn't take living here," Grace said with a grimace. "I don't know how she lasted as long as she did. Or how you do it."

He wouldn't have remained at the farm, either, except that he had no other choice. It was his duty to look after his mother and sisters, and staying was the only way he could do it. "Maybe it wouldn't be fun to have her here all the time, but I'd be able to keep her out of trouble."

"You're both better off living on your own."

As much as Clay felt obligated to take care of his

mother, maybe Grace was right. He wasn't sure he could tolerate living with her again. He'd grown too used to rambling around the farm by himself. "How's Chief McCormick getting away from his wife this weekend?"

"I have no idea. How does he do it any time?"

Clay shook his head. "Why won't Mom listen to me?"

"I'm sure she wants to. She just…can't."

"Can't?"

"I couldn't give Kennedy up if my life depended on it."

"Kennedy's your husband. Dale's committed to someone else."

She smoothed her dress. "I'm not saying what Mom's doing is right. I'm saying she's never been so completely in love, and that's why it's tough to make the sacrifice."

"She's more in love with him than she was with our father?"

"Chief McCormick is everything Dad wasn't. Solid, dependable, responsible, down-to-earth."

"He's not exactly a man of sterling character. He's cheating on his wife!"

"Of course that part's not admirable. But it's understandable—to a point. Mom's several years younger and far more attractive than Evelyn. Sex is…new and exciting again, and all that."

"At his age, it's as much about ego as it is about sex," Clay said. "Being able to get Mom probably makes him feel like a real man."

"And Mom's finally found someone who's treating her as if she's special."

"But it can't go anywhere," Clay said. "Imagine the scandal once everyone finds out."

"The backlash will be severe," she agreed, cringing

visibly. "I feel so sorry for Kennedy. Sometimes I wonder if he understood what he was getting into when he married me."

"Don't say that! He's lucky to have you."

"I hope he thinks so after Mom's affair is exposed."

"You say that as if it's inevitable."

"You can vouch for how hard it is to keep a secret in this town."

"Is Kennedy aware of it?"

"Yes. I thought it was only fair to warn him." Standing, she dropped a quick kiss on his cheek, and he knew she'd already stayed at the farm as long as she could tolerate. "Thanks, big brother. I'll try to convince Mom not to go this weekend."

"Good luck," he said. Lord knew that what *he'd* told Irene hadn't made any difference.

She paused on the steps. "By the way, Molly's coming out here for the birth."

"It'll be great to have her back. She hasn't been home since Christmas."

"She's seeing someone new. Have you heard?"

"No. Do you think this relationship's got a future?"

"I doubt it. She's only interested until they start making demands, and then she moves on." She tossed him a grin. "I wonder where she gets that from."

"Not me," he said.

"If you say so," she scoffed.

"Grace?"

Brushing the loose hair out of her eyes, she glanced back at him. "What?"

"Would you want to talk to Dad if you had the chance?"

She didn't take even a moment to think about it. "No," she said and gave him a final wave.

* * *

Allie was at the police station, sorting through the Barker files, when Lucas Montgomery's call came in. She had Whitney with her, coloring near her desk. Her father hadn't stopped by today, thank goodness. They hadn't spoken since breakfast and she wasn't ready to talk to him yet.

Fortunately, he usually didn't work on Saturdays. Two other officers, Grimsman and Pontiff, were on duty, out on patrol.

"Officer McCormick," she said into the phone. Her heart had started to race as soon as she saw the Alaska area code on her caller ID. She wasn't sure why she'd be nervous about talking to Clay's father, but she was.

"This is Lucas Montgomery."

"I recognized the number. I don't get many calls from Alaska. Thanks for phoning me back."

"No problem. What can I do for you?"

She tried to hear Clay in his voice, wondered if the two men looked much alike these days. She'd seen a copy of an old family photo in the file, but it was blurry and over a quarter of a century old. "As I explained to your wife, I'm from Stillwater, a little town in—"

"I know where you're from," he said. "And I know why you're calling. But I don't think I'll be able to help you. My wife said you have a few questions regarding the disappearance of some man I've never met."

Allie heard a trace of resentment in those last four words, beneath a thin veneer of good humor. "Not *some* man, Mr. Montgomery," she clarified. "We're talking about your ex-wife's second husband."

"I'm afraid I never knew him. I haven't spoken to Irene since I left."

"Not once?"

"Not once."

"So you don't know that your family's suffered through a great deal of suspicion and doubt concerning the disappearance of Lee Barker?"

"No, I don't. What I do know is that Irene isn't the kind of person who'd harm anyone. That's all I can tell you. I'm sorry if you were hoping otherwise."

"I wasn't hoping otherwise, Mr. Montgomery. I'm just searching for the facts."

"Isn't it a bit late for an investigation?" he asked.

"Excuse me?"

"Surely after nineteen years—"

"Nineteen years?" Allie interrupted, her breath lodged in her throat.

Silence fell over the line as if he'd suddenly realized his blunder, then he said, "It's been that long since I left."

"But you moved away when Clay was only ten years old." She could've used the actual date instead of Clay's age, but she wanted to remind Lucas of the little boy he'd abandoned.

"I'm not positive about that."

"You don't remember how old your son was?"

"Not exactly."

"It's been twenty-five years. A sixteen-year-old boy is quite different from a ten-year-old."

"Guess I lost count."

"So it's merely a coincidence that the nineteen years you just mentioned correlates perfectly with the length of time Reverend Barker's been gone?"

"I told you, I don't know anything about Reverend Barker!"

"Then it's even more amazing that you guessed the year he went missing, isn't it?"

There was a slight pause. "Listen, you—you're heading down the wrong road," he said. It was easy to tell that she'd managed to rattle him. "Like I said, Irene wouldn't hurt anybody. She's a good woman."

Yet he'd turned his back on her....

"Is it possible you know more than you're saying, Mr. Montgomery?"

"Are you calling me a liar?" he retorted.

For the first time, Allie wondered if he could've had something to do with Barker's disappearance. Could he have come back, found another man in his place, fought with that man and possibly killed him? That would certainly explain why Lucas Montgomery had made himself scarce for so long.

The thought came as a relief to Allie. She would much rather it was Clay's father than Clay. "I'm just doing my job," she replied. "Can you tell me where you were the night the reverend disappeared?"

"Yes. I have an airtight alibi. So don't go trying to pin his death on me."

Allie's hand tightened on the receiver. "I didn't say he was dead."

No response.

"Mr. Montgomery?"

"After so long, I think it's safe to make that assumption, don't you?" he said. "Anyway, I've been in Alaska for twenty years, and you can't prove I ever left. No airplane tickets. No train tickets. No gas receipts."

"I see you've been watching your share of *Forensic Files*."

"I've sat through a few."

"So you've never been back to see your children?"

Silence.

"Do you need me to speak up?" she asked.

"I heard you."

"And?"

"I haven't been back, okay?"

"Well, as far as I'm concerned, that's as much of a crime as anything else." She had no business passing judgment on him. But her own experience with Sam's rejection of Whitney and what she'd sensed in Clay last night put her too close to the situation.

"Go to hell," he said and hung up.

Allie returned the phone to its cradle. She hadn't handled that call as professionally as she should have. But she'd caught him lying to her. She was positive of it. Now she just needed to figure out why.

Whitney looked up at her. "Was that Daddy, Mommy?"

"No," she said. "It was someone a lot like him."

8

Reverend Portenski gripped the sides of the pulpit as he gave his weekly sermon, enjoying his own message—until he saw Clay Montgomery slip into the back of the church. The man scarcely made a sound as he came in and sat several rows behind everyone else—but it took only one person to notice him. Then the rumble of voices rose, and heads began to turn. Clay tolerated the attention with more dignity than he was ever credited with possessing. He stared straight ahead and ignored what was going on around him. But that didn't mean he liked it. Who would?

After a slight nod in his direction, a welcome Portenski forced himself to offer each and every time Clay showed up, he let his eyes seek out other parishioners with whom he felt more comfortable. Clay was an intimidating man. He'd probably seen and done things Portenski didn't even want to consider. The pictures in that dark hole explained why. But if Clay was as guilty as everyone believed, even the church couldn't bring him peace.

"Vengeance is mine, sayeth the Lord."

The confused expressions of those in the audience told Portenski he'd just spoken those words out loud, right in the middle of a persuasive argument on succoring the needy.

Clearing his throat to give himself a split second to

gather his scattered thoughts, he recovered by telling his listeners that it wasn't their place to judge whether or not a beggar deserved his current circumstances. "We should never turn away the needy. For aren't we all beggars before God?"

Several people murmured, "Amen." Portenski smiled approvingly and continued preaching—while trying to avoid Clay's piercing gaze. In another fifty minutes, he'd be rid of Mr. Montgomery, he told himself. And chances were good Clay wouldn't show up next week. His attendance was sporadic at best. But when the closing prayer ended, Clay didn't immediately walk out, as usual. He stood at the back, waiting.

Folding his arms, Clay leaned one shoulder against the wall as the rest of the congregation filed past him. Most people refused to even look at him. Joe's father muttered under his breath that he had no right to be standing in a church with decent people. Joe's mother and her friends glared at him shamelessly. But Clay didn't acknowledge them. He'd seen Allie McCormick's mother escort Allie's daughter out a few minutes before the service ended, saw the little girl turn and wave to her mother, so he knew Allie had come. He wanted to catch a glimpse of her badly enough to wait around. And, after what Grace had told him, he was hoping for a chance to speak to the reverend.

But it was Beth Ann who approached him as soon as she could cut through the crowd flowing toward the exit.

"Clay, it's so good to see you," she said.

"Good to see you, too." His response was automatic and subdued, but he regretted saying even that much when she pounced on the opportunity to read more into it.

"Really? Do you mean that?"

The longing in her voice made Clay uncomfortable. He wanted to say something to make the situation less painful for her, but being nice only gave her false hope.

"Listen, Beth Ann, I'm sorry—" he started, but a third voice interrupted before he could finish.

"Of course he means it. Clay likes to see all his friends. I'm glad you could make it to church today, Mr. Montgomery."

Surprised that Allie would involve herself, he turned to find her coming toward him from the other side. When their eyes met, she grinned, letting him know she'd rescued him on purpose.

"Officer McCormick," he said with a nod. Clay supposed he should smile politely and leave it at that, but he couldn't stop his eyes from wandering over her. She looked so pretty, so…wholesome in her white blouse and skirt. For a moment he completely forgot she wasn't the most beautiful woman in the world.

"What's going on?" Beth Ann asked, glancing between them.

Clay regarded her blankly, hoping to defuse her apparent jealousy, but it was too late.

"Are you hoping for your turn in his bed?" she asked Allie, instantly suspicious.

"You're in a church," Clay reminded her, but Beth Ann didn't seem to care.

Allie responded with far less than the denial Beth Ann had obviously hoped to provoke. "What I'd really like is a few lessons in pool," she said.

"Pool?" Beth Ann repeated, confusion wrinkling her normally smooth forehead.

Allie nodded. "Yes—billiards. Clay definitely knows how to play."

"That's not the only game he's good at," Beth Ann said. "If you're not careful, he'll hurt you, too."

Allie merely smiled. "If he doesn't want to tutor me, I'll learn from someone else."

"Until you realize there *is* no one else, at least no one like him," Beth Ann said sulkily and walked away.

Embarrassed, Clay wasn't sure what to say in the wake of such a departure. So he rubbed a hand over his jaw and waited for Allie to break the awkward silence.

"That was some endorsement," she said.

He tried to shrug it off. "She didn't grow up here, remember?"

"What does that mean?"

"I guess I have her fooled."

"Today. Considering the call she made from your farm, she tends to vacillate."

"She's not as bad as the past week might suggest."

Allie's smile changed, grew thoughtful. "That's generous of you."

"It's true," he said simply.

"I guess she's telling everyone she's ready to marry and settle down."

"I've heard." He shoved his hands into the pockets of his chinos. "She'll make someone a good wife."

"Someone?"

"Someone else."

"Why not you?"

"She can't play pool," he teased. "When do you want your first lesson?"

Allie lifted her chin. "How much is it going to cost me?"

He sent her a slow, devilish grin. "I'm not as cheap as you might've heard."

She feigned disappointment. "Now you're really breaking my heart."

"But I'll give you a lesson if you'll go out to dinner with me."

She glanced surreptitiously around the church. "When?"

"Tonight?"

His heart hammered against his chest as he waited for her response. He couldn't remember the last time he'd been nervous asking a woman out. In most cases, he wasn't the one extending the invitation.

She opened her mouth to answer him, then saw her father moving toward them. "I'll call you," she murmured and scooted out the door.

Clay was tempted to watch her as she left. But Chief McCormick had stopped in front of him and made a point of getting his attention.

"Leave her alone," he muttered.

Clay blinked in surprise. "What did you say?"

"You heard me," he replied and stalked out the door.

Allie hurried to her cruiser, which was the vehicle she usually drove around town. Whitney had grown restless in church and Evelyn had already taken her home for a nap, so she didn't have to worry about getting her daughter strapped into the back seat, which was fortunate because she didn't want to give her father a chance to catch up with her. She and her parents had barely spoken since their argument at the breakfast table yesterday. When they did talk, they acted as if nothing had happened. Judging by the look on Dale's face when he saw her with Clay, however, the truce was over.

She managed to slip into the driver's seat of her car and, pretending she didn't see her father coming after her, closed the door and drove off. She thought it'd be wise to give Dale a chance to cool down and get involved in a TV show or project before she saw him again—because it wasn't going to do any good to continue arguing. He couldn't convince her to stay away from Clay. Clay was part of her investigation and, after speaking with Lucas, Allie believed more than ever that the Montgomerys were the key to solving the case. Clearly, since Clay had stonewalled the police for nearly twenty years, the antagonistic approach wasn't working with him. She couldn't see the harm in trying a little friendship.

Besides, she liked Clay—just as much as she had when she was drunk, she realized with chagrin.

Beth Ann's words came back to her. *He'll hurt you, too,* she'd said. But Allie wasn't concerned. She had no expectations of a serious relationship. He might've asked her out to dinner, but she knew better than to assume he had more than a passing interest in her. A woman didn't have to know him very well to understand that he wasn't big on commitment. Of all the rumors that circulated about him, the one that said he was hard to get—which Allie translated as *impossible*—was the one she most believed.

Her cell phone rang. She rooted around for it while she drove, trying to find where it had fallen, hoping it was her brother. She'd called him earlier to complain about their father. Moving home was a mixed blessing. She appreciated her parents' support, knew it was good for Whitney to have them around, but it was so hard giving up the autonomy she'd enjoyed as a married adult. Maybe living with her father *and* working for him had started out okay, but after only six weeks it was putting a strain on their relationship. Danny had tried to warn her….

Where was her phone? As it rang again, she leaned

forward to feel under the seat, wondering if she should move into the guesthouse. Her parents wouldn't like it, but it would give her more privacy. And Whitney could still stay at her parents' on the nights Allie worked.

Eventually her fingers closed around her phone and she managed to pull it out from under the passenger seat. But after one glance at the caller ID, Allie tossed it aside. It wasn't her brother, it was her father—and they'd only get into a yelling match if she answered.

Since Whitney was probably asleep, Allie wasn't in any hurry to return home. She decided to use the next two hours to interview some of the witnesses whose testimony she'd read in the Barker files. It was Sunday, so most of them should be available.

She planned to begin with Jed Fowler. He'd been at the farm the night Barker disappeared; he'd also attempted to confess to Barker's murder nine months ago, during the last police search. And yet, apart from the three minutes it took to brush off enough dirt to determine that they'd dug up the skull of a dog and not a human, he'd never really been a suspect. Maybe he was strange, but he had no motive, nothing to gain from Barker's death.

Chances were much greater that he'd witnessed something and was keeping silent about it. But if that was true, why would he confess to murder instead of pointing a finger at the real culprit?

From what she'd read in the files, Allie thought she could venture a guess.

Clay remained near the doors of the church, grappling with his anger over Chief McCormick's parting words. He considered walking out—and never coming back. He wasn't sure why he'd returned in the first place. He didn't need Allie, her father or anyone else. But he wanted to speak to Portenski before he left—if the man would ever acknowledge his presence. For the last few minutes, the reverend had been moving around the pews, putting away hymnbooks and tidying up as if he didn't know Clay was still in the room.

When Clay cleared his throat, the preacher finally looked up and glanced around, apparently shocked to find them alone.

"Is there something I can do for you, Mr. Montgomery?" he asked. He had a mild voice and manner, which was fitting for a man in his position. And yet, as nice as Portenski was, Clay got the distinct impression that the reverend was reluctant to talk to him. Prior to what Grace had told him, Clay had simply assumed Portenski's reserve had to do with the fact that he believed what most people believed—that Clay or his mother was responsible for Barker's disappearance. Or if he wasn't certain, at least he wondered. But now Clay suspected there might be more to it.

"My sister mentioned to me that you spoke to her the other day."

A quick darting of the tongue wet Portenski's lips. "Yes, I—I wanted to make sure she felt welcome here. If she ever decides to join us again."

Clay took note of the color rising high on his cheeks. "You told her that God's wrath would destroy the wicked. Isn't that right?"

The reverend smoothed down the white tufts of hair growing over his ears. "I—um—yes, I did. It's true, after all, is it not?"

"Were you referring to my sister's destruction when you made that comment?"

The reverend's eyes widened. "Is that how she interpreted it?"

"Considering what most people in this town have accused us of, what else would she think?"

He flapped a hand in front of him. "That wasn't it at all! I was just trying to tell her that God knows all things and will set them right eventually. We must have faith."

"That's an interesting comment to make to someone you believe was involved in a murder."

The reverend muttered something, but Clay couldn't make out all the words.

"What was that?" he asked.

"I said I've never indicated that I believe Grace is *guilty* of any crime."

The inflection was too noticeable to be accidental.

Clay lowered his voice. "So you know." He wanted to add, "That Reverend Barker was a predator," but he had to be careful. He didn't need to reveal a stronger motive for murder than the greed they'd already attributed to him, especially on the heels of his supposed "confession" to Beth Ann.

Portenski's lips pursed. He seemed reluctant to respond—but he showed no curiosity or surprise.

"Reverend?"

The preacher remained stiff, uncomfortable. "I'm confident only of what I told her."

Clay stared at him for several seconds. "That God knows all things."

"Yes."

"Why?"

"I told you, it's true."

"That's it?"

"Of course."

Whatever the reverend was thinking, he wasn't going to tell. And, judging by his attitude, pressing him wouldn't loosen his tongue. Portenski had the determined look of a man who'd dug in for a storm.

Clay refused to waste the effort asking for answers he wouldn't get. But he had other questions, questions that were, in their own way, every bit as important. Questions he'd wanted to ask someone like Portenski for years. "And do you find God particularly forgiving?"

There was a slight delay in the reverend's response, as if Clay's change in tactics had caught him off guard. "According to the Bible—"

"Don't quote me the Bible, Reverend. I'm asking what *you* think."

"I'm just a man."

"A man who's read libraries of books on theology, philosophy and sociology." Portenski was known for always having a book in his hand, and often quoted from a variety of works during his sermons. "If you're not qualified to form an opinion, who is? We're all just men."

Portenski lifted his chin. "I believe that, for the deserving, mercy tempers justice."

Clay nodded. Grace was right. The reverend had found the missing pictures or some letters or…something. He must have; he knew too much. He was keeping silent, but not because he thought Clay was innocent. The "deserving" part of what he'd said indicated that he thought God's mercy would be reserved for Grace alone.

And Portenski was probably right. Although Clay hadn't actually killed Barker, he'd indirectly caused the events of that night, and he'd definitely had a hand in the cover-up.

His desire for mercy, for forgiveness and peace of mind,

had brought him back to church. But he was wasting his time.

After living such a lie, he could never be called deserving.

As Allie parked her police cruiser at the curb, Jed Fowler appeared briefly at his front window wearing a stark frown. She wanted to believe it was because he didn't recognize her. But that couldn't be the case. She was the only female officer on the force, and her father had been taking their vehicles to Jed's automotive repair shop for the past forty years.

Jed knew who she was, but he seemed ill at ease around women and children. A simple person, he got up early, worked until late and returned home to the same two-bedroom house where he'd grown up. His father had been killed in an automobile accident while Jed was just a boy. His mother, a cantankerous old woman who used to sit on the porch and rock for hours, glaring at the children who streamed by on their way home from the nearby elementary school, had died while Allie was in college. As far as Allie knew, Jed had lived alone ever since.

She strode up the walk, wondering if his mother was the reason he'd remained a bachelor. Quite possibly, the old woman had been so demanding that he was unwilling to welcome another female into his home. The stories that circulated about her were a bit scary. Allie remembered a group of her friends telling her they were walking home from a party late one night when they were startled by Mama Fowler. Jed's mother was sitting on her porch in the dead of winter, all bundled up in coats and blankets, and brandishing a shotgun, pointing it at anyone who so much as looked at the house.

With that background, no wonder he's odd, Allie thought.

She reached the stoop and lifted a hand to knock. But the door opened before she could touch it, and Jed's craggy nose and rheumy eyes appeared in the crack.

"Mr. Fowler?"

He made a noise that might've been a response, but he didn't open the door any wider.

Allie leaned close, hoping to win him over with a polite smile. "May I have a word with you?"

He glanced behind him as though he was looking for an excuse not to admit her.

"We could talk out here on the porch, if you like."

Yanking on the red ball cap she'd seen him wear around town, he stepped out, leaving the door ajar. Because he'd been reluctant to invite her in, Allie had assumed the house might not be neat enough for company. But from what she could see, there wasn't a thing out of place.

"You've probably guessed why I'm here."

The frown had left his face. Now he just stared at her, his bushy eyebrows forming a prominent ledge over his deep-set eyes. "No, ma'am."

"I'd like to talk to you about Lee Barker."

His eyes narrowed. "You're reopening the investigation?"

"No. Not officially. I'm doing what I can for Madeline."

"You want to help her?" he said.

"That's right."

"By finding out what happened to her father."

"Yes. I used to be a cold case detective before moving back here," she explained. "I learned a few things that I'm hoping will make a difference. Madeline deserves to know what happened, don't you think?"

Allie wasn't sure what kind of reaction she'd been expecting, but it wasn't the one she got. "Better off without him, if you ask me."

"What did you say?" He'd mumbled the words.

He pulled the bill of his cap lower. "Nothin'."

"You didn't like Reverend Barker?" Jed had been a regular at Barker's church until a few years before the reverend went missing. One day, Jed got up and walked out in the middle of the service and never returned. She remembered her mother launching a fellowship crusade to reclaim him, but nothing Evelyn or anyone else did made any difference. Jed had never joined the congregation again.

"Can't say as I did."

"I'd be interested to hear why, if you wouldn't mind telling me."

"He's gone. Don't matter now."

"It might," she said. He still didn't volunteer the details she was after, so she resorted to the questions she'd planned to ask in the first place. "You were at the property, fixing the tractor in the barn the night Barker disappeared. Is that correct?"

A single dip of his head served as confirmation.

"In the reports, you said Barker didn't come back to the farm that night."

No comment.

"Is that true?" she prompted.

"Yes, ma'am."

"Would you have seen him, or at least heard his car, if he did?"

"Tough to say."

"You had the radio on, right?"

"Yeah."

"Was it louder than you normally play it at your shop?" Allie knew he always had his radio tuned to a country-western station.

"Maybe. The kids were the only ones home, so I wasn't worried about botherin' anybody."

"The kids?"

"The Montgomery girls."

"Irene wasn't there? Clay wasn't there?" She knew they weren't, of course. She'd read the statements. But she needed to hear the words directly from Jed in order to get a sense of how he felt about the night's events. And to see if his story had changed over the years.

"Mrs. Montgomery—"

"Wasn't she Mrs. Barker then?" Allie asked, watching closely for his reaction.

He seemed undisturbed by the question. "I guess she was."

"Do you remember when she went back to her former name?"

If Allie was right about Jed's motivation for his strange and sudden confession at the farm—if it was true that he carried a torch for the attractive Irene Montgomery and had been trying to protect her—he'd be able to give her this information.

But his expression remained blank as he shook his head.

"Okay," Allie said. "Back to the night in question. Did you see Mrs. Montgomery that night?"

"She came out to the barn to tell me she'd be gone for a spell."

"Did she say where she was going?"

"Somethin' to do with the church."

Records confirmed that she'd attended choir practice

at Ruby Bradford's. She'd headed home thirty minutes after her husband had supposedly started in the same direction. "Did she seem eager to be on her way?"

He frowned as if this was a question he hadn't been asked before. "I don't know."

"How was she acting? Agitated? Worried? Preoccupied? Resigned?" Irene hadn't sung with the church choir since. When asked about it, she admitted that it was the reverend who'd insisted she join. He wanted her to set the proper example by supporting his auxiliary programs.

"She said she had to go and left."

"And then you were alone with the girls."

"No. Clay was there. At first."

"What were they doing? Do you recall?"

He shrugged. "I was just there to fix the tractor."

"Did anyone else come or go that night?"

"I heard some kids stop by."

"When?"

"Maybe half an hour later."

So he'd heard one car. "What happened then?"

"I saw Clay climb into a black truck with some other kids. They drove off a second later."

Those "other kids" were Jeremy Jordan and Rhys Franklin. They'd gone over to the home of Corinne Rasmussen, a girl Clay had been dating at the time. Corinne had since moved away, but she'd confirmed the visit in the original investigation. The files contained these details.

"So thirteen-year-old Grace and eleven-year-old Molly were home by themselves?" Allie clarified.

"I guess."

"It didn't concern you that they were alone?"

"Why would it? Grace was old enough to take care of her sister. Anyway, it wasn't any of my business."

"You were just there to fix the tractor."

"Yes, ma'am."

Frustrated, Allie studied him for a moment. He wasn't doing a heck of a lot to help her out. He offered only as much as he had to in order to answer each question. Was it just his taciturn manner? Did he distrust her because she was a woman? Or did he have some other reason for keeping quiet? "How well do you know Irene?" she asked, trying that tack again.

"She brings her car in now and then."

"That's it?"

"That's it."

"Were you friends at the time the reverend went missing?"

"She was his wife."

"She didn't deal with you personally?"

"Not unless the reverend wasn't around."

"Did that happen very often?"

"No."

"What type of interaction did you have when he wasn't there?"

Fowler shoved his hands deep into the pockets of his coveralls. "I told you, we didn't talk much."

Interviewing a man like Fowler wasn't easy. She hadn't gotten anything out of him that wasn't already well documented. But Allie kept at it. "You said you spoke to her when her husband wasn't around."

"She'd listen to what I told her so she could tell it to him."

"And Clay?"

"He was only a kid."

"What about now?"

"I don't do any work for him. Clay fixes his own cars."

"So you have no dealings with him at all?"

"Not unless we meet on the street."

"How does he treat you then?"

Fowler stared at her. "Like he treats anyone else, I s'pose."

"What about Grace and Madeline? Do you ever see them?"

"I've passed them in town—Grace more than Madeline since she moved back. She brought her Esplanade in for an oil change a few weeks ago."

He said it as if she was just another customer. If there was *any* kind of bond between the Montgomerys and Jed Fowler, Allie couldn't sense it. And yet he'd confessed when he thought Barker's remains had been discovered at the farm….

"According to what I've been told, nine months ago you tried to take responsibility for the murder of Reverend Barker. Is that true?"

No response.

"Can you tell me why you did that, Mr. Fowler?"

"I knew they were going to try and pin it on Mrs. Montgomery."

He admitted it? But he didn't even call her Irene…. "So you were trying to protect her?"

"I didn't want to see her go to jail."

"You'd rather go to jail yourself? That's a pretty big sacrifice for a lady you don't know all that well."

"She's been through enough." He stated it matter-of-factly.

Allie let her breath seep out. "Is it because you're in love with Irene Montgomery, Mr. Fowler? Is that why you confessed?"

"No."

"You're not in love with her?"

The telephone rang in the house. Fowler glanced back at it. "I've got to go. Someone might need a tow."

"Go ahead and answer it. I'll wait here."

He didn't have time to argue. Ducking inside, he left the door standing open as he headed down a hallway—presumably to the kitchen.

Allie took advantage of his absence to study the neat living room. From the look of the place, he'd kept the furnishings Mama Fowler had owned when she was alive. The crocheted doilies covering the arms of the sofa and the side tables had an old woman's touch. Even the television seemed ancient. An old Magnavox with rabbit ears on top, it sat next to a crystal candy dish that wasn't empty, as Allie might have expected, knowing that Jed never entertained, and a photograph of—

Who was that? Allie poked her head into the room. She might not have found the photograph so curious, except that there wasn't another sentimental object in sight—just a few landscapes hanging on the wall and a knitted afghan folded neatly on a footstool.

Fowler's voice filtered to her from somewhere else in the house. He was talking about a truck in a ditch and seemed fairly engrossed, so she slipped inside.

The scent that greeted her reminded her of a funeral home. This room didn't seem to be used much, and yet she spotted Fowler's work boots perfectly positioned beneath an antique oak hall tree.

He lived like a ghost, moving around without disturbing a thing. She thought his mother had died about fourteen years ago and yet the place felt as if Mrs. Fowler might walk in at any second.

Ignoring the creepy chill that skittered down her spine,

she picked up the photograph. It was an old black-and-white snapshot. Was it Mama Fowler? Another relative? Allie might've supposed so, except that someone had been torn out of the picture. She could see a man's arm next to the jagged edge.

On closer examination, she realized it wasn't a snapshot at all. It was part of a program for some event. At the bottom it read, "Join Reverend Barker and his—" The rest of the words were missing, along with the man in the picture. But what she'd read jostled Allie's memory enough that she suddenly recognized the woman. It was Eliza Barker, the reverend's first wife.

Allie held the picture closer, trying to see through the image to the writing on the other side. It was an invitation to a church Christmas party. From the date, it was probably the last party Eliza had ever attended. Barker's wife committed suicide three years before he married Irene. Allie remembered her as a gentle, soft-spoken woman who worked tirelessly to serve the members of her husband's church, but her suicide hadn't come as much of a surprise. Everyone knew Eliza suffered from depression. She'd even tried to start a support group for others who suffered as she did.

Finding her picture in such a prominent location in Jed's house, however, sparked Allie's curiosity. Had Eliza known Jed as more than just a parishioner? Allie didn't think so. If they'd had a relationship—a close friendship or even an affair—surely he'd have a real photograph of her and not simply a torn-off portion of a Christmas program.

Had he been obsessed with her?

The complete silence suddenly shattered Allie's preoccupation. Feeling the weight of Jed's stare at her back, she turned to find him standing at the entrance to the room.

She set the picture on the dusty coffee table, then wiped her hands on her skirt. "Does someone need roadside assistance?"

His face was flushed—with anger or embarrassment, she couldn't really tell. "Yes," he said. "I've got to go."

"No problem." She moved to the door, but looked back when he called her name.

"Don't come here again unless you've got a subpoena," he said.

Allie was frightened of Fowler. And she was uncomfortable in his neat but musty-smelling house. She was going to get in her cruiser and investigate some of the reverend's friends and neighbors who would be more forthcoming. But she had one last question. "Would you like to tell me why you have that program?"

"I received one just like everyone else who went to church that day," he said.

"I see," Allie responded. But she was willing to bet he was the only one who'd torn Barker out of the picture and framed it.

9

Clay's muscles shook as he pushed himself to bench-press more weight than ever before. Some days, in order to achieve any peace at all, he had to drive himself until he could scarcely think. Which was why he had a complete weight room in the basement of his house.

Today was one of those days. After his confrontation with Chief McCormick and the discussion that followed with Reverend Portenski, he was searching for the oblivion of absolute exhaustion.

Three hundred and fifty pounds hung suspended by his own power in the air above him. His body begged him to stop. But he wouldn't. He could still picture Allie in that pretty top at church, the flirtatious smile she'd given him when he said he wasn't as cheap as she might think—and the glower on her father's face as Chief McCormick demanded Clay leave her alone.

Maybe getting close to Allie would enable him to control—to a degree, anyway—what Allie learned about Barker and how she interpreted it. At least he'd know where she was in her investigation. He could see the value in that, for him. But he couldn't offer *her* anything. Unless she was just looking for a good time. Clay knew women enjoyed what he could give them in bed. Problem was, Allie McCormick wasn't like Beth Ann or the others who pursued him so relentlessly. Clay wasn't convinced he could get her to sleep with him even if he tried. She'd always been one of those straight-arrow types. *I've only been with my ex....*

One...two...three... Sucking air in between his teeth, he began to lower the barbell carefully to his chest. It wasn't wise to lift so much weight when he was alone. Maxing out, as he was doing now, was supposed to be done in the presence of a partner who could help in an emergency. But Clay didn't care about the risks involved. He preferred to lift alone, the way he did almost everything.

Briefly, the barbell touched his chest. Then he gritted his teeth and commanded his arms to lift it again. One...t-w-o...t-h-r-e-e, he groaned. For a moment, he didn't think he could do it. But he refused to give up before he was ready.

Push, dammit. Push! he ordered himself.

His whole body trembled with the strain. The weight began to rise, but it was only through sheer will that he finally lifted the barbell until he could fully extend his arms.

As he gasped for breath, Clay wanted to believe he'd done enough. He wasn't sure how much more he could take. But it was early. And he still wanted to see Allie, regardless of whether or not it'd be good for either one of them.

Another rep. He needed to keep lifting.

He managed two more, and then the phone rang.

Maneuvering the barbell into the holder over his head, Clay sat up and grabbed a towel to wipe the perspiration from his face. Allie had said she'd call him. He'd asked her to dinner.

But by getting to know her, he could lose as much as he stood to gain. Why bother? Without Barker's remains, she couldn't prove there'd even been a murder, whether Lucas was telling tales or not.

At least Clay hoped that was true. Since that night nineteen years ago, he could never be completely sure.

With a tired curse, he let the caller go to voice-mail and headed for the shower.

Allie hung up when Clay's voice, in the form of a recorded message, came over the line. She had several people still to interview and planned to go down her list. But Clay had had plenty of time to get home and she didn't want him to think her earlier lack of response and rapid departure meant she'd decided not to go out with him. Sure, she hoped to keep the peace with her parents, especially now that she was living with them and depending on them to watch Whitney while she worked. They'd always been close. But she had her limits. She wasn't going to allow them to tell her who she could and couldn't see.

To prove it, she'd go out with Clay in spite of her father. What was one dinner? They needed to talk. They'd been together a couple of times but had never thoroughly discussed the details of the night Reverend Barker went missing. In light of the photograph she'd just discovered at Fowler's, Allie had some questions Clay might not have entertained before. Also, Lucas denied that he'd spoken with his family during the two previous decades, but Allie knew from what he'd inadvertently revealed that he'd talked to *someone* during that time. She was hoping to get Clay to explain a bit more of how, when and why Lucas might have been in touch.

In any case, having dinner with Madeline's step-brother should prove interesting. Dealing with him usually was.

Pushing the End button on her cell phone, she decided to try again later and slowed to turn into the property across from Clay's farm. Bonnie Ray Simpson lived in the ramshackle old home set back a quarter of a mile from the road. Her aging husband, the victim of a recent stroke, and the wayward teenage granddaughter she was struggling to raise lived with her. According to the files and Allie's memory, Bonnie Ray had claimed she saw Barker come home on the night in question.

Allie wanted to see how definite Clay's neighbor was about that sighting. But as she looked over at the farm, wondering where Clay might have gone, she spotted the back end of his truck parked slightly behind the house. Had he missed her call because he was outside in the barn or somewhere else on the property?

Turning around, she pulled into Clay's driveway instead of Bonnie's and parked next to his truck. He hadn't answered the phone, so she didn't bother approaching the front door. She walked to the chicken coop in back, calling his name as she scanned the fields and the area between the outbuildings.

No one responded and nothing moved except the chickens pecking at the ground and the leaves on the trees, stirred by a gentle wind.

She crossed to the barn. Clay spent a lot of time restoring antique cars. She was betting she'd find him tearing apart one engine or another. But the barn doors were bolted shut and secured by a heavy padlock.

To the right, she recognized the small room that had been Barker's office. She'd accompanied her father there once to hand in her brother's permission slip for a youth campout. That was a long time ago, but she had a vivid recollection of the middle-aged, soft-looking Barker sitting behind his wooden desk, wearing a pair of reading glasses she'd never seen on him before.

Tossing a quick glance over her shoulder to make sure she wasn't being watched, she hurried closer to the window. Sunlight reflected off the glass, making it difficult to see. But when she raised a hand to shade her eyes, she found herself peering into a room that had been stripped of absolutely everything—even the carpet and the dark paneling that had once covered the walls.

Obviously, Clay didn't plan on Barker's coming back. Allie could understand, now that Barker had been gone for so many years. But she wondered why Clay hadn't turned the space into his own office. Or used it for some other purpose. Maybe he was in the process of doing so, she thought. But—she squinted to see more clearly—it appeared that someone had stabbed at the bare Sheetrock with a knife or some other sharp object.

Automatically, she began searching for the instrument that might have caused the damage, but the deep rumble of an engine distracted her. She looked between the buildings, toward the sound, just in time to see a tow truck heading toward town.

Was it Jed Fowler? Had he followed her here?

Hurrying toward the road to catch another glimpse of the truck, she charged around the corner of the house as fast as she could in high heels.

A strong arm reached out and grabbed her, halting her in midstride and causing her to step right out of one shoe.

"What are you doing here?"

Allie blinked up at Clay. She'd seen a number of

closely guarded emotions flicker across his face in the past three days, more than she'd ever seen him reveal before—but now his expression was positively stony.

"You didn't answer your phone," she explained. She looked past him, trying to see the road again. But the tow truck was gone.

"And?" Clay prompted.

She gave him her full attention. "And when I was on my way to Bonnie Ray's, I spotted your vehicle and thought you must be working outside."

"I was having a shower."

She could tell. Water dripped from his hair onto his bare shoulders. He hadn't taken time to put on a shirt or shoes before coming out of the house.

"I'm sorry. I just wanted to let you know that I'm interested in dinner."

He flicked his hair out of his eyes. "So you can dig a little deeper into my past?"

"So we can work together to discover what happened to your stepfather and bring Madeline and the rest of your family some closure." Allie suspected he wouldn't like that answer, but she knew he couldn't complain about it, regardless of his true feelings.

"And your father?" he asked.

"Don't worry about my father. He's…confused right now."

"About?"

"The nature of our relationship."

"Which is…"

She wasn't completely sure herself, but she knew what it needed to be. "Professional, of course."

"Of course," he repeated.

"So where should we eat?"

He wiped away a drop of water running down his chest. "I don't like crowds."

"We could find some out-of-the-way café. Or…wait, I know the perfect place."

He hesitated as if he might refuse.

"Have you changed your mind?" she asked.

"Maybe."

She sent him a challenging grin. "Why? Do I make you nervous?"

He chuckled softly—the cat laughing at the canary. "What time?"

"Is it okay if we go late? After I put Whitney to bed?"

"Your call," he said.

"Fine." She told him how to get to the back of her parents' property and promised she'd be waiting at the guesthouse. From there, they'd drive on to the destination she had in mind. "Pick me up at eight-thirty."

His eyes moved over her. The blouse she was wearing wasn't particularly revealing. It wouldn't raise eyebrows even in a church, which was why she'd felt perfectly comfortable wearing it to the service today. But Clay had a way of making her feel as if he could see right through it.

Her heart began to pound for no reason at all and she realized then, more than ever, that police officer or not, she wasn't as immune to his sex appeal as she preferred to think.

The nature of our relationship is professional. Of course.

"See you at eight-thirty," he said and went back inside as if he didn't care whether she rambled around the farm. But now that he was aware of her presence, she knew she wouldn't get very far if she started snooping again. Clay was infamous for guarding his own.

With a sigh, she wiggled her foot back into the high heel she'd lost, climbed into her car and headed to Bonnie Ray's. The place she'd chosen for dinner with Clay was private indeed. Which could work in her favor, if it put Clay at ease and he actually talked to her. Or the seclusion could be a liability, if Clay was as dangerous as her father had suggested.

Was she foolish to take the chance? Possibly. But not because she feared Clay would hurt her physically. It was the promise of what he could do to make her feel *good* that worried her. The last thing she needed was to get intimately involved with her prime suspect.

Clay picked up Allie and they took his truck, but she insisted on driving, so they switched seats.

She drove about forty-five minutes from Stillwater to an isolated fishing shack upstream from Pickwick Lake. Then she cut the engine, grabbed the picnic basket she'd wedged into the seat between them and climbed out.

Clay wasn't sure whether or not to follow her. He didn't know where Irene and Dale spent time together, but he figured it had to be fairly close. Neither of them was ever gone for long. And Clay doubted the chief would risk meeting Irene at the guesthouse on his property in town. This small fishing hut, which Allie had described as her father's favorite getaway, sounded like a much more viable option. It was always available to Dale, very private and somewhere Evelyn probably never went.

Clay stared at the cabin, which Allie had already entered. He'd never dreamed she'd take him to such a place. He hadn't even known it existed. Now that he did know, however, he could easily imagine Allie's father calling Irene and asking her to meet him here for a few hours on an available afternoon.

Not that imagining such a rendezvous created a picture Clay wanted to see….

"Aren't you coming?" Allie called from the front step, her body silhouetted by the flicker of a kerosene lamp. She seemed uncertain about his delay, but she didn't act as if she'd just stumbled on proof that her father was having an affair.

Releasing his breath, Clay got out of his truck and approached the cabin.

"This is definitely private," he said.

"My dad comes out here almost every Sunday," she told him. "He likes to fish."

"With you?"

"When my brother and I were younger, he'd bring us along. These days he mostly comes alone."

Or so he wanted everyone to believe, Clay thought. "What about today? He didn't come up?"

"No, he had too much to do. I saw him at home before I left."

More good news. "I can see why he likes it here."

The *qui-ko-wee* of a lone whip-poor-will, which rose from the damp woods surrounding them, seemed louder than any Clay had ever heard. He liked that sound and the sense of seclusion provided by the dense vegetation. But he hesitated at the cabin door, still afraid he might find something of his mother's inside.

"You seem…reluctant to be here with me," Allie said, frowning up at him. "What's wrong?"

"Nothing," he said and stepped across the threshold.

Only about twelve by fifteen feet, the shack looked like an old miner's cabin. There was a double bed pushed up against the wall. A dining table sat in front of a rock fireplace that had a spit and an iron hook dangling from above. Three wooden logs, crudely fashioned into chairs, were arranged by the table. White drapes hung at the window. The other furnishings included a small bookcase near the bed, some detached cupboards, a shelf above the fireplace with cooking utensils hanging from it and a knotted rug that covered the wooden planks of the floor.

"There's no bathroom?" he said.

"The outhouse is downstream a bit. This time of night you'll need a flashlight or you'll never find it."

"How long has your father owned this place?"

"Most of my life." She gestured around her. "Luxurious, isn't it?"

Maybe it wasn't luxurious, but it was appealing. After all the unwanted attention he'd endured in his life, Clay felt as if he'd just stepped into another world, as if he could hide out here and avoid the prying eyes that watched him wherever he went in Stillwater.

It was easy to see how Chief McCormick and Irene might feel the same sense of security. Clay was almost certain this had to be their meeting place. But, fortunately, he saw no sign of his mother's having visited once, let alone more often.

"Maybe someday my father will make improvements," Allie said.

Clay shook his head. "I hope not. I like it the way it is."

"If you had to cook here very often, you wouldn't be so eager to keep it primitive," she said. "I personally think it could use running water and electricity. And I'm not fond of trudging down to the outhouse in the middle of a dark cold night." She moved the picnic basket from the floor to the table. "But considering how remote this place feels, it's really not that far from civilization."

She tilted her face up, expecting a reaction to her remarks, but he'd already forgotten what she'd said. Clay was beginning to marvel at the fact that he hadn't originally considered Allie very attractive. She was so quick-witted and optimistic, so full of life and energy. She made him *feel* again—eagerness, hope, a deep-seated arousal— just when he'd decided he was beyond reach. Stillwater had become such a stagnant place, one that, for him, still revolved around the events of nineteen years ago. And yet, now that Allie was back, everything seemed to be changing....

He welcomed the way she made him feel, knew he needed it. At the same time, he feared the hope—because he knew no one could really change anything in his life. Certainly not the past...

"What?" she said when he simply stared at her.

"It's perfect," he said.

She smiled as if she was a little surprised he liked it so much. But he hadn't been talking about the cabin. "I hope you're hungry."

"What's for dinner?" He eyed her basket. "Or do the pointed questions come first?"

"Don't worry about the questions. I'm going to ply you with wine before we start. Maybe I'll get more out of you that way," she said with a wink.

He arched his eyebrows. "More *what* out of me?"

She ignored the double meaning. "More than you normally say, which isn't much." She pinched her bottom lip, an action Clay found distracting, to say the least. Her lips were so full, so kissable. He was imagining what they might taste like, when she drew him back to the conversation. "Why is that? Why do you keep such a tight rein on yourself?"

Clay was beginning to believe they were far too alone…. "I don't. Haven't you heard? I do exactly as I please."

She shook her head. "That's not true. You push everyone who reaches out to you away. And yet I sense a deep desire to connect."

"That's bullshit," he retorted, but he couldn't meet her eyes. The way she watched him made him feel as if she could decipher every need, every longing. "I don't trust just any idiot who comes along, that's all."

She folded her hands on top of the picnic basket. "Are you willing to trust me, Clay?"

He couldn't trust anyone. *Especially* her. But he didn't say that. He steered the conversation in a different direction. "Tell me what you think happened."

"To Barker?"

"Who else?"

"As far as I'm concerned, it's still a mystery."

"Come on," he said. "After everything you've heard, you have to wonder—am I the guilty party?" He advanced on her to see if she'd back away. "I don't even go to church regularly. That makes me a heathen right there."

She stood her ground. "Not in my opinion."

"You're avoiding the bigger issue," he said softly. "What if it's not safe for you to be alone with me?"

He loomed over her, hoping she'd cower in fear or retreat—so he could dismiss her as easily as he did everyone else in Stillwater. He had to destroy the confidence she seemed to have in him. He was pretty sure it was the way she treated him, as if he was good and not evil, that affected him so deeply. But she didn't blanch or move. She seemed perfectly relaxed as she glared up at him. "You don't intimidate me," she said calmly.

"Then maybe you don't know what's good for you," he scoffed. "I bet no one's even aware that you're out here."

"Who would you have me tell?"

"Not your father, that's for sure."

"Good. We're in agreement there."

"So no one knows."

"Does it matter?"

"It could if I'm the monster everyone thinks I am."

Her expression turned thoughtful. "You're not a monster, Clay. But that doesn't mean you're perfect."

"Do I have to be?"

She studied his face, but he glanced away before she could guess how badly he wanted her to accept him as he was. "For what?" she asked.

To atone for the past. But it was a pointless question. He already knew he could never be good enough. And that was his problem, not Allie's. He was the one who had to live with his role in what had happened. "To get fed tonight," he said.

She jerked her head toward a small stack of firewood. "As soon as you build a fire, we'll eat."

The flames cast a golden haze of moving shadows over Clay, softening the harsher angles of his face. Allie wished she could see him more clearly, but once she'd warmed the gumbo over the fire and poured it into the sourdough bowls she'd brought, he filled two wineglasses with Merlot and turned off the kerosene lamp.

She'd considered turning the lamp back on, but, in the end, decided that she liked the darkness. It encircled them like a protective shroud, evoking the kind of intimacy that set them apart from the concerns of everyday life. She thought that might help Clay loosen up and talk to her. But she was a little concerned that it might loosen *her* up, too.

They ate mostly in silence. Then, because the chairs were so hard, they carried their wine over to the bed. Allie lay on her stomach, cradling her glass in her hands; Clay leaned against the wall and stretched his legs out in front of him.

"I could get used to coming here," he said, gazing into the fire.

Allie had guessed he'd like the place, but she'd been surprised by how vocal he'd been about it. Clay wasn't all that vocal about anything. "I'll bring you again sometime."

He raised his glass to her in a mock toast. "Providing I have more secrets to share, eh?"

She grinned. "You must have something I want."

"I can play pool, remember?"

"And if I'm ever in the market for a 1950s Jag, I'll know where to go."

He shook his head. "Wow, such enthusiasm. You really build a guy's ego, don't you?"

She ran her finger around the rim of her glass. "I suspect your ego can withstand one less female swooning at your feet."

"Swooning?" He took another sip of wine. "I never dreamed someone so prim and proper could be such a smart-ass."

"Prim and proper?" she echoed. "What makes you think I've ever been prim and proper?"

"Maybe it's the badge."

"Not everyone who wears a badge could be called prim and proper. Why would you describe me like that?"

"I guess it started with the long skirts you wore in high school. And the way you hugged your books to your chest and walked to class with such purpose."

"You remember that?" she said with a laugh. She hadn't thought Clay had ever really noticed her.

"Along with the speech you delivered as valedictorian. What was it— 'Building on the Foundation of the Past'?"

"You just nailed the topic," she said, astonished.

"They printed it in the paper. It was a damn good speech. If you had a past worth building on."

"My parents made sure I had what I needed," she said. But she knew he hadn't been nearly as lucky. Once his stepfather went missing, his mother had been forced to take whatever job she could, and it was a standing joke in town that she'd work for slave wages. She'd had to. No one in Stillwater had wanted to give the person they held responsible for the reverend's disappearance any breaks.

Clay wore the same clothes to school for several days in a row and never ate lunch. He didn't have the money. Like his mother, he worked at the farm and took whatever odd jobs he could find. Some days he showed up at school so ragged around the edges he could scarcely stay awake in class. But he always looked after his sisters, even his stepsister, Madeline. And he would've died before admitting that he was going without because he had to. He made it seem very cool and rebellious, as if he liked what he wore and wasn't in need of anything at all.

Most of the kids actually bought in to the tough image he'd projected but, as an adult, Allie could see it for what it was—a young man's sacrifice and pride.

"They care about you," he said. "You should listen to them."

"And stay away from you? Is that what you're getting at?" she asked bluntly.

His eyes settled on the small amount of cleavage showing above her shirt. "For starters."

"Yeah, well, thanks for trying to protect me, but I'll tell you what I told them. I'm a big girl. I'll think for myself."

"A *big* girl?" he scoffed. "Hardly."

"I'm big enough."

"For what?"

"To do whatever I want to."

His grin slanted to one side, as if he found what she'd said rather endearing, like a puppy barking at a much larger dog.

"Stop with the patronizing bullshit," she said irritably.

"Hey, I think you're tough." He lifted his hands in a show of sincerity, but his grin had turned into a full-fledged smile. The kind you didn't get very often from Clay Montgomery. As if he was enjoying himself. As if he liked her. "You carry a gun, don't you?"

She cocked her head to the side. "Don't make me shoot you."

He laughed softly. "Are all lady cops out to prove something? Or just the ones who weigh less than a hundred pounds?"

"I weigh a hundred and *five* pounds," she said. "Anyway, haven't you ever heard that good things come in small packages?"

"I'm growing more convinced of that by the moment," he said, staring at her mouth.

Allie's heart was now beating in her throat. She wanted to fill the silence but wasn't sure she could speak. She felt as though all the oxygen had been sucked from the room.

Finally, he broke the tense silence. "What happened to your marriage?"

She scowled. "I thought I was the one who got to ask the uncomfortable questions."

"You know the saying—all's fair in love and war."

"Which is this?" she asked.

His gaze returned to her lips. "You tell me."

She swallowed hard. It sure as hell wasn't war…. "He struggled with mood swings, had very little patience and different priorities," she said.

Clay seemed to have lost the thread of the conversation.

"My ex," she clarified.

"What were his priorities?"

"Affluence. Freedom."

"And yours?"

"Children."

"The other day you told me he didn't want children."

"Right. He couldn't stand to have anything slow us down and resented the financial obligations and responsibilities. But mostly he hated sharing me with anyone else."

"Did he tell you no children before you were married?"

"No. He mentioned it before I got pregnant, though. We argued about it all the time and decided to compromise at one."

"And then?"

"And then he'd hardly look at Whitney and got jealous whenever she interrupted us or required my attention."

"Where did you meet this guy?" he asked.

Allie liked that response. It told her that Clay found Sam as unbelievable as she did. "At college. He's a bright guy, ambitious, social—and intensely possessive and selfish. I eventually realized that I couldn't tolerate having a husband who wouldn't even babysit our child if I needed it. I began to feel more and more torn between the two of them. Then, one day I came home to find that Sam had picked up Whitney before I got off work because the babysitter had a family emergency. He'd tried to call me, but I was working an important case and couldn't be reached. So he brought her home, locked her in her room and let her cry for hours."

"That's the point where I'd make him very sorry."

She laughed. "I was the one who was sorry—sorry I'd ever married him. To my mind, there was no excuse for such neglect."

"Sounds like he didn't deserve either of you."

"Yeah, well, he's with someone else now, and it's for the best."

"Are you happier on your own?"

"I'd never go back to him, if that's what you're asking." She rubbed her free hand over the goose bumps on one arm. Now that it was later, the air was growing cold despite the fire.

Leaning over, Clay unfolded the quilt at the foot of the bed and pulled it over her.

"Thanks," she said.

He grinned. "Don't say I never did anything for you."

"Okay, I won't." She drained her glass and set it on the bookcase. "Now can I ask *you* a few questions?"

"Am I going to need more wine to survive the interrogation?"

"Possibly."

"Where are you going to start?"

She frowned apologetically. "With your father."

He grimaced. "Great."

"Should I get you another glass of wine?" she asked, sitting up.

"Actually, I'm pretty sure I wouldn't want to talk about him even if I was falling-down drunk. So you might as well go ahead."

Switching positions on the bed, she sat beside him with her back against the wall, and covered them both with the blanket. "When did he come back here?"

"Where's here?" he asked.

"Stillwater."

He blinked at her. "He didn't, as far as I know."

"He's never contacted you?"

"No."

She hated having to press him about this particular subject. She knew that what his father had done still hurt, although Clay liked to pretend otherwise. "What about your mother?"

He stared into his wineglass. "He didn't contact her, either."

"Would she tell you if he did?"

"I think so. For a while, I was all she had."

For a long while, Allie added silently. "You've always been close."

"She told me most everything."

Allie suspected Irene had shared far more about her very adult problems than was good for a teenage boy. But, as Clay had just said, he was all she'd had. And somehow, at sixteen, he'd taken on the responsibilities of a man. He'd run the farm and picked up various part-time jobs. The way he'd supported her and his sisters was admirable, but no one in town ever talked about that.

Allie wondered why he never seemed to get any credit for the good things he'd done. He'd graduated from high school while doing the work of two men and acting as his family's patriarch. And then he'd put himself through college, completing a four-year degree in only two and a half.

"Your mother's lucky to have a son like you," Allie said.

He finished his wine. "Someone about twenty years older would've been a greater help."

"You did your best. What more could she ask?"

He grew quiet, pensive.

She craned her neck to look at him. "What is it?"

"Nothing. I'm just tired."

He tilted his head back against the wall and Allie scooted a little closer, seeking the warmth of his body. He responded by putting his arm around her, as if it was the most natural thing in the world. She sensed that his first inclination was to shelter, to protect.

Did that mean he was protecting someone else—his mother, for instance—in the reverend's disappearance? Allie was about to ask him about that night, when she realized Clay was asleep.

Reluctant to disturb him, she rested her cheek against his chest and counted the steady beats of his heart. Clay wasn't what she'd expected. He was far more sensitive, far deeper. She was willing to bet a lot of people, including her father, would be surprised to learn that. Allie thought she'd never met anyone more misunderstood.

We've got to leave, she told herself. But she was exhausted, too. She decided they could afford to rest for another ten minutes….

The next thing she knew, birds were chirping in the trees. It was morning.

10

Allie's first thought was that she'd just spent the night with Clay Montgomery. Her second was that he hadn't even tried to kiss her. She wasn't sure whether she was relieved or disappointed. She had to admit his lack of action was a blow to her self-esteem. She'd never expected Clay to pursue her. She knew she wasn't his type. But she'd slept in his arms for hours and he'd acted as if he wasn't even tempted….

"We have to get back," she mumbled, pulling away from the comfort his body had provided. "I need to be at home when Whitney wakes up."

He'd opened his eyes the moment she began to stir and was looking at her as if, unlike other mortals, he didn't need to go through the various groggy stages of rising to full consciousness.

Allie yawned, guessing that instant alertness came from a lifetime of standing vigil over the farm. Couldn't Clay ever truly relax?

"What's wrong?" she asked when he didn't respond.

"Nothing."

Immediately standing up, he started gathering the left-overs of their picnic while Allie tried to stretch the kinks from her muscles. "Do you always wake up going a hundred miles an hour?"

"What?" he said.

"Never mind." With a final stretch, she stood, too, and began to help.

"So, did you learn any deep dark secrets last night?" he asked as he carried the basket out to his truck.

She followed with the tablecloth. "Are you kidding? You know I didn't. You got off pretty light."

"How'd I manage that?" he said with a boyish grin.

She liked the way his hair stuck up on one side, the dark shadow of beard growth covering his prominent jaw. He looked rumpled—and sexy. "You went to sleep. What was I supposed to do, wake you?"

They both knew she could've done exactly that. But Allie was no longer so anxious to badger Clay for details about that long-ago night. She was beginning to hope, *really* hope, that he'd had no part in whatever had happened. And it was easier to avoid the answers to certain questions if she didn't ask them in the first place.

"What makes you think Lucas has been back to Stillwater?" he asked.

After loading the picnic supplies in the back, they'd both gone to the driver's side. Clay opened the door and waved Allie in, then got in after her.

Allie slid over a few feet so he could drive, but not all the way. She had the oddest desire to sit close to him. Probably because she wasn't quite ready to return to regular life.

"He acted kind of suspicious when I talked to him on the phone," she said.

Clay's face was unreadable. "In what way?"

"He claimed he didn't know anything about Barker. Yet, a few seconds later, he accidentally revealed that he knew it'd been nineteen years since Barker went missing."

Clay said nothing.

"That's strange, don't you think?" she prompted.

"Anything's possible with my dad."

"I guess he could've heard about the investigation through the media," she went on, "but it wasn't that widely publicized. And he's been living in Alaska for two decades."

"He has some distant relatives here in Mississippi."

"Do you think he stays in touch with them?"

Clay shrugged. "He could."

His dad might have maintained contact. But that didn't explain why Lucas had jumped to the conclusion that Barker was dead, when only the guilty party, and anyone the guilty party might have told, really knew for sure. And it didn't explain why Lucas hadn't simply told her that he'd heard about Barker from family or friends.

"Do you know much about Eliza?" Allie asked, gazing out the window as they turned onto the highway and began to travel at a greater speed.

"Eliza?"

She glanced over at him. "Barker's first wife."

"Not really. Besides what Madeline's said."

"Barker never talked about her?"

"No. I found some old pictures in his office, but I gave those to Maddy when I finally dismantled the place."

"When was that?"

"Last summer."

"Why haven't you used the office for something else?" she asked.

He had one arm slung across the back of the seat, his hand so close he could've touched her hair, but Allie could tell he wasn't as relaxed as he appeared. "I don't need the space."

What Clay had done to the office was extreme, considering the fact that he had no real reason for gutting it. But Allie didn't want to ask about that, for fear of getting too close to details she'd rather not know.

"Can you tell me why Jed Fowler might have hated your stepfather?" she asked, changing the subject.

Clay took a little longer than he should have to answer, as though he was warring with himself over whether or not to be truthful. "No," he said at last.

Evidently, he'd decided he couldn't. Which set Allie's cop instincts buzzing. Clay had too many secrets. They frightened her. For him.

"We can never be completely honest with each other, can we?" she asked earnestly.

He took his eyes off the road long enough to stare across the seat at her. "That depends on what you want."

"I don't know what you mean."

"Yes, you do."

Was he acknowledging that he felt a spark between them, the same spark she felt? That the truth, once known, would stand in the way of what they both secretly wanted? She could've asked for clarification, but he wasn't a man who spelled out his feelings. And she was too confused about her own emotions to press him on his. So she let him drive the rest of the way in silence.

As they neared her parents' property, Allie couldn't help glancing nervously at the clock. It was only six-fifteen. She should arrive before Whitney woke up for school, which usually didn't happen until seven. But Allie's father was likely pacing the floor, waiting. Or maybe he'd gone to the guesthouse looking for her.

Fortunately, when Clay pulled down the back road, the guesthouse looked as empty and dark as they'd left it. If

Dale was awake, he'd be expecting Allie at the main house. "I don't think we should see each other again," she said as she grabbed hold of the door handle.

"Neither do I."

His quick, decisive rejoinder caused a painful jab. But Allie was determined not to show her disappointment. "Right. So we agree."

She opened the door, but he caught hold of her jacket before her feet could touch the ground.

"What is it?" she asked.

He cursed under his breath but didn't release her.

"What?" she said again.

"When are we going back?"

Allie didn't ask where. He was referring to the cabin. They'd acknowledged what they thought they should do; now they were addressing what they *wanted* to do.

"I'm on graveyard all week," she said.

She could tell he believed she was turning him down. With a nod, he let her go.

"But Friday would work," she added, lingering of her own volition.

His eyes fastened on hers. Agreeing to see him again confirmed that she wanted to be with him enough to go against her better judgment.

"We're at the part where you say okay," she told him when he didn't respond.

He nodded, looking somber. "Okay. I'll pick you up here."

Allie knew she'd be crazy to nurture the romantic feelings she was beginning to have for Clay Montgomery. And yet the temptation to return to her father's fishing shack, to spend another evening with him, was too enticing to resist. She'd stop seeing Clay after next weekend. One more outing would be okay. He didn't want her sexually, she told herself, or he would've made a move when they'd shared the bed. He needed company, a friend.

"Same time?" she asked, her heart beating wildly.

With a nod, he said, "I'll bring the food," and, as soon as she'd grabbed her picnic basket out of the back, he drove away.

"Dale's furious," Clay's mother said over the phone, her voice a harsh whisper, which indicated she was calling from work.

Clay was squatting near a broken water pipe out on the south forty. When he heard this, he put the lid on the special cement he'd been using, and stood. "About what?" he said, but he didn't need to ask. Dale had obviously found out that he'd been with Allie last night. If Clay were Dale, he'd be furious, too. He wouldn't want his daughter dating someone in Clay's position.

But Chief McCormick had at least one reason to be grateful, Clay thought. A lot more could've happened at the cabin than did. Clay had never exercised so much self-control when he held a woman that close. He'd never had to. The girls he dated started climbing all over him almost at hello. Yet last night, he'd shared a bed with Allie, felt her pliant body curl into his, breathed in the scent of her clean hair and soft skin—and hadn't so much as brushed his lips across her neck. Knowing she was too good for him, but having her completely available to him, was one of the most bittersweet experiences of his life.

And, like the stupid glutton for punishment he was, he'd asked for more of the same kind of torture next weekend.

"You *know* what," his mother said.

"Do I need to remind you that seeing Allie was your idea?" Clay pulled a rag from his pocket and wiped the dust from his face.

"I've changed my mind. I—I didn't know how much it'd upset—" her voice dropped again "—you-know-who."

"Your lover. Who's married." Clay laughed without humor. "Doesn't it bother you that he can sleep with you while demanding that your unmarried son stay away from his unmarried daughter?"

"It bothers me," she admitted. "But it's not that he doesn't like you."

"Right," he said, but she ignored the sarcastic interruption.

"It's that he's extra protective of Allie. She's his baby. He doesn't want to see her hurt again."

"She's only a year younger than I am. Why's he treating her like a kid?"

"I just told you. He doesn't want her to get hurt again. She has a child now, Clay. She needs to find a good father for Whitney."

Clay winced. "And that excludes me?"

"It's not as if you've had many long-term relationships," she said. "What woman have you dated more than a handful of times?"

"What woman that I've dated would you want me to marry?" he countered.

"None of them. You tend to like a woman who has a bust measurement larger than her IQ. But Allie's different."

He chose the women he chose on purpose. So there was no danger of wanting more than he could have. So he wasn't callously breaking the heart of one innocent woman after another while trying to fulfill his own needs.

But he wasn't about to explain that to Irene. "I don't like what's happening to you," he said instead.

"I don't know what you mean."

"You're not yourself. This relationship is clouding your judgment, making you do things you ordinarily wouldn't."

"That's not true."

"Yes, it is. And besides that, it's dangerous."

"For who?"

"For all of us, but especially Grace. She has the most to lose."

Irene made no response.

"Are you even listening?" he asked.

"Grace isn't the only one who wants to be loved, Clay."

He knew that from personal experience. But he still had to protect his sister. And standing by while his mother had an affair with the chief of police wasn't the way to do it. "Find someone else," he said. "Someone who's free to love you back."

"Stop it," she said. "I don't want to hear any more."

"Listen to me!"

"No, I won't! What's wrong, Clay? Why do you hate it so much that I'm finally happy?" she asked. "Just because you're determined to be miserable for the rest of your life, you want me to be miserable, too? Is that it?"

Clay's chest grew tight. "Is that what you think?"

"Yes!" she said and hung up.

But she called right back, and this time she was crying. "I'm sorry. That wasn't fair and I know it. It's just… I love him so much, and he says he loves me, but I can't ever really have him, can I? There's no way to make it work."

"No," he admitted.

She sniffed and gulped for air. "So what do I do?"

"The only thing you can do, Mom. Cut it off as soon as possible and then do your best to survive the bleeding."

Allie was supposed to be sleeping while Whitney was in school, but instead she was staring at her picture of Clay. Madeline had left her several messages. Clay's stepsister wanted to talk about the case, present some ideas and leads she thought Allie should follow up on. But Allie didn't particularly want to talk to her. She was losing enthusiasm for the case and knew she'd have trouble hiding it. For the first time in her life, she honestly believed there might be some truth to that old cliché about letting sleeping dogs lie.

Not returning Maddy's call wouldn't help, though. Her cell phone rang *again*, and caller ID indicated Clay's stepsister's name. Knowing Madeline would only keep calling if she didn't pick up, Allie hit the Talk button. "Hello?"

"How's it going?"

"Good, you?"

"I'm great."

She didn't sound so great. She sounded as if she was forcing herself to be cheerful when she was really just eager—eager for answers Allie didn't have.

"You finished going through the files yet?"

"Almost."

"Anything stand out?"

Nothing Madeline would want to hear. But to fill the silence, and pretend she was still moving forward, she mentioned that she'd questioned Jed.

"Did he say anything new?"

"Not really."

Allie could feel the other woman's disappointment, which made her want to ask her next question very carefully. She had no idea whether the torn program at Jed's house meant anything. He was odd enough that he might've kept it simply because Eliza had given him a kind word now and then. And Maddy's mother had to be a painful subject for her. "Do you know if your mother and Jed were ever friends?" she asked, putting a little lift in her voice to make the question sound as casual as possible.

"*Friends?* I don't think I'd say that. But I was only ten when…when she died, so maybe they knew each other better than I realized."

"You don't remember ever seeing him at the house?"

"No…but he helped us out when our car stalled once. I remember him towing us back to his shop and giving me a quarter for a Pepsi. And there was the time he got scarlet fever. He refused to go to the hospital. My mother helped nurse him so he could stay at home. But she was always doing that kind of stuff for people… Why?"

"I'm just trying to figure out why he quit coming to church. I wondered if they might've had a falling-out."

"Oh, no. No one ever had a falling-out with my mother. She was…" She seemed aware that her admiration for her mother was breaking through the anger that usually kept all mention of Eliza at bay. "She didn't have any enemies," she finished.

"Right. I didn't think so."

"Who are you going to talk to next?" Maddy asked.

Allie held Clay's picture a little closer. "I don't know," she said. "I spoke to Bonnie Ray but she just repeated what was in the files. And we're pretty busy at the station."

Silence.

"I'll make a list of other people to interview, though, okay?" she added.

There was another pause, as if Madeline wanted to ask

"When?" But she didn't. "Great. Okay. I know it's hard to get it all done."

Especially when your heart isn't in it. Allie sighed. "That's it for now, then. I'd better go."

"Allie?"

"Yes?"

"Tell me you won't give up."

Thinking of her rendezvous with Clay, Allie cringed. "Maddy…"

"I know, you'll do your best," she said and disconnected.

Over the next few days, Clay worked even harder than usual. He rebuilt fences, added soil amendments to the fields, and started to relandscape the front yard, all in an effort to keep himself too busy to think about Allie. But it was no good. On Tuesday night, his mother came over and told him she'd broken off her relationship with Chief McCormick. From her abject despair, he knew it was the truth, and was glad, especially for Grace. With the baby due in less than a week, she didn't need her world to fall apart. But Clay felt hypocritical telling his mother she'd made the right decision when, by seeing Allie, he was asking for the same kind of dilemma. He and Irene were both reaching for someone they couldn't have.

Cut it off as soon as possible, and then do your best to survive the bleeding.

He should be taking his own advice. Sooner rather than later. But he didn't attempt to contact Allie until Thursday night, after he'd already gone to bed, when he couldn't put it off any longer. Since he didn't have her cell number, he had to call the police station while she was at work.

"Stillwater Police Department. Officer McCormick."

Glad she'd answered the phone herself, Clay muted the television, shoved his pillows behind his back and sat up. "It's Clay."

"What's going on?" She sounded pleased to hear from him, which made him even more reluctant to cancel their plans for the following night.

"Nothing much."

"No late-night trips to Let the Good Times Roll?"

"Not tonight."

"The farm's looking nice. I couldn't help noticing when I was out there," she said.

"Thanks. How's your father treating you?" After his mother had told him how unhappy Dale was, Clay had worried that Allie's father might take his displeasure out on Allie. He'd wanted to call her just to see, but he knew he couldn't do anything about it, anyway.

"He's been in a bad mood all week," she said.

"Who told him you were with me?"

"I did. We weren't doing anything wrong. I didn't see any reason to lie."

She wasn't ashamed of being with him, and that made Clay feel better. He didn't want the fact that they'd gone out to cause problems for her, but neither did he want to be her guilty secret. "What did he say?"

"He said I'd ruin my future and that I had to think about Whitney. That was about it. To be honest, he didn't say as much as I thought he would. He seems a little…preoccupied these days."

"With what?"

"I'm not sure. I'm actually worried about him."

Had Irene's decision made more of an impact on Dale than Clay had expected? Was that the reason for his preoccupation? "Why?"

"He hasn't really been himself since I got back."

"From the cabin?"

"From Chicago. But this week he's been worse than usual."

A trickle of unease made Clay kick off his blankets and get out of bed so he could wander over to the window. "In what way?"

"Gruffer. Highly irritable. I don't know what's bugging him. Danny's noticed it, too, when he's talked to Dad on the phone."

"Danny's your brother, right?"

"Yeah. In Arizona. He says Dad's been distracted. But what really has me frightened—" She stopped as if she wasn't sure whether or not to continue.

"Is…" he prompted.

"I shouldn't be telling you this."

Clay hated the fact that he probably already knew the reason behind her father's strange behavior—and hated pretending he didn't. "You don't have to tell me," he said and sort of hoped she wouldn't.

There was a long pause. "I'd like to tell someone I can trust."

He pressed his forehead to the cool glass. She wanted to trust *him?* "What is it?" he asked, closing his eyes.

"I found a tube of bright red lipstick under the seat of my father's car."

Clay gripped the phone more tightly and began to pace. This was exactly what he'd been afraid of. His mother had broken up with McCormick—but had she done it in time? If news of the affair came out now, it'd cause just as much damage. "It doesn't belong to your mother?" he asked.

"No. She's never worn such a flamboyant color. She rarely wears any lipstick."

"Was it in his squad car?"

"Yes."

Clay pivoted and headed back across the carpet. "Then it could belong to almost anyone, right?"

"Conceivably, but…I don't know. That's not all. This is going to sound silly, but…there's this cute bear mug my dad uses. At first I assumed he grabbed whatever cup he saw. But no. He goes for the teddy bear every day. And he has the number of a florist in Corinth written on his Rolodex."

"Why's that so odd?"

"I don't remember him ever sending my mother flowers."

"Maybe he's planning to do it in the future."

"No. Something's not right. My mom covers it well, but I don't think he's giving her the attention he used to. When he's home he barely acknowledges her."

"They've been married a long time."

"That's no excuse."

Cursing to himself, Clay pivoted again. "What are you going to do about the lipstick?"

"Keep it until I can figure out what's going on. I'm thinking about searching the cabin when we go there tomorrow night."

"We were just there," he said. "Wouldn't you have noticed anything unusual?"

"I didn't really look. But if my father's having an affair, he has to be meeting the woman somewhere. Maybe it's at the cabin."

Clay imagined combing through the place with Allie, shoving any proof he might find in his pocket, and decided he couldn't do it. He didn't want what his mother had done to hurt his sisters—or Allie—and would carry Irene's secret to his grave. But he couldn't pretend to be Allie's friend, let her believe he was there for her when he was actually serving his own purposes. Maybe he wasn't a saint, but he wasn't going to abuse her trust like that, either.

"I'm afraid I won't be able to help you," he said.

A couple of seconds ticked by before she responded. "You're canceling?"

He cleared his throat. "Yeah. I've got a conflict."

"No problem," she said, but he could tell she was only being polite.

"Why don't you take a friend," he said. "You shouldn't be going alone."

"No. This isn't something I want to share with anyone else. I'll do it myself."

He dropped his head in his hand and massaged his forehead. "I'm sorry," he said, even though an apology wouldn't improve matters.

"Don't worry about it. We were never meant to be together, anyway."

She wasn't speaking in anger. It was an acknowledgment. And she was right. "I know."

"Is that the real reason you're not coming tomorrow night?" she asked.

"Yes."

He heard her sigh and wanted to tell her how badly he wished it could be different. But what was the point?

"Can I say one thing?" she asked.

He braced for the worst. "What's that?"

"I've never met anyone like you," she said and hung up.

Allie sat in her father's chair, staring glumly at the teddy bear coffee mug that seemed so damn out of place on his desk. She'd taken that cup to the sink every night for the past week, thinking her father would use another one when he came in the following morning. But every time she returned to work, she found the cute "Life would be un-bear-able without you" cup sitting beside his calendar. Obviously, it was a cup he deemed his own and not one to be shared around the station. But where had it come from? And why did he like it so much?

Allie wished she knew. On second thought—she sank lower in her seat—maybe she didn't. She felt bad enough. She had to admit that she was better off accepting the fact that she and Clay had too many secrets between them, secrets that could have devastating effects on *any* relationship, let alone one involving a cop.

But since last Friday, she'd thought of little besides seeing him again. Not only was he breathtakingly handsome, he'd been through enough in life to make him interesting, layered, unique—not shallow and selfish, like her ex.

The door swung open, and Allie barely hid her grimace as Hendricks walked in. She'd sent him out on patrol an hour ago, and he was already back. Not that it surprised her.

Taking one look at her, he asked, "What's wrong?"

The question caught Allie off guard. She hadn't managed to hide her real feelings? "Nothing, why?"

"Normally you're in the storeroom, digging through the Barker files as if you plan to strike gold. Don't tell me you're getting discouraged."

Reluctant was a more accurate word. When she'd talked to Madeline earlier in the week, she'd gotten excited about the case all over again. Clay's stepsister was so sure that he and his family weren't involved. Allie had wanted to solve the mystery just to prove Clay was as innocent as she hoped. To finally dispel the doubt and suspicion, so there was nothing to fear.

But then she'd begun to read the reverend's pocket Bible, which Madeline had dropped off at the station the day before. Judging by the notes in that Bible, the reverend seemed obsessed with sins of the flesh and, simultaneously, with his new stepdaughter. She wasn't sure the two were related in Barker's mind, but if so, what that Bible revealed made for some unsettling possibilities. Madeline attributed her father's words to his zeal for righteousness and his love of Grace. But whenever Allie began to puzzle out the most likely scenario, she immediately lost her enthusiasm for pursuing answers. She hoped Barker was living in Alaska, like Lucas Montgomery, or in some other remote place. Or that he'd been murdered by a stranger.

It was possible, she told herself. But in her more pragmatic moments, she had to admit the chances of that weren't high. In her experience, random murders were rare, especially when theft wasn't a motive. Homicide was almost always committed by someone who knew the victim, and it was generally the person who had the most to gain.

The Montgomerys had the most to gain in Barker's disappearance....

"I'm giving it a rest tonight," she told Hendricks. She couldn't think about the case right now. She was too disappointed about not seeing Clay tomorrow night, even though it was for the best. And she was too worried about her father. Was Dale having an affair? Betraying her mother? Betraying the whole family? If so, with whom?

The door opened again and Joe Vincelli strode in. Beth

Ann Cole was hanging on his arm, but Allie wasn't surprised to see them together. Last night, around midnight, she'd stopped in at Let the Good Times Roll, just to make sure there weren't any fights or folks needing a ride home, and found Beth Ann sucking on Joe's tongue and grinding herself against him right there on the dance floor. It was such a flagrant display that Allie had nearly cited them for public indecency.

She wished she had….

"Hello, Joe," she said. "Beth Ann. What can I do for you?"

"We dropped by to see how you're coming along with my uncle's case," Joe said.

As Allie stood, she placed the teddy bear cup behind her father's standing file folders. She knew moving it was probably unnecessary, but she instinctively wanted to hide it. "It's slow going. Cold cases generally take lots of time."

"Is my statement going to make a difference?" Beth Ann asked.

"It's in the file," Allie said.

Hendricks's shoes creaked under his weight as he made his way over to them. "It should be a big help."

"What does 'in the file' mean?" Joe demanded, ignoring him.

"It means it's there with everything else, and I'll take it into consideration," Allie responded.

"Will it get some attention?"

"If it warrants attention. But the case isn't even officially open, so don't expect too much."

Joe's expression darkened. "What are you talking about? Clay confessed. If that isn't enough to reopen the case, what is?"

"Last time I talked to Beth Ann, she didn't seem too sure of anything," Allie said.

"I was sure of Clay's confession." Beth Ann looked to Joe, who gave her an encouraging nod. "And I remembered something else."

"What is it?" Hendricks asked anxiously.

"Clay told me he buried the body right there on the farm."

Hendricks rubbed his hands together as if he believed every word, but Allie had to grit her teeth to stop from calling Beth Ann a liar. She couldn't let this case get any more personal than it already was. She had to allow people to prove what they really were.

Reminding herself of that, she managed to reel in her temper. "He did?" she said, trying to sound neutral.

Beth Ann flipped her long blond hair out of her face. "He did. And I said, 'Aren't you afraid the police will find it?'"

"What did he say?" Hendricks asked.

Beth Ann flashed Allie's fellow officer a smile for his eagerness. "He said, 'I'm not worried about that. The cops around here aren't smart enough to catch me.'"

Obviously, Beth Ann and Joe were hoping to provoke Allie into acting against Clay, whether she had justification or not. "That's an interesting and very detailed conversation," she observed. "It's a wonder you didn't remember it when I had you in here a week ago."

"I was upset."

"Who wouldn't be?" Joe chimed in, slinging his arm around her neck. "That bastard threatened to kill her if she told anyone."

"That's right," Hendricks breathed, enthralled by the drama.

"That's why I didn't come forward before," Beth Ann said. "I told you that, didn't I, Allie?"

Allie folded her arms. "That's Officer McCormick."

Beth Ann blinked in confusion. "What?"

"I'm Officer McCormick to you."

She stiffened, but Joe was already talking. "So what are you going to do about it? Are we finally going to see some action against the Montgomerys?"

"I can't do anything until I figure out who really killed your uncle," Allie said. "If anyone did."

The frown between his eyebrows deepened. That, together with his narrow face and pointy eyeteeth, made him appear more wolfish than usual. "You're saying it's *not* Clay?" he nearly shouted, ignoring her qualification.

"I don't think so," she said, but Allie wasn't sure if the facts supported her opinion or she just didn't want to accept the possibility.

"You're crazy," he told her scornfully. "Who else could it be?"

"I'm afraid I can't answer that yet."

"See?" Beth Ann looked smugly up at Joe. "She's hoping to get with him. She wants Clay."

"I've contacted him regarding the investigation. Like I've contacted a lot of other people," Allie said, trying to stem the accusations.

"But you're not hoping to sleep with those other people," Beth Ann said.

Anger drove Allie forward, until she stood mere inches from Beth Ann's face. "You've lied to me on several occasions," she said. "Unless you have something truthful to say, get out. Now."

A muscle flexed in Joe's cheek. "I'm going to the mayor."

Mayor Nibley was a friend of Joe's family, and she could cause problems for Allie, and for Allie's father, which wouldn't help their relationship. But Allie refused to let Joe intimidate her. "You do what you have to," she said. "And I'll do what I have to. Now leave before I arrest you both for disturbing the peace."

"You're the one who's disturbing the peace," Joe said.

"Because I won't pile on when it comes to Clay?"

"Because you won't do your job!"

"You can't prove something that didn't happen," Allie said. She was taking a big gamble, assuming so much. All the circumstantial evidence pointed to Clay. But she couldn't imagine him doing what everyone thought. At least not in cold blood.

Joe gave her a look of utter contempt. "This isn't over."

Allie had more to say but, fortunately, Beth Ann managed to drag Joe outside. The door swung closed behind them, then a long silence fell, during which Hendricks gaped at her.

"I don't think you want to be on Clay's side," he said at last.

"Maybe it's time someone was," Allie responded and stomped into the bathroom where Hendricks couldn't follow her.

11

Dale shot up out of his seat the moment Allie walked through the station door the next morning. The veins protruding in his neck told her he was every bit as angry as she'd figured he'd be.

"You wouldn't listen to me. You wouldn't keep your head down and stay out of the line of fire," he shouted.

Allie didn't know what to say. When her mother had nudged her awake and told her she was needed at the station, she'd known it was time to face the backlash from Joe's visit. But her father's reaction was even worse than she'd expected.

"Calm down. You'll give yourself a heart attack." She took a seat across from him, but she knew Dale wouldn't relax until he was good and ready. They were alone, so he could yell all he wanted without fear of being overheard.

"What were you *thinking?*" he demanded. "Being seen around town with Clay Montgomery. Getting drunk with Clay Montgomery. *Sleeping* with Clay Montgomery."

She hadn't told her father they'd gone to his cabin. He assumed she'd gone to Clay's farm, and she planned to leave it that way. "Maybe I had a little too much to drink the night we played pool," she said. "But I didn't get drunk with Clay. Not the way you think. And Clay didn't even touch me when we were out last weekend. We fell asleep, okay? *Nothing happened.*"

"But you know everyone around here believes he's guilty of murder. And you're a police officer, for God's sake!"

"No one's been able to prove Clay was responsible," she said. "Besides, like I just told you, nothing happened."

"Well, something happened this morning," he said.

Foreboding settled deep in Allie's bones. "What's that?"

"What you get when you thumb your nose at the people who've been dying to bring Clay Montgomery down."

"I don't know what you're talking about."

"The mayor's already called me three times, mad as hell. When she was struggling to win the election, she promised the Vincellis that she'd get to the bottom of Barker's disappearance. It was part of her damn platform. I had her convinced we were doing everything we could, that there wasn't enough proof to press charges. And that was okay—before you riled up the Vincellis. Now she wants a full-fledged investigation. No holds barred."

Allie caught her breath. Until that moment, she'd been studying her father's ruddy face, wondering if he was really cheating on her mother. But this last statement got her full attention. "What?" she murmured.

"You heard me. You've wanted this ever since you came home. Well, now you have it. You'd better solve the damn thing and do it fast, or we'll both be out of a job."

Allie's jaw dropped. She didn't want to investigate Barker's disappearance anymore. These days she had difficulty even reading through the notes and statements in the storeroom, terrified she'd uncover some piece of evidence that implicated Clay. "I've changed my mind," she said. "There's not enough there. I can't solve it."

"It's too late," he said. "You don't have a choice. You solve it or we'll be packing our bags. And they'll bring charges against Clay regardless."

"It's official? You're reopening the case?"

"It won't be open long."

"They'll never get a conviction based on what we've got!"

"That depends on the jurors, doesn't it? And if they're from around here, you never know."

Shit! Allie knew Clay's enemies were powerful enough to guarantee a panel of jurors to their liking.

She nibbled nervously at her bottom lip. "We can't put an innocent man in prison, Dad. That's where this is all leading, isn't it? They want to put him away and they're tired of waiting for the proper evidence in order to do it."

"Who says Clay's innocent?"

"I do!"

"That's your heart talking, Allie. And that's what scares me."

What about *Dale's* heart? Where was his heart in all of this? And what about his marriage? Allie wanted to ask if he was seeing someone else, but right now she could only accuse him of drinking out of the wrong mug. Clay was right; that tube of lipstick could belong to anyone who'd ridden in his car. Her father didn't give rides to many women, but that didn't mean he couldn't or hadn't. "I was just trying to help Madeline," she said.

He shoved some papers aside and finally sat down. "If they lock up her brother, you won't have done her any favors."

"That isn't what I wanted."

"I know. I've been trying to keep you out of this...."

His words trailed off, and he shook his head in frustration.

"That family's been through hell, Allie. You think I want to see that happen? I actually had Clay's best interests at heart when I asked him to stay away from you. But the two of you wouldn't listen to me. And now I have no alternative except to pursue the case."

Allie considered the information she'd sifted through already, Lucas's odd reaction on the phone, the picture Jed Fowler kept in his living room. What did it mean for Clay? For Madeline? For the rest of the Montgomery family?

She thought of Clay holding her at the cabin, remembered her desire to feel his mouth moving on hers.... "Clay didn't do it," she said.

Her father lifted a skeptical eyebrow. "It doesn't matter, does it? Someone has to pay. They're going to get him one way or another."

"No, they're not," she said. "He didn't do it, and I'm going to prove it."

Allie smiled at her daughter. "Hold still, babe, okay?"

Whitney could hardly contain her excitement long enough for Allie to tie the bow in her hair. "They'll be skating. On ice!" she said breathlessly.

"I know."

"And in the morning we're going to eat breakfast on a little cart in our room!"

Whitney had been planning this trip with her grandmother for the past several days. They were driving three hours to Nashville to see Disney on Ice and then, because it would be late, they were staying the night. Whitney had hardly talked about anything else. Fortunately, she didn't need much in the way of a response, because Allie hadn't been paying a lot of attention. She was too focused on trying to figure out how to stop the Vincellis from manipulating her father into pressing murder charges against Clay—and whether her search of the cabin would yield proof that her father was having an affair.

"Belle and Cinderella and Snow White will be there," Whitney went on. "And Beast."

"It'll be wonderful," Allie murmured absentmindedly.

Evelyn stuck her head in the bathroom. "How's my girl? She all set?"

Wearing a cream-colored dress, with a strand of pearls at her neck and matching pumps on her feet, Evelyn had put on some makeup. But Allie couldn't help noticing that the lipstick she wore was a very light pink. Soft. Muted. Like always. "Whitney's ready," she said.

Allie's daughter jumped up and down and clapped her hands. "Do I look pretty, Boppo? Do I? Huh?"

"You look beautiful, darling. Now, don't mess your hair." Evelyn gave her a warm embrace. "You remind me so much of your mother at this age."

"Are you sure tonight won't be too much for you?" Allie asked. "Driving so far alone? Maybe I should go with you."

Evelyn waved a dismissive hand. "Don't be silly. You don't have a ticket for the show, and there's no need to sit in some hotel room, waiting for us. This is our little adventure, right?" she said to Whitney.

Whitney came in perfectly on cue. "Right!"

Allie had assumed that her mother was spending so much time with Whitney because, prior to Allie's return, Evelyn hadn't been able to see her only grandchild very often. Danny had married three years ago, but so far he and his wife remained childless. Having Whitney in the same house was new for Evelyn and she was definitely enjoying it. But now Allie had to wonder if her mother wasn't channeling all her energy into her grandchild to make up for losses and disappointments in other areas of her life.

"Mom?" Allie asked.

Evelyn adjusted the clasp on her pearls. "What?"

"Doesn't Dad mind that you'll be gone all night?"

"Of course not. Why would he?"

"Because he'll miss you?"

"He'll be fine. He knows we'll be back tomorrow." She opened her purse and began to show Whitney all the treasures she had stashed inside.

"Are you and Dad getting along okay?" Allie asked.

Evelyn seemed to grow even more interested in the contents of her purse. "And see this?" she said to Whitney. "These are mints. To freshen our breath."

Whitney beamed at being treated like an adult. "Oh, I'm going to want one of those," she said reverently.

"Mom?" Allie persisted.

Evelyn snapped her purse shut and straightened. "What?"

"Are you and Dad doing okay?"

"Of course." She smiled, but Allie couldn't tell whether it was sincere. "Why do you ask?"

"He's seems a little…"

"Temperamental?"

Allie watched Evelyn closely. "I guess."

"Don't worry." She smoothed back a strand of Whitney's hair. "It's the diet."

"He doesn't like to eat his peas," Whitney confided.

Allie doubted her father was denying himself. From what she could see, he'd actually gained a few pounds. Was her mother afraid to question what was really going on for fear she might find the truth too painful?

If so, Allie certainly didn't want to be the one to inform her. But who else was there?

"I'll see that he finishes his vegetables tonight," she teased and walked them out to the car.

Her mother and daughter waved as they drove off, then Allie began packing for her own trip. She wanted to reach the cabin before it grew dark—and she wanted to leave before her father came home. She hadn't told him she'd be gone, hadn't wanted to invent any excuses.

If she was lucky, he'd assume she'd gone with Evelyn and Whitney.

Allie was on her way out of town when she spotted Grace Montgomery—Grace Archer since the wedding—at the stand she occasionally ran in front of what used to be Evonne Walker's house on the corner of Main Street and Apple Blossom. Since Grace had married Kennedy Archer, she'd taken a sabbatical from working as a lawyer. She preferred to stay home with her stepsons, and certainly didn't need to work for financial reasons. She didn't need to sit at the side of the road selling baked goods, garden produce and handmade items, either. But when Evonne died a year or so earlier, the Walker family had inherited her house and Grace had inherited her special recipes—recipes that were such a tradition in Stillwater, Allie couldn't imagine them disappearing. Evidently, Grace felt the same way. When the Walkers put the house up for sale, Grace had bought it and was in the process of turning it into a shop that would sell the same things Evonne had made. Until the improvements were complete, however, she continued to run her stand right there in the front yard, just as Evonne had always done.

Everyone knew it was in tribute to a woman Grace had truly admired. Grace wasn't the only one to miss Evonne. The entire town mourned her.

Kennedy's two boys were with Grace, as usual. They seemed especially close to their new stepmother. Which was a little surprising. Like Clay, Grace could be remote and guarded. Allie had tried to approach her on a number of occasions, but if Kennedy was around, he generally moved to intercept anyone who might corner his wife and make her feel uncomfortable.

Kennedy wasn't around today. So Allie decided to stop. She wanted to get to the cabin as early as possible, but she was also aware of what lay ahead of her on the Barker case. She needed to find some clue, some kernel of truth that would lead her to Barker's real murderer—before the situation spiraled out of control.

She hoped Grace would be the one to provide that kernel of truth.

Parking at the side of the road, she turned off the engine and climbed out.

"Hi, Officer McCormick!" Nine-year-old Teddy, the younger of the two boys, hurried over to meet her. He loved police officers and had once told her he wanted to be a policeman when he grew up.

"Hello, Teddy."

Heath, Teddy's older brother by two years, hovered near the end of the table. "I'll collect your money when you're ready," he announced.

If Allie had her guess, he'd be the one to take over at the bank. "Okay," she said chuckling as she picked up a bar of handmade soap.

Grace was selling two fruit pies to Mrs. Franklin, the wife of a retired pharmacist who'd been an institution in Stillwater since Allie could remember. When Clay's sister glanced up and saw Allie, she didn't seem too pleased.

"These smell good," Allie said to Teddy, stalling for time.

"Those are violet," Teddy told her.

"Lavender," Grace corrected as Mrs. Franklin left.

"They're nice," Allie said.

Heath handed her a wicker basket to hold her purchases, and she set the bar inside, along with some lavender lotion. "Evonne would be proud of the way you've stepped into her shoes," she told Grace. She was sincere in her praise, but that comment didn't start the conversation she was hoping it would.

"Thank you," Grace said politely, then shifted her attention to the curb as another car pulled up.

Allie turned to see that it was Reverend Portenski. He nodded a general greeting as he approached the stand, but his eyes kept flicking—rather nervously—to Grace.

Grace immediately busied herself restocking the brownie and cookie platters from covered plastic dishes stored under the table.

"What can I get for you, Reverend Portenski?" Heath asked.

"The peaches are good," Teddy suggested at his elbow.

Portenski picked up a bottle of peaches. "Yes, I think you're right. I'll have some of these." He glanced at Grace again; she didn't look up. "And a jar of dill pickles."

Teddy got the pickles for him while Heath hurried to the cash drawer behind the table. "That'll be ten dollars."

Allie put a plateful of brownies in her own basket. Because she'd been in such a hurry to leave the house, she'd packed a very meager dinner. The brownies might sustain her if the search took longer than expected. Or possibly help console her, as much as anything could, if she found something she'd rather not see.

"No fresh tomatoes yet?" Portenski asked Grace.

"Not yet," she replied.

"That's too bad. The ones you had last summer were the best."

Grace didn't respond, but Teddy spoke up. "They'll be ripe in a few weeks."

Allie sensed a strange kind of tension between Grace and the reverend, but she didn't understand the cause. Grace never went to church. Maybe the reverend had invited her to come out and she'd refused. Or he wanted to invite her and was afraid she'd refuse. Grace certainly didn't seem any more open to talking to him than she did to the police in general, or Allie in particular.

Allie watched the reverend struggle to gain her attention—in between adding a dozen fresh eggs to his purchases and examining the jams and jellies. But then a truck drove by, a truck Allie recognized. It was Jed's old Chevy, and she focused on that instead.

She still suspected he was the one who'd driven by the farm the other day, when she was peeking in the window of Barker's old office. If he hadn't followed her, it was an odd coincidence that they'd been heading in the same direction. And Allie was always suspicious of a coincidence.

He was such an unusual man. What was he doing with that picture of Eliza Barker? she wondered for the millionth time.

"I, uh, I spoke with your brother." Portenski was talking to Grace again, but the fact that he'd lowered his voice to almost a whisper caught Allie's notice.

"I'm afraid I might have given you the wrong idea with what I said the last time we talked," he murmured.

Allie had to strain to hear him, but Grace spoke more loudly.

"It's fine," she said. "No need to mention it."

It seemed obvious that Clay's sister didn't want to

address the issue, but the reverend was intent on saying what he'd come to say. "I want you to know I'm sorry. For everything."

Grace fidgeted nervously, and Allie did her best to look preoccupied. "You have nothing to be sorry for," Grace said.

He seemed relieved by her response. "Thank you." He gave Heath the money he owed for his purchases and started to leave, but Grace surprised Allie by calling him back. "Reverend Portenski?"

"Yes?" he said, a trifle too hopefully.

"You can help me by helping my brother."

Portenski must have understood what she meant, because he didn't ask *how* he could help Clay. The two of them stared at each other for a long moment. Then he nodded and got back in his car.

Allie handed her shopping basket to Heath. "I'm ready."

He added up the cost, gave her a total, and she withdrew twenty-five dollars from her purse.

"Come again," he said.

She accepted her change. "I will."

Grace turned away, expecting her to walk off, but Allie stood where she was. "Grace?"

Grace was putting labels on more bottles of peaches. "Yes?"

"I'd like to talk with you."

Any warmth that had been in her pretty, blue eyes when Allie drove up had long since fled. "About what?"

"I want to help your brother, too."

Silence. Then, "How do you propose to do that?"

"At this point, I'm not sure," Allie admitted. "That's why I'm coming to you."

"What can I do? I've already told you everything I know about the night my stepfather went missing."

The slam of a car door broke Allie's concentration. Jed had parked in front of her Camry and was approaching the stand.

"You've heard about Beth Ann's claims," Allie said quickly.

"She's lying."

"I know that and you know that, but we have to prove it."

"What can I get for you this week, Mr. Fowler?" Teddy asked, rushing over to meet him.

Allie sensed Fowler and the boy coming up behind her, and instinctively shifted to put more distance between them. But she didn't turn to look at Jed again. And he didn't answer Teddy. He merely handed the boy a jar of peaches and a sweet-potato pie, along with the exact change.

When Teddy began to whisper excitedly to his brother about how busy they were, and how much money they were making, Allie assumed Jed was on his way back to his truck and forgot all about him in favor of appealing to Grace. If there was a way to reach her, to enlist her support, it was through her love for Clay. Allie felt certain of it. In the past, Grace and Clay might have had their differences, but they'd always maintained a unified front.

"What do you say?" she asked. "Will you sit down with me? Answer a few questions I've never had the chance to ask?"

"I don't know," Grace said, her eyes troubled. "I don't see what that'll change. We've already been over it."

Allie wanted to tell Grace that the Vincellis had friends in high places who were trying to strong-arm her father into pressing charges. But she hesitated to go that far. Grace was too close to the end of her pregnancy. Allie hoped to solve the Barker disappearance, but she didn't want to throw Grace into an early labor or spoil the excitement she had to be feeling about the baby. "Will you think about it?"

Grace nodded, and Allie reached out to touch her arm. "Trust me, I'm on your side," she whispered earnestly, then nearly ran into Jed Fowler when she started to leave.

"Excuse me," she murmured. Irritated that Jed seemed to be lurking around every corner, she got in her car and drove away.

Allie reached the cabin much later than she'd hoped. A semi pulling two trailers full of dirt had overturned on the highway ahead of her, causing a traffic jam that lasted more than two hours. And then it had started to rain. By the time she arrived, it was pouring and completely dark.

"Just my luck," she muttered, staring miserably at the fat drops pelting her windshield. She was tempted to turn around and go back. She didn't really want to be out here alone so late at night. And she definitely didn't want to find what she was looking for.

But she'd already made the drive. It didn't make sense to give up before she'd even gotten out.

Grabbing her small dinner and the plate of brownies, she made a dash for the door. But she hesitated once she stood under the small overhang, staring at the dark cabin. She felt jittery, afraid, because she hadn't been able to answer the questions she'd been asking herself the entire drive: What if my father *is* seeing someone else? Would I tell my mother? Confront him? Or keep his dirty secret? What would be best for both my parents?

Despite her father's bluster, Allie loved him as much as she did Evelyn. But she wasn't sure how she'd feel toward him if she caught him cheating. To her, the fact that he was a cop made the situation that much worse. She expected more from a police officer. She didn't want to lose respect for the man she'd always admired.

"Please, don't let me down," she whispered. Then she took a deep breath, retrieved the key from under the mat and went inside.

The place smelled like Clay. Allie couldn't believe it. It'd been a whole week, and yet she could still detect his cologne. Or maybe she was only imagining that she could pick up his scent because she wished he was with her.

She scanned the room. Nothing that said "adultery" jumped out at her, even now that she was looking with a critical eye. But her father wouldn't leave evidence of a clandestine affair lying around where anyone could find it, would he?

She had to search for the small, insignificant details he might have overlooked.

Clay flipped through the channels on the television, trying to distract himself. Allie was probably at the cabin already, searching for proof of her father's infidelity. Whether or not she'd find it, he couldn't guess. He hadn't seen anything suspicious. But he hadn't checked the drawers, under the bed, the bookcase or cupboards. There was no telling what small thing his mother might have left behind. And if Allie found anything to fuel her suspicions, it'd only be a matter of time before she reached the truth.

Unless his mother could remain strong and stay away from Dale. Then there might be a chance.

But Clay didn't have much hope of that. He'd spoken

to Irene earlier. "I'm fifty-one years old, and my life is more than half over. What else do I have to look forward to?" she'd wailed. "Why am I denying myself?"

He'd tried to remind her. He'd also invited her to the farm, so she'd have company, but she'd declined. He would've gone to her place and kept watch over her, except he didn't believe that, ultimately, it would make any difference. If Irene was going to see Dale, she'd just arrange a meeting after he left. He couldn't stand guard on her around the clock.

Besides, he was agitated and torn himself. He couldn't stop thinking about Allie up at that cabin alone, discovering that her father was sleeping with his mother.

He shook his head. Allie would hate him by association. She might even guess that he'd known all along and wonder if he'd been secretly laughing at her.

The possibility that she might feel he'd betrayed her bothered him. But he didn't owe her anything. He had to protect his family from the people of Stillwater, including the police, *including Allie*. She was a cop.

And yet—he blew out a long sigh and changed the channel—and yet he wanted to shield her from the hurt she'd suffer as a result of learning the truth.

Flipping off the television, he stood. If she was going to find proof of her father's affair she'd have it by now. He'd drive there, console her if necessary, see that she made it safely home.

But if she *hadn't* found anything, they'd be in the same situation as last weekend, alone together, with only a nineteen-year-old secret to keep them apart—a secret that was all too easy to forget when he felt her beside him.

Muttering a curse, he forced himself to sit back down. He wasn't going anywhere. Allie wasn't his concern. He couldn't care about her and his family, too. Loving one would only betray the other.

Allie pointed her flashlight under the bed, then lifted the mattress. She was looking for sex toys, cast-off lingerie or lipstick-smeared shirts. But she found nothing.

She went through the bookcase, searching for pictures or notes or pornography. Nothing there, either.

She pulled everything out of the cupboard, checking for champagne or the presence of foods her father didn't like or wouldn't eat. She looked everywhere else she could think of—but once again came up empty-handed.

Standing in the center of the room, she turned slowly around, wondering if she'd missed anything. But she couldn't imagine what. One room, without much furniture, didn't give her father a lot of hiding places. Besides, he wasn't even aware that she suspected him, so she doubted he'd get too creative.

And that meant she'd been wrong.

Feeling a tremendous surge of relief, she laughed out loud. So what if her father was drinking out of a teddy bear mug? So what if she'd found the number of a florist on his Rolodex or a tube of lipstick in his car? She didn't care—because it didn't mean anything. He wasn't having an affair, or there'd be proof of it here at the cabin. She felt certain of it. Where else would he find the privacy an affair required? He couldn't meet his lover anyplace in town. He'd be instantly recognized.

Hunger pangs reminded Allie that she hadn't had dinner yet. Throwing another log on the fire she'd built for light as much as heat, she left the kerosene lamp burning, grabbed a flashlight, some soap and a towel and went to the outhouse before heading down to the river to wash her hands. It was still raining outside, but she didn't mind getting wet. She wasn't going to stay at the cabin much longer. She'd eat, then drive home, where she'd give her father a heartfelt hug and revel in the knowledge that her mother's life wasn't about to be destroyed.

The sound of shattering glass brought Allie's head up. There were a few other cabins in the area, but she didn't know exactly where and they were pretty spread out. She was fairly sure the noise had originated from her own place.

Dropping the soap and towel, she ran up the bank to the cabin, careful to turn off her flashlight and hang back out of sight as she approached it. But the window wasn't even cracked. She could see the glimmer of the fire through the glass. So...

A rustling in the woods not far away sent her pulse racing. Was it a small animal of some sort? "Is someone there?" she called, just in case.

No one answered.

She stepped out of the woods, her flashlight held low to the ground. But as she examined the clearing, she realized that someone had broken her car window. The rock that had been used to smash it was lying a few feet away.

Stunned, she crouched down for cover and searched the clearing again. But she could see no one, hear nothing except the soft beat of rain. Whoever had used that rock seemed to be gone, so she hurried over to check the damage. Why would anyone—

"Oh, God," she whispered. Slipping her hand gingerly through the jagged hole to unlock the car and open the door, she began to feel underneath the seat. Her gun was missing. Someone had stolen her Glock.

"Shit." Automatically, she reached for the portable radio she carried almost everywhere. But whoever had stolen her gun had taken the radio, too.

How had someone stumbled upon her car in this remote location and in the middle of a storm? Where had that person come from? And, more important than anything—at least at this moment—where had he gone?

Using the door for protection, Allie moved her flashlight in a wide arc. Who'd done this?

She couldn't see anything but trees.

Too bad she hadn't brought her squad car. That might have discouraged the theft. But she never took it outside jurisdiction.

She needed to get her cell phone, alert her father, then get the hell out of the woods. She didn't want to be sitting here alone in the middle of a storm while some unknown person was running around with her gun.

Turning off the flashlight, she picked up the closest stick she could find and crept toward the cabin to peer through the open doorway. Empty. A more thorough check revealed that there was no one hiding under the bed or behind the door. But her purse, which she'd left on the table, was gone, too—and with it her cell phone and car keys. In its place, next to the plate of brownies she'd bought from Grace, was a rain-soaked note.

The paper nearly fell apart as she unfolded it, but she managed to make out the blurry words that appeared to have been typed on a computer.

Leave the past alone, or Barker won't be the only person missing.

12

Rain pounded on the roof of the cabin as Allie huddled by the fire. She'd covered the window with a blanket so she couldn't be seen from outside and shoved the bookshelves in front of the door. It wasn't a perfect plan, but without a car or any way to call for assistance, she couldn't do much more. Except hope that the dry wood lasted until morning, and that the offender who'd paid her a visit was gone for good.

Noises from outside kept her on edge. Branches banged against the sides of the cabin; the rain thrummed loudly and steadily on the roof. Even the crackle of the fire made it difficult to determine whether or not she heard someone moving around.

It was unlikely, she told herself. If the person who had her gun had intended to hurt her tonight, he would've done it already. She had a kitchen knife for a weapon, but a knife wasn't much use against a gun. Considering her isolation, she was easy prey. So she doubted her visitor had hung around with plans to harm her. For now he—or she—was only out to deliver a message.

She knew that and yet she couldn't relax.

Holding her breath, she closed her eyes so she could focus on differentiating between the various rustling, tapping and scratching noises. But, in the end, concentrating didn't help. Her nerves were working against her. She couldn't tell what was real and what she'd imagined.

Calm down. Her palm began to sweat on the handle of the knife, but she didn't release it. She tried to occupy her mind by puzzling out who might've written the note. It had to be someone who knew her and what she was working on, someone who was familiar with the Barker case and had a personal stake in it.

Unfortunately, that didn't bring a lot of possibilities to mind. Most people in Stillwater *wanted* her to get to the truth. The Montgomerys were the only ones she knew of, besides Jed Fowler perhaps, who weren't particularly forthcoming.

Could it be Clay?

The thought crept in, even though she'd been carefully avoiding it. She'd told no one else where she'd be tonight.

But he was too smart to write a note that would make him look worse than he already did. And he'd told her not to come to the cabin alone. Would he encourage her to bring a friend if he planned to break into her car and frighten her half to death?

She didn't think so. It had to be someone else. Someone who wanted her to believe it was Clay....

Joe Vincelli? Joe's father or another member of the Vincelli clan? Beth Ann?

A car door slammed, and Allie froze. Maybe she was about to find out.

Scrambling to her feet, she pressed herself against the inside wall of the cabin listening for the sound of approaching footsteps. Whoever it was wouldn't be able to get in through the door. But he—or she—could break the window.

A loud knock made her knees go weak.

"Allie? Are you in there?"

Clay! She recognized his voice immediately and nearly

called out to him. But she was afraid she'd been a fool to trust him so much. Had she been blinded by his legendary sex appeal?

It was possible. *Anything* was possible. At the moment, she doubted herself, doubted everyone.

"Allie, open the door," he said. "What happened to your car? Why's the passenger window broken?"

The doorknob rattled. Icy tentacles of fear tightened every muscle—and yet Allie's first instinct, even now, was to let him in. She would have, if not for the echo of her father's voice in her head…*you got into his car, knowing he could be dangerous…*

"Allie, answer me! Are you okay?"

If Clay intended to hurt her, he'd had his chance last weekend.

Her reaction wasn't logical, but fear rarely was. Fear said if she lowered her defenses and she was wrong, he could kill her, bury her in the woods and drive back to town as if he'd never even left the farm—and no one would be the wiser. She'd simply be gone. Like Barker. Just as the note promised.

The fingernails of her free hand curled into her palm as she heard Clay move to the window. Would he break it?

She waited, heart racing, as she wondered if she'd have to defend herself against the man she'd started fantasizing about.

But when she heard his voice again, he was heading toward the river, probably searching for the outhouse she'd told him about, hoping he'd find her there.

"Allie!" The wind tossed his voice about. Her name seemed to echo against the trees, mixing with the melee of thunder and wind and rain. He must be getting soaked.

If he wasn't responsible for the night's events, what was he doing out here?

Think, she ordered herself. *Think, think, think!* She needed to clear her head; her imagination was getting the best of her. She didn't believe Clay had killed Barker, at least not purposely. And she couldn't believe he'd harm her now. She trusted him.

Enough to bet her life on opening the door?

She remembered the humiliation she'd sensed in him when she'd made him remove his shirt the night Beth Ann had accused him of murder. Beneath the tough exterior, Clay was a good man. Her gut had told her that from the beginning and her gut was all she had to rely on.

Taking a deep breath, she set the knife aside and started to shove the bookcase out of the way. But then she heard a muttered curse right outside the cabin, too close to be Clay. Clay was still calling for her down by the river.

Was the person who'd taken her gun still there? If so, why?

Joe's face, angry and vindictive, flashed through Allie's mind. The only answer she could come up with was that this was some kind of setup. No doubt Beth Ann had convinced Joe, along with half the town, that Allie wouldn't put Clay behind bars even if he deserved it. Maybe Joe had gotten tired of waiting for justice and decided to take the law into his own hands. Joe and his father and brother had been fishing with Allie's father a couple of times, so they knew about the cabin. It was possible that Joe had enticed Clay to the lake on false pretenses.

And if that was true…

Allie's stomach tensed. If that was true, she'd just let Clay walk into a trap.

She had to warn him. Now! But it had taken her a full

fifteen minutes to slide the bookcase in front of the door. She couldn't move it in a matter of seconds.

Unable to stop the terrible images bombarding her brain—images of Joe creeping up behind Clay with her Glock—she tore half the books off the shelves, kicked the unit over and used the wall to give her some leverage as she pushed.

"Allie?" Clay was still calling her.

"Stop! Get down!" she cried out in panic and frustration. But she knew he couldn't hear her. Each agonizing second seemed to last an hour as she moved the bookcase inch by inch.

Finally, she was able to open the door enough to slip through. "Clay!"

Clay's truck was parked right in front. Even without a flashlight she could tell that someone had punctured two of his tires.

Someone who didn't want him to leave. Which frightened her more than anything.

"Clay, get down! Don't say a word!" she yelled. Her cry echoed back to her as she charged after him. But it was too late. A shot rang out before she'd taken five steps. She heard a gasp to her left. Then someone went crashing through the woods to her right.

Time seemed to stand still as, not far away, Allie heard an engine start. The shooter was escaping. She didn't even try to follow. She'd never be able to catch him. But that wasn't what kept her rooted to the spot. It was the sickening realization that someone had just taken a shot at Clay. And she'd heard him fall.

The pungent smell of wet earth filled Clay's nostrils as he lay on the ground, blinking against the rain falling into his face. What had happened? One moment, he'd been searching frantically for Allie. The next, he'd heard a gunshot and something—presumably a bullet—had knocked him off his feet.

Had someone taken a shot at him? As surreal as that seemed, it was the only explanation. He wanted to believe the gunshot was a freak accident, but then he remembered Allie yelling, trying to warn him.

What was going on? He remembered the shattered window in Allie's car. She wasn't safe. He had to get up.

But his arm…

Muffling a groan, he tried to see what was wrong with it. It ached and burned. His head hurt, too. But he had to reach Allie somehow. The person who'd shot him could be after her.

"Allie?" he called. Except he was pretty sure her name didn't actually leave his lips. He was yelling, but only inside his head.

"Clay? Answer me if you can. Please! Clay? Help me find you."

She was the one who was calling. She was pleading with him, searching for him, but he couldn't seem to respond. Why?

The beam of a flashlight swept through the trees. She was coming toward him.

He cursed the target her light made. She had to turn it off, run, hide….

Squeezing his eyes shut, he tried to clear his muddled brain. Had he blacked out when he hit the ground? "Allie, get out of here," he said. The words were a mere croak, but at least this time he heard his own voice and, when he redoubled his efforts, he was able to yell louder. "Get out of here! Do you hear? Go!"

"Clay!" she cried, breaking into a run.

"Not this way!" he yelled. Slowly, his faculties were returning. He clambered into a sitting position and used the tree to pull himself to his feet. Dizziness nearly overwhelmed him, but he fought it back. She wasn't listening, dammit. She was hurrying toward him.

"Allie—" he started. But then she was there, helping to support his weight while she shone her flashlight, examining him closely.

"Are you hurt?"

He wanted to shield her, in case another bullet came from the same direction. But he didn't have his accustomed mobility. He wasn't even sure he'd still be standing without her. "My arm."

The beam of her flashlight rose, and he heard her gasp. She'd spotted the warm, sticky blood he'd felt soaking into his clothes. But when she spoke, her cop instincts seemed to take control because she sounded quite calm. "It doesn't look too bad."

He knew she was saying it for his benefit, but he had bigger concerns on his mind right now. Like getting shot again. Or seeing Allie shot. "Whoever did it could still be out there—"

"No, I heard him go. We've got to get you to the cabin," she said urgently.

"The cabin?" he said. "Let's get the hell out of here."

"We can't," she told him. "We don't have a vehicle."

As soon as Allie got Clay out of the rain, she helped him strip off his wet clothes. She was afraid he'd go into shock if she didn't get him warm. He was soaked clear through, and his pupils were dilated.

"Do you have a cell phone?" she asked.

"No."

Great. "That's okay. You're going to be fine," she said over and over. She wasn't sure who she was trying to convince, him or herself; she didn't feel nearly as confident as she tried to appear. Before she joined the cold case unit in Chicago, she'd responded to calls that involved some serious wounds, but she'd never come across a victim she couldn't immediately rush—or have rushed— to the hospital.

In any event, it didn't matter if she sounded a little panicked, because Clay didn't seem to be listening, any- way. Allie got the impression he had to concentrate just to remain conscious.

"Are you in a lot of pain?" she asked.

"No," he said.

She could tell by the grim set of his jaw that he was lying, but decided to play along. "That's good." She pulled the blankets over his naked body then rummaged through the cupboards, searching for anything that might help them.

She located a first-aid kit that was at least fifteen years old. Thankfully, the bottle of ibuprofen she found right af- terward was almost new. "Here, have some of these," she said, dropping four pills into his palm. "They might take the edge off."

He swallowed the pills without water and without argument.

"Doesn't look like a big deal," he said, gazing down at his arm.

Bits of dirt and grass clung to the blood smeared on his bicep, and a fresh trickle flowed from a tiny hole in his deltoid.

Was the bullet still inside?

That thought made Allie nauseous, which surprised

her. She'd dealt with some gruesome murders, considered herself to have a strong stomach. But this was different. Clay wasn't a stranger.

Allie wiped away the blood with a dish towel, because it was all she had. More blood surged out, so she applied pressure until the bleeding slowed. She could see where the bullet had gone in and—she leaned forward, then sagged onto the bed in relief—where it had come out. It had passed straight through the muscle.

"Don't tell me you're going to faint," he murmured.

"No, I'm just glad we don't have to perform any kind of crude surgery. There's a lovely exit wound on the back of your arm. If it didn't hurt so badly, you could probably turn it far enough to see for yourself."

He winced. "I'll take your word for it."

"I'm getting the bleeding under control."

"Glad to hear it," he muttered.

She tied the dish towel around his arm to keep pressure on the wound. "I'll be right back."

He reached out to stop her, but she stood up too fast. "Where are you going?"

"To the river for water."

"No, I don't want you out there. Get under these blankets before you catch pneumonia."

Allie immediately pictured the body beneath the covers, the body she'd helped undress. She knew Clay was only being practical. They were almost out of dry wood and had to stay warm somehow. The shock to his system was probably making it difficult for him to bring his body temperature up, even though he was dry and covered with blankets. But she should clean his wound first. There was no telling how much bacteria he'd encountered when he fell in the mud.

Besides, she couldn't climb into bed wearing wet clothes and, although she had more worrisome issues to deal with at the moment, she felt self-conscious about getting naked. She was too attracted to Clay. Had he been a stranger, she could've reacted to the necessity of the situation without feeling so nervous and aroused.

"I will once I clean it," she said.

"Isn't there some antiseptic?"

"No. It's long gone. I need some water."

He scowled. "Morning will be soon enough for that."

Allie was so cold she could scarcely feel her fingers or toes. But she knew it was important to do all she could for Clay's injuries. "Hang on. I'm already wet, so now's the best time."

"Just come here," he said stubbornly, but she got his truck keys out of the pocket of his jeans. She wanted to see if he had anything in his vehicle that might prove useful. Then she grabbed a pan and hurried out.

The wind and the rain lashed at Allie's clothes and hair. She hunched against it, grimacing when she saw Clay's truck sitting at an awkward angle because of the two flat tires. She'd get the son of a bitch who'd shot him, she promised herself. Another foot to the right and Clay might've been dead when she reached him.

Rage roiled inside her, tempting her to dash off to look for tracks—before they were completely obliterated by the storm. But she couldn't. Clay needed her.

Planning to comb every inch of the area come morning, she searched his truck. She could smell Clay's cologne, but he kept his truck as utilitarian and clean as his house. In the glove compartment, she found only a tire gauge, some napkins, his registration, proof of insurance, a seven-inch knife and a box of condoms.

Obviously, he was prepared. He just wasn't prepared for getting shot.

She considered trying to drive them out of there despite the ruined tires, but she couldn't risk getting stuck in the mud in the middle of nowhere. And she couldn't lose valuable time running around, looking for other cabins. She had no idea if she'd even find an occupied one. At least for the moment they had a warm place and a bed.

Worried that she was leaving Clay for too long, she ran down to the river and filled her pan. When she returned, she found him curled up, shaking, struggling to get warm. The fact that he might be slipping into shock scared her so badly she abandoned the water, stripped off her clothes, and dried herself off as well as she could.

The mattress creaked slightly beneath her weight. Allie knew Clay had to be aware of her. But he didn't seek her body, as she'd expected. And that scared her even more.

"Clay?"

"Hmm?"

She wanted to pull him to her that very second, to reassure herself that he was as strong as ever. But until she got warmer, she'd only leech what little heat he'd managed to generate away from him. "Are you okay?" she asked, briskly rubbing her arms and legs to hurry the process.

"Umm."

His response sounded like an affirmative answer, but she wasn't about to take any chances. As soon as she dared touch him, she fixed the dish towel as a field bandage. Then she slid over and wrapped her body around his. She no longer cared about nudity or propriety or anything else. She didn't even care if he figured out how deeply he affected her. She only wanted to make him better.

"Feels good," he mumbled a few minutes later.

"Can you sleep?" she asked.

He didn't answer. She worried that the pain might be too much for him. But after a few minutes, he seemed somewhat improved. She could feel a steady, strong heartbeat, and his chest began to rise and fall in a regular rhythm.

"Thank God," she whispered and prayed he'd remain safe through the night.

The pain in his arm dragged Clay out of a deep sleep while it was still dark. He couldn't immediately remember why he hurt, but he knew he wasn't alone. A woman was hugging him from behind. Her small firm breasts were pressed against his back, her legs were tucked under his buttocks and her warm breath moved his hair, tickling his neck. But it was her hand that distracted him the most. She'd looped her arm around his waist as if she'd been holding him tightly to her. But now that her body had relaxed in sleep, her hand dangled very close to—

He shifted, wondering what the hell was going on.

"You okay?" she muttered sleepily.

Allie McCormick. At the sound of her voice, it all came back to him. The broken window. Tramping through the woods. Gnawing fear for her safety. The crack of gunfire. But, strangely enough, the fact that she was lying next to him seemed the most pertinent. They were in bed at her father's isolated cabin. Naked and alone. And he wanted to touch her....

"I'm fine." Easing out of her arms, he turned to face her. Embers still glowed in the fireplace, but he could make out only a few rough shapes. His other senses took in more. The warmth emanating from her body. The feel of her soft legs entwined with his. The scent of her on his pillow.

"Clay?" she whispered, reaching for him.

Her hand encountered his stomach. At that point, he thought she might recoil and find some excuse to get out of bed.

But she didn't. Her fingers moved toward his injured arm, but he deflected her questioning touch.

"Are you sure you're all right?" she asked.

"Positive." He was sure about a few other things, as well—like the testosterone suddenly pounding through him.

"I'm glad." The hand that had touched him a moment earlier touched him again, moving slowly over his chest as if she was eager to explore every groove and contour.

Squeezing his eyes shut, he told himself not to react. She was just reassuring herself that he was okay. Or she was half-asleep and didn't know what she was doing. Otherwise, she wouldn't be touching him so…erotically. She had to realize that the closer she got to him, the more she alienated herself from her family and friends.

Her hand traveled up to his neck and eventually cupped his cheek in a movement so tender it made Clay's stomach twist with longing. But he couldn't respond. One eager kiss or receptive moan on her part, and he'd be on fire.

Drawing a deep breath, he fought to hang on to his self-control. But then her thumb brushed his bottom lip and he couldn't help tracing the edges with his tongue.

Her sigh made his muscles bunch with desire, and he took her thumb all the way into his mouth.

The bed moved as she inched closer.

"You really had me worried," she said.

He felt the tips of her breasts against him and nearly let his good arm encircle her, pull her to him.

No. Think of her father. Think what it would do to her.

But she didn't stop. She was threading her fingers through his hair, and he could feel her breath on his neck.

Clay lay suspended between what he knew he should do and what he *wanted* to do. He had to warn her at least. There was a condom in his wallet from the box he'd bought at the gas station. But if they made love, he didn't want her to be sorry about it later, didn't want to feel responsible for her regret.

"Allie?"

"What?"

"I—" Her nipples grazed his chest again, causing a reaction powerful enough to silence him. His determination to restrain himself kept him from reaching out, from taking what she offered. But he couldn't push her away. Especially since she seemed a bit tentative, as if she imagined he might not be interested.

"Can you go back to sleep?" she asked.

Not a chance. "No."

"Am I…disturbing you?"

"Hell, no."

She seemed relieved, but that didn't help *his* situation. He couldn't think of anything except the softness of her skin. He wanted to bend his head and take one nipple in his mouth while his hands wandered elsewhere, eliciting the responses he craved from her…

Don't think about it. He didn't want her to be ostracized later just because she'd been with him.

But he couldn't *help* thinking about it. *Remove her hand.* The command came with authority, but the pleasure of her touch was too intense. And then her tongue slid invitingly over his bottom lip and every cell in his body rose up against him. He longed to move decisively, aggressively. To roll her onto her back and kiss her as he buried himself inside her—and to forget all the reasons he shouldn't. But he merely parted his lips and met the tip of her tongue with his.

She made a sound that told him she liked it and arched into him. What they were doing couldn't possibly be good for her, though. He wasn't husband or father material. And she had a child.

"Clay?" she said. The quaver in her voice meant that his earlier response hadn't completely squelched her insecurities.

He didn't answer. If he explained what he knew to be true, he'd have to act on it. But he wasn't sure how long he could hover between yes and no.

Finally, he pulled away.

He could sense her embarrassment and confusion. He hated that, but what could he do? Rejecting her advances was the lesser of two evils. Especially since it would encourage her to keep her distance from him in the future.

They lay in silence for minutes that felt like hours.

"I'm sorry," she said at last. "I know you're in a lot of pain."

He was too aroused to care about the wound in his arm. He'd have to be unconscious not to want her. "It's not the pain."

She didn't say anything.

"I don't want the people you know and love to look at you the way they look at me," he explained, because he couldn't take her thinking that she'd made a fool of herself by approaching him.

His heart beat several times before she responded. "You've slept with other women in Stillwater."

"No one like you."

"What's that supposed to mean?"

"You're different. You know that. You're a cop, one of *them*."

"I'm also a woman."

"Expectations are different for you."

"So you're doing me a favor?"

"I'm trying."

There was a slight pause. Then she said, "I'm not sure I'm able to appreciate that right now. When you were shot, I—" She didn't finish, but he could hear the huskiness in her voice, the worry and concern. The shooting had really shaken her, made her want to reassure herself in the most primitive way possible.

He let go of a long breath. "It's not easy for me to say no," he admitted. "It's…harder than you know."

Her finger began tracing a line through his pectorals and down his stomach. "How hard?"

He guessed she wasn't talking about the difficulty of the situation. "Hard enough," he told her gruffly, but he didn't move. He held perfectly still.

"Maybe I should decide about that." Her finger had reached his navel. She was moving slowly, giving him plenty of time to stop her. But he didn't. He couldn't wait until she touched him. His heartbeat radiated throughout his entire body as she drew closer and closer—and then her hand curled tightly around him, and he knew trying to resist would be hopeless.

With his good arm, he brought her into full contact with him. "You're making a mistake," he said, taking her mouth in a harsh, hungry kiss.

"Good thing you're worth it," she said and buried her face in his neck as he used his hand to make her tremble.

13

It'd been more than a year since Allie had made love. She missed the physical intimacy of having a man in her life. But being with Clay was nothing like what she'd experienced in the past. Clay's lovemaking was full of an urgency she'd never known, as if it wasn't enough for him to claim her body—he wanted her soul. The crazy thing was, she knew better than to give it to him, yet she did so eagerly. With every kiss, with every touch, with every thrust of his hips, she gave up a little more of herself. He was alive, and somehow that was all that mattered in this cloistered cabin. The rest of the world could not intrude.

She *was* making a mistake, she dimly realized. She was letting him spoil her for anyone else. But she was too caught up to care. With one hand he angled her hips so she could take more of him.

Euphoria, combined with raw, desperate need, caused every muscle to quiver. Allie moaned as Clay's mouth closed over her breast, suckling her just hard enough. He knew how to amplify every sensation, how to take it to the extreme.

"What are you feeling?" he murmured, his voice ragged, breathless, as he kissed her mouth, her ear, her neck.

"You. I feel you. You're in me, around me, everywhere."

"Then let go. Give me what I want, okay? Trust me."

Worry lingered in some distant corner of her mind. "Be careful of your wound," she said. But he didn't act as if he had an injury. Pinning her hands over her head, he nuzzled her neck. Then his mouth trailed back down to her breasts.

Allie had never felt so alive, so hyperaware of another human being. As the rhythm intensified, she was no longer sure where Clay's body stopped and hers started, and she didn't care. The separate parts didn't matter, only the unified, glorious whole. They were nothing without each other.

Her muscles tensed, then several spasms rolled through her so hard her whole body shook.

Clay chuckled softly as she shuddered in his arms. "That's it. One more," he said, but she could sense him struggling to hold back and wanted to relish a little power of her own. Pressing him onto his back, she made sure he lost all control.

When Allie woke up, it was light. She blinked, feeling lazy, satiated, content—until she saw red on the pillow in front of her. Then she sat up so fast black spots danced before her eyes.

The dish towel she'd wrapped around Clay's wound had fallen off, and his blood had smeared the bedding. But, once the dizziness passed, she could see there wasn't as much as she'd feared.

"What's wrong?" he asked, lifting his head.

"You've been bleeding."

He groaned and fell back on his pillow. "Is that all?"

"Is that *all?*"

"The way you had my heart going, how can you be surprised?"

He'd turned his face into the pillow, which muffled his voice, but Allie knew he was teasing her. "We've got to get you cleaned up," she said, straining for a look at his wound.

"Not here. We don't have any dry firewood to purify the water."

"I can wash off the dried blood, at least." She started to climb out of bed but realized she didn't have anything except the wet clothes piled on the floor. She hesitated. It was one thing to strip in the dark. It was quite another to go strolling naked about the cabin in broad daylight. Especially when Clay couldn't help but compare her to the likes of Beth Ann.

"What's the matter?" he asked.

She pulled the sheet off the bed with her as she moved. "It's freezing in here."

He scowled. "You don't want me to see you."

Clay never missed anything. Feeling a blush warm her cheeks, Allie glanced away. "We made love half the night. You've already seen me."

"I've felt you," he clarified. "I haven't seen you."

Take what Beth Ann has and cut it in half, she wanted to say. But she refused to reveal her insecurity. "It's too cold."

"I never expected you to be the self-conscious type, *Officer.*"

"I'm not!"

He sat against the headboard and cocked a disbelieving eyebrow at her.

"I'm not—what did you call me? Prim and proper?"

"The way you're hiding behind that blanket isn't too convincing."

"Do you know who shot you?" she asked, trying to

change the subject. During the night, she'd briefly told him about her missing gun and the note. But they'd been too preoccupied to discuss it fully.

"No idea." A crooked grin curved his mouth. "So…I'm number two."

She knew he was referring to the number of men she'd slept with. In her mind, he was number one, and she was pretty sure she'd think of him that way for a long time. She'd never experienced anything like last night. But she wasn't about to tell him that. "Stop gloating," she said.

"I'm not gloating. I'm wondering how I got so lucky."

"Are you kidding? You were bleeding. I felt sorry for you," she said with a smirk.

Clay's blue eyes sparkled. "How can I get you to feel sorry for me again?"

She laughed, shaking her head. "If you could make love the way you did last night, you're fine."

"I'd be a lot better if you'd take off that sheet."

"No."

"What if *I* take it off?" he challenged.

Allie recognized the desire in his voice. She'd expected last night to be an isolated incident, a breakdown of her customary resistance, due to an unusual situation. But he wanted her again. Now.

And, just as Beth Ann had predicted, she wanted him.

Frightened by how shaky he could make her feel with just that look, Allie caught her breath. She nearly dropped the sheet and climbed back into his arms. But warning signals were ringing loudly in her head. She'd gone too far last night—too far for her job, and too far for her emotional well-being.

"We have things to talk about." She forced herself to look away as she returned to the subject of last night's shooting. "You haven't received any threatening letters or calls, have you?"

He seemed taken aback by her businesslike tone. "No."

After dunking another dish towel in the pan of water, she gently washed his arm.

He didn't speak while she worked, but she could feel his defenses snapping back into place. She'd seen a different side of Clay, a warm, loving side he didn't show many people. It was difficult to watch him transform into the remote man she'd always known, and even harder to acknowledge that it was because she'd backed away from him first.

"Care to hazard a guess as to who might want you dead?" she asked.

"After last night, I'm sure your father will top the list."

"We're not talking about that part of last night." She set the wet towel and water aside.

He scowled. "We're pretending it didn't happen?"

She chose not to answer. "If you had to guess, who would you say shot you?"

"Joe," he replied. "Except Joe would know better than to leave me alive, in case I ever found out it was him." As Clay shoved a pillow behind his back, the gold medallion dangling on his chest glinted in the sunlight streaming through the window.

Allie picked it up. She'd wondered about it before, felt it last night as he moved on top of her. "This is Catholic, right?"

He didn't seem particularly eager to answer.

"Clay?"

"Saint Jude."

"Pray for us," she read. She could feel his eyes on her. "Jude's the patron saint of hopeless causes, isn't he?"

"I don't know."

Allie looked up at him. She was pretty sure she was right. She'd seen a similar medallion on a homicide victim in Chicago. "But you're not Catholic."

He stared at her from beneath his thick lashes, and she got the impression that he was trying to figure her out, like that first night at his farm.

"Are you?" she asked.

"It belonged to my father."

"He gave it to you?"

"No, my mother did. It was the only thing he left behind."

The fact that he still wore it indicated that Allie had been right about the depth of the scars Lucas had inflicted on his young son. She didn't like to think about the heartache Clay must have endured. She felt too drawn to him, especially after last night.

She let the medallion fall back against his chest and hurried to bandage his wounds. She needed to put some space between them as soon as possible.

"Did you find any evidence that your father's having an affair?" he asked.

Allie felt the tension between them but didn't know how to relieve it. "No, nothing at all. Thank God. I actually feel a little sheepish for doubting him."

She expected Clay to say something to indicate that he was pleased for her. It was what almost anyone would do. But his thoughts remained a mystery.

Finished, she stepped away from him. "Are you okay?" she asked.

He met her gaze. "I don't know."

He wasn't talking about his wound. She understood that. She wasn't sure she was okay, either. Something had happened last night beyond the physical act of making love, and it had affected them both.

Turning his attention to his wound, Clay tried to rotate his shoulder to see the back of his arm and muttered a curse.

"Don't do that," she said. "You could make it bleed again."

"It's fine."

She drew the sheet around her a little higher. "What enticed you to come to the cabin?" she asked.

"What do you mean?"

"Did you receive a phone call, telling you I was in trouble? Or a request to meet someone here?"

"No."

She frowned in confusion. How else had the shooter brought Clay to this remote location? "So why'd you come?"

He regarded her levelly. "You have to ask?"

"Tell me."

"You were here."

Allie let her eyes sweep over him, trying to commit every detail to memory.

When he caught her admiring him, he held out his hand in subtle invitation.

Allie tried to resist but couldn't. Reaching out, she wove her fingers through his. Then he pulled her toward him and began tugging on the sheet.

She didn't stop him. She closed her eyes as the sheet fell to the floor. A moment later, she heard the bed creak as Clay leaned forward, felt his lips move along her collarbone, over her breasts, as light as a butterfly's wings. "Clay…"

Pulling her into his arms, he rolled her over him, and

laid her on her back. He was acting differently than he had last night, when they'd made love with such passion. Today Clay touched her with a reverence she'd never experienced.

She watched him take in all the details she'd been afraid to show him.

"Perfect," he said, his hand following his eyes. "Just like I imagined."

What was she going to do? Allie asked herself. She was falling in love.

She almost kept him from touching her. She had to return to real life. But that would come soon enough. Instead, she sighed in blissful satisfaction as he began to love her.

Wrapping her arms around his neck, Allie reveled in the scent and feel of him, in the heightened sensations only he could evoke—until someone tried to open the door. Then she cried out and stiffened in panic.

Clay tried to shield her body with his. But it didn't help. A second later, she heard a crack. Then the door flew open and crashed against the inside wall, and Allie's heart nearly stopped.

Her father stood there, holding the ax handle he'd used to break the lock.

The look of contempt on McCormick's face burned Clay worse than his gunshot wound, although he had to admit he had it coming. He'd known better than to touch Allie. He just hadn't been able to resist.

"Give us a minute," he said gruffly. The anger he felt, mostly directed at himself, lent his words plenty of authority. But he doubted Chief McCormick heard him. The older man was already backing away. He threw down the hatchet and stomped out, probably because he couldn't bear what he'd just seen.

Allie scrambled out from under Clay and grabbed her clothes. "I'll handle this."

He buried his head beneath the pillows, cursing his own weakness and stupidity.

"He's all bark," Allie said. "He'll calm down."

Clay had little hope of that. Still, he stayed where he was as she pulled on her wet jeans and shirt and hurried outside.

He expected to hear a blistering argument—but Chief McCormick didn't even raise his voice. If she hadn't left the door ajar, he probably wouldn't even have been able to hear them.

"You're fired," he said. "Turn in your badge, your car and your gun as soon as you get back to town."

Silence met this statement. Clay couldn't believe it himself. Was Chief McCormick serious? What would Allie do without a job? She had a child to care for—McCormick's grandchild!

He got out of bed and started dressing.

"I'm a good police officer. You can't fire me because I slept with a man you don't like," she said.

"A man I don't *like?* He's a suspect in the only murder case we've got."

"He's also a man I've known since high school, and he was just like anyone else a few days ago. When I moved back here, you weren't even interested in reopening the Barker case! It was all me, digging around to help Madeline."

"Things have changed, and you know it."

"Not in the name of justice. The Vincellis have their own agenda, that's all."

"And you think sleeping with Clay is going to help? Are you trying to ruin your life?" he retorted. "What about Whitney?"

"Whitney is my concern. I'll take care of her."

"How? You don't have a husband anymore. You don't have a job. You don't have a home of your own. Without me, you don't have anything!"

Clay froze, waiting for Allie's response.

"You and Mom invited me back," she said evenly. "You wanted me to move home as much as I wanted to come."

"That was before."

"Before *what?*"

"Before you started acting like a bitch in heat!"

The hypocrisy of McCormick's statement made the blood boil in Clay's veins. At least he and Allie were single. At first Clay had thought Allie would fare better if he let her deal with her father alone. But he couldn't stand back and allow McCormick to mistreat her. Clay was equally responsible.

Striding out of the cabin, he leaped from the porch to the ground because he didn't have the patience to bother with the steps. *A bitch in heat?* Allie had slept with two people in her life. A few minutes earlier, she'd been too self-conscious to let him see her naked despite what they'd shared during the night. "Watch your mouth," Clay warned.

"You stay out of it," McCormick said. "This is between Allie and me."

"Not anymore."

"You're challenging me, Montgomery?" Chief McCormick's hand hovered near his gun, but Allie moved between them.

"Stop it! I won't have the two of you fighting."

Clay assumed she'd explain the extenuating circumstances leading up to last night. But not Allie. She was too proud to justify her actions. Tears glistened in her eyes, but her throat worked as she fought them back. "We're stranded," she said. "If you'll just give us a ride to town, we'll figure out how to get our cars home."

McCormick blinked several times, then focused on the toppled bookshelf visible through the open doorway. As if finally realizing that it hadn't happened as part of their lovemaking, that much more had taken place at the cabin than finding his daughter in bed with a man he didn't approve of, he turned to her. "What's been going on here?"

"You can read the report," Allie said stiffly. "I'll file it when I turn in my badge." Pivoting, she stalked past Clay and collected her shoes from the cabin before marching over and climbing into the front seat of her father's cruiser.

Clay remained where he was. He'd been worried about his mother putting his sisters at risk. But after nineteen years of caution, he was making some big mistakes of his own.

McCormick stomped around him and went into the cabin. Clay glanced over at the patrol car, but Allie didn't look back at him. She stared straight ahead, the set of her jaw testifying to her misery.

He could've avoided this whole debacle, Clay thought. If only he'd stayed home and minded his own business— the way he usually did.

But then he remembered that the window of Allie's car had been broken before he'd arrived.

Maybe it was a good thing he'd come. Whoever had shot him might've attacked her had he not shown up—

"What's this?"

Clay turned to see McCormick holding his shirt. It was

so bloody he'd left it on the floor and donned his sweat-shirt instead.

"What does it look like?" he said and got into the back of the cruiser.

Allie's mother hovered over her the entire time Allie was packing her belongings. Allie felt bad about the rift between her and her father, and was worried about how she'd support her daughter. But even if her father would allow it, she couldn't go back to the Stillwater police force. They weren't interested in devoting the man-hours it would take to actually solve the Barker case. They were only looking for a quick escape from the pressure, a way to get Clay.

She needed her own space. Complicated as her life had become, that was clear.

"Why not move into the guesthouse?" her mother asked hopefully. Wearing a pained expression, Evelyn had been waiting for the right moment to intercede. But Allie hadn't given her much of a chance. She'd been rushing from one drawer to the next. Whitney's clothes and half of her own belongings were already jammed into a large suitcase she'd had to sit on to latch. The rest she was tossing into boxes she'd stored in the garage.

"No, thanks," she muttered.

Her father had made himself scarce since their return to town. Allie couldn't guess what he was thinking. But she refused to be dependent on him any longer. She had some savings, enough to pay a security deposit and a few months' rent. She'd start looking for work on Monday.

"Where are we going, Mommy?" Whitney asked, watching her with eyes almost as wide as Evelyn's.

"Not far, sweetheart." After she'd dropped off her

badge and cruiser at the station, along with a report that explained the theft and subsequent shooting, Allie had picked up a newspaper and placed a few calls. Stillwater didn't have much of a rental market. But she'd managed to lease, on a month-to-month basis, a small two-bedroom house.

The only problem was that it happened to be directly across the street from Jed Fowler's.

Allie wasn't too happy about living in Jed's neighborhood. But at least she'd be around the corner from Whitney's school.

"Why are you making such a snap decision?" Evelyn asked. "Give your father time to cool off, then sit down and talk about this with him, like adults."

Letting him cool off wouldn't help. They were on opposite sides of this issue. She hated to uproot Whitney again, but she and her father couldn't live under the same roof. The tension would be worse for her daughter than the change. "I have nothing more to say to him," she said.

"You're mad at Grandpa?" Whitney asked.

Allie tried to temper her response. "We're having a disagreement, that's all."

Whitney moved closer. "So you want to leave before he gets home?"

"That would be best." She'd rather save Whitney from hearing an upsetting argument. She had other reasons for rushing, too. She was determined to canvass the cabin and surrounding woods for evidence—before the sheriff's department could take over. She'd gone through the area once already, when Officer Grimes had taken her back to get her car. But she hadn't wanted to run into Clay, who'd be coming back for his truck, so she'd made only a cursory pass. She was embarrassed that she'd lost her objectivity so quickly. And she wasn't proud of herself for getting personally involved in a case.

Whitney hugged Evelyn's leg. "Will I still get to see Boppo?"

Seeing the panic in her daughter's face, Allie knelt in front of her. "Of course. Boppo can visit us whenever she likes."

"*Visit* you?" Evelyn echoed. "I won't be watching Whitney while you work?"

"Not until I get a job."

"*You quit the force?*"

Allie dumped the rest of her shoes on top of the quilt that had been a wedding gift. "No, Dad fired me. But…he was probably right to do so." Otherwise, she would've caused even more trouble for him. And, hurt and angry though she was over what he'd said, she didn't want to do that.

"What's wrong with him?" Evelyn muttered, obviously confused.

Remembering the photograph stuck between her mattress and box spring, Allie retrieved it and slipped it into her pocket. "He doesn't like the company I'm keeping," she said. Then she started dragging the first of her boxes down the hall.

Clay was cleaning up the dishes from his supper when he finally gave up trying to ignore his ringing phone.

"I've been trying to reach you all day. Where have you been?" his mother asked without any of the customary greetings.

Clay hadn't wanted to talk to anyone until he'd decided how he was going to handle the situation with Allie and her father. He couldn't leave it as it was. She'd lost her job because of him. "I've been busy."

"I came by earlier. No one was there."

"I was out running errands." He'd had Grace drive him to Jed's shop, where he'd purchased two tires before she took him to the cabin to get his truck. Then he'd paid Joe a visit. Joe claimed he was in bed asleep when Clay was shot. But there wasn't anyone to corroborate his whereabouts. So it wasn't easy to give him the benefit of the doubt.

"Word has it you were shot last night," Irene said.

"That would be true." He was wearing a makeshift bandage he'd put on himself. But he didn't plan to keep it on for long. The tape bothered him, and the wound was already beginning to heal.

"You didn't think your mother might be worried about you?"

He slipped the pan he'd used to fry grits into the soapy water. "Who told you? Grace?"

"No. I haven't been able to get hold of her, either. Madeline overheard it at the grocery store. Can you imagine what *that* must've been like? To hear from a stranger that her brother had been shot? We've both been worried sick."

"I'm sorry." He'd had too much on his mind, hadn't expected word to get out quite this fast. "Anyway, it's nothing." It was making love with Allie afterward that had made a serious impact.

"What happened?"

"Someone took a shot at me from the trees."

She gasped. "Who?"

"I don't know. But I'm fine. The bullet passed through the flesh of my arm, that's all."

"Have you seen a doctor?"

He used a pot scrubber to get his pan clean. "There's no need."

"You were shot and you didn't even go to the doctor?"

"I told you, I'm fine."

"Where were you when this happened? At the farm?"

"At Chief McCormick's cabin."

She said nothing.

He paused in his work. "You've been there, haven't you?"

"What do *you* think?"

He went back to scrubbing. "I think you should be glad you broke things off with McCormick when you did."

"Why?"

"Allie went there searching for proof that her father's having an affair."

"You *told* her?"

"Of course not. She's beginning to suspect."

"Why?"

"Did you give him a teddy bear mug?" he asked, rinsing the pan and setting it in the drainer.

There was an uncomfortable silence. "Yes…"

Clay let the water drain out of the sink. "There you go."

"Did she find what she was looking for?"

If there'd been any doubt in Clay's mind, the fear in his mother's voice would've confirmed that she'd spent plenty of time at the cabin. "No. But make sure you never go back."

"We broke up, remember?"

"Doesn't hurt to give you a little warning."

"Who would want to harm you?" she asked.

He ran some clear water through his rag, wrung it out and started wiping the counters. "The list isn't as short as we might hope."

"But…why now?"

"Allie thinks someone's afraid I'm not going to get what's coming to me."

"It has to be Joe," she said. "That man's awful. Just awful."

Joe had been particularly hateful since Grace's return nine months ago. Something about her triggered the worst in him. He wanted her and hated her at the same time. And now that Allie was back, and she wasn't siding with the Vincellis the way Joe thought she should, he was angrier than ever.

Joe… Clay shook his head. He didn't have an alibi for last night. But why would he write Allie a note, telling her to leave the past alone? Joe *wanted* her to investigate.

"I'm not convinced it was Joe." Which was the only reason Joe was still walking around in perfect health.

"Who else could it be?"

"I don't know, but I need to talk to Chief McCormick. Face-to-face. Can you tell him to pay me a visit? Tonight?"

"What?" she said.

"You heard me."

"What do you want with him?"

Clay grabbed a towel to dry his dishes. "A trade."

"What kind of trade?"

"Nothing you need to worry about."

"Does it have to do with Allie?" she asked.

"Maybe."

"I heard you're sleeping with her. Is that true?"

"The chief tell you that?"

"Of course not. We're not talking. Anyway, he's too protective of his daughter to tell anyone. Madeline heard it."

"Who from?"

"She didn't say."

Clay winced at the twinge of pain he felt lifting his

dishes into the cupboard and switched hands. The person who'd spread that gossip was most likely the person who'd shot him. Who else, besides the chief, knew he and Allie had been together?

"It's not true," he said. He knew it'd be better for Allie if he simply denied it and hoped she'd do the same.

There was a long silence. "Now you're lying to *me?*"

Hell. "We were together one night."

"I see."

"You're the one who started the whole thing, so don't give me any grief about it."

"I never said you should sleep with her!"

"You didn't act as if you'd be opposed to the idea. Anyway, it's not worth arguing about. We're not seeing each other anymore."

"Well, I'm not seeing her father, either. So I can't deliver your message."

"Call him." Clay closed the cupboard and chucked his towel toward the hook where he normally hung it. "You must have some way of getting in touch with him. Or I'll call him myself."

There was a long pause. "Clay, what's going on?"

He started bagging up the garbage under his sink. "Is the chief aware that I know about the two of you?"

"Of course not."

That explained why McCormick had felt free to disparage Allie. "Maybe it's time he found out."

"No! Clay, I've done what you wanted me to do, now leave him alone."

Clay tied the bag shut and dropped it. Much as he was tempted to use McCormick's own mistakes against him, he couldn't. Threatening to divulge the chief's extramarital affair would only make McCormick angrier. And it would be a bluff, anyway. Clay could never really tell because of the people it would hurt, including Allie and his own mother.

In any event, he didn't need to blackmail McCormick. He had something else the chief wanted, and he suspected McCormick wanted it badly enough to give Clay almost anything in return.

"Are you going to call him, or am I?" he asked his mother.

"Will you tell me what you're doing?"

He kicked the garbage bag toward the back door. "I'm cleaning up my own mess."

She sighed. "Fine. I'll call him."

"You have a private way of getting in touch?"

"I have a number that goes directly to a voice-mail account. He used to check it and call me back when he could. Now I don't know what he'll do."

"He probably checks it more often than ever," Clay said. "Just tell him I'll be expecting him here at the house."

14

Turning off his headlights, Chief McCormick sat at the side of the road and studied the farm where Clay Montgomery lived. He wasn't convinced he was doing the right thing in coming here, especially this late. After what had happened at the cabin that morning, he feared a confrontation might turn violent. But the message that Clay wanted to see him had come through Irene, which worried McCormick more than a little. She rarely mentioned her son. Most of the time, Dale managed to pretend she had only a distant connection to that whole business with Lee Barker.

Did this late-night summons mean she'd told Clay about the two of them?

That thought alone made Dale's pulse race. Current circumstances were bad enough; he didn't need any more trouble. Although he was relieved not to be sneaking around anymore, he couldn't quit thinking about Irene, couldn't stop missing her. The mayor was breathing down his neck, threatening his job if he didn't charge *someone* with the death of Reverend Barker. And, according to the call he'd received from his wife, Allie and Whitney had moved out.

But he'd had to take a stand. He would not allow her to get mixed up with Clay Montgomery. What kind of husband would Clay make? He was standoffish at best. And if he ever went to prison, justifiably or not, where would that leave Allie and Whitney? Besides, considering his own past relationship with Irene, he'd be a fool to bring the two families together. In such proximity, the truth was bound to emerge. And he couldn't have that. He was taken with Irene, *craved* her, but he didn't love her the way he loved his wife.

Putting the transmission in gear, Dale pulled slowly into the gravel driveway, wondering how he'd let his life come to this. He'd never planned on having an affair. He'd just grown so infatuated with Irene—and it had all stemmed from seeing her so often at Two Sisters, where they both ate lunch.

He remembered making eye contact, the tentative smiles they'd exchanged and how they'd begun to time their exit so they could walk out together. Even after she'd slipped him her number, it had taken him a full two weeks to get up the nerve to call her. Part of him—the decent part, he supposed—hadn't wanted to break down. But in the end, he couldn't resist, despite her alleged involvement in the Barker case.

That case hadn't seemed so important back then. The investigation had stalled out years earlier, and Dale had never dreamed it would become such an issue again. Besides, the better he got to know Irene, the easier it was to ignore the whole Barker mess. The woman he knew would never purposely harm anyone.

But that didn't mean she wouldn't cover for Clay…. Maybe he'd shrugged off that possibility in the past, but he couldn't anymore. The mayor was pressing him too hard.

His cell phone rang. He took it from the seat, hoping

it was Irene. She wasn't supposed to call him on his cell but whenever his phone rang he couldn't help wishing….

The number on the screen indicated that it was his wife.

Should he answer it or not? He wasn't cheating on her anymore, but he had a feeling something terrible was about to happen.

Maybe because of that disastrous scene with Allie…

He hit the Talk button. "Hello?"

"Dale?"

"What?"

"It's getting late. Where are you? Why haven't you called?"

"I've been busy."

"Doing what?"

"Paperwork."

"You usually let me know if you can't make it for dinner."

"I'm sorry. I was…distracted." Since Irene had broken off the relationship, he'd let down his guard, mostly because he felt fatalistic about the whole affair. If he put Clay in jail for Barker's murder, what would stop Irene from telling whoever she wanted? At that point, she'd have nothing to lose and would probably retaliate. Maybe in the past they'd purposely avoided mention of their respective families. But he knew how much Irene loved her son.

"I just called the station," Evelyn said. "They told me you left twenty minutes ago. I thought you'd be home by now."

"I'm out on patrol. I'll be there shortly."

"You said you were doing paperwork."

"I was."

There was a slight pause. "Have you tried calling Allie?"

"No."

"Are you going to?"

He rubbed his temples, hoping to relieve the tension headache building behind his eyes. He felt terrible about what had happened. But he was doing Allie a favor. He didn't want to see his daughter hurt, and Clay was too dangerous for her—on many levels. "No."

"Why not?"

"She knows why."

"Dale—"

"I don't want to talk about it." If Allie could walk out on them that easily, for the likes of Clay Montgomery, she didn't deserve the help they'd offered her.

Evelyn hesitated, then backed off. He knew she'd bring it up later. No one could get around him like Evelyn. But he was grateful for the reprieve. "You sound tired," she said. "How are you feeling?"

"I'm fine," he told her. But he wasn't fine at all. Besides being angry at Allie, he was disappointed in himself and lovesick for Irene. How had he let his obsession with another woman cloud his judgment so completely?

"Dinner's waiting," Evelyn said. "Hurry home, okay?"

He pictured the handful of peas and the miniature piece of fish he'd find on his plate and missed the candlelight steak dinners he'd once enjoyed, in a town several miles away, with Irene. "I'll be there as soon as I can."

Hanging up, he got out of the car and approached the dark farmhouse as if it might spring to life and attack him. The shiny windows acted like mirrors beneath the moonlight. He couldn't see inside, but he imagined Clay looking out at him and shivered. Maybe Irene wasn't capable of intentionally harming anyone. But her son was. In Dale's opinion, Clay was capable of almost anything.

The door swung open before Dale could even reach it, and Irene's son appeared, his large form silhouetted in the light spilling from the hallway. The sound of a television resonated from some other room.

"Come in," Clay said.

"We'll talk here," Dale muttered. "What do you want?"

As Clay watched him, Dale tried to cover the fact that he was a little spooked. Clay had a way of putting people on edge. Maybe that was why most folks kept their distance. Most folks except the women who frequented his place—which now included Dale's own daughter.

"I want to make a deal," Clay said.

"I don't make deals."

"You'll be interested in this one."

"Why?"

Clay shoved his hands in his pockets. He was wearing a long-sleeved shirt, so Dale couldn't see his injury. The way he moved didn't suggest he was in pain, but Clay was one tough son of a bitch. Dale could feel the younger man studying him, drawing conclusions Dale couldn't even guess at. "It has to do with Allie," he said at last.

The hair on Dale's arms stood up. He hated the thought of this man, who seemed so dark and mysterious, so dangerous, being intimately involved with his bright, attractive daughter. He hadn't invited Allie back to Stillwater for *that*. "What about her?" he said, his words clipped.

"Hire her back—"

Dale narrowed his eyes. "You think you can tell me what to do?"

"—and you'll have my word that I won't pursue the relationship."

Dale let his eyebrows slide up. Why would Clay offer to walk away for so little? He hadn't even mentioned the Barker case. "Anything else?" he asked.

"That's it," Clay replied. "No punishment, no bullshit. Patch up your relationship and move on as if she'd never met me, and you won't have to worry about me touching her again."

"Fine," Dale said immediately.

Clay's half smile turned even more cynical than usual. "I thought we might be able to come to some sort of agreement. Thanks for stopping by," he said and shut the door.

Dale stood on the porch in stunned silence. Clay hadn't said anything about Irene. Did that mean he didn't know?

Of course he didn't know. Or surely a man like Clay would've used that information to improve his own position. He wouldn't have given Dale exactly what he wanted and asked for nothing in return.

Feeling the tension in his shoulders ease, Dale walked to his car and whistled the entire ride home. Maybe he'd survive the next few weeks after all.

Allie didn't feel quite at home in her new house. She hadn't had a chance to unpack much of anything, couldn't get comfortable lying on the hard floor in a sleeping bag, even though she was right next to Whitney. Her mother kept calling, begging her to reconsider and move home again. When that failed, her brother had phoned her from Arizona to see if he could help her and Dale settle their differences. And, on top of that, every time she heard the slightest sound, she jumped up to stare at Jed Fowler's house.

God, that man gave her the creeps.... His truck had been parked in the driveway for hours, yet his place had been dark since nightfall. What did he do after he came home from work? Eat and go straight to bed? Light candles in the back instead of turning on a few lights?

Forcing herself to think of something else, Allie left Whitney sleeping in her bag and wandered listlessly through the small two-bedroom rental. She was making note of all the cleaning and organizing yet to be done. Fortunately, her mother was bringing some furniture from the guesthouse in the morning. But she wasn't sure when she'd be able to put her house together. She wanted to revisit the cabin tomorrow. She hadn't been able to go back there today because someone from the sheriff's department was already investigating. He'd called to get a statement from her and indicated that he was going to contact Clay, as well. He also said he'd found the shell casing *and* the slug.

The deputy she'd spoken to seemed competent enough. But for Allie, the incident was far too personal to leave the resolution to someone else.

A thump brought her back to the window. It was probably a cat or a raccoon jumping onto the roof—but her overactive imagination suggested it could be Jed's car door.

Was he up?

She squinted, trying to decide whether she saw movement behind his dark windows. But the sound of an engine caught her attention, and it didn't belong to Jed. Her father's squad car was coming down the street.

"Great," she muttered. She didn't relish another confrontation. But now that she was living across the street from Jed and it was growing so late, she couldn't help feeling slightly relieved to have company, even if it was her father.

She waited until he reached the front step. Then she opened the door so he wouldn't ring the bell and wake Whitney.

"Did Clay already call you?" he asked in apparent surprise.

Clay hadn't called. She'd heard from Madeline, several times, though. Tomorrow Clay's stepsister was bringing a twin bed for Whitney she had in her garage, since Evelyn had only one bed to lend her. But Allie hadn't heard from Clay since her father had brought them to town. She knew they'd both been a little overwhelmed by what had happened before, and after, her father arrived. But she still missed him. "I don't know what you're talking about. Was he supposed to call me?" she said, pretending it didn't bother her that he hadn't.

"Er...no." He brushed some dirt from his pant leg. "Why aren't you asleep?"

"Why aren't *you* asleep?" She folded her arms and leaned against the doorjamb. Maybe her new neighbor made her uneasy, but she wasn't about to let her father know that her situation was less than perfect. The way he'd spoken to her at the cabin had been unforgivable. *A bitch in heat?*

"I've been doing damage control," he said.

He clearly blamed her as the reason, and Allie felt she had to accept some of the responsibility. She shouldn't have gotten so involved with Clay. The fair, unbiased friendship she'd intended to offer had quickly spun out of control. But when he was hurt and bleeding, nothing seemed to matter except the relief of knowing he was still alive.

"What do you want?" she asked briskly. What had happened had happened. There was no going back now.

Allie didn't think she'd go back, even if she could. She'd never had another night like that one.

Her father fiddled with his police belt, giving her the impression that what he had to say wasn't easy to get out. She would've guessed he was trying to extend her an apology—except he wasn't the type to apologize. He meant well but struggled when it came to expressing emotion.

"I've changed my mind," he said with a scowl. "You can work at the station. But only as my personal assistant," he added.

Allie's jaw dropped. "What?"

"You heard me. You want work, those are the terms. And be glad of them. I've never hired anyone else back."

"I don't remember you firing anyone." She thought of Hendricks. "Even officers who deserve it."

"This is Stillwater."

She rubbed her forehead. "How well I remember."

"So?" he said. "Take it or leave it."

"No." She closed the door, then stood amid the boxes filling her new living room, feeling frustrated with herself, her father, the whole situation.

Whitney coughed and stirred in her sleep, trying to kick off the cover of her sleeping bag. Afraid that her daughter was coming down with bronchitis, like last year, Allie crossed the room and turned up the heat. It was poor timing if Whitney was getting sick, but they'd manage without Dale's job offer. Even in Stillwater.

She was about to lie down again and try to get some sleep. But her father didn't drive off, as she'd expected. He knocked.

Grumbling a curse, Allie went back to the door. "Yes?"

He muttered something she couldn't make out.

"I can't hear you," she said.

"Stop being a stubborn fool."

"Now I'm a stubborn fool? I thought I was a bitch in heat."

He looked slightly ashamed. "I got a little carried away this morning."

"You don't say."

His scowl returned. "You had no business sleeping with Clay. Word about the two of you is spreading all over town. You think that's going to help him, for folks to believe you're partial to him? When everyone expected you to finally come up with the truth?"

She knew it wouldn't help anyone. That was why she felt so bad. "You're right. And I'm sorry for that. But I'm out of the spotlight now. I shouldn't cause you any more trouble."

"Dammit, Allie." A muscle twitched in his cheek. "Okay, you win. You can have your regular job back. Just stay away from Clay Montgomery."

She needed to stop seeing Clay, at least until things settled down. Since he hadn't called her, she assumed he'd come to the same conclusion. But that didn't mean she was going back to work for her father. She'd already crossed too many lines; she couldn't be impartial in the investigation the mayor was insisting they launch. "I can't, Dad. I wouldn't be any good to you," she said. "I think it's best if I sit this one out."

His thick eyebrows rumpled. "It's a job. What about Whitney? How will you put food on the table?"

"I'll manage."

"She's my granddaughter."

"She'll be fine."

They stood staring at each other. Allie was so caught

up in the moment that at first she didn't realize Jed Fowler had poked his head out of the house across the street. Even when she sensed him watching, she couldn't be completely sure she wasn't imagining it. The streetlight was too far away to reveal what he was looking at.

"I've got to get some sleep," she said, wanting to go back inside and lock the door against both men.

"That's it? You won't come back?" her father asked.

"I won't come back."

He drew himself up straight. "Suit yourself," he said and stalked to his cruiser.

Reverend Portenski tried not to show the depth of his concern as he listened to Evelyn McCormick. He usually enjoyed her visits. They shared books, debated the nature of God, planned various outreach efforts on behalf of the church.

But this was the first time she'd ever come to him in tears.

"I don't know what to do, Reverend," she said. "Dale can be harsh, but he's always been a good father."

"There's no doubt about that," he concurred.

"So I'm not complaining."

"Of course not." Portenski could tell Evelyn didn't want to malign her husband's character—and yet she was angry with him.

"It's just that I'm afraid what he's done will only tempt Allie to get more involved with Clay. I mean, without our influence, what's to stop her?"

Nodding, Portenski conjured up an expression of understanding and commiseration, but his mind had turned to the Polaroid pictures he'd put back in the hole beneath the floorboards. Those pictures constituted a pretty powerful motive for murder. Allie, as a police officer, would know that instantly. If she ever saw them…

Did she realize who she was flirting with? That she was ruining her relationship with her parents for a man who could soon be dragged off to prison? The Vincellis were pressing hard for just that.

"She's always been a good girl," Evelyn went on. "Dale's pushed her too far, that's all."

"How does Dale feel about the situation?"

"He admits saying some things he's not proud of."

"I see."

"If only he'd waited until later, when we could've spoken calmly with her, the situation might've turned out differently. I mean, she would've had to listen to reason. We all know what Clay's done."

Portenski didn't respond to that comment. "Women seem to like Clay."

"Well, he's a handsome man, but considering his past…"

"Has he broken off his relationship with Beth Ann?" Portenski asked.

"That's what I'm hearing."

"And now he has his eye on Allie."

"Apparently."

"Chances are, the affair will be brief," he said, hoping to convince himself of that, as well. He didn't like holding the missing piece of the puzzle, didn't like the responsibility it placed on his shoulders. He was damned if he revealed the pictures, and damned if he didn't.

"But a lot can happen, even in a brief relationship," Evelyn argued. "It'll destroy what's left of her reputation, make her an enemy to most of our friends." She lowered her voice. "And what if she were to get pregnant?"

Portenski shuddered at the thought. He'd always been partial to young Allie. "Allie's very levelheaded. Surely she understands the dangers."

"Normally, I'd agree with you. But her divorce was hard. She's on the rebound and...vulnerable in a way she's never been vulnerable before."

"I see."

"Do you think I should send Dale over to her house again?" Evelyn asked.

"Will he go? Is there any chance the two of them could work this out on their own?"

She twisted the tissue he'd given her. "I'd have more confidence in that if they weren't so darn alike. Now that they're at a standoff, this could go on forever."

"Why not talk to Allie yourself?"

"I've tried, Reverend. I've asked her to move home, for Whitney's sake, for my sake, for her sake. Danny's called her, too. And I'm worried about Whitney—she's had a terrible cold all week. But Allie won't hear of it."

"How's Allie getting by financially?"

"Her savings, I guess. I helped furnish the house, but she won't even let me buy groceries for her."

"Will she let you see Whitney?"

"Yes, and I'll babysit once Allie finds work, of course, but I had to insist on that much."

"Where does she plan to work?"

"She's trying to get on with the Iuka police force."

"Will she be able to? Without a recommendation from Dale?"

"I'm sure she'll use her track record at her old department in Chicago."

Portenski rubbed his chin, trying to decide the best way to proceed. "Are you sure she's still seeing Clay?"

"It was less than a week ago that Dale found them at the cabin together. And it's true, you know, the rumors that they were…intimate." Tears streamed down her cheeks.

"Maybe her falling out with the two of you has opened her eyes."

Evelyn chuckled bitterly as she dabbed at her face. "No. If anything, it's made her more determined to go her own way. Dale has all but thrown her into that Montgomery boy's arms."

Portenski got out of his chair and rounded his desk, pausing at the corner. "Evelyn…"

"Yes?"

"Will you let me know if the relationship continues?"

She hesitated. "What are you going to do?"

He'd given away too much. Averting his gaze, he fixed a peaceful smile on his face. "I'm going to pray for her." *For all of us.*

Evelyn nodded and stood up to leave. "Right. Of course. Thank you, Reverend."

Portenski patted her shoulder as they said goodbye at the door, then slowly returned to his desk. He couldn't stand by and allow any member of his flock to get hurt by what had happened in the past—not while he had the power to stop it. Could he?

Sinking into his chair, he pressed his thumb and forefinger to his eyes. He knew what those Polaroids would do, to Grace, to Clay, to Irene, to Madeline and, especially, to his beloved church. Barker's deception and perversions would try the faith of the whole congregation.

But Allie was the daughter of a good friend, a good woman.

Maybe this was God's way of finally making his will known.

* * *

Allie parked and got out of her car. This was her fifth trip to her father's fishing hideaway in as many days, but the sight of that cabin still evoked memories of Clay and the time they'd spent there. Not that she needed much of a trigger to recall those hours. She'd hardly been able to think of anything else. Especially when the house grew quiet at night… But she hadn't heard from him since.

"It's for the best," she told herself and tried to focus on what she'd come up here to do—finish her search of the crime scene. But, just in case, she paused long enough to check the messages on her new cell phone. Although she'd had the window of her car fixed, her purse, phone and keys hadn't turned up yet. Unfortunately, neither had her gun.

She had three messages. The first was from her mother. *Allie, please. I don't know why you're being so stubborn. You should at least move into the guesthouse. Think of how much easier it'd be for—*

She cut Evelyn off in midsentence. She wasn't moving home under any circumstances.

Feeling a nervous flutter in her stomach, she went on to the second message, hoping, in spite of herself, that it was from Clay. As far as she knew, he didn't have her new number, but he could get it from one of his sisters easily enough.

It wasn't from Clay. It was from Madeline. She'd been adding various pieces of furniture to Allie's motley collection. But this wasn't about furniture. Although her brother was okay, she was still very upset about the shooting. *Do you know who did it yet, Allie?*

The last message wasn't from Clay, either. Hendricks was responding to a call she'd made to him earlier. Allie found it a bit ironic that Hendricks, a man she'd never admired and didn't really like, was now nicer to her than any of the other men with whom she'd worked. He seemed more intrigued than offended by the fact that she'd turned traitor to those who ran Stillwater.

No one's brought in your purse. Sorry about that, he said. *I hope you canceled your credit cards and changed your locks. And, according to what I hear, the sheriff doesn't have any leads on whoever shot your* good buddy.

The emphasis he placed on *good buddy* made Allie cringe. If she'd had any illusions that they were actually friends, his words would have shown her the reality. He wasn't on her side. No one was. Now that she'd aligned herself with Clay, she could scarcely walk down the street without receiving a dirty look from someone. She'd expected it, of course—and yet it stung.

"Welcome to life as the Montgomerys know it," she muttered to herself.

Your father wouldn't want me to share this with you, of course, Hendricks continued. *But since you asked, I've been up at the cabin with a deputy from the sheriff's department a coupla times. The casing and slug they found came from a .9mm Glock, so it was probably your gun. No big shock there. But that shooter must've known what he was doing 'cause he didn't leave us a scrap of evidence that would tell us anything we don't already know.*

Allie wasn't surprised. She hadn't found any prints on the note, either. Whoever had pulled it from whatever printer it'd come from had worn gloves.

Let me know if there's anything else you need. It's not the same here without you.

She frowned at his deceptively friendly tone. He wasn't sincere, but it really wasn't the same for Allie, either. She loved police work and hadn't received a response to the résumé she'd submitted in Iuka. But it was too late to go back to her old job. Besides, she still couldn't tolerate the politics behind what was happening at the station in Stillwater.

Double-checking to make sure those were the only messages she had, she hung up. Was she just another idiot in a long string of idiots to lose her heart to the darkly mysterious Clay Montgomery?

Not wanting to face the probable answer to that question, she dropped her phone inside her purse, then set her camera bag on the ground and retrieved her most expensive lens. Over the past four days, she'd spent the hours Whitney was in school examining the crime scene, going over it inch by painstaking inch. But, like the sheriff's department, she'd come up empty-handed. There was no blood where the perp had broken her car window, no recognizable tire tracks in the woods, no sign of her gun, no fibers caught on a tree branch, no footprints, nothing.

Hiking both bags onto her shoulder, she scoured the clearing once again. Then she climbed up the hill behind the cabin to look down on the scene as a whole. Some areas along the river were so overgrown she couldn't pass through them. But if the perpetrator had thrown some object into the river—like her gun—it might've snagged on a rock or a root on its way downstream.

If she could find a place from which to take a few pictures, a perch with enough visibility, she could use her powerful telephoto lens to capture parts of the river that were up to a quarter of a mile away. Then she could load the photos onto her computer and study them up close.

There was only a slight chance, she decided as she struggled to find the right view. But she wasn't about to give up. Whoever had stolen her gun and attempted to kill Clay had no respect for her training and background.

She planned to change that. For the sake of her wounded pride. But mostly because of what had been done to Clay. As much as she told herself she was stupid to care about him, the memory of hearing that gunshot made her blood run cold.

"I'll get the bastard who did it," she promised and hunkered down on an outcropping of rock. It wasn't the perfect angle but—she peered through the lens of her camera—it wasn't bad. She took a few shots, then clambered farther up the hill, swatting at the mosquitoes that were so prevalent in early summer.

She was just climbing onto a particularly large rock to get some more pictures when a spot of red caught her eye. At first she discounted it as unrelated to the case. It was highly unlikely the perpetrator had come this far from the road and the cabin.

But then, as she stared at it, she realized what it was.

15

"Finally! My God, Clay, are you all right?"

At the sound of his youngest sister's voice, Clay shifted the phone to his other ear, shoved a kitchen chair out from the table with his foot, and slouched into it. He'd been lifting weights again, concentrating on building up the strength in his legs while giving his arm a chance to heal. Lately he always seemed to be prowling around the house, looking for something rigorous enough to occupy his mind and his body, and lifting seemed to be his most effective diversion. Especially during the past five days, while he'd been trying so hard to keep his promise to Chief McCormick. He didn't see any point in phoning Allie to say they couldn't see each other again. It was better to leave the situation exactly as it was. Hearing her voice would only weaken his resolve.

"I'm fine," he told Molly, balling up the T-shirt he'd removed just before she called and using it to mop his forehead.

"I heard someone shot you!"

Clay had taken off the bandages he'd worn the first two days, and could see that the wound had already scabbed over. "It's only a scratch."

"That's not what Grace told me."

"Are you going to take Henny-penny's word for it, or mine?" he asked with a lazy smile.

"Henny-penny's, I guess, because Mom's been just as worried as Grace."

In the middle of her suffering over the loss of her married boyfriend, maybe. Clay didn't know who was feeling more deprived these days—he or his mother.

"And Madeline's been more upset than both of them," Molly added.

"I'm fine. You'll see for yourself when you get here. You're still coming, right?"

"I fly in next week. Has the sheriff's department figured out who shot at you?"

"No. They're relying on our local department for help, and I don't get the impression the Stillwater P.D. is too interested in solving the case."

"Why not?"

"This may come as a surprise, but I'm not as popular as our beloved stepfather was."

"Shows you what they know. There's no comparison between the kind of man you are and the monster Barker was."

"Yeah, well, that's the best-kept secret in town, remember?"

"I remember. What's the latest word on Grace's baby? Any labor pains?"

His chair squeaked against the hardwood floor as he shifted. "Not yet. But she's only two days overdue."

"*Only?* Doesn't that mean she's done?"

"Jeez, you know less about having babies than I do," he said with a laugh. "What, there are no newborns in the Big Apple?"

"All my friends are single. Besides, I make it a point

not to worry about that sort of thing. There'll be plenty of time for that later."

For her, maybe. He propped his legs on the opposite chair. "Don't want those maternal instincts kicking in just yet, eh?"

"Not until I find the right man."

"From what I hear, you're not looking very hard."

"You're older than I am," she said.

Exactly. But when he saw where the conversation was going, he made an effort to guide it back to safer ground. "The doctor said he'll let Grace go for two weeks before he induces."

"Induces? Wow, I think you're the first man I've ever heard use that term—about having a baby, I mean."

He chuckled. "You know me. I'm up on all things feminine, thanks to my softer side."

"You mean the one most people don't know about?"

"Crying isn't good for my image."

"I don't think anything could harm your image," she said wryly.

"How's New York?"

"It's the place to be. I'm still waiting for you to visit me here, by the way."

"Maybe I'll do that someday," he said, although they both knew chances were better that he wouldn't.

The phone clicked, telling Clay he had another call, but he didn't bother to check who it was. Probably Beth Ann. Again. He'd contacted her earlier to determine whether or not she'd had anything to do with the shooting. She'd adamantly denied it, and provided him with an alibi that had been easy to verify—she'd been at the pool hall the night of the shooting. Then she'd called him several times to make sure he believed her. She'd even offered to bring him some homemade soup. When he'd insisted he didn't need soup, she'd launched into a big spiel about how they should at least be friends.

They hadn't been friends when they were sleeping together. He didn't see why that would change now that they weren't. But he'd told her he might call her later, just so he could get off the phone.

"You could bring Allie McCormick to the city with you," Molly said.

Clay tossed his sweat-dampened T-shirt across the room. Evidently Grace, Irene and Madeline had been doing some talking. "Why would I want to do that?"

"Because you like her."

"Who says?"

"You'd *have* to like her, to sleep with a cop. Not to mention that she's the daughter of the man our mother's having an affair with."

"Mom broke off that relationship."

"I know, but do you think that's going to make any difference to Allie if she finds out?"

"I'm hoping it'll mean she won't find out."

"I don't blame you." She spoke to someone in the background, then came back on the line. "So does she know how you feel?"

"Molly, *I* don't even know how I feel," he said, growing exasperated. "Anyway, it doesn't matter."

"Why?"

"Why do you think?"

"Clay—" Molly started. Fortunately, Clay's call waiting beeped again. And this time, he was eager for the interruption.

"Hang on a sec."

He was pretty sure she muttered something about how he

was a stubborn son of a bitch who didn't know what was good for him, but he didn't hear the rest of it because he switched to his other call in the middle of her diatribe. "Hello?"

"It's me." Grace.

"What's up?"

"The baby's coming."

He jumped to his feet. *"Now?"*

She laughed. "Yes, but don't freak out, okay? It's going to take some time. I just wanted to tell you we're on our way to the hospital. Would you like to come along or wait for word at home?"

"What about the boys? Do you need me to watch them?"

"No. We've got a sitter lined up."

"Then I'll grab a shower and head over to the hospital," he said. "Molly's on the other line. I'll let her know it's time."

"Great. Tell her I'm looking forward to seeing her next week."

As Grace hung up, Clay wondered what it must be like for Kennedy—to know he was about to be a father again. Was it as satisfying as Clay imagined it would be?

"Clay?" Molly said.

Taking the stairs two at a time, Clay hurried to his room. "Yeah, I'm back."

"Who was it?"

"Grace. She's having the baby."

"You're kidding me! Right this minute?"

He started running the water in the shower. "Sometime tonight."

"How exciting! Did you think she'd ever be this happy? That she'd ever recover from…what happened?"

"No." He peeled off his shorts and kicked them aside.

"You're part of the reason she's recovered so well. You know that, don't you?"

No. He only knew he was part of the reason she'd been hurt in the first place. Although Clay understood that it was Barker's fault, not his, he couldn't get past the fact that he'd left his sisters vulnerable the night it all went wrong. "Gotta go, Molly," he said, pausing at the shower door.

"Call me later?"

"I will," he replied.

And he did, at midnight, when he was staring into the small, red face of his newborn niece.

Allie sat at her kitchen table, glaring at the red ball cap she'd found near the cabin. She knew it belonged to Jed Fowler. For one thing, it had the logo of his auto shop stitched on the front. For another, she'd seen him wearing it at least a dozen times.

But why would Jed shoot Clay? It didn't make sense. If he wanted to hurt Clay, all he had to do was implicate him in Barker's disappearance. Public opinion being what it was, his word would probably be enough to put Clay away for a very long time. After all, Jed was there that night. Instead, Fowler was the only person in town to stand by the Montgomerys.

Allie rubbed her lip, trying to piece it all together. Logic told her he wouldn't shoot Clay, but she couldn't think of any reason for him to be near the cabin. And she'd seen him at Grace's fruit-and-vegetable stand right before she drove to the cabin. Had he followed her there, as she suspected he'd followed her a few days earlier?

She wanted to discuss it with Clay. But he hadn't responded to the message she'd left him last Tuesday, and she was reluctant to call him again. She didn't want to pester him like some lovesick fool. She understood now that last weekend had meant much more to her than it did to him.

Or maybe their relationship was just more complicated than he was willing to tolerate. If that was the case, she could sympathize with his concerns.

She stared at the phone, tapping her fingers on the table. Currently employed or not, she was a cop. She needed to take charge of the situation despite her feelings. Maybe Clay knew something about Jed that would help her sort this out.

Finally overcoming her pride, she picked up the phone.

It rang five times before his answering machine came on.

This is Clay Montgomery. Leave your name and number at the beep.

She noticed he didn't promise to return his calls. "Clay, it's me. I'd like to talk to you, if you've got a minute. It's about the shooting," she said. Then she left her number, again, and disconnected.

What now? she wondered. She was tempted to get a flashlight and poke around inside her neighbor's truck and garage, looking for her gun. But did she really want to break the law?

With a sigh, she went back to the phone. She hated to turn Jed's hat over to the police department that had so recently fired her. But she needed a search warrant to go any further with what she had, and she certainly wasn't going to get one by approaching the judge as a civilian.

Hendricks answered, as she'd expected him to. "'Lo?"

"Hendricks? It's Allie."

"Did you get my message?"

"I did, thanks. Listen, I have something you might be interested in."

"What's that?"

"Jed Fowler's baseball cap."

"What would I want with that?"

She toyed nervously with the drawstring of her pajama bottoms. "I found it at the cabin today."

There was a long pause. "I didn't see it when I was there, Allie."

She hesitated, surprised by his response. "It was up on the hill."

"You're sure?"

"What's that supposed to mean?" she demanded.

"Nothing. I just can't imagine why Jed's cap would be at the cabin. That's all."

Allie stood and began to wipe off the counters. She'd done most of the dishes earlier but had been too preoccupied with Jed's cap to finish the job. "Maybe we should find out why," she suggested.

"How do you propose to do that?"

"Have the sheriff's department get a search warrant for Jed's house and vehicle. See if he has my gun."

"They're not gonna go after a search warrant."

"Why not?"

"Because now that they've taken all the statements and collected the evidence, they're relying on us to finish up. And your father knows Jed would never shoot Clay."

She turned off the water she'd been running in the sink. "Do you have any other suspects?"

"Not yet, but that won't make any difference."

"Why not?"

"Your father has more important things to do."

Allie dropped the wet rag she'd been using to clean the kitchen table. "What's more important than attempted murder?"

"Murder one."

"What are you talking about?" she asked.

"The D.A.'s finally agreed to prosecute. Your father's planning to charge Clay with Barker's murder."

Allie's stomach knotted painfully. "When?"

"First thing tomorrow morning."

Holding the new baby was a bittersweet experience. The complete innocence, even the scent of the child evoked a mixture of tenderness and hope that warred with the darker feelings that were far more familiar to Clay. He was unaccustomed to these emotions but still didn't want to go home to the secrets that haunted him. He longed to feel as normal men did—to feel as he had when he was holding Allie naked against him. Alive. On fire. Crazy with the desire to possess more of her than her body and to let her possess more of him. He wanted to let himself care, to grab hold of someone and hang on. At last.

Unfortunately, that was the one thing he couldn't do. He'd promised Allie's father he wouldn't contact her, and he planned to keep that promise. Everyone knew she was better off without him. He knew it, too. And yet, when he returned to Stillwater, he went out of his way to drive by her parents' house. He even considered calling her cell phone. If she picked up, maybe he'd ask her to come outside so he could tell her about the baby.

He imagined her sexy mouth curving into a smile when he gave her the news. She had her own child; she'd understand. He wouldn't touch her. He just wanted to *tell* her.

But when he didn't see her car in the driveway, he

realized she must be at work and decided to leave well
enough alone. For the good of everyone, he had to be satisfied with the life he led, had to relegate himself to relationships like the one he'd had with Beth Ann. Maybe he'd
grown tired of the emptiness—and maybe those relationships had their pitfalls—but superficial associations were
better than having no love life at all, weren't they?

Braking for the light at Fourth and Main, he glanced to
the left, which led to his farm, then to the right, which
would take him to the trailer park where Beth Ann lived.
If he relented and started seeing her again, would he get
over Allie?

Probably not, but at least he'd be able to fill the empty
hours so he wouldn't think of her so often.

Remembering the plaintive sound of Beth Ann's voice
when she'd asked to see him earlier, he turned toward her
house. He knew better than to sleep with her, refused to
let her trap him. But there were still ways she could help
him forget….

"Mommy, what are we doing?"

"Just taking a drive, baby." Allie reached behind the
seat to adjust the blanket she'd brought to cover Whitney.
She hated waking her daughter and dragging her from bed
in the middle of the night. Whitney wasn't quite over her
cough. But Allie couldn't leave her home by herself and
Clay wasn't answering his phone. She had to rouse him
from bed if he was sleeping, or find him if he wasn't at
home. She didn't want her father's appearance on his
doorstep in the morning to come without warning.

Once she told him what was happening, and he understood the odds stacked against him, maybe he'd skip town.
Allie hoped so. Why should he stay? He wouldn't get a

fair trial. And she preferred not to watch what the Vincellis and their friends had in store for him.

"Mommy?" Whitney said.

Allie turned onto Main Street. "What?"

"Can I take off my seat belt? I want to lie down."

"No."

"But I'm sleepy."

"Sorry, sweetheart. We won't be long, okay?" Allie tapped the steering wheel with her fingernails while she waited at the next light, eager to reach Clay's farm. But then she realized that the pool hall was still open and decided to check there before heading out of town.

"Is this where we're going?" Whitney asked in confusion when Allie turned down the narrow side street that led to the back parking lot.

"No," she murmured. "I'm looking for a black truck."

But Clay's vehicle wasn't among the fifteen or so that remained. Allie was about to turn around, when Joe Vincelli and his brother Roger came out of the building.

She paused, watching them. They swayed as if they'd had too much to drink, then Joe pivoted to shout at someone who lingered in the doorway.

Allie frowned as he laughed. He was certainly in high spirits. Had he heard about Clay? Were he and his brother out celebrating their victory?

Joe's gloating turned Allie's stomach. She turned her car around, but Joe noticed her before she could drive off. He waved to Roger to block the road so that she couldn't exit the lot.

"What the hell are you doing?" she asked, rolling down her window.

He put a hand on her roof and leaned in. "I was hoping you had your boyfriend with you."

"I don't have a boyfriend."

"Jeez, does that mean you'll sleep with me, too?" he said, and he and his brother laughed uproariously.

Allie clenched her jaw. "Do you mind? I have my kid in the car."

"What, you don't want her to hear what Mommy's been up to? Can't say as I blame you."

"You've been enough of an embarrassment to your parents," Roger chimed in.

"Get out of my way," she said. "Both of you."

Joe challenged her with a haughty smirk. "What if we don't want to?"

"Then you're going to wind up getting yourselves arrested."

"Not by you, babe."

"Last I heard, you no longer had a badge," Roger added.

Joe leaned closer, close enough that Allie could smell the beer on his breath. "You must've wanted Clay pretty bad, huh? Tell me, was it as good as you hoped?"

Allie forced a cocky grin. "As good as it gets."

Joe's eyes narrowed. "Well, I hope that'll be enough to tide you over, then, because there won't be any more where that came from. Clay's going to prison. For life."

"Says who?"

"You know it's true."

"Maybe you'll join him there," she snapped.

The smile disappeared from Joe's face. "Why do you say that?"

"Attempted murder is a serious crime."

"It wasn't my cap you found in the woods," he taunted.

Allie's heart skipped a beat. No one knew about the cap except Hendricks. He must've called Joe the moment she hung up.

Or maybe that cap was a plant. An attempt to get rid of Clay and the one man who'd tried to protect him for the past nineteen years.

"If you're behind that shooting, you'd better watch out," she said.

"Because…"

"Because I'm going to nail your ass to the wall."

"Is that a threat?" He glanced at his brother. "I think that was a threat, don't you?"

Allie longed to wipe the smug expressions from their faces. "It's the truth."

"You're not in Kansas anymore, Dorothy." Joe pounded the roof of her car.

Keeping her foot firmly on the brake, Allie punched the gas at the same time. The sudden revving of her engine and the powerful lurch of her car frightened Joe enough that he stepped back and Roger dived to the side.

Laughing for the Vincellis' benefit, Allie drove away.

"Who were those men, Mommy?" Whitney asked, sounding frightened as their tires squealed around the corner.

Allie rolled up her window. "They're bad guys, honey."

"Are they going to hurt us?"

"No. If I have my way, they're going to jail."

"Oh."

Allie checked her rearview mirror to see Whitney snuggling deeper into the blanket.

"Can we go home now?" she asked with a yawn.

"In a few minutes," she replied.

She drove to Clay's house, but when she arrived, she found all the lights out and his truck gone. Where was he? She drove by his mother's duplex, Grace and Kennedy's historic mansion, Madeline's quaint cottage, even the

small retail space Madeline leased for the newspaper—
all with no luck.

At that point, Allie couldn't think of anywhere else to
look. She sat, letting her car idle in the church parking lot,
until she realized there was one more place. The thought
of finding Clay there made her ill. But it would certainly
explain why she hadn't heard from him.

"Clay? It's really you?" Beth Ann squinted against the
porch light she'd turned on. "What are you doing here?"

"Just...dropping by," he finished lamely. He wasn't
entirely sure why he'd come, except that he needed to
talk to someone, to share the news about the baby and
what it'd been like at the hospital. Grace and Kennedy
had been glowing with happiness. His mother had forgotten her misery long enough to marvel over her first
grandchild. And Madeline had barely been able to
choke back the tears as she held her little niece. Molly
was the only one who'd been missing, and she was
coming next week. For once, being with his family had
felt...healthy, normal. Like any other family. It made
him believe there was hope, made him yearn for a
family of his own....

"Are you okay?" Beth Ann asked tentatively.

"I'm fine."

"Come in."

The moment he stepped inside, she slipped her arms
around his waist and pressed her cheek to his chest. "It's
good to see you," she murmured.

Clay tolerated the hug but immediately felt cornered.
Coming here wasn't what he'd thought it would be. Too
much had changed over the past few weeks. He didn't
even feel like the same man.

But now that he was here, he forced himself to sit and accept a glass of wine.

"Are you tired?" she asked when he'd drained it and set it aside. "Do you want to go to bed?" She grinned enticingly. "I'll give you a blow job."

She was assuming they'd pick up where they'd left off. He tried to talk himself into doing just that, into taking Beth Ann into the bedroom and using everything but the kind of sex that created a baby to obliterate what he was thinking and feeling. But he couldn't. He didn't want Beth Ann. He wanted Allie.

God, what had he done to himself, going to that cabin?

"What's wrong?" she said when he didn't answer.

"Nothing." He made an effort to wipe the scowl from his face. "Did I tell you Grace had her baby tonight?"

"No. What is it?"

"A little girl."

"Really?"

He nodded, but he could tell Beth Ann didn't particularly care about Grace or the baby. Neither did she make an effort to understand how important the whole experience had been to him. She was trying to figure out why he was telling her this so she could use it to get what *she* wanted.

"That's good."

"Kennedy said Grace did great."

She nodded, but seemed preoccupied.

"What is it?" he asked.

"Are you and Allie…over for good?"

"We're not going to talk about Allie," he said.

She offered him a quick, placating smile. "Okay, we won't, but I just want to tell you that…I know what happened between you two at the cabin."

He watched her, wondering where she was going with this.

"And I won't lie," she went on. "It bothers me. A lot. But—" she smiled "—at least you're back where you belong."

The moment she said it, Clay knew she was wrong. He wasn't back. He felt nothing, not even sexual desire. "No, Beth Ann. I—you said you wanted to be friends. I just came to tell you about the baby."

Her jaw hardened. "Does that mean you're still seeing *her?* Is that why she rented that house? So you can stay over anytime you want, and she won't have to answer to her father?"

Clay sat forward. "What are you talking about? Allie lives with her parents."

"Not anymore." She sniffed, apparently feeling vindicated that he hadn't known. "I guess you should've left her alone, huh?"

"What happened?" He'd purposely kept to himself the past week, hoping the rumors would die down and allow life to return to normal for Allie. But he'd talked to his sisters, seen Madeline at the hospital tonight. Did they know? If so, why hadn't anyone told him?

They'd probably been too preoccupied with the baby. Or they had avoided the subject because they knew he'd feel responsible.

"She and her father aren't speaking."

"She's not back on the force?" McCormick had agreed…

"No."

"How do you know?"

"Her mother told Polly Zufelt's mother who told Polly."

Polly worked at the Piggly Wiggly with Beth Ann. "So how's Allie managing?"

"Beats the heck out of me. Polly told me she won't even accept groceries from her parents."

"Son of a bitch," he muttered.

Beth Ann looked even less pleased. "What's that supposed to mean?"

"What about her little girl?"

She wrapped her short, sheer robe more tightly around herself. "That's what she has that I don't, isn't it? A child? What is it all of a sudden, with you and children?"

He stood and headed for the door. "I've got to go."

She followed him. "I'll give you a baby, Clay. I've already told you that. I'll give you anything you want."

He didn't even pause. "No one can give me what I want," he said and walked out.

Allie pulled up in front of Beth Ann's mobile home just as Clay was coming out the door. She'd tried to prepare herself for how she might feel if she actually found him here. But the sight of his truck in the drive had been enough to make her sick. Seeing him in the flesh, with Beth Ann at the door wearing some sort of lingerie, nearly knocked the wind out of her.

"What an idiot," she muttered, leaning her forehead against the steering wheel.

"What's wrong, Mommy?" Whitney asked from the back seat.

"Nothing," she said. Clay hadn't made her any promises. She shouldn't have expected anything else. It was just that—after what they'd experienced—she couldn't imagine letting another man touch her.

He started toward her car, looking surprised and confused. Allie told herself to roll down her window and say what she'd come to say. Get it over with and forget him. But she couldn't. The lump in her throat made it impossible to speak with any clarity, and she didn't want him to know how badly he'd hurt her.

Swallowing the tears that threatened, she drove off and left him standing at the curb.

16

Clay called Allie a dozen times before she finally picked up.

"Hello?"

"It's me," he said.

"I know."

Of course she did. Or she would've answered a long time ago. It was nearly three in the morning. "I want to see you. Can I come over?"

"No."

He said nothing. He knew she'd jumped to the wrong conclusion when she'd seen him at Beth Ann's house. But he didn't attempt to justify his actions. He'd gone there to mess around with Beth Ann. He just hadn't been able to do it. Besides, what difference would it make? If thinking the worst helped Allie stay away from him, she was better off.

"How did you know I was at Beth Ann's tonight?" he asked.

"I didn't." She hesitated. "I was searching for you. Everywhere. It was…the last place I could think of to look."

He ran a finger slowly over one eyebrow. "Why did you want to find me?"

During the ensuing silence, he could sense her reluctance to continue. But finally, she said, "They're coming after you tomorrow."

"They?"

"My father and probably a couple of other officers."

"They have another search warrant?"

"An arrest warrant."

Clay had always known it could come to this. But now? As far as he knew, the police didn't have any more evidence than they'd had all along.

"What's changed?" he asked.

He heard her sigh. "The political climate. If this was happening anywhere else, they wouldn't have a prayer of getting a conviction."

"But here?"

"Where are you going to get an unbiased jury? Everyone already believes you're guilty."

Clay glanced around the kitchen, where almost everything had occurred that fateful night, and heard once again his stepfather's angry voice and outright lies, his mother's screams. He saw Grace in the corner, her face chalk-white as the tears she was silently crying dripped from her chin. Molly had huddled beside her. Then there were the powerful blows of his stepfather when he'd tried to step in to defend his mother, and his desperation to conquer or be conquered. Clay had known in those few minutes that he couldn't let his stepfather win. Maybe he was only a kid, but he alone stood between his mother and sisters and the man who was a danger to them.

And the violence wasn't the worst of it. What followed topped even that—the panic that came with realization, the permanence of what had happened, the blood splattered everywhere, the heavy lifeless body Clay had had to drag from the house.

Clay's muscles still ached when he thought of all the digging he'd done that night. He'd been physically and emotionally exhausted, had wanted to lie in bed for a week—then wake up and learn it'd been a terrible nightmare.

But it had been real. All of it. He'd had to get up the next morning and the next and soldier on as if nothing had happened. There was no one else to take the lead, to provide the support his family needed.

Closing his eyes, he drew a calming breath. "Thanks for letting me know."

"That's it?" she responded.

"There's nothing more I can say, Allie."

"Then why not use the time you've got left to get out of town? Go to Alaska, like your father did, or somewhere else, and don't come back."

Clay pinched his neck, hoping to ease the tension in his muscles. "You're telling me to run?"

"I'm scared for you. Go now. Before they can arrest you."

"That's interesting, coming from a law-and-order type."

"As far as I'm concerned, they're not playing by the rules. Why should we?"

We. He jammed a hand through his hair. He didn't want her in this with him. After what she thought she'd seen at Beth Ann's, she should hate him, hope for the worst. "There's no 'we,' Allie. I'm in this alone. Do you hear?"

Silence. He cursed, wishing he could offer her…something. But telling her how he felt would only make this harder on both of them. "I can't go anywhere," he added.

She sniffed, which made him wonder if she was crying. "Why not?"

Because the police would get another search warrant

and find what was in his cellar. Then there'd be no question about what had happened. He'd have a much better chance going up against the flimsy evidence they already possessed. "The time's come to put an end to this, don't you think? The reverend went missing, and the town wants someone to pay. If I stand trial, chances are they'll leave my mother and sisters alone."

"But you didn't kill him."

Her words caused a terrible longing. "How do you know?"

"I know. And I hate that what happened between us last weekend is probably what's angered everyone enough to do this. We shouldn't have…"

She let her words dwindle away, but he finished for her. "Made love?"

"Yes."

He smiled in spite of what tomorrow would bring. "Are you kidding? When I close my eyes, I can still taste you, feel you—"

"Clay, don't," she said, her voice breathless.

"Whatever comes next, I don't regret it," he said and hung up.

The following morning, Allie was awakened by a call from Grace Archer.

"Your father just arrested my brother," she said.

Allie scrubbed the fatigue from her face. The hour or so she'd been sleeping since getting Whitney off to school wasn't nearly enough, not when such a bad day loomed before her. She'd spent the entire night worrying about what would happen to Clay and wishing she could do something to stop it. But she didn't have any answers. "How'd you get my new number?" she asked distantly, stalling, trying to head off the poignant emotions that were already descending on her like a heavy burden she'd barely put down and had to take up again.

"Madeline."

With a sigh, she relaxed into her pillow. "I'm sorry, Grace…for Clay."

There was a long pause. "How sorry?" she asked at last.

The question took Allie aback. "I don't know what you mean."

"At Evonne's, you said you were on my side."

She pushed herself up on one elbow. "I am."

"Do you care about my brother?"

Allie didn't really want to face that question. But if answering it honestly meant she might be able to enlist Grace's help and support… "I'm in love with him," she said.

There was another significant pause. Then Grace spoke again. "Can you come to my house tonight?"

"What for?"

"Madeline says you're out of work."

"And…"

"I have a job offer for you."

"Doing what?"

"Clay's going to need a good investigator, isn't he?"

Allie threw off the covers and sat up. "Will you be handling his defense?"

"Of course."

"But you're just about to have a baby."

"I had her last night. Her name is Lauren Elizabeth, and she's beautiful. Perfect."

Had Allie not been so exhausted, she would've smiled at the pride in Grace's voice. "Congratulations. How are you feeling?"

"Fine. Except for this."

"So you're out of the hospital?"

"Kennedy will be taking me home in a few hours."

She was calling Allie from her hospital bed? "Are you sure you shouldn't rest for a week or two, enjoy your new baby and let someone else handle—"

"Nothing's going to stand in the way of helping my brother," she stated flatly. "I'm not letting two whole weeks slip by without taking advantage of them."

Suddenly Allie felt more alert. "What's his bail amount?"

"They haven't set it yet," she said. "The bastards—excuse me—the *police* arrested him on Friday, knowing he won't be arraigned until Tuesday."

"Which means he has to spend four days in jail."

"Exactly. But regardless of the bail amount, I'm getting him out. I'll raise the money, even if I have to sell my own house."

Allie bit her lip as she considered the odds. It'd be her, the Montgomerys, Grace's husband Kennedy—and possibly Jed Fowler, except that finding his cap at the cabin suggested she might be a fool to trust him—against the whole town, including Allie's own father.

Shit. She fell back into bed and covered her eyes with one arm. "What time do you want me at your place?"

"Seven."

"Okay," she said, resolute. "The D.A.'s going to be sorry he ever pursued this case, right?"

"If we're lucky," Grace said, but she sounded more determined than optimistic.

After Allie disconnected, she stayed where she was, staring up at the ceiling. She'd just admitted how she felt about Clay. Was she crazy? She'd seen him coming out of Beth Ann's trailer last night!

But she wasn't basing her decision to help in his

defense on whether or not he returned her feelings. She was basing it on the fact that she believed he was innocent. That gave her no choice.

Allie stepped back behind the curtains as a car turned down her street. She'd been waiting for Jed Fowler to get home from work so she could talk to him about his cap, but the Buick that rolled past belonged to a neighbor on the far corner. Jed didn't show up for another fifteen minutes—but when she saw him pull into his driveway, she left the house and crossed the street.

Fortunately, she didn't have to worry about her daughter. After school, she'd taken Whitney to her Boppo's. Whitney had been begging to go, and Allie didn't want her there for the conversation with Jed or at Grace's later tonight. Why risk having Whitney repeat what she'd heard to Evelyn and Dale?

Although Allie was pretty sure Jed knew she was waiting for him, he took his time getting out of his truck. He'd asked her not to come to his place without a subpoena. But she needed answers now more than ever. If she could figure out who'd shot Clay, she might be able to raise enough doubt and uncertainty about the motivation behind Clay's arrest to get the D.A. to drop the case.

"Did you hear?" she said when Jed finally opened his door.

He squinted at her, and she guessed he was remembering that he'd told her not to come over again.

"They arrested Clay Montgomery this morning. For the murder of Reverend Barker."

He shook his head—in disgust or disbelief, she didn't know—grabbed his lunch pail from his truck and started for the house.

"I have something that belongs to you," Allie called after him.

When he turned back, she pulled his red cap out of her new purse. "Look familiar?"

"Where'd you get that?" he asked, wiping the grease-covered fingers of his free hand on his gray coveralls.

"At my father's fishing cabin."

His lips formed a grim line.

"You know where that is, don't you?" she asked.

"Nope."

She made a show of studying his cap. "Then how did your hat get up there?"

He shoved his lunch box under one arm. "No idea. Haven't seen it for several days."

"Where'd you leave it last?"

"Don't know."

"In the truck?"

"Maybe."

"At your shop?"

He shrugged.

"Someone broke into my car, stole my gun and shot Clay with it," she said. *"At the cabin."*

He didn't respond.

"I don't suppose you know who might've done that."

"The Vincellis are saying you shot him yourself," he said.

Allie stiffened in surprise. "Why would I do that?"

"To muddy the waters, I guess."

"Muddy the waters?"

"Pretend there's someone else who's trying to keep the truth from coming out."

She thought of the blood pouring down Clay's arm. "That's quite a chance to take with someone's life, don't you think?"

"It's amazing what some people will do," he said.

For love? Was that why he'd tried to confess?

She wanted to ask. But he disappeared inside the house, leaving her standing in his driveway.

McCormick had been expecting Irene's call. He'd known she wouldn't sit back and take her son's arrest without *some* reaction. But he'd expected her to use the number he'd given her—not contact him at the station. When Hendricks announced that Irene Montgomery was on the line, demanding to speak with him, Dale nearly had a heart attack. The mayor, the Vincellis, Beth Ann, even some of the folks who'd given statements on the Barker case years ago, were gathered around him, celebrating Clay's arrest.

"Okay…uh…thank you," he said to Hendricks as all eyes turned toward him, even those of his wife.

Assuming an impersonal expression, he picked up the receiver. "Chief McCormick."

"How could you?" Irene said.

Glancing around the crowded room, he cleared his throat to buy a few seconds to prepare his response. "Yes, that's true, Mrs. Montgomery. I'm sorry, but there's been some new evidence that's come to light—"

"What evidence?" she snapped.

"A witness who—"

"Beth Ann?" she screeched. "She's a damn liar, and you know it!"

He strove to keep his voice steady, calm. "I'll be happy to explain everything to you. But now's not a good time. I've got a lot of *people* here at the station. Let me call you back."

"No! Dale—"

"I'm afraid I have to insist."

She started to cry. "When?"

"As soon as possible."

"You'd better," she said and hung up.

Evelyn stepped close to him as he set the phone back in its cradle. "I feel sorry for her," she murmured. "What must it be like to have your son hauled off to jail?"

"I'm sure she knew he was guilty all along," Joe said, confirming Dale's impression that he'd been listening in. "Right, Beth Ann?"

Beth Ann no longer seemed so eager to go after Clay, but Joe was putting pressure on her to stick with her story. "Right," she muttered.

"He said they all knew about it," Joe clarified. "All the Montgomerys. Beth Ann already told me that."

They'd been citing Beth Ann's testimony as the case breaker, but Dale doubted she was telling the truth. Clay might be dangerous, but he wasn't an idiot. He wouldn't tell Beth Ann what she claimed he had. But now that she'd made her statement, the whole town had proclaimed it as gospel—the truth at last—and made her a minicelebrity. She'd become a pariah if she changed her story.

She wasn't the most credible witness in the world. But her testimony fit the circumstantial evidence and selective snippets of testimony taken from several other witnesses. Thanks to the active involvement of Stillwater's most influential citizens and the exchange of a few favors, that might be enough to get a conviction.

Dale simply wanted to forget about Barker, and he believed the only way to do that was to try the most likely culprit. In the best-case scenario, Clay would be acquitted and could never be charged with Barker's murder again. In the worst, Clay would go to prison. If that happened, Irene would need a strong male figure in her life. As self-serving as that was, Dale couldn't overlook it.

He moved through the crowd, smiling, shaking hands and nodding as he accepted congratulations all around. Everyone acted as if the trial was already over and Clay had been convicted. But Dale knew Allie was right. They didn't have much of a case. This would be a battle of political power over due process.

"We've got him now…. It's about damn time…. There's nothing wrong with being sure on something like this. A man's future is at stake…. The point is he didn't get away with it."

Most of the time, Dale didn't even bother looking up to see who was talking. "What a damn mess," he muttered to himself, then felt his wife's hand on his arm.

"Is something wrong, dear?" she asked in concern.

"No, nothing," he replied. They spoke about the judge being the mayor's uncle, and the fact that Hendricks's father sat on the County Board of Supervisors, both of which would help the prosecution. Then, after Dale reassured Evelyn a second time that he was fine, she left to attend her book group.

He excused himself as soon as she was gone. Once he'd climbed into his squad car and closed the door, he called Irene.

"Irene, honey, I'm sorry," he said when she answered. "There was nothing I could do about Clay. You know that, don't you?"

"You didn't even warn me," she said.

He cringed at the tears in her voice. "You told me not to call you anymore. I was trying to honor your wishes."

"By arresting my son?"

He ran a hand over the whiskers on his chin. In all the excitement, he'd forgotten to shave this morning. "I didn't want to arrest him. I've tried to protect you, and him. It's just…since Grace moved back, the Vincellis have been buzzing like a hornet's nest—"

"Don't give me that," she said. "This isn't because of Grace. It's because of Allie. You're punishing my son for not staying away from your daughter."

He didn't want Clay and Allie together, but he couldn't admit it to her. "That's not true."

"What can I do?" she cried. "How can I stop this?"

Dale had reached the outskirts of town, where he felt more secure. He drove down a deserted country road, then cut the engine. "Nothing, babe. Nothing at all."

"I'll come back to you if that'll help."

"I wish it was that easy."

"You want me, don't you?"

So badly, he ached inside. Only she could satisfy him. But he couldn't help Clay. It was up to the attorneys now. "I want you," he said. "But I can't let Clay out of jail. I'm not the one who's running this show. It's the mayor and Supervisor Hendricks, honey."

She was openly sobbing now. "What am I going to do?"

"Stand by him," he said. "The D.A. doesn't have much of a case. It's all circumstantial."

She sniffed. "Do you think he'll get off?"

"Maybe," he said, hedging because, now that things had gone so far, he had no idea what might happen. Grace, or whoever handled Clay's defense, would no doubt fight to have the trial moved to a different location, where his opponents didn't have so much control. But he doubted she'd succeed. If Grace argued that there was significant prejudice against her brother, the prosecution would point to the fact that they'd waited nearly twenty years to charge him. That certainly didn't make them appear overeager.

Irene's voice turned to a hopeful whisper. "Do you still love me?"

As much as Irene liked to talk about the possibility, he knew he'd never leave his wife. But, in a way, he did love her. If he'd met her in another time, another place, if he was a younger man... "Yes. You know that. I'll do anything I can for you, okay? I'll try to get you anything you need."

"I need *you*. I can't go through this alone."

She made him feel so strong and capable. He knew he was being silly, acting like he didn't have any sense, but Lord, was he addicted to her. "I'll be there for you."

"But we shouldn't see each other."

"You just said you need me."

"I do."

There was a long pause. Surely she wouldn't change her mind again.

"One battle at a time, right?" she eventually said.

He breathed a sigh of relief. "One battle at a time," he replied. Then he called the florist in Corinth and ordered Irene a dozen long-stemmed red roses.

"What would you like on the card?" the woman asked.

"I can't wait to be with you," he said. "Call me when you're ready."

Allie wasn't sure what to expect when she arrived at the beautiful old Georgian where Grace lived. Set off the highway south of town, it was the only historic building in Stillwater besides the old post office. The yard was large and well groomed, with lots of mature trees and a fountain. Stepping stones passed through a rose-covered trellis and went around to the back of the house, and a tree swing that had been there since Allie was in high school hung from a giant oak on the side. In front, three wide steps led to a deep veranda that was partially covered with wisteria vines.

Allie wondered what it was like to have grown up in such poverty and then to have married so rich. Grace seemed happy. But—Allie thought of Clay in jail—the taint of some things never went away.

As she crossed the porch, Allie noticed two pairs of small rubber boots at the far end of the veranda near a single glass door that probably led to a bathroom or mudroom. But it was the carved, double doors in front of her that opened when she rang the bell.

"Thank you for coming," Grace said and beckoned her inside a grand foyer.

Grace had her hair in a messy knot and wasn't wearing any makeup, but she had deep blue eyes like Clay's and the same elegant structure to her face. Few women looked so beautiful right after giving birth. Perhaps Grace wasn't as slender as usual, but she'd always had a curvaceous figure, and a few extra pounds only added to that effect.

"Good to see you," Allie said. "How's the baby?"

Grace smiled. "Fine. She's sleeping in her bassinet upstairs. I'll bring her down and let you take a peek at her when we're finished here."

"And the boys? Are they around?"

"No, I had Kennedy take them over to Grandma and Grandpa Archer's for a visit. They didn't want to leave the baby, of course, but I'm not ready to let her go out."

Allie remembered the joy she'd experienced at Whitney's birth. She also remembered wanting to share that joy with her husband—and how negatively he'd reacted. He'd spent most of the first few months working late or going out with his buddies because he couldn't stand the care and devotion she lavished on their child. "There's nothing like having a baby," she murmured.

"No," Grace said. "There isn't."

Allie adjusted the strap of her purse. "I'm sorry about Clay. And I'm especially sorry that it had to happen at a time like this."

Worry clouded Grace's eyes. "I doubt the timing was a coincidence."

"You think the mayor and the Vincellis were hoping to catch you at a weak moment?"

"I do. They're hoping I won't be available to help him. But I won't let them get away with what they're doing. Clay doesn't deserve to go to prison."

"I know."

"We'll meet in here," Grace said, taking her to a drawing room that contained a large sofa and two chairs. Two walls were covered by built-in bookshelves and the other two walls had very large windows with expensive, heavy draperies. Allie might have commented on the beauty of the room, which was tastefully decorated in cranberry, green and ivory, but there were two people seated on the sofa staring up at her. Two people she hadn't expected to see: Madeline Barker and Irene Montgomery.

"Hi, Allie," Madeline said. "Come and sit down."

"Good to see you, Maddy," she said.

"I'm so glad you're willing to help us."

Irene's red, splotchy face suggested she'd been crying. Allie tried to convince herself that Clay's mother was only upset about his arrest. But the way her lips tightened made Allie think Irene blamed her for what had happened to Clay.

No doubt all three women had heard about the time she'd spent at the cabin with him. And no doubt they all knew how her father had reacted to finding them together—or she wouldn't be in need of a job.

Feeling extremely self-conscious, she took a seat in one of the chairs across from them.

"His arraignment's on Tuesday," Grace announced, adjusting the volume on the baby monitor which sat on the small table next to her.

"Any idea what they'll be asking for bail?" Allie asked, since she was likely the only one who hadn't heard anything about this.

"I'm guessing half a million."

"That's outrageous!" Madeline cried.

Grace's eyes glittered with righteous indignation. "Kennedy told me they're going to claim he's a danger to society."

"How does Kennedy know that?" Allie asked.

"His mother told him. She's so well connected she hears everything."

Allie tried not to look at Irene. "And if they get a high bail…"

"We'll cover it," Grace said. "Clay mortgaged the farm to be able to clean the place up and do some repairs, but it's been several years since he did that and it wasn't a large note to begin with. He has plenty of equity. So we'll refinance when I run out of my own money."

"He has clear title to the property?" Allie asked.

"He bought us out a few years ago," Madeline explained.

"Getting back to the subject…from what Kennedy's mother says, they're going to throw everything at us they possibly can," Grace said.

"Beth Ann's testimony won't stand up," Madeline said.

"Beth Ann's sticking with her story?" Allie asked in amazement. She'd assumed that Clay's visit to Beth Ann's trailer might have changed the other woman's mind.

"That's the rumor," Grace said.

"Aren't—aren't they still seeing each other?" Allie felt herself flush as she became the center of attention.

Madeline stared at her blankly. "He's seeing you, isn't he?"

"Not really," Allie admitted.

Irene dabbed at fresh tears. "The Vincellis are using Beth Ann, and she's not strong enough or smart enough to stop it. They'll coach her, and the attorneys will coach her. You said that yourself just a minute ago, Grace."

Grace ignored her mother. "What else do they have that's new, Allie?"

"Nothing," she said. "Unless they can come up with the remains, a murder weapon, fiber evidence, *something*, I don't think they have much."

"Jed Fowler could change his testimony," Grace said.

"What makes you think he might do that?" Allie asked.

"Someone called here this morning."

"Who?" Allie and Madeline spoke in unison.

"He wouldn't identify himself."

They all scooted forward. "What'd he say?"

"That Jed's the one who shot Clay at the cabin."

"No! Jed would never hurt Clay," Madeline argued.

Allie didn't respond. She stared at Grace. "Is that all he said?"

"No, he claimed there was proof but then disconnected before he told me what it was."

Jed's cap. Joe had known about it last night at the pool hall, soon after Allie had told Hendricks she'd found it. Had Joe or Hendricks called Grace?

If so… Allie's jaw tightened. Hendricks had acted as if the cap was unimportant. But maybe he didn't know that it played a significant role in what was happening. That someone was going to use it to lean on Jed, hoping to persuade him to change his story so they could build a stronger case against Clay.

Allie's heart began to pound as she saw the brilliance behind such a plan. If the situation was what she imagined it might be, Joe, the mayor or whoever else was out to get Clay, had played her like a pawn. They knew she'd take the attack at the cabin personally, that she'd search for evidence. So they'd planted what they wanted her to find. And not only had she found it, she'd reported it and turned it in. She'd done that a few minutes ago, on her way to Grace's house. The fact that *she'd* found the cap, someone who was friendly with Clay and an ex-police officer to boot, lent Clay's opponents even more credibility.

Allie didn't think Joe was smart enough to manipulate the situation to that extent. And the mayor didn't have sufficient motivation—did she? Who else wanted Clay prosecuted badly enough to remove Jed's testimony from his defense?

"What is it?" Grace asked.

Allie covered her face and shook her head.

"What?" Madeline prompted. "I know Jed would never do anything to hurt Clay. It had to be a…a crank call or something."

"Or something," Allie repeated. "I have a feeling someone's trying to get Jed to change his story."

"He wouldn't do that," Irene said. "He tried to confess to Barker's murder so Clay wouldn't go to jail."

"Do you know why?" Allie looked squarely at Irene for the first time since she'd arrived.

"No. No one ever knows why Jed does what he does. But he's proven his loyalty."

Grace picked up where her mother had left off. "Exactly. So what could they threaten him with that would be worse than what he's already risked?"

It's amazing what some people will do...

Fowler had seemed almost...disgusted when he made that statement. Why? Was he referring to what he'd tried to do to save Irene and her kids from harm?

Allie dropped her hands. "We're probably okay, unless... Is there any reason he might be angry with you, Mrs. Montgomery?"

Irene straightened the ruffle on her purple blouse. "Me? Of course not. I rarely see him, and we usually don't speak when we do bump into each other."

"He's painfully shy with women," Allie said. "But he had to be trying to protect you when he confessed. I can't think of any other reason he'd do what he did."

Irene gave a little shrug. "I have no idea why he'd care about me. We hardly know each other."

"Could it be that he's admired you? From afar?"

"I wouldn't know," she insisted.

"So you've had no argument with him? You've never done anything that might make him feel angry or disaffected?"

"Like what?"

"Like being seen with another man?"

Irene's eyes flicked toward Grace. To Allie, it seemed that they were filled with sudden fear, as if something had just occurred to her. But she didn't say what it was. "No, nothing."

17

"I might have made a mistake."

Those were not the first words Clay wanted to hear after spending twenty-four hours in jail. Especially from Grace.

He took the seat provided for him in the small, windowless room set aside for attorney–client conferences and regarded his sister. "You look great," he said. "How's the baby?"

"Good." She bent closer. "Did you hear me?"

"Did Lauren come home from the hospital with you?" he asked.

Grace gave him an impatient scowl. "Yes. She's doing fine. I'm doing fine. The weather's been unseasonably warm. Listen, we don't have very long. Would you please focus on the reason I'm here?"

He stretched his legs out in front of him. "You have a brand-new baby. You shouldn't have to be doing this right now."

"You shouldn't have to be doing it, either," she said.

"*I* don't have a choice."

"Well, I'm not going to sit back and enjoy Lauren while you're locked up." She arched an eyebrow in challenge. "So could we talk about the problem at hand?"

"What's there to say? You'll try to get the trial moved

someplace else, where I'll have a better chance. The other side will contest it, but the judge is Mayor Nibley's uncle, so they'll win. Then you'll have to fight to get a few jurors who won't say, 'Roast him,' before they've even heard the testimony or seen the evidence, and—"

"I hired Allie to help me investigate," she interrupted.

Slouching lower in his seat, Clay pressed his thumb and finger against his closed eyelids. Okay, so *this* was the mistake. "What were you thinking?"

"I wanted someone who was talented and capable, and who was passionate about defending you."

"Granted, that doesn't leave you a large pool of people to draw from. But there're always strangers. You know, professionals who hire out?"

"She *is* a professional, Clay."

He wanted to remember Allie the way she'd been at the cabin, didn't want her mixed up in the mess that was brewing. If she joined forces with his sister, her father would never forgive her. Neither would a lot of other people in Stillwater. And what was the point? What difference could she really make? The trial wouldn't be fair in the first place. "I don't care. You can't involve her."

Grace fiddled with the pen she'd taken out of her brief-case, then tossed it on top of her blank legal pad and shoved back her chair. "It's too late. She's already involved."

"Aw, hell. Grace—"

She put up a hand. "Let me finish. When she came over last night, Mom and Madeline both—"

"Mom?" Clay echoed. "Grace, Mom's not strong enough to handle this right now. You have to tell her it'll all work out and exclude her from any conversation that isn't entirely optimistic."

"I realize that. But after they arrested you, it was all I could do to stop her from marching down to the police station and confessing."

"That would only get us *all* in trouble."

"I explained that. But she's frantic. I have to include her."

He shifted uncomfortably in his seat. He didn't like being locked up. He'd been limited before, but at least he'd had his work and his cars and an occasional trip to town. In here, it felt like all hell was about to break loose and he wouldn't have the chance to fight back. "I suppose Madeline wouldn't let you exclude her, either?"

"Of course not. They're worried about you. They have to feel as if they're helping."

"Which only makes your job harder."

"When has dealing with our past ever been easy?"

He sighed. "True."

The door opened, and a deputy poked his head in. "You okay in here, ma'am?"

"I'm fine," Grace said.

The man smiled appreciatively at Clay's attractive sister. "Let me know if he gives you any trouble."

"Get out," Clay snapped.

The glitter in the deputy's eyes suggested he was going to respond, but Grace quickly moved between them. "Please, you're not helping."

"Your client had better watch his step," he growled, but he closed the door.

Grace waited several seconds, then picked up where they'd left off. "Anyway, Madeline thinks she'll be able to help."

Clay's stepsister had been his savior *and* his worst enemy. She hotly defended him against anyone who implied that he'd ever done anything wrong. Her loyalty and Jed Fowler's was what had kept him out of jail this long. But Madeline was also one of the people who wouldn't give up searching, wouldn't let anyone forget. Thanks to her—and the Vincellis, of course—suspicion swirled around Clay constantly, and probably always would, whether he went to trial or not. "In what way can she help?"

"She's planning to post a notice in the paper, offering a reward for any information leading to the arrest of the man who shot you."

"Who's putting up the reward?"

"Kennedy."

Clay studied her. "What do Kennedy's parents have to say about that?"

"We didn't ask them. We don't care. You're family to Kennedy now."

Clay shook his head. "He'll do anything for you."

She finally smiled. "Yes, but he's doing this for you."

"So my defense team consists of an ex-assistant district attorney with a new baby, my overwrought mother, a step-sister who can't know the real truth and a cop I got fired."

"So far."

He stretched his neck. "That's quite a team."

She regarded him steadily. "It's better than you make it sound. Allie's definitely an asset."

"Too bad you have to fire her," he said.

Grace rubbed a finger over her bottom lip. "I know it's risky to include her, but—"

He leaned forward. "Risky? It's idiotic! Are you trying to beat the charges or put me away for good?" Clay had more pressing reasons to get her off the case—but he didn't want to tell Grace just how much he cared about Allie.

"Clay, she'll keep digging whether we join forces with her or not. After Mom and Madeline left last night, she told me about the note someone left at the cabin, and that she found Jed's baseball cap nearby."

"*Jed's?* That has to be a mistake."

"It's not."

"But Jed wouldn't shoot me. And he'd have no reason to leave Allie that note."

"Allie thinks it's a setup."

"What would anyone have to gain by implicating Jed?"

"It's a way to obfuscate the truth, a way to send anyone who's trying to track down the real offender on a wild-goose chase. And whoever doesn't like you probably doesn't like Jed, either. So he's expendable. After all, his insistence that our dear old stepdad didn't come home that night is what's stood between you and prosecution all these years."

"That and the fact that they have no physical evidence," Clay pointed out dryly.

"At this stage, it's not about evidence. It's about an old grudge."

Sobering, Clay moved closer to the table. He'd lose his mind if they sent him to prison. He could take almost anything, but he couldn't take being locked up. "I know."

"Allie thinks, and I agree, that our opponents might be trying to lean on Jed, to tell him they won't go after him for attempted murder or some other charge if he'll testify against you."

Clay frowned. He wasn't sure why Jed Fowler had been such a good friend to them, but the mechanic had to know more about the night Barker died than he'd ever said. Otherwise, he wouldn't have tried to confess when they dug up Butch's bones, which Clay had purposely relocated after he'd moved Barker's body to the cellar. "We've never had a close relationship with Jed. We don't even know why he's stood by us. Which makes him a question mark. We can't predict what he'll do."

She toyed with the pen she'd dropped a moment earlier. "Allie said something else that concerns me."

"What's that?" Clay was growing more agitated. He'd expected to be up against the circumstantial evidence he already knew about. He'd had no idea there'd be more. Whoever was out to get him was going to great lengths to insure he went away for life.

"She asked Mom if Jed's ever seen her with another man."

A jolt of alarm brought Clay to his feet. "Why would she ask that?"

"She believes Jed's secretly admired Mom for years."

"We've guessed as much."

"True. But listen to this. She thinks we'll be okay—unless Jed's become disaffected with her for some reason."

Clay paced the small room. "Is she suggesting that's already happened?"

"No, but she's wondering about it."

Muttering another curse, Clay shook his head. Little did Allie know Irene *had* been seeing another man—*her own father*. She was going to get hurt. He could feel it coming and chafed at his helplessness to stop it. "This just gets better and better, doesn't it?"

The jingle of her cell phone woke Allie from a deep sleep. She fumbled through her bedding, searching for it, and nearly knocked the lamp off her nightstand. It wasn't until she heard her daughter running toward her, the ring growing louder, that she realized she'd left it out in the kitchen and Whitney was bringing it to her.

Rubbing her eyes, she rolled over as her daughter reached the side of her bed, saw that it was broad daylight and panicked. "Oh, no! Are we late?"

"For what?" Whitney asked.

"For school!"

Her daughter laughed. "It's Saturday, silly. I don't have school on Saturday."

"Right. Thank goodness." Taking the phone, Allie slumped back onto her pillows and covered the mouthpiece while she asked Whitney what she was doing.

"Watching cartoons," Whitney said and ran into the living room.

Allie watched her go, relieved to see that she seemed to be adjusting to the move, then put the phone to her ear. "Hello?"

"Allie?"

It was her mother. Which came as no surprise. Since she'd moved out, Evelyn checked in with her often and brought more furniture each time. "Hi, what's up?"

"Why didn't you wake me when you picked up Whitney last night?"

"I didn't want to disturb you."

"I wouldn't have minded."

"There wasn't any need."

"But it would've given us a chance to talk."

Her father had been at home. Allie hadn't been eager to wake anyone. "We can talk now, can't we?"

"I guess," she said. "How are things over there? Do you have enough to eat?"

"We're fine."

"Maybe we should go out today and get some groceries—a few staples. Then I won't have to worry so much about you. It might take a while to find work, you know."

Allie considered the job she'd just accepted. She knew her mother wouldn't be pleased to hear that she was helping with Clay's defense, but she didn't see any point in trying to hide it. Gossip being what it was in Stillwater, Evelyn and everyone else would probably know by the end of the day.

"Actually, I already have a job," she said.

Evelyn immediately pounced on that. "*Really?* Wonderful. Where?"

Allie swallowed a groan. "I'm helping Grace with Clay's case."

Silence. Allie gripped the phone a little tighter but refused to speak first. Finally, Evelyn said, "You're kidding, aren't you?"

"No, I'm not."

"Allie, this…this obsession of yours with Clay Montgomery has gone far enough, don't you think?"

"Obsession?"

Her mother ignored her. "It's up to the courts to decide his fate now."

"How can they come to the right conclusion without the facts, Mom?"

"What facts? You're a good detective, Allie. But even you haven't been able to come up with anything new."

"I can't give up. Someone just tried to kill him. What's going on is not as clear-cut as everyone would like to believe."

"You know it was Joe who shot Clay. So take your old job back and go after him. He deserves it. But then forget about Clay."

"I'm not convinced it *was* Joe."

"Then you should be. When I was at the Piggly Wiggly a few minutes ago, I heard Joe's ex-wife tell Francine

Eastman she thinks Joe has your gun. She said she stopped by to get some money he owes her and saw something that looked like a gun at his house."

"Why hasn't she reported it?"

"There's been nothing but trouble between those two. And she's just getting her life back. She doesn't want to step into the middle of this."

"No one does! But what's happening is a farce. All the people who've been out to get Clay are finally gaining the upper hand. And I'm not going to watch the Vincellis and others with a personal agenda use the law for their own purposes."

"Can't you see what Clay's doing?" Evelyn argued. "Do you think he's been lavishing his attention on you because he *likes* you?"

Allie felt her jaw drop but was too offended to be able to respond right away.

"Clay doesn't like anyone," her mother went on. "He's using you. He knows he needs allies—solid, reputable allies—so he's trying to elicit your support, hoping you can save him. And he doesn't care if he ruins you in the process."

"That's not true," Allie said. "Clay doesn't suck up to anyone, for any reason. He doesn't even want me in his life. He told me—" What good would it do to explain this to her mother? The people of Stillwater wanted a scapegoat and they thought they'd found the perfect candidate. "Never mind."

"Think about the number of women he's slept with," Evelyn said. "You're just another conquest to him. A calculated conquest because now, in addition to getting exactly what he wanted from you at the cabin, you're going to help him."

Allie hung up. She knew she shouldn't. Her mother was her last support. But Allie was so angry, she couldn't stop herself.

"Mommy?" Whitney called.

Allie forced back the rush of emotions that were assaulting her all at once. "What, honey?"

"Did Boppo ask you?"

"Ask me what?"

"If I can stay with her tonight?"

Allie didn't know what to say. They hadn't gotten that far.

"Did she?" Whitney pressed.

The phone rang again. Allie answered instead of answering her daughter.

"Are you really choosing Clay over your family?" her mother asked.

Allie cursed silently. "Of course not."

"You are if you're going to help the Montgomerys. Your father will take it as a personal affront, and although I've tried to remain neutral, this will compel me to choose his side. Do you realize that? I have to be loyal to my husband."

"This isn't about loyalty. At least not entirely. I need the job," Allie said.

"If you weren't being so stubborn, you could go back to work for your father."

Working for the police department would give her a lot more stability. She'd have a long-term income and benefits, which she wasn't going to get helping Grace. And she had Whitney to think of. Her responsibility to her daughter and the emotional pressure she faced from everyone else would make it infinitely easier to fall in line with her parents.

Except that no one seemed to care about actually *solving*
the case. They wanted someone to punish for Barker's disappearance so that the Vincellis would finally be satisfied
and everyone could go on with their lives. And, unlike his
mother and sisters, Clay was defiant, angry. In fact, the
depth of the anger running through him was a little fright-
ening at times. That made it easy for some people to believe
he was capable of such a crime. But Allie cared about the
truth.

Or maybe she just cared about Clay.

"I can't," she said.

"Not even for Whitney's sake?" Evelyn asked.

Allie hugged her extra pillow to her chest. "I'll make
sure she gets everything she needs."

"But she loves us. Putting a rift between you and us
will hurt her."

"Mom, we don't even know what happened to Barker.
Clay deserves a fair trial, don't you think?"

Her mother's voice rose. "He'll have his sister to defend
him. She's never lost a case."

"She's never had so much at stake before, or been up
against odds like this!"

"Let her deal with it! She'll be fine without you."

"I have to do what I think is right," Allie insisted.

There was a long silence, then her mother said, "Are
you sure it's your conscience you're trying to satisfy?"
And this time it was Evelyn who hung up.

"Mom-my?" Whitney wailed, losing patience. "Why
won't you answer me?"

Allie wanted to throw her phone across the room but
set it gently on the nightstand instead. "I'm sorry, honey,"
she called back. "You can't stay with Boppo tonight. She
forgot that she already has other plans."

"But she just asked me! We were going to bake cookies!"

"Why don't I see if your friend Emily can spend the night with us?"

"What about Boppo?" Whitney asked.

"Maybe you can go there next week," Allie said. "But it's not looking good," she muttered to herself. Then she turned her thoughts to what her mother had said about her gun. Cindy thought she'd seen it at Joe's house? Considering that Joe had the strongest motivation to shoot Clay, *and* he had no alibi, she thought the police could establish probable cause for a search warrant. But the situation being what it was, she knew she'd never convince her father to try. He wouldn't act against the Vincellis right now. No one would.

And that meant she had to do something herself, and she had to do it fast—before Joe got rid of the evidence.

"Whitney?" she called.

"What, Mommy?"

"We'll make arrangements for you to stay with Emily, instead. Okay?"

Dale stood in the shed where he kept his tools and glanced at his watch. He'd just finished edging the lawn. It was part of his Saturday-morning routine, a routine that usually relaxed him. But he was growing anxious. Irene should've received the flowers by now. Typically, she responded right away when he gave her something; he was hoping that was still the case. He had to see her. If they could be together, even if it was just one more time, it'd be easier to deal with everything else going on in his life. His estrangement from Allie. The mayor and the Vincellis interfering with his job. The shooting at the cabin.

Wiping his hands on a paper towel that he promptly tossed in the trash can by the door, he reached into his pocket for his cell phone and dialed the voice-mail account he'd set up for her use.

Sure enough, he had a message.

Feeling a tremor of hope, he pressed "one" to hear it.

But his wife's voice intruded, coming from behind him. "Dale, what's taking you so long out here?"

He turned to find Evelyn standing in the doorway. He was tempted to close the phone and shove it in his pocket, but Evelyn trusted him so much she wasn't particularly nosy. And Irene was beginning to mention the "beautiful roses."

He motioned for Evelyn to be quiet. "I'm checking my voice-mail to see if anyone needs me at the station," he lied, his heart thumping with more than its usual share of guilt.

Evelyn was always very respectful of his wishes, but today she ignored his plea for silence. Wringing her hands, she scowled and said, "I've got to see Reverend Portenski. I'll be back in a few minutes."

Obviously, she was unhappy. He would've asked her what was wrong. But Irene was telling him how much she loved him, how much she longed to be with him—and how she planned to remove the skimpy lingerie he'd bought her the next time they were together.

Instead of stopping Evelyn, Dale breathed a sigh of relief as she pulled out of the driveway and then dialed Irene.

"Hello?"

"It's me," he said.

"How come you're calling me now? You're usually home on a Saturday morning."

"Evelyn's out."

"Thank you for the flowers," she said. "And the note. I needed the note more than anything."

"I want to make love to you," he said.

"Now?"

If they had time, he would. But the cabin was too far, and after what had happened there, he didn't dare take her back, anyway. Their favorite little hotel in Corinth wasn't much closer, not close enough for a quick rendezvous. "Soon. It'll give me something to look forward to."

"I don't want to wait," she said, her voice pleading. "I need you now."

He was afraid she'd change her mind about seeing him if he didn't arrange something in the next few days. "I'd say we could get together tonight, but I'm not sure where we could go that would be safe, darling."

"You have that guesthouse."

He was desperate, but not crazy. "Not there."

"Come on. No one'll see us."

"It's right next to my *house,* for crying out loud."

"No, it's not. It's down by the pond. You can't even see it from your house. You've told me often enough that you'd like to move me there."

That was wishful thinking, and she knew it. But she could be so childlike. He tried a different line of reasoning. "That wouldn't be any fun. I'd have a heart attack from the stress."

She started crying. "If I'm that bad for you, forget it. Forget everything—"

"Irene, stop," he begged. "I want to touch you so badly I can't think of anything else. It's just—" Suddenly he had an idea. "Wait. What about the farm?"

"The farm?" she echoed, sniffling.

"It's empty now, isn't it? And it's private. I could go the back way and hide my car in the barn."

"No. Molly will be in town this afternoon. She flew in early because of Clay. She's renting a car in Nashville right now."

"She'll be staying at the farm?"

"She could. She usually stays with Clay."

"But Clay's not there this weekend. She won't stay at the farm alone."

"That's true," she admitted. "And she'll be excited to see Grace's new baby. I'm sure she'll stay with Grace. But they'll expect me to be with them this evening."

"You can get away. Say you've got a headache, that you're going home to bed and leave a bit early."

"But someone's bound to see the lights in the farm-house," she said.

"Then we won't turn on any lights. You can hide your car in the barn, too."

She didn't answer.

"It's perfect, honey," he pleaded. "It's close and it's private. Where else is there?"

"But Clay's in jail—"

"Not for long. Grace will get him out." He knew Irene would assume he meant for good, when he was only talking about making bail. But he didn't want to get specific; she was too worried about her son.

"He won't like it," she said.

"How will it hurt him?"

Silence.

"He doesn't know about us, right?"

"Of course not," she said immediately.

"Good. Then meet me there tonight."

"What will you tell your wife?"

"I'll say that one of my men called in sick and I've got to fill in."

"What time?"

"Ten."

He heard a soft sigh. "If that's what you want."

"It's what I want. And bring that nightie you were talking about in the message," he added.

The lumps in the cheap mattress dug into Clay's back as he stared at the bunk above his. Fortunately, the county lockup was mostly empty, so he didn't have a cellmate. He could imagine how much worse his stay would be with two or three other guys sharing the same small space—the lack of privacy, the smell, the noise. Of course, he had all that to look forward to, and more, if he went to prison. But for now, he could take comfort in the fact that there was no one besides the jailer who delivered his meals to interrupt his thoughts.

He kicked at a piece of lint on the ground. Actually, having twenty-four hours a day strictly to himself might not be so good. Because he couldn't stop thinking about Allie. And her little girl. They'd be better off if Allie didn't try to help him. The fact that she was willing to take a stand against everyone she knew and loved, for his sake, made Clay yearn for things he couldn't have. And he hated the thought of her being mistreated, which would surely happen if she continued to take his side.

Rotating the shoulder of his hurt arm, he pinched the site of his bullet wound to stop the unmerciful itching that had started this morning. It was healing well, but the situation could've been very different. There were those who hated him and everyone associated with him. His sisters and mother couldn't change their affiliation, of course. But

Allie could. If he was locked up, he'd be unable to protect her. She probably understood that, but he doubted she understood how important it was to him to keep her safe. He didn't want to drag her down with him.

That was the worst part of jail, he decided. It wasn't the luxuries and comforts he was missing. It was being so damn helpless. He could do nothing to insure the happiness of those he loved, and after so long he didn't know how to live for anything else.

"Grace had better do as I told her," he muttered, rolling off the bed to walk around his cell. He'd instructed his sister to tell Allie to get a real job, that Clay didn't want anything to do with her. He knew he was being harsh, but he *had* to be harsh. Otherwise, Allie wouldn't listen. And the momentary sting those words might cause would be infinitely kinder than screwing up her life. Let her make up with her folks, go back to the force, find a suitable father for Whitney. A man who could give her everything Clay couldn't.

For a moment, Clay let himself imagine being that man. Coming in from the farm to sleep with her at night. Helping raise her little girl. Making Allie pregnant with his own child.

With a faint smile, he remembered the red-faced bundle that was Grace's baby, Lauren, and the way Lauren had turned her tiny mouth toward him when he'd touched her cheek. Holding that baby had shown him, more clearly than ever, exactly what was important in life. Most men took their ability, their *right*, to have a family for granted. They had no idea how badly they'd want that if they couldn't have it.

Regardless of his future, Clay wanted a good life for Allie. But he had a feeling Grace wouldn't deliver his message. His sister was stronger now than she'd ever been, more confident in her own decisions. For some reason, she thought Allie's participation might make a difference.

Grace was going to give his defense everything she had—and that included Allie, whether he liked it or not.

18

Joe usually spent Saturday evenings drinking with his buddies. According to his ex-wife, he drank too much. But tonight, Allie was grateful for his rather reliable interest in heading to the pool hall. As she stood with her back to the fence behind Stillwater Sand and Gravel and gazed through the trees, she could see that the house his parents provided for him was completely dark.

Leaving her car, which she'd hidden among the giant piles of sand and rock crowding the machinery, Allie moved closer. She didn't feel particularly good about breaking and entering. But she didn't see that she had any better choice. Before coming over here, she'd called Hendricks and tried the sheriff's department, and they'd simply referred her back to her father.

Wearing tennis shoes, jeans and a dark shirt, Allie slipped through the tall white ash and silver maple trees that lined the back of Joe's yard and approached the screened-in porch. She had a flashlight, but she didn't want to use it until she was inside. Fortunately, the moon was nearly full, so she could make out most objects in her path. She just hoped Joe didn't have a dog.

Reaching the back of the house, Allie stood by the screen and listened carefully for any noises from inside.

The night was as quiet as it was still.

He's gone. She tried to open the screen door.

It was locked.

Cursing under her breath, Allie began to dig through the large canvas bag she'd brought with her. She'd put a small knife in there, as well as her flashlight and some other tools. She could slice a hole in the screen, reach through and unlatch the old-fashioned catch. But she abandoned that plan almost as soon as she thought of it. If Joe spotted the hole later, he might become suspicious, and she didn't see any reason to give her little search away, especially if she didn't have to. Surely she could find an open window somewhere. Few people in Stillwater bothered with tight security. And the month of June was already upon them, with its oppressive heat and humidity.

Wiping the nervous perspiration from her top lip, she began to circle the house. She didn't find anything very hopeful on the first floor, but a second-story window stood open. She guessed it was Joe's bedroom. She could see the curtains flutter ever so slightly and assumed he'd left a fan running.

The problem was getting up to that window without being seen from the street. It was at the front of the house, right above the porch and facing the highway; there were no trees to give her cover.

She bit her lip, trying to decide what to do. Did she cut the screen or try to climb up to the second story?

This time of night, there wasn't much traffic….

Seeing no cars in either direction, she pulled the strap of her bag over her head so she could wear it across her body and began to climb onto the porch railing. The trellis that continued up from there didn't seem too sturdy, but she was fairly certain it'd bear her weight. Once she was on the roof, getting to the window would be—

The sound of an engine reached Allie's ears as she clung to the side of the house. She calculated how long it'd take her to get to the window and how long it'd take her to climb back down and decided she didn't have time to do either. That engine was growing louder by the second.

Forgetting her fear of falling, she scooted up the trellis, clambered onto the porch roof and lay flat. Cringing, she waited for the vehicle to pass.

But it didn't pass. It slowed and turned in at the driveway.

Joe was home.

Dammit! Allie held perfectly still as the engine died. Then the truck door opened and slammed, and footsteps approached the house. Keys jingled directly below her as Joe crossed the porch. She told herself to get the hell out of there as soon as he stepped inside the house. But that open window was only a few feet away. If he stayed downstairs for a few minutes, she could take a peek....

Gathering her nerve, she crawled over to the window and listened again, in case he had a dog. The sound of a television drifted up to her, but no barking, whining or thumping. No "hello pooch" from Joe.

Quickly climbing over the ledge, she dropped silently into a room that contained a whirring fan, a rumpled bed, a chest of drawers and a desk scattered with papers. His closet stood open and had dirty laundry spilling out of it; another foot of discarded clothing covered the floor.

Hurrying to the fan, Allie turned it off so she could hear if Joe came up the stairs. Then she pulled out her flashlight and used his desk chair to search the top shelves of the closet. She found a small bundle wrapped in a T-shirt that felt promising. But when she opened it, she discovered a bunch of sex toys, including a giant vibrator and some S&M paraphernalia.

"Definitely not what I wanted to know about you," she muttered. Shoving the bundle back where she'd found it, she turned her attention to Joe's dresser. There was a recent issue of a girlie magazine tossed in with his underwear. Below that, she spotted an old high school yearbook. She almost pushed it aside, too. But she could still hear the television downstairs, so she slowed long enough to flip through it.

It was from Joe's senior year. In the front pages, some of his male friends had drawn crude pictures. Kennedy had told him to take it easy over the summer. And various girls had written the usual sentiments. "I can't believe it's over. Call me, okay?" There was a long love note from Cindy, Joe's girlfriend at the time and the woman he ended up marrying and divorcing—twice.

Why would Joe have his high school yearbook in his underwear drawer? she wondered. He and Cindy must have broken up and reunited half a dozen times since they were teens, which meant he'd been moving back and forth between the house they'd shared and this one. Allie would've expected something so old and inconsequential, at least at this point in their lives, to fall by the wayside. Or end up in the attic or garage. But Joe kept it with his personal items.

Allie found that very interesting. Especially when she realized that there was one particular page in the senior portrait section that had a packaged condom as a bookmark. It was the page with Grace Montgomery's photograph. Her picture was a simple snapshot, not a fancy portrait from one of the expensive studios like most of the others. But it wouldn't have stood out all that much if someone, presumably Joe, hadn't written across her face: "Fucking bitch, you'll get yours."

Was this a recent addition? The condom didn't look that old. Allie got the impression the writing wasn't, either.

That Joe blamed Grace for taking his best friend away from him was no secret. He and Kennedy had hung out together all through high school and beyond, until Grace had returned to town last year and Kennedy had fallen in love with her. But the emotion behind the sentiment Joe had expressed toward Grace in the yearbook seemed more malevolent than resentful.

Then Allie heard a creak on the stairs.

She cocked her head, listening to be sure. The footsteps came closer. Turning off her flashlight, she threw the book back in the drawer and closed it, jammed her bag under Joe's bed and wiggled in behind it. The dust made it difficult to breathe, but she was too scared to breathe, anyway. She wasn't sure she was far enough under the bed to avoid being seen. Joe had so much junk under there, including what felt like a couple of dishes, she couldn't move any farther.

The light went on. With her cheek pressed to the carpet, Allie could see Joe's feet as he entered the room and prayed he wouldn't notice that she'd turned off the fan.

He didn't seem to. The springs above her creaked as he sat down to remove his boots.

Thank God. He was going to bed. Once he fell asleep, she'd slip out and search the rest of the house.

But he didn't disrobe. He put on a pair of tennis shoes and called someone.

"You ready?...Hell, no, it'll take longer than that...I'm beginning to believe he's buried in that damn barn....So? Maybe Jed was in on it. They must've buried him some-where close by. They wouldn't have had time to do anything else…Where did you see her?… Doesn't matter. She won't be at the farm. She'll be with Grace or her mother… Right. Just don't let anyone see you pull in. If Clay finds out we were there, he'll bury us right next to my uncle… You should've seen what he did to Tim Fox when he caught him messing around with Grace…. I don't care how long ago it was, I know him better than you do…. Yeah…. Doesn't matter. Kennedy will post as much as it takes…. We could always finish up tomorrow or the next night, if we have to…. That's good… Okay… Don't forget to bring a shovel."

He hung up, grabbed something off his dresser and walked out.

Allie started to scramble out from under the bed. She was choking on dust and shocked by what she'd just heard. But Joe returned a second later to turn off the light.

Reverend Portenski paced back and forth in his study. Evelyn McCormick had left hours earlier but, hard as he'd tried to forget her visit, he couldn't. She was a good woman and so worried about her daughter. She'd come to him looking for peace, advice, support.

Should he do what was best for him? Or for her? And what about everyone else?

He had to come forward, didn't he? He'd been able to justify his silence this long only because he couldn't have saved the girls the Reverend Barker had abused. He didn't even recognize them; Portenski hadn't moved to town until he'd heard about the opening at the church. Those Polaroids had been old when he'd found them, the children in them all grown up. And except for Grace, he doubted the victims were still living in the area, because no one had ever filed any complaints.

What was done was done, right? Keeping his mouth shut protected Madeline from a very harsh reality, the church from a terrible shame, and the Vincellis, who were a proud family, from the worst possible humiliation. They wouldn't want these pictures to come out, even if it meant Clay would go to jail for the rest of his life. This town had long touted Barker as a saint.

The Montgomerys wouldn't be eager to see them made public, either. Grace was a sensitive soul who'd barely survived what had happened to her. Portenski didn't want to bring her any more unhappiness. She'd asked him to help her brother, and he wanted to do that. Maybe he was uncomfortable around Clay, but a part of him admired the younger man's strength. Another part sympathized with the tough decisions he'd made.

But how could he protect the Montgomerys, the Vincellis *and* the McCormicks?

Portenski tugged at his bottom lip. What should he do?

With a sigh, he knelt down and began to pray.

"Father, enlighten my mind. Instruct thy servant that I might be fair to all involved."

He paused, searching, waiting for the answer. There was nothing in his mind except silence. Then, at last, a thought crystallized.

"Truth is the secret of eloquence and of virtue, the basis of moral authority; it is the highest summit of art and of life."

Henri Frederic Amiel, a nineteenth-century Swiss philosopher had written those words. Portenski knew they hadn't come directly from God's mouth. But why should he remember them now, unless they were intended as his answer?

Amiel had written something else that merited consideration. *"The man who insists upon seeing with perfect clearness before he decides, never decides. Accept life and you must accept regret."*

It was a sign, Portenski decided. A sign that the time had come to act; whether he would later regret it or not.

Allie froze halfway out from under the bed, terrified that Joe had spotted her. But he didn't do anything to indicate he had. He flipped off the light, then jogged down the stairs, slammed the door and started his truck. He was too focused on what he was about to do—which, as far as she could tell, was search Clay's farm.

Let him search. He won't find anything. The police had already searched twice. Clay was innocent.

Getting up, she began going through the rest of Joe's drawers. She'd use the time to look for her gun....

But she stopped only a second later. Clay was innocent of cold-blooded murder. In her heart, she knew that had to be true and refused to believe her emotions were clouding her judgment. But he harbored more than his share of secrets. She was frightened of what those secrets might be, and how they might be interpreted if they got out. He must have some reason for protecting the farm as vigilantly as he did.

What would Joe and whoever he was meeting find?

She wasn't sure. But she couldn't take the chance that they'd come up with something they could use against Clay.

Abandoning her own search, she rushed downstairs, let herself out the back door and ran for her car. She had to stop them before it was too late.

Allie was pretty sure she'd arrived in time. She'd tried contacting Grace and Madeline while she was on the road, to ask them to meet her at the farm. But Grace's line was busy, and she hadn't been able to reach Madeline. As a last-ditch effort, she'd called Madeline's boyfriend, Kirk. He'd said Molly had come to town and they were all at Grace's. Since she couldn't reach anyone, he'd promised to meet her himself, but she'd obviously arrived before everyone else—including Vincelli. The farm looked deserted.

Parking in front, she hurried to the house. The door was locked. She went around back, choosing the soft earth rather than the wraparound porch so the boards wouldn't creak, and scaled the steps. The back door was locked, too.

Standing by the chicken coop, she gazed up at the second story and thought she saw a glimmer of light in some distant room—a bathroom, maybe? It winked out so fast, she decided it had to be the moon reflecting off a window.

Or was she imagining things?

She was uneasy enough to conjure up almost any sight or sound. She knew Joe had a mean streak. Providing Cindy was right about her gun, it was Joe who'd nearly killed Clay. If he found Allie here, maybe she'd become his next target.

Shot with her own gun. Not a nice thought. But she had to admit it was possible. Joe hated the Montgomerys, and hate was a very powerful motivator.

She tried to call her father for backup. He seemed to believe Clay was the only person in Stillwater capable of violence, despite the theft and shooting at the cabin. But she knew Dale would come, anyway. If she could get hold of him.

On the third ring, her call transferred to voice-mail.

"Damn," she muttered, but Kirk would be here shortly.

While she waited, she decided to check for cars. The farm was far enough from town that Joe and whoever was with him would've had to drive. And if they were smart, they wouldn't park too far away, in case they needed to leave in a hurry. Their best parking options would be the dirt road along the back of the property, the open area where Clay kept his heavy equipment, behind the barn or down by the creek.

Allie moved automatically toward the barn, since Joe had mentioned it and it was closest. But she hadn't yet reached the building when she noticed that the large sliding door Clay had installed so he could drive his cars in and out with ease wasn't closed all the way.

Clay wouldn't go anywhere with that door open. He was far too private and too cautious.

"Damn Joe," she whispered. He'd beaten her here, after all. Were they already digging? He'd said something about starting in the barn. But there was no light peeking through the door. Surely they wouldn't dig in the dark.

The house…

She turned back, now confident that the glimmer of light she'd seen earlier had been more than the moon's reflection. But at the last second, she decided to do Joe and his friend the same favor they'd done Clay at the cabin, and flatten their tires. Even if Joe wasn't the one who'd shot Clay, he deserved a little payback. And that way, if they heard her coming, they couldn't escape quickly and lie about the fact that they were here.

Taking the flashlight and knife from her bag, she ducked into the pitch-black of the barn.

Something small darted past her. The fact that it might've been a mouse nearly made her scream.

"It's okay," she muttered, managing to reel in her reaction. "Calm down."

Snapping on her flashlight, she turned to face the cars

parked close to Clay's classic Jaguar. But what she saw stunned her, and it took several seconds to make sense of it. Joe's truck wasn't anywhere to be seen. It was Irene Montgomery's blue Honda that sat in front of her, which wouldn't have been such a terrible surprise—except that her father's cruiser was parked beside it. She could see the decorated baby-food lid Whitney had made him in school hanging from the rearview mirror.

Why? Why would they *both* be here? If they were meeting for some legitimate reason, they wouldn't feel the need to hide their vehicles….

Allie pictured the fear that had entered Irene's face at Grace's, when she was asked if Jed had ever seen her with another man, and a sick feeling began in the pit of her stomach. "No," she whispered. "No."

She listened to her heartbeat for several seconds before she could get her feet to move. She didn't want to go to the house. She was afraid of what she might see. She knew now where that bright red lipstick she'd found in her father's car had come from. It was exactly the same shade Irene wore almost every day.

But she had to do *something*. Joe was on his way. If finding her car in the driveway wasn't enough to stop them from snooping around—

"Oh, God," she groaned, hurrying cautiously out of the barn. She had to get her father and Irene away from the farm. If they were caught, her father would be ruined, her mother devastated as well as publicly humiliated. And the vengeance this town would exact from the Montgomerys would send Clay to prison in spite of the most brilliant defense they could muster.

How could her father do this? she asked herself over and over.

Despite the lump rising in her throat, Allie searched the area between the chicken coop and the shed, listening for voices or movement. She heard nothing. So she locked the barn door behind her, to slow Joe down, and approached the house.

Irene…and her father.

Shaking her head as if she could rid her mind of that painful thought, Allie moved as quietly as possible. If she wasn't careful, she could draw Joe's attention to the house when she'd rather leave him trying to jimmy the lock on the barn. But that meant she'd have to find her own way in, warn Dale and Irene and help them sneak out. She could simply tell them to hide, but if Kirk didn't arrive soon, Joe would break the lock on the barn, discover the cars and instigate a search for the living instead of the dead.

Slipping the crowbar she'd brought out of her bag, she wedged it between the back door and the frame, cast a final, wary glance over her shoulder, and tried to force it open.

The resulting noise made her cringe. It sounded so loud she thought Joe and her father would both come running and meet her right there on the porch.

If her father heard anything, however, he was too afraid to give his presence away. And she saw no sign of Joe.

"Good news," she mumbled. It might've been good news, if only she'd been able to get in. But the door held.

After another silent curse, Allie tried the crowbar again and, despite the noise, finally met with success.

So much for stealth. And so much for Clay's privacy. Three different parties would likely be tramping through his house tonight. She could only imagine how much he'd like that.

Stepping inside, she replaced the crowbar in her bag and used a kitchen chair to hold the door shut behind her. She didn't want Joe to see it hanging open. Then, careful to keep the beam pointed at the floor, she turned on her flashlight and hurried through the kitchen to the stairs. She was tempted to call out a warning, but refrained. She didn't dare. She wasn't sure who might hear her.

Allie had never gone so far into Clay's house. It bothered her that he wasn't here. But she didn't have time to dwell on the sense of loss that made her heart feel even heavier. Instead, she ran up the stairs as quietly as she could.

The rooms off the second-story hallway were all open. Except two.

She'd find her father behind one of them with a woman who wasn't her mother. *Shit...*

Taking a deep breath, she opened the first door. It was Clay's room, and it was empty. The subtle masculine scent that lingered brought him back to her, made her remember that night at the cabin when he'd held her naked against him. She longed to be with him again. Even now. But he was in jail, and might be going to prison for good. Meanwhile, her father was having an affair. And Joe was pressing his advantage.

The world had gone crazy. *Everything* was wrong. But Allie couldn't let panic and pain defeat her. She had to find her father and Irene. The rest she could deal with later.

Moving to the other door, she tried to open it but found it locked. They had to be there.

She knocked softly. No response.

"Dad, it's me, Allie. Open up."

Nothing.

"Dad, listen. Joe's on his way here," she murmured as

close to the panel as she could get. "He's planning to search for his uncle's remains. If he finds your cars, he'll start looking for a lot more than that. You've got to come downstairs with me and pretend we had a meeting here."

She heard movement. Had they received her message? Were they scrambling to get dressed? She couldn't be sure. "Dad? Did you hear me? I locked the barn, which is where he plans to start, but I doubt that'll detain him for long." She hesitated. "Hello? Answer me! Joe is—"

"Not as stupid as you think," someone interrupted from behind her.

Allie's heart lodged in her throat as she turned to see the man she'd been hoping to avoid step out of a third room and flip on the light.

"How'd you know I was coming here tonight?" he asked.

Allie did her best to bluff. "Clay's behind bars, isn't he? I figured you'd take advantage of his absence."

He didn't seem completely convinced she was telling the truth, but he was too excited about having the upper hand to dwell on the mystery. "It's a good thing I'm here," he said. "This explains so much, doesn't it? Now I understand why your father never wanted to investigate the people who murdered my uncle. He was too busy getting down and dirty with Clay's mother and her big tits." Joe shook his head. "Tsk, tsk. Poor Evelyn. How's *that* going to look? A churchgoing man like Dale. The chief of *police*, no less. Nope, can't be good."

Allie glared at him. "You're trespassing. You have no right to be here."

He raised an eyebrow. "And you do?"

"More right than you've got. At least Clay likes me."

He chuckled. "Yeah, we've all heard how much."

"How'd you get in?" she asked. There were no sounds coming from the bedroom, so she was trying to stall for time, hoping her father and Irene had managed to climb out and were right now scurrying away.

"It was easier to break a window in the basement than to bother with the door, I'll tell you that much."

"Who's here with you?"

"What makes you think I'm not alone?"

What she'd overheard. But she couldn't say that. "Joe, listen—"

Kirk pounded on the door downstairs. "Allie? Allie, are you in there?"

"That's enough," Joe said. Painfully gripping her arm, he dragged her against him as he banged the flashlight he carried in one hand on the door. "Hey, McCormick. I've got your little girl out here."

Allie tried to wriggle free, to let Kirk in, but Joe held her fast. "Are you the one who shot Clay?" she asked Joe.

Laughing, he shook his head. "Are you kidding? Assault with a deadly weapon is a crime."

"Cindy saw my gun at your house."

"Cindy's a stupid bitch. She didn't see anything."

She could hear Kirk coming in through the back. "You hate Clay enough to do just about anything."

"I won't cry when he goes to prison for life," he muttered and hit the door again. "McCormick! I know you're in there."

"You're letting hate twist you into a monster," she told Joe.

"And your father's a saint? Like the Montgomerys? No doubt he's trying to crawl out the window right now. But he won't get far before he runs into Roger," he said and that was when she knew Joe's brother was waiting outside, blocking her father and Irene's only escape.

"Allie?" Kirk ran up the stairs.

"You're too late," Joe said, and he was right. The shrill cry of a siren broke the silence, drawing closer and closer. Then the sound died abruptly.

"You called the police?" Allie cried.

"In addition to a few other key individuals. Figured this could use a little documentation," he replied with a grin.

Kirk made him release her, but it was only a few minutes later that Officers Hendricks and Pontiff, together with Allie's mother, came hurrying up the stairs—Pontiff first, then Evelyn and a huffing and puffing Hendricks.

"What is it?" Evelyn asked when she spotted Allie. "Why was I supposed to meet you here?"

Allie made sure her expression told Joe what she thought of him. The unfeeling bastard had dragged her mother out to see this firsthand.

"Sometimes the truth hurts," he murmured carelessly in her ear.

Kirk reached out to steady her, but Allie couldn't hold back the tears. Especially as she watched Hendricks and Joe force open the door to the bedroom and turn on the light. Sure enough, her father was inside. He had his clothes on, but there was a lipstick smudge on his shirt, his face was beet red and his hair mussed.

Although Dale was trying to shield her from view, Irene was there, too, and looked even worse. Her hair, which was normally teased high, was completely flat on one side, and her mascara was running with her tears.

But the worst was yet to come. Striding into the room, Joe picked up a scrap of fabric that had been shoved under the bed. "What's this?" he said and held it up for all to see.

It was a tiny sheer teddy.

19

As the sun came up, Allie sat at her kitchen table, staring into the cup of coffee that had grown cold more than an hour ago. She'd brought her mother home with her and tried to feed her—with no success. Finally, she'd given her a sedative and put her to bed in Whitney's room. She already knew she'd never forget Evelyn's gasp of pain as they both stood facing the proof of Dale's infidelity.

The images that once again entered Allie's mind threatened to make her ill. Pushing her coffee away, she squeezed her eyes shut in an attempt to block out the worst of what she'd seen and heard. But it was no good. Everything came back to her: her father's halting apology, Irene crying that Dale was the only man she'd ever loved, Joe calling them both the most degrading of names, Kirk almost punching him, the mayor showing up in the midst of the chaos. It was difficult to believe that less than a year before, Allie had been married and living in Chicago, and longing for Stillwater as if it was still the perfect haven it'd always been for her.

Maybe she and Sam hadn't had the best relationship, but her life had been far saner than it was now. She was divorced, Dale and Evelyn would probably soon follow, she'd lost her job, and her father was about to join her in the ranks of the unemployed. Beyond all that, she loved a man who was, most likely, going to prison.

God, she wanted to be with Clay….

"Home's supposed to be…safe," she muttered. She'd come back to Stillwater to recoup, rebuild. Instead, she felt as if her life had fallen apart bit by bit—and at a faster rate *after* she'd returned than before.

She wondered how her brother would take the news of what had happened last night. Briefly, she considered calling him, but couldn't make herself go through with it. She had to come to terms with this new reality first. Actually, she wasn't sure how she'd *ever* tell Daniel that their father had been sleeping with Irene Montgomery. Finding out that Dale was having an affair was bad enough. Betrayal was never easy to accept. But cheating with *Irene Montgomery?* That created all sorts of additional complications.

If Allie had her guess, it was only a matter of time until Joe began to fight for another search of the farm, saying that her father had purposely avoided the barn when they were digging there before. As she left this morning, he was already claiming that Dale knew all about Barker and had been keeping quiet for Irene's sake.

Allie remembered her father's comment that the Montgomerys had been through enough. *Did* he know what had happened?

Covering a yawn, she got up and tried to busy herself by cleaning up—throwing out the leftover eggs she'd cooked for her mother, washing the dishes, putting them away. But she had no energy, could hardly move. Thinking about the conversation she had to have with her daughter when she picked Whitney up from Emily's in a few hours didn't help. How was she going to explain why Boppo was coming to live with them? And later in the day, Allie had a meeting with Grace. They'd arranged it yesterday. Would

Clay's sister be surprised about Dale and Irene? Or did she already know about the affair? What about Madeline and Molly? And Clay? Surely Kirk had called them all by now. Except Clay, of course.

Remembering Clay's evasive answers when she'd told him that she was afraid her father might be cheating on her mother, and his reluctance to come to the cabin after that, she guessed Clay had known all along. It bothered her that he'd heard her deepest fears and hadn't leveled with her—but not because she couldn't understand why. His silence emphasized the fact that he had other people to protect, other people who meant more to him than she did.

Of course. What they'd had was…fleeting, unreal. A one-time encounter. She knew that and yet she had a hard time really believing it. Making love with Clay had felt so powerful, so visceral and meaningful.

Suddenly claustrophic, Allie dried her wet hands and walked outside. It was a mild Sunday morning. No one on her street seemed to be up yet.

She sat in the plastic chair she'd placed on her porch and stared across the street at Jed Fowler's. She *had* to find out who shot Clay. She also had to prove that Clay wasn't guilty of murder and that her father hadn't turned a blind eye to the fact that he was.

A neighbor's cat jumped from the top of her mailbox to the ground, reminding her that she hadn't retrieved yesterday's mail. Chances were good that there'd only be a stack of bills. But, like Madeline, she was expecting her tax return. Thinking the money might help her survive until her life improved, she walked down the driveway and checked inside the box.

There was a large package jammed inside. After struggling to pull it out, she realized it hadn't come through the mail. It had no return address or postage. Just her name in big bold letters across the front.

Who'd delivered this? And when?

She checked the box again, and found a page of coupons and a few bills. Nothing else.

Instinctively, she looked around her, but whoever had brought it was long gone.

When she opened the package, she could see why.

The man the jailer led down the narrow gray hall outside Clay's cell stood several inches taller than Clay, which made him six-eight or so. Shackled and wearing handcuffs, he was on his way to the empty cage next door, but he was smiling as if his arrest and subsequent lockup didn't bother him at all.

Leaning against the bars of his own cell, Clay watched, wondering why this Goliath of a man seemed so damn happy. It couldn't be because anyone was making him feel welcome here. The jailer handled him more roughly than he had Clay and responded curtly to every question.

"When's dinner?" the man asked. "I'm looking forward to my three squares a day, you know? It's a bitch on the outside. You gotta feed yourself."

"You'll eat when it comes," the jailer responded. The officer's disgust was obvious, but his rudeness didn't disturb the new inmate. The man laughed as the jailer clanked the door shut and stalked off. Then he turned to Clay.

"How's the food?" he asked.

"Terrible," Clay said. "Is it supposed to be good?"

The man shrugged. "Sometimes it's not bad. Beats foraging out of a garbage can."

Clay studied him in return. "Is that what you normally do?"

"Hell, no. It's just a little trick I learned."

Clay pushed away from the bars and moved closer. "Trick?"

"There's always something worse. If you think about what's worse, what you have doesn't seem so bad."

"You should go on the Positive Mental Attitude circuit," he said, flopping onto his bed. "Except I don't think your attitude is winning you any points with the police."

The man waved an indifferent hand. "Who cares about those assholes? Anyway, I don't want to do public speaking. I can make a lot more money robbing banks, and for that I don't have to sell tickets."

Propping his head on his hands, Clay tried to make himself comfortable. "That's what you're in for? Robbery?"

"Armed robbery. And an accidental shooting they're calling assault with a deadly weapon."

"Accidental," Clay repeated.

"That's what I said."

Tired of the square pattern on the mattress above him, Clay sized up the newcomer again. "Isn't it hard to be a bank robber when you're so tall? You don't exactly blend into a crowd."

"Oh, maybe *that's* what's wrong," he said, smacking his forehead.

Clay couldn't help laughing. "Well, if you decide to go straight, there's always basketball."

"Not an option for me, *amigo*. I can't handle a ball to save my life. And you can blame my mother for that."

"Your *mother?*"

"Well, you can't blame my dad. No one knows who he is."

Clay thought of his own father. "Sometimes even that's a blessing."

"Maybe."

"That doesn't explain why you can't play basketball."

"When my mother decided to turn her life around and became *devout*, my life did not improve. From that point forward, she wouldn't allow me to own a ball."

Clay leaned up on one elbow. "Why not?"

"She didn't believe in sports. They're competitive," he said with another shrug. "Someone has to lose."

"It's a cruel world," Clay said.

"Exactly."

"I suppose everyone wins in a bank robbery?"

"She doesn't know about my career. She's living in a cult in Oregon and refuses to acknowledge me."

Clay shook his head at what this man had been through. "You're right. There's always something worse."

"Glad I could make you feel better about *your* life," he said with a hoot of laughter.

They fell silent for several minutes, and Clay relaxed, hoping to doze off. It wasn't as if he was getting much sleep when he was constantly worrying about Allie and his family and what might be happening at the farm.

"What are you in for, anyway?"

Clay opened his eyes. The other inmate had wandered right up to the bars separating them. "Me? Nothing. I'm falsely accused."

"Aren't we all."

Now that he'd been interrupted, Clay doubted he could drift off again, so he sat up. "Want to tell me how you accidentally shot someone?"

"The shooting wasn't the part that was accidental," he admitted.

"Oh?" Clay raised his eyebrows. "Then which part was?"

"The part where I let the dumbass see me," he said, laughing some more.

This man had tried to kill a witness. On purpose. Clay no longer found the situation funny. "Attempted murder?"

"That's what they claim," he replied with a wink.

"That's what they claim," Clay muttered to himself. Obviously, he was locked up with someone who, despite his apparent good nature, had no conscience.

Suddenly, Clay didn't feel like talking anymore. He couldn't relate to this man. They had nothing in common, and he hoped they never would.

Lying back, he threw an arm over his eyes to signal the end of the conversation. He'd be out of here soon, he told himself. Tuesday would have to come eventually. There was no reason to think about this inmate or the fact that he'd meet a lot more men who were an even greater danger to society if he went to prison. But as he let his mind wander, he realized something that hadn't occurred to him before. He'd assumed that whoever shot him at the cabin had acted out of anger or vengeance.

But what if the motivation behind the shooting was more random than that? The guy in the next cell had tried to kill a man just for being in the wrong place at the wrong time. The shooter at the cabin might have been doing the same. Which meant Clay must have seen something, or come close to seeing something, that could give the guy away.

Now if only he could remember the people and cars he'd spotted as he approached the cabin that night…

"Are you okay?" Madeline asked.

Allie tightened her grip on the cell phone. She'd gone to

Clay's farm for privacy. Now that her mother was at her house, she craved some time alone, a few minutes to deal with her own emotions. Especially after seeing the pictures she'd found in the package that had been delievered to her earlier.

Taking them from her purse, she lined them up very carefully on Clay's kitchen counter. She'd had them all day and yet it still made her teeth chatter and her body quake to look at them.

She forced herself to answer Madeline in a calm voice. "I'm fine."

"You must be heartbroken."

Allie hugged herself. Madeline had no idea. But Clay's stepsister wasn't referring to the pictures. It wasn't difficult to guess she didn't know about them. She was talking about the scandal involving Allie's father that had erupted last night. In typical Stillwater fashion, word was rolling through town like a tidal wave, and Allie was as humiliated and embarrassed as she'd expected to be. When she thought of her father in that room with Irene, she still felt a very poignant ache in her chest.

But these pictures… They were more heartbreaking than almost anything else could possibly be. They'd upset her so badly she couldn't even keep her appointment with Grace. She didn't know what to say to Clay's sister. Should she bring up the abuse Grace had suffered? Tell her about the pictures?

"It hasn't been easy," she said into the phone. "But… somehow my mother and I will get through it." *How had Grace survive? How did the family cope?*

"I have to admit I suspected Mom was seeing someone. She's been a little secretive for…gee, months and months. But I never dreamed…" Madeline let her words fall away and tried again. "I mean, I feel guilty by association. Ashamed. I want to apologize."

Allie managed to keep her brain working well enough to answer, but it took a real effort. Her mind had drifted to Barker's Bible and the supposed "love" he felt for his stepdaughter. It wasn't love. He'd been sexually obsessed.

"There's no need for you to feel guilty, Maddy," she said. "I know you're not responsible for what your father, I mean—" she cleared her throat "—*stepmother* has done."

Maddy seemed a bit confused by Allie's mistake but didn't comment on it. "I didn't know, I swear."

"Did Clay?" Allie asked, gazing through his kitchen window toward the barn outside.

"I doubt it."

She turned to glance around the kitchen. She'd had to kick out the cardboard they'd used to cover the broken window downstairs in order to get in. But it had been worth it to find a place where she could be alone and was unlikely to be disturbed. Her mother was refusing to accept Dale's calls or speak of the affair. And she was ignoring Allie—as though Allie was to blame for the situation—and lavishing one hundred percent of her attention on Whitney. Evelyn was trying to buffer herself from the pain. But Allie knew she'd have to deal with it at some point and worried that this would only put off her recovery.

Then there was Joe. Allie was afraid that even though his chances of getting a search warrant had improved by a large margin, he'd be back late tonight to find what he could. Clay's absence was too good an opportunity to pass up.

"I'm sure Grace didn't know, either," Madeline was saying. "She would've told me."

Allie picked up a Polaroid of Grace at twelve or thirteen

years old. She couldn't tell where it had been taken but Grace was naked and spread eagled, her wrists and ankles tied. Another showed Barker with his mouth between her legs, his head slightly distorted as if he'd held the camera out and taken the picture himself.

Of course Grace would tell Madeline if their mother was having an affair, Allie thought sarcastically. Clay and Grace told Madeline everything, right?

Swallowing a sigh, Allie shook her head. Madeline had no idea. The Montgomerys loved her and treated her well, but they kept their secrets to themselves.

And she could see why. There were pictures here that revealed such depravity she couldn't even bear to pick them up.

Swiping her arm across the counter, she sent them fluttering to the floor. She didn't try to hold back her tears. What she'd seen wounded her in a way she'd never been hurt before. How could any man, least of all a minister, do what Barker had done? Experience had taught Allie how evil some people could be. In Chicago, she'd gained quite an education in that department. But this was different. The perpetrator wasn't a stranger. He was a man who'd dressed up as Santa Claus and dangled her on his knee, a man who'd encouraged her to be chaste and good and to save herself for marriage—the worst kind of hypocrite.

And the victims! Although older than Allie, they were women she'd known. Rosy Lee Harper had overdosed on sleeping pills at sixteen. Allie still remembered getting out of school to attend her funeral. And Katie Swanson had run away at—Allie couldn't quite remember because she'd been so young at the time—fifteen? Almost everyone in town had gathered to help find her, even Barker. He'd led the search! They'd combed the entire area until they received word that she'd been found dead on the highway, the victim of a hit and run. Both girls came from very poor families who'd relied heavily on the support of their minister.

Allie pressed her lips tightly together to squelch a sob. God, what Barker had done, what he'd caused. Poor Grace. She was the lone survivor.

Was that because of Clay?

Allie's conversation with Madeline had been filled with more silence than words. Madeline was being patient, but Allie shouldn't have answered the phone. She'd just… wanted to reach out to someone. She'd irrationally hoped that Madeline would set the world right again, or at least explain *why*. But the only person who could do that had disappeared nineteen years ago.

"I'd better run," Allie said at last. Madeline couldn't save her from the confusion and pain. No one could—and *she* wasn't even involved. She was just viewing the evidence.

"Allie…"

From the sympathetic way she said her name, Allie knew Madeline had heard the tears in her voice. "I'm okay," she said.

"I'm so sorry."

"Don't be. We can't control what other people do."

"I know, but…please call me if I can help."

"I will," she promised and disconnected. Then she collected all the pictures and shoved them back in her purse, because she couldn't stand to look at them anymore. What was she going to do? If she turned them over to the police, they'd convince everyone that Barker had come to some violent end—and they'd give Clay a very compelling reason to have harmed him.

What happened the night the reverend went missing? Allie wondered for the millionth time. Had Clay discovered what Barker was doing to Grace and put a very decisive stop to it? Only yesterday, she would've bet her soul that Clay hadn't been the one to kill his stepfather.

But today, after seeing the pictures, she believed that if anything could make Clay resort to murder, what Barker had done was it.

A bump jolted Allie out of a deep sleep. Blinking, she gazed around her, taking in the neat but sparsely furnished room, bathed in a dim, eerie glow. The light in the adjoining kitchen was the only one she'd left on, but after a moment she could tell that she was in Clay's living room. She'd fallen asleep on the couch.

Sitting up, she tried to identify the noise that had disturbed her. The darkness felt heavy, oppressive. It was late. Too late for friendly visitors.

Had she heard a cat, jumping from the railing to the porch? Or was it…a car door?

It hadn't been a big bump. It was more of a quiet—

Thump.

There it was again. Nerves prickling, Allie reached for her purse and hugged it close to her body. Joe's goals in coming to the farm would have nothing to do with her purse. She doubted he'd glance twice at it. But she had to protect it, just in case. She couldn't let those pictures fall into the wrong hands—

Swish… Click…

That was no cat. Someone was in the house.

Thrusting her purse under the couch where it wouldn't

be seen, she grabbed the closest lamp. Then she crept silently to the wall near the opening to the kitchen and pressed herself against it. The movements she heard seemed to be coming from the area around the back door.

Creak…creak…creak, creak, creak… Someone was crossing the kitchen floor.

Heart pumping, Allie leaned forward and peered around the door frame to see who it was. She held the lamp high, ready to bring it crashing down on the head of the intruder. But what she saw surprised her. It was Grace, carrying her new baby in an infant seat.

"Grace?" she said, immediately lowering the lamp.

"Hi."

Allie put the lamp back on the end table and stepped into the light, feeling particularly rumpled and red-eyed. "How'd you get in?" Before they'd left last night, Kirk had hammered a few boards across the broken door. She could see that those boards were still intact and couldn't picture Grace climbing through the window with her baby.

"I have a key to the mudroom." She nodded toward the small room just off the kitchen.

"Is something wrong?" Allie asked.

Grace gazed at her steadily, then put her sleeping baby on the floor near her feet and sat at the kitchen table. "A lot is wrong, isn't it?" she said with a weary smile. "But I'm not here with any more bad news. I sent Kennedy over to make sure the farm was secure, and he saw your car in the driveway."

"I'm sorry. I should've told you I'd be here. I didn't mean to make you come out so late at night."

"The baby was fussy, anyway. When she gets like this, I take her for a car ride." She adjusted Elizabeth's blanket. "Puts her right to sleep."

Allie envied Grace's sweet infant the bliss of being

unaware. "I was afraid Joe might come back," she explained.

"I know."

Silence fell for several minutes. Then Grace cleared her throat. "How's your mother?"

"She's been better, of course."

"And you?" she asked. "Are you okay?"

Allie wished everyone would quit asking her that. She was disappointed, hurt, upset and worried—about her mother, her father and Clay. But Grace had suffered a soul-deep kind of pain, and at such a tender age. It'd been worse than anything Allie could have imagined. Yet Grace had received no friendship or support. She'd been reviled and gossiped about and judged—even accused of having hurt Barker! "No, I'm not okay," she said softly.

Grace nodded. "I'm sorry. If it had to happen, I wish it was someone else and not my mother who was involved."

Natural defensiveness made it difficult not to blame Irene for more than was probably fair. Especially since Allie didn't know her all that well. But in a situation like this, the fault couldn't lie with only one person. And, after those pictures, the affair seemed less important than it otherwise would have. Allie couldn't stop thinking about what had happened to Grace and the other two girls in those photos.

"It's not the affair that has me upset," she blurted out.

Grace's eyes widened.

"I mean, it's heartbreaking, but…" Allie could no longer find the words to express what she was feeling. She didn't want to make Grace acknowledge something that had to be excruciating for her. But Clay's defense hinged on his lawyer sister. If they were going to work together to help him, they had to be honest with each other, didn't they? Whoever had delivered those photographs had done it for a reason. Allie wasn't the only one to have seen them.

"Grace…" She forced the name around the lump in her throat but broke down immediately after.

Concern brought a worried frown to Grace's elegant face as she stood and came toward her. "What is it, Allie? Is it about Clay?"

Wishing she could gain control of her wayward emotions, Allie wiped her tears with the back of her hand. "I know, Grace," she said, forcing back the sobs. "I know what Barker did to you."

Grace turned pale and teetered on her feet as if she might collapse. Allie started to reach out to her—but Grace stepped back, straightened and tilted her chin at such a defiant angle that she appeared absolutely regal, far above anything so degrading as the obscene images in those photographs.

"How?" she asked, her voice toneless.

Allie longed to embrace her, to comfort her if possible—and to reassure herself that they were both okay, despite everything. She needed some antidote to the anger pounding through her. She wanted to take on the world, to fight anyone who even looked at Grace wrong.

She could imagine those same emotions amplified in Clay, who loved Grace so much and had always tried to protect her. He must've felt like a failure when he realized; he must've sworn that nothing so vile would ever get past him again.

And then he must have—

Allie refused to think it. He wasn't the only person who could've acted. But now she knew it had to be one of the Montgomerys. If Clay wasn't the actual culprit, he was protecting whoever it was.

"Someone left a package in my m-mailbox. It contained—" Allie struggled with more tears "—p-pictures," she choked out.

"Portenski." Grace swayed as if the mention of those pictures had been a physical blow. Again, Allie wanted to touch her, to reassure her, but she suspected Clay's sister needed the space, and that physical contact, no matter how well intentioned, would be the wrong thing to do.

"Did you say *Portenski?*" she asked. "You think Portenski gave them to me?"

"It had to be him," she whispered. "He must've found them at the church."

"When?"

"I don't know."

"Was the camera there, too?"

"No." Grace stared at her for several long seconds, but Allie guessed she wasn't really seeing her at all.

"Grace?" she said gently. "I'm sorry. I'm sorry for everything, even though I know sorry isn't nearly good enough."

Grace's throat worked as she swallowed, but there were no tears in her blue eyes. "You didn't tell Madeline…"

"Of course not."

"So what are you going to do with the pictures?"

"What do you think I should do?" Allie asked.

Grace hesitated. "If I say burn them, will you tell the police I asked you to destroy evidence?"

Allie shook her head. She wasn't going to tell the police anything. They weren't striving for justice, only to make the right people happy.

"Then burn them," Grace whispered vehemently.

Allie curled her fingers around Grace's ice-cold hand. Grace didn't respond, but she didn't withdraw, either. "What if Portenski has more?"

"If he wanted to turn them over to the police, he would've done it already. He wouldn't have given them to you."

Nodding, Allie let her breath go. That made sense. She didn't understand why he'd entrusted her with them, but—

A thought suddenly occurred to her. "Are you sure they didn't come from Jed?" The pictures, the note at the cabin… Maybe he knew the truth, too, and sympathized with Grace.

"I can't see how," Grace said. "But…maybe. Maybe he found—" her voice broke "—*them* while he was working in the barn."

"Then maybe Barker *did* come back that night. Maybe an argument ensued, and—"

"Jed didn't kill him."

Allie felt a chill roll down her spine. From the way Grace had spoken, she knew who did. If Allie had ever doubted it, she didn't anymore. "If it wasn't Jed, who was it?" she asked.

A ghost of a smile touched Grace's lips. "Not Clay," she said. Then she picked up her baby and left. She didn't ask to see the pictures, didn't ask to witness Allie burning them. But Allie did exactly that, right there in Clay's fireplace. She watched every disgusting photo twist and writhe in the heat, as she hoped Barker was twisting and writhing in hell, then go up in smoke.

Except for the photos of Barker with the other two girls. Allie decided to keep those safe. She knew they were a risk to Madeline's happiness. That Clay and Grace would rather she destroyed them, too. But there could come a day when the truth won out. Then the Montgomerys would need the evidence for *their* side.

20

Clay stood at the periphery of the dance floor, drinking a beer. It felt so good to be out of jail, he didn't care if he moved from that spot all night. Molly was in town to see the baby, but Grace and Lauren had gone to sleep early, so Clay had taken his youngest sister dancing.

Right now, coming to the pool hall felt like a pretty great idea. Molly seemed to be having fun dancing with a cowboy who'd just moved to Stillwater.

Clay smiled as he watched her. He enjoyed Molly's laughter and animated conversation for a lot of reasons, but mostly because it had so little to do with the past, or what he was enduring in the present. Of everyone in his family, she seemed the least affected by what had happened the night Barker died. She'd been so young at the time, she hadn't understood what their stepfather had done to Grace. She only knew there'd been an argument and a terrible accident, and that they'd had to cover it up because they couldn't risk having their mother carted off to prison. Without Irene, they would've been split up and forced into foster care.

Leaning one shoulder against the wall, Clay took another long pull on his beer. As an adult, Molly probably knew more about the abuse that had occurred than she had as a child. But it was still largely in a cerebral sense. Grace refused to talk about Barker, so Clay guessed Molly had never heard the gruesome details. Neither had she seen the pictures he and his mother had found and destroyed that night in Barker's office. Unlike Grace, who'd acted like an automaton during those long hours, running and fetching everything he and Irene asked for, even helping scrub up the blood because they were so desperate for time, Molly had covered her ears and run off to her bedroom, where she'd stayed until the following morning, when it was all over.

Less than two years ago, she'd told Clay that The Night was more like a bad dream for her than anything else.

Lucky girl...

He saw Molly staring at him over the shoulder of the cowboy she was dancing with, and tipped the top of his beer bottle her way.

She waved, indicating that she wanted him to join her on the dance floor. But he shook his head. He wasn't interested in finding a partner. Maybe he was out of jail, which made him feel practically euphoric, but he was only out on bail. He faced a difficult trial in the not so distant future. And that wasn't all he had to worry about. Since the discovery of her affair with Dale McCormick, Irene had closeted herself in her little duplex and wouldn't come out. According to Madeline, she hadn't even been to work.

Clay would've visited his mother and attempted to console her, but he was angry with her for going back to McCormick and making a bad situation even worse. For hurting Allie...

He grimaced. Somehow, every thought led him back to the police chief's daughter. Although Grace said she was okay, he wanted to contact her to see for himself. But he couldn't. How could he expect her to pick up her old life and move on as if he didn't exist if he was still calling her?

"Hi, Clay. You're looking good."

Helaina, a woman he used to date, had sauntered up to him.

He nodded but barely acknowledged her beyond that. He didn't want to encourage her to hang around.

Unfortunately, she didn't seem to notice that his response lacked enthusiasm. "I'm surprised to see you out and about," she said.

"Why?" He held up his bottle. "Might as well enjoy a beer while I can still order one, eh?"

She sidled closer, reminding him of a cat eager to rub up against him. "Do you really think they're gonna put you away?"

"I think they're gonna try."

Her bottom lip came out. "It'll be a real loss to womankind if they succeed."

He cocked an eyebrow at her suggestive tone, and she responded with a sultry smile. "Having a beer is good. But there are other things you should do while you have the chance," she murmured, moving so that her breasts brushed his arm.

The fact that he might soon be permanently denied the pleasure of a woman made Clay crave sex more than ever. But not with Helaina. Or any of the other women he'd known in the past. He wanted Allie—so badly he dreamed of her almost every night. "Thanks, but I've got my sister here with me," he said.

"She's not big enough to find her own way home?"

"It wouldn't be very nice of me to leave her, would it? She just got into town this morning."

Helaina's heart-shaped face flushed with disappointment, but she shrugged. "You have my number."

He started to give her a noncommittal response—but

the words congealed in his throat. The door across the room had opened and Allie walked in. She was wearing an attractive skirt that hit her above the knees, along with a pair of cowboy boots and a tight-fitting brown sweater. And she was alone. He knew she hadn't come to socialize when a frown of concentration wrinkled her forehead and she began to search the crowd.

Helaina followed his gaze. "What?" she said. "Don't tell me you're still seeing Miss Goody two-shoes."

"I'm not seeing anyone." For Allie's sake, he wanted the rumors to die down. But she'd already spotted him and was coming straight toward him.

"Can we step outside?" she asked as soon as she reached him. "I'd like to talk to you for a moment."

Clay could feel Helaina's attention, knew she was listening to every word. "Not tonight," he said.

Allie blinked in surprise. "Excuse me, but I'm not asking you to dance. This is important."

He scowled. "It can't be important. We don't have any business together."

"Oooh," Helaina said, her voice lively with interest.

Allie's eyes cut to her, then returned to him. "What, exactly, are you trying to prove? I'm doing my best to *help* you."

"I don't need you," he replied, sounding as indifferent as he could. "For anything."

Allie's chest lifted, as though she had to gasp for breath, as if he'd just stabbed her or something. But the way his heart pounded and his stomach tensed, Clay knew he was probably feeling worse. He hated himself for saying what he'd said. It was the biggest lie he'd ever told, but he saw no alternative. As soon as he got out of jail, he'd left Allie a message telling her to find another job. She'd left him a message saying she wasn't walking away from his case whether she had a job or not.

The only way to get her to give up on trying to save him was to convince her he wasn't worth saving.

She glared at him for several seconds, during which he forced himself to act as careless as possible. He even saluted her before taking another drink of his beer. But it was Helaina, laughing behind her hand, that seemed to be the final straw.

Tears filled Allie's eyes, but she raised her chin and spoke clearly. "Whatever you want," she said and stalked off.

As Allie hurried through the crowd, the crushing pain made it difficult to breathe. Several people tried to stop her. She paused to respond to a few, mechanically going through the usual greetings, but it was mostly a blur. Grace had told her that Clay believed whoever had shot him had done it to avoid being identified. So she'd gone back to the cabin and interviewed every gas station attendant and store clerk along the route. Ralph Ling, an attendant at the gas station just before the turnoff to the lake, had some very interesting things to say. But what could she do if Clay refused to listen?

I don't need you...for anything. Those words hurt so much, she could hardly bear to think of them. And the angry glares she received from many of the people who used to smile didn't help.

Finally reaching the gravel parking lot behind the pool hall, she headed for her car. She just wanted to know that Clay wouldn't go to prison for a crime he didn't commit. And she wanted...

God, she wanted more than that. She wanted *him*. There

was no use denying it. Beth Ann had been right. Allie had assumed she'd be fine because she'd known what to expect. But she'd been overconfident.

There's no one else, at least no one like him....

No kidding, she thought bitterly. She tried to wrench open her car door, but a male hand closed over hers before she could.

Clay had tried to let Allie go. He'd stood perfectly still while she disappeared into the crowd. Hadn't moved when someone called to Helaina, drawing her away. Hadn't so much as flinched when someone behind him said, "He cast Allie aside already? Me, I would've given her a few more days, taken her back to my house and—"

Because he couldn't tolerate hearing the end of that statement, Clay had bolted to the bar to order another drink. But he hadn't stopped there, the way he'd intended. He'd kept on walking, past the pool tables, the dartboards and the restrooms. Before he knew it, he was in the parking lot and jogging to catch up with her.

"I'm sorry," he whispered, turning her to face him. "I'm so sorry."

Her eyes were full of confusion and pain when they lifted to his, which shredded the last of his restraint. He told himself to explain, to somehow convince her to leave. But he couldn't get the words out.

Bending his head, he kissed her instead—instantly drowning in the wet warmth of her mouth.

"I'm no good for you, Allie," he murmured. Some distant voice in his head told him it wasn't too late to put her in the car and send her off. But he was desperate to feel her against him. And she was kissing him back as if she felt the same driving urgency. They couldn't touch each other intimately enough, couldn't get close enough.

Dimly, he could hear the music in the pool hall and realized he needed to find them some privacy. So he led her inside a small shed, where the owner of Good Times kept some lawn-and-garden equipment.

He barely managed to shut the door and wedge a narrow saw blade in the latch so it couldn't be opened from the outside, before he sat her on a crudely made shelf and greedily slid his hands up her skirt.

Allie gasped and spread her legs, and he felt his body's instant response. "I lie awake at night craving the taste and feel of you," he whispered. "I want you more than I've ever wanted anyone."

He felt her move, sensed that she was reaching above them. Then he heard a *snap* and light flooded the small, crowded room. She'd found the pull-chain to the bulb on the ceiling. "I want to watch you make love to me," she said. "I want to see it this time, your face, your body, everything."

Clay guided her hand to his pants, then held his breath as she undid the buttons. Her eyes never wavered from his until she was finished. Then she looked down—and he thought he'd never seen a sexier smile.

"Can you come home with me?" Clay whispered, easing her back onto the shelf.

Allie was covered in a light sheen of sweat and feeling weak from the bone-melting pleasure. Her clothes were halfway on and halfway off, and she still had her legs wrapped around his waist.

"I need to check on Whitney. If she and my mom are asleep, and everything's okay, I'll drive over. For a little while."

He pulled up his pants and started helping her dress. "This is crazy," he said. "This is setting us both up for a terrible disappointment. You know that."

She stopped fussing with her clothes and reached up to smooth the hair off his forehead. "I only know that I'm in love with you."

He winced as if it hurt him to hear her say it. "I don't want you to be in love with me. I don't want to feel the pain of missing you. And I don't want you to feel it, either. I have nothing to offer you. Don't you understand that?"

"All I'm asking is that you love me in return."

"And what good is that?" he asked bitterly. "Will it keep you safe and warm? No. Will it mean we can be together? No. I'm going to prison!"

"You're not there yet," she said stubbornly.

He shoved an impatient hand through the hair she'd just smoothed. "Let's be honest. You're a police officer. What are my chances?"

"I don't know," she said, refusing to go where he was trying to lead her. "A lot could happen before and during the trial."

He buttoned his pants in quick impatient movements. "You're avoiding reality."

"I'm being optimistic." She finished righting her bra and sweater, then hopped off the shelf and pulled down her skirt.

He caught her chin to make her look up at him. "Allie, if you don't stay away from me and make things right with your parents, where will you be if I go to prison? Do you think I want to imagine people around here thumbing their noses at you? Treating you like shit for loving me? Do you think I want to be responsible for the rift between you and everyone you care about?"

"Maybe I won't stay here," she said. "But wherever I go, I'll be waiting for you."

He froze as if he couldn't believe what she'd just said. Then a tormented expression crossed his face, and she could've sworn she saw tears glistening in his eyes.

He snapped off the light before she could really tell. "I want more than that for you," he whispered hoarsely, but she had the impression that, for himself, he craved exactly what she'd promised him. And that was enough to give her hope.

"You're not the only one who has a choice," she said quietly.

It was Molly who answered the door when Allie arrived at the farm. Allie felt a little silly standing on the doorstep at nearly one-thirty in the morning, but Clay's youngest sister didn't seem to think anything of it.

"Hi," she said. "Come on in. Clay's in the kitchen whipping up some eggs and grits and bacon."

Allie nodded. The scent of bacon seemed to pervade the whole house. "Smells great."

Molly gave her an exaggerated grimace. "Yeah, well, we'll see how it turns out."

Faced with Allie's questioning look, Molly quickly explained. "*I* was going to make it, but he took the spatula away from me. *You* know how he is—large and in charge!"

She'd raised her voice on the last sentence so Clay would be sure to hear her. "How many eggs did you expect me to let you ruin?" he asked from the kitchen.

"So I burned a few," she said with a shrug. "I live in New York. I eat out. But I would've gotten the hang of it eventually."

"I'm hungry," he grumbled. "I didn't want to wait all night."

Allie chuckled at their banter as she followed Clay's sister into the kitchen. Then Clay turned toward her, wearing the comfortable-looking, well-worn jeans he'd had on at Good Times and a simple white T-shirt, and her heart leaped into her throat. Everything about him appealed to her—his rugged face, his muscular body, his fierce independence, his stubborn pride, his determination to take on the whole world if necessary…and the way he made love. Especially the way he made love. He knew how to be just the right amount of gentle and just the right amount of rough.

She felt warm thinking about what had occurred in the toolshed earlier. No wonder Beth Ann was having such a difficult time getting over him.

"What?" Clay said, watching her closely.

"I was thinking about the night Beth Ann was here and called the police on you," she lied.

One eyebrow slid up in a sardonic expression. "You were smiling."

"It was the first time I'd ever had a half-naked woman come charging at me from the shadows. And the glower on your face when you answered the door—"

"What I remember is that you made me strip for you," Clay interrupted pointedly. "And the fact that you were taking an awful lot of pictures. You wanted to see my chest. You wanted to see my back. I'm surprised you didn't have me flex for you."

Allie could tell Clay thought he'd bested her, that she'd back off because of Molly. But she wasn't quite finished yet. "It was worth it," she said wistfully. "I still have one of those pictures tucked between my mattresses."

"You're kidding," he said.

She gave him a teasing grin. "Maybe, maybe not."

"I'm going to check," he promised.

Molly glanced from Allie to Clay, then frowned at the food Clay was neglecting. "Wait a second. Am I going to have to finish breakfast?"

Clay turned back to his work. "Hell, no. Then we'll never get fed."

"I don't think it's food you want right now," Molly grumbled.

Clay threw Allie a guilty look but finished the eggs and bacon.

"How long are you staying?" Allie asked Clay's sister as Clay handed them each a plate.

"I fly back on Sunday."

"What do you think of the new baby?"

"She's beautiful. I just wish…"

"What?" Allie coaxed.

"That Clay and Grace didn't have to worry about the trial. That *I* didn't have to worry about it, either."

Mention of the future put an immediate damper on everyone's mood. "It'll be all right," Allie insisted.

Molly ate the last of her food and went to rinse her plate at the sink. "I think it's great, you know. The way you're sticking by him."

If only she could find something that would save him. "Thanks."

When they were finished eating, Clay stacked their plates on the counter, then took her hand. "I'm getting tired. Let's go up to bed while I still have some energy."

Allie resisted his attempt to pull her toward the stairs. She couldn't imagine marching up to his bedroom and making love with him while his sister was in the house and knew exactly what they were doing. "Actually, I should get home."

He scowled. "Really?"

"Really. But I…was hoping we could talk for a few minutes before I go."

"We could talk upstairs in my bed," he said hopefully.

She laughed. "I was thinking of here or in the living room."

"I'll let you two be alone," Molly said. "I'm beat."

"Good night," Allie said.

Molly waved as she headed up the stairs. "'Night."

Clay took the chair next to Allie, stretched out his long legs and locked his hands behind his head. The definition in his arms and chest made Allie's mouth go dry. Had she been crazy to turn down a trip to his bedroom? Probably. But Molly was so close….

"What is it?" he asked.

Besides the fact that she wanted to undress him right here in the kitchen? "You know the last gas station before you leave the highway to go to the cabin?"

The expression in Clay's eyes changed, intensified. "Of course. I stopped there. That's where I bought the condoms we used."

Allie was glad Molly had left. "It is?"

"Yeah."

"Did you see anyone you recognized?"

Clay's forehead furrowed. "No. I've gone over every second of that night. All I remember about the place is that the attendant was muttering about some guy getting blood on the floor. But whoever it was had already pulled out when I arrived."

"You didn't see him?"

"We might've passed. I wasn't really paying attention. I was too busy arguing with myself."

"About what?"

"I knew I didn't have any business planning to sleep with you," he said with a grin. "But I also didn't want to show up unprepared in case the temptation proved too great."

She laughed. "It's a good thing you came prepared."

"I'm still prepared," he said softly.

Desire coiled tightly inside Allie. She wanted to let Clay lead her upstairs, but she knew she'd be too embarrassed to face Molly in the morning. "I'd better get home," she said.

"Molly doesn't care, Allie."

"I know. It's just…" She felt her cheeks grow hot at the thought of Molly overhearing them.

"Jeez, you *are* a straight arrow," he said with a laugh.

"No! I'm not." She shrugged. "Okay, maybe I am."

He pulled her chair around so they were facing each other, maneuvering her weight as easily as he might transfer a sack of groceries from one spot to another. "It's okay. I like that about you. So what did you find at the gas station?"

"The attendant, Ralph Ling, remembered something interesting."

"What?"

"A man came in around midnight with blood dripping from his hand. He hurried into the bathroom to clean himself up but, like you said, Ling wasn't too pleased about the mess because he'd have to mop again."

Resting his elbows on his knees, Clay took her hands in his. "Did Ling say who this man was?"

"He'd never seen him before."

"Why was the guy bleeding?"

"He told Ling he'd stopped at the side of the road to let his dog have a potty break but accidentally dropped the leash. The dog bounded into the woods, and he fell while chasing after it."

"He fell in the woods? Or he cut his arm when he broke your window?"

"Exactly," Allie said.

"Did Ling see the injury?"

"I'm afraid not."

Clay rubbed the inside of her wrists with his thumbs. "What about the dog? Did Ling see the dog?"

"Ling watched the guy drive off and said, unless it was a very small dog, he was alone. And no stray dogs have shown up in the area since."

"That's odd, isn't it?"

"Besides that, Ling said the guy was acting a little weird."

Clay raised his eyes to hers. "In what way?"

"He wore a baseball cap pulled very low. When he approached the register to buy some Band-Aids, he pulled it even lower and turned his head away, as if he was worried about the security camera."

"There was a camera?" Dropping her hands, Clay stood. "Tell me he was filmed."

"Ling thinks he might've been. But they cycle the tapes, so he's not sure whether or not it's been destroyed. Even if he found it, he needed the owner's permission to give it to me, and we couldn't reach him."

"When will you hear?"

"I got a message from him just before I walked into Good Times tonight. I'm supposed to pick it up tomorrow afternoon."

Clay rubbed the back of his neck. "What about the sheriff's investigation? Haven't they talked to this Ling?"

Allie hated to tell Clay this, but she knew it probably

wouldn't surprise him. "I don't think the sheriff's department is doing anything to find the man who shot you. They're pretty much leaving it to my father."

"Professional courtesy?"

"Something like that."

He crossed to the sink and gazed out at the night, but he didn't say anything, so she continued. "Right now, I'm actually glad. If they were investigating in earnest, they might've gotten hold of the tape. Now we'll get it."

"Have you told Grace about Ling?" he asked without turning.

"No. I tried calling her on my way back to town, but got her answering machine. Then I tried you, with the same result. That's when I drove by the pool hall and saw your truck."

"She'll be happy," he said.

"This could mean a lot to all of us."

He sighed. "It's late. I'd better let you head home."

She nodded, and he walked her out to her car. The heat was growing more intense as June progressed, and with it the oppressive humidity. But Allie liked the scent of damp earth and confederate jasmine that embraced her at the farm.

"It's nice here, isn't it?"

"It beats prison," he replied, opening the car door for her. She started to get in, but he gave her arm a gentle yank to get her to look back at him. "How are you handling your father's affair?"

"With your *mother?*" she asked wryly.

His expression was difficult to read, but that was more often the case than not. And tonight they were in darkness, except for the security light on the barn. "Yeah," he said.

"You knew, didn't you? You already knew the night I told you what I suspected."

He nodded. "I tried to stop it, but…some people can't avoid a brick wall even when they see it coming."

Was *she* one of those people? Clay had been trying to warn her that falling in love with him would only cause her pain. He'd put her on notice at almost every opportunity. Was he right? Would she live to regret losing her heart to such a man?

Probably.

"I know the feeling," she said.

He stared down at her. "It's not too late."

"Are you kidding? It was too late the night Beth Ann called me to the farm."

Lifting her chin with one finger, he kissed her tenderly. "Then you really do have my picture between your mattresses," he teased.

She delved her hands into his thick hair and stood on tiptoe to kiss him again, more aggressively. "You don't know that."

He shook his head and let go of her. "Call me when you get home, so I'll know you're all right."

"I will."

He caught her arm. "Allie?"

"What?"

"Will you come over for dinner tomorrow night?"

There was something different in his voice, something that said the invitation wasn't as simple as it seemed. "Sure," she said cautiously.

"And bring Whitney?" he asked.

Whitney? Allie swallowed hard. As long as she kept Whitney separate from Clay, her daughter's life would remain relatively untouched, no matter what happened. But if Allie brought Whitney to the farm and let her meet him…

She opened her mouth to say she'd think about it. But

she knew he was testing her, to see if she'd meant the promises she'd made, and the flicker of hope in his eyes was too much for her. She couldn't bear to extinguish it. "Of course," she said.

"I'll be good to her," he promised solemnly. "You know that, don't you?"

"I know that."

"Good night." He gave her a quick peck and waited for her to get behind the wheel before closing her door.

Allie backed out of the driveway and headed toward town, but once she knew her taillights could no longer be seen from the farm, she pulled off onto the shoulder and sat staring into the darkness all around her. Clay was starting to open up, to grab hold of the relationship.

Had she been reckless in making the reassurances and declarations she'd made, in giving him hope?

She cringed at the thought. He'd lived his life in a certain way because that was how he could bear it. She had no business mixing things up, making him vulnerable.

And yet, they deserved to fight for what they felt, didn't they?

Taking a deep breath, Allie started her car and continued home. She couldn't change anything now. She cared too much about him to even try.

Once she arrived, she crept into her room and into bed. Whitney occasionally spent the night in Evelyn's room, but tonight she slept in Allie's bed.

Allie was glad to have her there. She needed to hold her daughter close. Gathering Whitney's small body into the curve of hers, Allie kissed her temple.

"I love you," she whispered and prayed she was making the right decision about including Whitney in her relationship with Clay.

21

Allie could hear her father's voice in the kitchen.

"No. Please, tell me he's not here!" She groaned and rolled onto her stomach to bury her head beneath the pillow. But she could still hear the argument between her parents and knew she had to get up and play referee or there was no telling what kind of scene her daughter might witness. Whitney had to be out there. She wasn't in bed.

Allie put on her robe and marched into the kitchen. Her mother stood against the counter in her own robe, arms folded stubbornly across her chest. Her father faced her mother, wearing his police uniform. According to Grace, the town had given Dale his termination papers, so he wouldn't be wearing the uniform much longer.

Allie wondered what he was going to do then and almost felt sorry for him. *Some people can't avoid a brick wall even when they see it coming....* She agreed, and yet she found it difficult to forgive Dale. Maybe it was because he'd always set himself up as an example, so when he made a mistake it was more shocking than if someone else had. Especially a mistake of this magnitude.

"Is there any chance I could persuade the two of you to take a drive together?" she asked, nodding meaningfully toward Whitney, who was sitting at the kitchen table downing a bowl of cold cereal while staring up at them with wide eyes.

"Don't leave," Whitney said. "I want to hear."

Allie raised her eyebrows at her mother.

"There's no need," Evelyn said. "Your father was on his way out."

"No, I wasn't," he retorted. "I just got here."

Evelyn stiffened. "I want you to go."

Dale sighed heavily. "You have to talk to me sometime, Evelyn. Whether you like it or not, you're still my wife."

"Not for long."

He looked crestfallen at the vehemence of her response. "Please…I—I know I deserve the way you feel about me, but at least hear me out."

Allie hated to see her father, who'd always been so confident, humbled to such a degree. But he'd brought it on himself. There was nothing she could do to help him. Right now she didn't even *want* to help him. Or maybe she did. It was all so confusing.

"What's there to say?" Evelyn asked.

"I'm sorry. I've been trying to tell you that since—" he glanced nervously at Whitney "—since you found out. But you wouldn't let me."

"You think that's enough?" Evelyn marveled. "I'm *sorry?*"

For the first time, the expression on her face revealed how truly devastated she was. "We had forty years together, Dale. Forty years you threw away for—"

"Mom!" Allie interrupted, afraid of the word she might choose to finish that sentence. "Can't you at least step outside? If nothing else, you can talk about the division of property."

"I'll get half of everything," her mother said. "I've been a loyal wife since the day I married him."

"I made a mistake," he said miserably.

Evelyn clamped her shaking hands together. "Are you telling me—" she hesitated "—you saw her only once?"

Dale didn't respond.

"No, of course not." The emotional strain was taking its toll, and Evelyn was beginning to break down. While Allie thought that was probably good—her mother needed to deal with her grief instead of denying it—Allie really didn't want this happening in front of her daughter. It could make an indelible—and damaging—impression.

"Never mind, Whitney and I will go for a drive," she said.

Evelyn held up a hand to stop her. "No, your father's the one who has to go."

"But Grandpa's sorry," Whitney said. "Can't he stay, Boppo? Can't you make him breakfast like before?"

Evelyn didn't answer. She was too busy staring at her husband. "You must care about her," she whispered. "I can't believe you'd do what you did to me unless you cared about her."

His gaze fell to the floor. "I do care. I won't lie about that. But I care a lot more about you."

Silence filled the room as tears began to slip down Evelyn's cheeks.

Allie felt more torn and confused than ever, but she reached out to console her mother.

Evelyn resisted her touch and managed to blink away her tears. "Then why?" she asked Dale. "Why did you do it?"

He hung his head. "I—I'm getting old and falling apart. I didn't want to see it. I didn't want to diet and check my blood pressure and see myself in the mirror as I really am, to acknowledge that I've lost more hair and gained more weight. Irene made me forget all that. She fed me cheesecake and wine and…and I felt like a younger, stronger version of myself. I know that's not much of an answer. It doesn't really make sense to me, either. But it's all I can come up with."

"You look good to me, Grandpa," Whitney said.

He smiled sadly at her.

"I don't know what to say," Evelyn replied. "I don't know how I feel or if we can get over this."

"Will you at least try?" he asked earnestly.

Allie knew that, in a town the size of Stillwater, the embarrassment alone had to be overwhelming. And that was only one of the emotions her mother must be feeling.

"I'll think about it," Evelyn said. "That's all I can promise."

"Thank you," he said. "Would you come home?"

Evelyn shook her head, and he backed off right away. "Just think about it."

"She will," Allie said. "And now you should go."

He started for the door. Allie followed to let him out. She wasn't sure how she felt toward her father, but she knew there was love for him inside her somewhere. It was just mixed up with everything else.

After he'd stepped outside, he turned back. "You should know something, Allie," he said.

"What?" She expected him to tell her not to judge him too harshly, that everyone makes mistakes. Or that he'd appreciate her help in trying to talk to Evelyn. But nothing prepared her for what actually came out of his mouth.

"I think it was Hendricks who shot Clay."

It took a moment for those words to register. "You've got to be kidding me."

"No."

"What makes you think so?"

"Yesterday, I found your gun hidden in the evidence room, yet I've seen no report of its having been turned in."

The evidence room was usually locked, and all the officers had access to the key. "That means it could be anyone on the force," she said.

"No. Hendricks is the only one who works alone. I'd bet money it was him."

"But why would he want to kill Clay?"

"Maybe he didn't," he said. "Maybe he wanted the money for a down payment on a new truck."

"He's driving one?"

"I saw it a few hours ago."

Allie waited impatiently for Madeline to pick up the phone.

Clay's stepsister answered on the fourth ring. *"Stillwater Independent."*

"Maddy?"

"Yeah?"

"It's Allie."

"What's up, Allie?"

"Has the reward you posted for information on the shooting turned up any leads?"

"No."

"None?"

"Not one. I would've called you right away. Why?"

Allie swallowed a sigh. "Just checking."

There was a slight pause. "I'm sorry."

"We're all sorry," she said.

The clutter and absolute filth of Hendricks's house was appalling, and so was the stench. It was all Allie could do not to call after his wife, who'd answered the door and gone to get him, that she'd meet him in the front yard.

A teenage boy and girl lounged on the worn orange couches in the family room to her left, playing video games. It was early afternoon, but they were still wearing T-shirts and pajama bottoms and hadn't combed their hair. To her right, a toddler with a sagging diaper and no other clothes foraged in the kitchen cupboards, pulling out one cereal box after another and eating what he wanted.

The stairs creaked. Trying not to gag when the toddler ate something off the floor, Allie looked up to see Hendricks's wife, Colleen, returning. "He said he'll call you later, when he wakes up. He's exhausted. You know how it is when you work graveyard."

Allie hesitated. She was about to insist on speaking to him now. With everything that'd been going on, she was desperate for answers. But she figured it might be smart to get the tape first and see what was on it. She'd have a lot more leverage if Hendricks showed up clearly enough to be identified. "No problem," she said. "Let me give you my new number."

It took a while, but after digging through several drawers in the kitchen and living room, Colleen finally came up with a pen and paper and wrote down Allie's number.

"How's that cut on your husband's hand?" Allie asked as they walked to the door.

Colleen shook her head. "It's healing, but it needed six stitches."

Allie caught her breath. She'd been bluffing, but the bluff had paid off. "That's what I heard," she said sympathetically. "How did it happen?"

"At work."

"At the department or—"

She must've sounded a little too eager, because Colleen's simple, trusting smile faded and her expression grew guarded. "I'm not sure. You'll have to ask him."

"I'll do that." Allie stepped out and waved toward the brand new Ford F–150 sitting in the weed-filled driveway. "Nice truck. Maybe I'll be able save enough for one of those someday."

"It's nice, but I'm a little worried about the payments."

"You financed it?" Allie asked.

"Of course," Colleen said, then the door closed with a decisive click.

"Do you have it?" Clay asked.

Allie transferred the phone to her other ear and glanced at the tape on the passenger seat of her car. "I do."

"What does it show?"

She could hear the caution in his voice, the effort he was making not to expect too much. "The tape's old and grainy," she said. "But I can see a heavyset man buying Band-Aids. He's acting fidgety and wearing a baseball cap."

"A red one?"

"The tape's black-and-white. But it's not Jed's hat, if that's what you're wondering. It has a different logo."

"Is there any way to tell who it is?"

Allie slowed to navigate a particularly tight curve. "From the man's build, it looks an awful lot like Hendricks."

"Who?"

"Officer Hendricks," she said and explained what her father had told her earlier.

"But why would Hendricks steal your gun and leave you that note?" Clay asked.

She turned down the music she had playing in the background. "I think he was trying to be clever, to make me believe it was you."

"So you'd finally fall in line with the Vincellis and everyone else?"

"I guess. I was the lone holdout, and he was trying to convert me."

"Why? He doesn't really have a vested interest in the situation. He's not related to the Vincellis. He sees them at church and they're sociable to him. But he's married with kids. I've never even seen him with Joe or his brother."

"Money," Allie explained. "The Vincellis or someone else paid him to do it."

There was a long silence, as if Clay was thinking it through.

"If you hadn't stopped at the same gas station, he probably wouldn't have shot you," she went on. "I don't think you were actually supposed to be involved."

"He must've seen me when I pulled in and thought I saw him, too."

"That's my guess."

"So he returned to the cabin to make sure I didn't tell anyone." He paused. "For a cop, he didn't do a very good job of silencing me."

"It was so dark, and what he was doing probably scared the hell out of him. The next day, when he realized you weren't dead, it was too late to be any more thorough. But I doubt he would've had the nerve to try again, anyway."

"By now, he must think he got away clean."

"Since the video isn't clear enough to prove it was him beyond a reasonable doubt, maybe he *will* get away clean," she said sadly.

"Did you check the inside of your car before you had the window fixed? See if he left any blood behind?"

The day was growing warm. Allie could feel her clothes sticking to her and adjusted the air-conditioning vents to hit her more directly. "I checked. There wasn't anything. But—" An idea suddenly occurred to her. "What about the gas station?"

"What about it?"

"Hendricks didn't do anything to clean up, right? He left that to the attendant."

"Who was already getting out his mop when I arrived."

"I admit it's a long shot, but it's possible he might've missed a spot or two, if not on the floor, then in the restroom. Maybe while I'm this close, I should go back and see."

"Will the owner let you snoop around like that?"

"I think so. He's fascinated by the fact that I'm investigating a shooting." Slowing, Allie found a safe place to pull off the highway and turn around.

"Do you have what you need to collect a sample if you find it?" Clay asked.

"Of course. I carry my forensics bag in my trunk."

"Still?"

"Always."

"But even if you find his DNA, what's to stop Hendricks from saying he had a nosebleed there three months ago?" Clay asked. "You told me the station cycles its security tapes, so we wouldn't be able to go back and prove he was lying—that he wasn't there earlier."

"He doesn't know that," she said. "And his wife already admitted that he had a cut on his hand."

"She did?"

"She clammed up right afterward, but I got that much.

Anyway, I think this is how we play it—we tell Hendricks you saw him the night you were shot. If we're lucky, he'll panic and swear he's never been to that particular gas station. Chances are, before that night, he hadn't. He's certainly never been invited to the cabin. He drives my father crazy."

"He drives everyone crazy."

"Then we introduce the tape," she continued, "showing a man of Hendricks's exact height and weight buying Band-Aids, together with a DNA profile that puts him right where he said he's never been. Hopefully, that'll persuade him to give us what we really want."

"The name of the person who paid him."

"That's it," Allie said, but her mind wasn't on the conversation anymore. A truck had come right up on her bumper and was honking to get her attention.

"Does Whitney like steak?" Clay asked, changing the subject.

Allie twisted to look behind her, but the glare of the afternoon sun reflected off the windshield of the other vehicle, making it impossible to see the driver.

"Allie?"

"Someone wants me to pull over," she said.

"Why?"

"I don't know. But if you don't hear from me in five minutes, call the police."

Clay called Allie back immediately after she'd disconnected. He wanted to know who was flagging her down. *Now.* But she wasn't answering.

Hello, this is Allie. Leave your name and number and I'll get back to you as soon as possible.

Hanging up, he dialed again—and again got her

recorded message. Finally, he pushed the phone across the table and stalked to the window above the sink, where he stared out, feeling pensive and uneasy.

He didn't have a cell phone so he couldn't leave. Should he wait for her to call? Continue trying to reach her? Summon the cops, just in case?

It had only been three or four minutes, but he couldn't wait any longer. He was going to call the police, then head up there himself.

But the phone rang just as he picked it up.

"Allie?" he said immediately.

"I'm fine," she replied.

"What's going on?"

"I can't explain right now. Jed and I are going to the cabin. I'm sorry, but it looks as if I won't be able to make dinner."

"I'm not worried about dinner," he said. "I'm worried about you. What does Jed want?"

"I'm not sure yet. But I'll call you as soon as I know."

"Should I come up there?"

"No. We'll be finished before you could ever reach us," she said and disconnected.

Clay wasn't about to sit home and wonder. Grabbing his car keys, he charged out of the house—and right into a middle-aged man several inches shorter than he was who'd just climbed the stairs to the front door. With his graying dark hair tied back, he looked like some kind of Willie Nelson wannabe.

But even after twenty-five years, Clay recognized his own father.

Allie couldn't move, couldn't breathe. She sat in the log chair she'd taken at the cabin, her stomach churning as she stared at Jed Fowler. "Why wouldn't you speak to me when I came to your house?" she asked.

He didn't answer, but he'd nearly run her off the road, trying to initiate this private meeting. When she'd realized who was driving the blue truck that had come so close, she'd stopped at the most public place she could find, a small strip mall not far from the gas station where Hendricks had gone, and had her finger on the Send button of her phone, with 911 already programmed in. But Jed had managed to convince her that he merely had something to say, so she'd called Clay to tell him who she was with and that she was fine. Then she and Jed had come to the cabin.

After all the effort he'd put into getting her alone, it was *still* difficult to drag anything out of him.

"Jed, please," she said. "You have to speak more freely. I…I need details. I have to understand."

"I didn't trust you," he said simply.

"Why not?"

"I thought you'd go along with the rest of 'em."

"The rest of them," she repeated.

He shoved his hands in the pockets of his work coveralls. "The Vincellis. Your father. The mayor."

"What makes you think I won't?"

There was a two- or three-second lag before every answer, but at least Jed was *willing* to talk about the Barker case. That was something, after keeping his mouth shut for nineteen years. "I've been watching you," he said at last.

She'd noticed. His unwavering attention had made her very uncomfortable and suspicious. So did the fact that he'd been following her. To Clay's farm. To Grace's stand. To the gas station where she'd picked up the tape. Today he'd been driving a truck someone must've brought in for repairs, because she hadn't recognized it or she would've realized who he was a lot sooner.

"Are you the person who left me that package?" she asked.

He looked puzzled for a moment. Then the confusion cleared. "You mean the one in your mailbox?"

Her phone rang, but she turned it to silent and slipped it into her purse. She was finally getting somewhere and was afraid it would spook Jed if they were interrupted. "Yes."

"It came from Portenski."

Just as Grace had said.

"I saw him deliver it," he added.

Jed had been watching her very closely indeed. He'd even been keeping an eye on her house while she slept! "Do you know what was inside it?"

"No."

"Pictures."

He grimaced.

"Do you want me to tell you what was in them?"

"No."

He said only that one word, but she could tell he was having a strong emotional reaction. "Why?"

He sighed heavily. "I can guess."

"How?"

"I could tell by the way Barker looked at her."

Allie sat up straighter. "By the way he looked at *whom?*"

"Grace. I was afraid it was happening again."

A chill ran down Allie's spine. "*Again?* You knew it had happened before?"

He stared at the floor as if he was ashamed. "I could've stopped it."

"But?"

"Eliza wouldn't let me."

Eliza. Jed was talking about Barker's wife. The framed program he kept in his living room flashed through Allie's mind.

"But I had no proof," he went on. "Only what she told me she suspected. And she was terrified of him. She wouldn't let me say a word to anyone. She promised me, when she was ready, she'd have me take her away from Stillwater. She said that was when we'd turn in the pictures she'd found."

More pictures? Or were they the same ones? "Were you and Eliza lovers?" she asked.

"Like your father and Mrs. Montgomery? No."

There was no judgment in his words. He was merely clarifying. So Allie felt comfortable doing that, too. "What was the nature of your relationship?"

"We were…friends," he said simply. "She was always… so sad. I…I wanted to help her. But…"

"But?"

"I didn't act soon enough."

"Or she gave up the fight before you could."

"Is that what you think?" he asked, responding quickly for the first time. "That she took her own life?"

Allie felt her eyes widen. "Isn't that what *you* think?"

The way he clenched his jaw told her it wasn't what he thought at all. He thought… "You're not saying Barker *killed* her!"

When he didn't deny it, Allie knew that was exactly what he was saying. "That's why you've got her picture in your living room," she breathed as the truth dawned on her. "As a reminder."

Again, he said nothing but Allie knew she was right.

That framed program was his tribute to a friend he'd cared about, a friend he felt he'd let down. "Is she the one who told you what Barker did to—" Allie swallowed hard and forced the words out "—the girls?"

"She told me she found some pictures. Told me they were despicable. That her husband was worse than the devil himself. And that was the last day I saw her alive."

Allie's heart raced as she tried to fit the various pieces together. Had Barker resorted to murder to cover up his sick obsession? Had he killed his wife, Madeline's *mother?* Was Stillwater's beloved pastor a sadistic pedophile *and* a murderer?

"Why didn't you go to the police after Eliza died?"

"With what?" he asked.

"You didn't have the pictures?"

"No. And everyone considered Barker to be some kind of saint. Who would believe what I had to say?"

"That's why you've stuck by the Montgomerys all this time," she said.

"Barker deserved what he got."

Allie agreed, but that was up to a court to decide. Not the Montgomerys. As much as her heart sympathized with Grace and Clay, with all of them, she knew no court in Mississippi would condone the fact that they'd taken the law into their own hands.

"What happened the night Barker went missing?" she asked. She'd expected to keep prodding Jed, but now that he'd revealed as much as he had, he responded readily.

"The reverend came home early."

Allie covered her face with her hands. Did she really want to hear this? There was a possibility that what she learned would forever stand between her and Clay. But could she hide from the truth? Could she risk her daughter's well-being on a man who had such dark secrets?

Of course not. As much as she *wanted* to trust blindly, she couldn't.

Jed waited as if he understood her reluctance.

"And?" she said at last.

"I called Irene at Ruby's. That's where she was, for choir practice."

"How? Weren't you out in the barn?"

"There was a phone there, right outside the door to Barker's office."

"I see. And what did you say?"

"Nothing."

"You didn't say anything."

"What could I say?"

Allie thought of Jed trying to tell Irene that he thought her husband was about to molest her daughter. "So what did you do?"

"I kept calling, asking for her and hanging up, trying to get her home, just in case he..."

His voice fell off, but Allie knew what he meant.

"Then what?" she said.

"Irene came home. But when I started up to the house to speak with Barker about the tractor, I heard yelling."

"Go on."

"I was afraid for Irene and the kids, so instead of heading back to the barn—" he frowned and scratched his sun-reddened neck "—I looked through the window."

Allie said a silent prayer that he wouldn't tell her something she'd feel obligated to report to the authorities. "And what did you see?"

"They were in the kitchen. Barker was beating Irene. Then Clay got into it, trying to protect his mom."

At sixteen. Poor Clay… Allie could imagine him trying
to fend off his mother's attacker regardless of any disad-
vantage. She could also imagine where his actions might
have led. "Did he…kill him?"

Allie could scarcely hear for the beating of her heart.
Grace had told her no, and Allie had believed her. But
would Grace tell her the truth?

"No," Jed replied. *No…* Relief flooded Allie. Clay
hadn't done it. "But Barker would've killed Clay, if not
for Irene," he added.

"What was Barker doing?" she asked.

"Beating him bad. I was about to go in and break it up
when Clay made a run for the living room. Barker grabbed
him by the hair and pulled him back. Then Irene panicked
and picked up something—I couldn't tell what it was, don't
know to this day—and brought it down on Barker's head."

Allie's eyes were riveted on Jed's. "And then he
dropped," she finished.

"And then he dropped," Jed echoed.

"You could see him?"

He nodded. "He wasn't moving."

It was beginning to get dark outside, so Allie lit the
kerosene lamp. She needed to do something with her
hands. She felt so jittery, so rattled. "What happened after
that?" she asked as she blew out the match.

"They buried him."

"Where?"

"Behind the barn."

The flicker of the lamp's flame cast moving shadows
on the table. "Weren't they afraid you'd see them?"

"They were too afraid of everything else to worry
about me, I suppose. They tried to move careful and
quiet-like, but…"

"It was too late. You'd already seen what happened."

Another nod.

"Only you didn't let them know."

"Figured we were all safer that way."

"Why do you think they didn't go to the police?"

Jed's expression didn't change. "For the same reason Eliza didn't."

"Grace might've told them about the pictures."

"Who knows if she knew where to find them. And even if they had them…" He clucked his tongue, and Allie knew what he was thinking. Even if they did, they were pictures that would humiliate a thirteen-year-old girl in the worst possible way. Pictures that would require she testify at her mother's trial in a town where she and her family weren't liked in the first place.

"You should've seen Grace that night," he added.

Allie doubted Grace would've been strong enough to go through a trial. And what if they'd lost? What if the court had ruled that Barker wasn't killed in self-defense? What if the prosecutor managed to convince a jury that Irene had murdered her husband because she'd found out what he was doing to her daughter?

Allie couldn't remain sitting any longer. She stood up and circled the room, careful not to look at the bed. Clay's blood was still on the sheets; no one had cleaned up since he was shot. The last few times she'd gone to the cabin, she'd been too busy searching for evidence. "So why are you breaking your silence after so long?" she asked. "Why are you telling *me?*"

Jed's whiskers made a rasping sound against his callused hand. "Because I don't think Clay ever will. And I don't think he'll let Grace tell you, either."

Allie had to agree. Clay was too loyal to his family. And

knowing Clay, he'd view it as a burden he wouldn't want her to carry.

"I thought knowing the truth might help you defend him," Jed murmured.

"At least I know what we're up against."

"I had to do something this time. Clay doesn't deserve to spend the rest of his life behind bars."

And Jed didn't need any additional regrets. Allie understood. He'd spoken more words in the past hour than he'd probably ever strung together at one time, which proved how passionate he felt about Eliza and Barker and the Montgomerys. But Allie had one more question. "So why didn't the police find Barker's remains when they searched the farm?" she asked.

Jed shrugged. "They should've. They were searching in the right place."

And that was why Jed had confessed to Barker's murder. Suddenly it all made sense. Jed hadn't tried to confess because he was in love with Irene. He felt responsible because he hadn't stopped Barker when Eliza had told him what Barker was.

What Barker was... Allie shook her head in stunned disbelief. Madeline wanted the truth. But wasn't a truth like that the worst thing a daughter could ever hear?

22

"Alaska isn't like any place you've ever seen." Lucas smiled as if Clay and Molly had every reason to smile with him. Their father had been going on about the beauty of his adopted state and his love of flying ever since Molly had invited him in. And he'd been talking as fast and animatedly as Clay remembered, as if Clay had given him some sort of welcome, which he hadn't.

"With a mouth like that, you should've been a used-car salesman," Clay said.

Molly glanced nervously at him. Lucas merely blinked. "What?"

Evidently, Clay's response wasn't one Lucas had been expecting. Clay was a little surprised himself. He'd dreamed of seeing his father ever since Lucas had left them. At first, he'd imagined a happy reunion, a day when his father would finally realize how much he loved his family and return to apologize and make everything better.

But after that summer when Clay and his mother and sisters had subsisted almost entirely on oatmeal and they hadn't even been able to pay the electric bill, Clay's dreams had become far less optimistic. During the Barker years, whenever he thought about meeting up with his father, there was always some degree of violence involved. Usually, Clay threw a single punch that broke the old man's jaw.

Clay was still considering whether or not to make that dream a reality. But Molly seemed more willing to accept him. And his father no longer looked like a worthy adversary, which came as quite a disappointment. Age was taking its toll, and he wasn't nearly as big as Clay remembered.

"What did you say?" Lucas said, referring to Clay's comment.

"Don't mind him," Molly said quickly.

Until that moment, their father had avoided meeting Clay's eyes.

"I said, with a mouth like that, you should've been a used-car salesman."

Lucas chuckled uncomfortably. "Why's that?"

Clay let his gaze drift over the Flying Makes Me Higher Than a Kite T-shirt, blue jeans and brand-new flip-flops his father was wearing. "Because I've never met anyone who fits the stereotype more—all talk and no integrity."

"Clay—" Molly started, but he ignored her, keeping Lucas pinned beneath his unswerving regard.

Their father wiped his forehead as if it was getting too hot in the room. And it was. The humidity was causing beads of sweat to trickle down the middle of Clay's back.

"I deserved that," he said. "You've got every reason to be angry, Clay. I understand—"

"You don't understand anything," Clay interrupted. "What makes you think you can step foot on my property?"

"I came because I wanted to help."

Molly moved closer to Clay. "He just got here," she said softly.

"I don't care." Clay's hands curled into fists in spite of his determination not to swing them. "We don't need his

help. I already did his job." Not that Clay felt he'd
managed very well. He'd had so little to work with—not
much maturity, very little wisdom and no resources. He'd
had to become a man at thirteen. "If he'd never left, Grace
wouldn't have been hurt," he pointed out. "We wouldn't
even have known Barker."

Instead, they had to live with their stepfather's remains
in the cellar, as well as the terrible memories he'd created.

What a difference Lucas could've made—for everyone.

To his credit, Lucas put up a hand to silence Molly
instead of letting her argue for him. And he didn't cower
as Clay had expected. "I thought you could use some
support," he said.

"*Now?* Where were you when Molly was eight years
old? Where were you when Grace—" Clay's throat constricted at the memory of her ghost-white face. How could
Lucas love her and Molly so much less than Clay did?
Lucas was their *father*.

And how could Molly talk to Lucas as if he'd done
nothing wrong?

Clay couldn't begin to understand, which only made his
anger blaze hotter. Swallowing hard, he decided to end the
conversation. Lucas didn't deserve a single kind word
from Molly. He didn't deserve anything. Their father
simply hadn't cared enough. What he'd wanted for himself
had mattered more than all of them.

"It's time for you to go," Clay said. "We have nothing
to say to you."

Lucas smiled at Molly. "You turned out to be a beautiful woman."

"Shut up," Clay said, disgusted.

"Maybe I shouldn't have come back at…at this late
date, Clay," his father said. "But someone called me, a

female police officer. She was asking a bunch of questions, and I—" he sighed "—I might've made some mistakes in what I said. I've been worried about that. I didn't want to make the situation worse for you. I—I wanted you to know that if I blew it, it wasn't intentional. My wife said I should—"

"Your *wife?*" Clay echoed.

"Lorette."

"That's her name?" Molly asked eagerly.

Clay clenched his teeth as Lucas nodded. Lorette. Who was this woman? he wondered. Whoever she was, she must be something special, something they weren't. "Well, you can tell *Lorette* that it was a nice thought, a kind thought of her to have for complete strangers. But like you said, you shouldn't have come. As far as we're concerned, you don't exist."

Molly said nothing. Clay could feel how torn she was, how difficult she found it to lose her only chance to speak with their father. He'd tried to keep his mouth shut for her sake, had even let their father walk into his living room, which he'd never dreamed he'd do. But he couldn't tolerate the man's presence any longer.

Head bowed, his father stared at his shoes. "You're right," he said. "I'm sorry."

"Go with him if you want," Clay muttered to Molly.

He couldn't stop her, didn't want to cause her any more pain. If she could accept so little from Lucas and be okay with it, he was happy for her.

But she didn't go anywhere. She drew closer and slipped her hand in his, as if he was her father and not Lucas.

As Lucas started out the door, Clay expected to feel some sense of victory or relief. At last he'd seen the man who'd hurt him so deeply—and he'd sent him packing without a trace of kindness or forgiveness.

Lucas had deserved exactly what he'd gotten.

But, somehow, the encounter only made Clay feel worse.

"It's okay," Molly said when he looked down at her.

"It's not okay," he said, and doubted it ever would be.

After Jed left, Allie stripped the linen from the bed and hauled it out to her car so she could take it home and wash it. Then she went back inside to finish tidying up. If her parents split up, her father would have to sell the place and share the equity with her mother. And she and Clay were the last people to use the cabin. It was the least she could do.

The probability that her parents would get a divorce depressed Allie, but the physical motions of straightening the cabin felt good. It meant she could put one thing right—and in quick order. She wasn't sure what to do about anything else, especially the information she'd learned from Jed. She was relieved that Clay wasn't responsible for Barker's death, that she'd been right in that regard all along. But now she knew Clay was partially responsible for the cover-up that had followed. Which put him at odds with the law, regardless of the fact that he was innocent of murder.

How had he and Irene disposed of Barker's car? Would it ever turn up? And where had Clay or one of the other Montgomerys moved the body? Barker wasn't behind the barn where Jed had told her he'd been buried.

His remains couldn't be far. Clay wouldn't risk having them discovered.

Allie shook her head. Why did the skeletons in Clay's

closet have to be so literal? He could never leave the farm, or Stillwater. She had to be crazy to get involved with a man like that.

But she was already involved, wasn't she? She loved him in spite of his problems. He wasn't an ordinary man. Who else could have survived what Clay had been through without cracking under the pressure?

As far as she was concerned, he and the rest of the Montgomerys had suffered enough. She'd go back to Stillwater and talk to Hendricks this evening. Once she proved that Joe or one of the other Vincellis had hired him to cause trouble for Clay, she'd have some leverage she could use to get the prosecution to back off. The mayor and the D.A. might be good friends with the Vincellis, but they wouldn't want to be discredited. Proof that someone was out to get Clay should make them view their lack of evidence in a different light. Or maybe it'd encourage the judge to throw the case out of court.

"That's it," she mumbled as she wiped off the table. "That's what I'll do." She'd stay the course, even though she knew she was heading past the point of no return. From now on, she would be, without reservations, completely on Clay's side, whether their relationship worked out or not.

A noise from outside startled Allie. Then the glimmer of headlights hit the window. At first she thought Jed had returned. But the man who knocked on the door wasn't Jed.

It was Joe.

Jed had stood by him and his family for so long that Clay had difficulty believing he would ever hurt Allie. He'd relaxed the moment he learned it was Jed who wanted to talk to her, and not Hendricks or any of the Vincellis. But she wasn't back yet, and he was beginning to worry. He'd tried her cell phone, several times, and gotten her voice-mail.

"What's wrong?" Molly asked.

His sister had been quiet ever since their father had left. Clay didn't know what she was thinking, but he doubted she felt any better than he did.

He hated the doubts that nagged at him, didn't want to take responsibility for her disappointment or make her feel obligated to remain loyal to him when her heart wanted something else.

"I'm going out to look for Allie," he said.

"Where is she?"

"I'm not sure. She's not answering. But it's getting late. She should've been back by now."

"What do you want me to do with dinner?"

"Eat and put the rest in the fridge."

"You care about her a lot, don't you?" she asked.

"No," he said. He knew it was a lie. But every time he began to hope for something better, the past intruded once again.

"Oh, really?" His sister folded her arms. "Because I think you're in love with her. And I think she loves you, too."

He scowled. "You don't know anything."

"I know you," she said. But he didn't respond. He walked out and left her standing in his living room.

She followed him as far as the door and turned on the porch light. "Do you want me to go with you?" she called after him, but he shook his head.

Allie didn't invite Joe in; she didn't want to be alone with him. The memories of the shooting that had occurred during her last stay at the cabin put her on edge. But she was convinced Joe had hired Hendricks to make Clay look bad, to make her suspicious of the Montgomerys, not to kill him. Hendricks had shot Clay on his own, *right?*

"I talked to your mother," Joe said.

"After what you did at the farm, she was willing to speak to you?" Allie asked incredulously.

His expression became a study in mock empathy. "Like I told her, I feel terrible that she was caught up in that *nasty* business."

Allie clenched her jaw. "You seemed pretty gleeful to me."

"Only because it revealed Irene to be the whore that she is. You know what I think of the Montgomerys."

That wasn't all of it. Joe had been targeting Allie, too, reveling in the fact that she and her mother felt hurt and betrayed. Couldn't Evelyn see that?

"I still can't get over the fact that she told you I was here," Allie said. When she'd called Evelyn to check on Whitney, she'd mentioned where she was as a natural part of the conversation. But she hadn't expected Evelyn to tell anyone, least of all Joe.

Obviously, her mother was more trusting than Allie was. But why wouldn't she be? She'd known Joe and his family for years and years and, like Dale, she believed Clay to be the only threat to the community.

Joe stuffed a wad of tobacco in his cheek and walked back to lean against the grille of his truck. "We had a really nice chat, Evelyn and I," he said. "I apologized for having to expose what Irene's done to your family, and she talked about the Montgomerys and how they've hurt so many people." It wasn't easy to make out his expression in the dark, but she saw a flash of teeth, as if he was smiling. "She talked about you, too, and your *confusion* over Clay right now. She's really upset about that, you know."

Allie wasn't willing to have this conversation with him. "Why are you here?" she asked bluntly.

"It's nice." He breathed deep. "Smell the pine, hear the cicadas."

"You didn't answer my question."

"Is this where you fucked Clay? In that bed?" He jerked a thumb toward the bed she'd stripped, and she sensed a salaciousness in his interest.

"If you have something to say to me, say it," she said.

He seemed to give up badgering her, for the moment. "Hendricks called me."

She lifted her chin. "I thought he might."

"He said you wanted to ask him some questions."

"I do."

He spat at the spongy earth. "'Bout what?"

Allie felt cornered with the small cabin at her back. She stepped farther out so she could run if need be. "About you. You must know that or you wouldn't be here."

He took his time settling the chew in his cheek. "I didn't pay him to kill Clay, if that's what you think."

She considered possible responses. She'd wanted Hendricks to confess before she spoke to Joe. The money for that truck had to come from somewhere. But Joe's sudden appearance preempted the possibility of preparing for this confrontation. "Maybe you didn't hire him to shoot Clay. But you paid him to scare me, didn't you? To try and make me think it was Clay who was threatening me?"

He pushed away from the truck and moved into the sliver of lamplight cast through the open doorway. "No."

"Then it had to be your family."

His eyes turned cold and flat enough to raise the level of caution already surging through Allie's blood. "*Had* to be?" he said, speaking around the bulge in his cheek.

Joe had caused trouble in the past, usually when he was drunk. Although he didn't seem drunk now, the Montgomerys—and particularly Clay—had long been a sore subject for him. He seemed to have grown more bitter toward them as the years passed.

"Who else would want me to think Clay had something to hide?" she asked, edging toward her car in case she decided to make a dash for it.

"The whole town thinks Clay has something to hide," he said.

"So they *all* paid Hendricks to do what he did?" she countered.

Another stream of tobacco juice hit the ground as Joe cut off her retreat. "I told you, I didn't hire Hendricks to do *anything*. Neither did my family."

"Is that why you drove all the way here from Stillwater? To tell me you're innocent?"

"To tell you you're heading down the wrong path. I don't need you creating problems for me."

She mentally measured the distance to her car. Could she make it?

No, he'd be on her before she even opened the door....

"What could I do without proof?" she asked.

"You could try to convince my mother that I was involved."

Allie narrowed her gaze. "Don't tell me you're afraid it'll upset her. You're not that considerate."

He spat at her feet, barely missing her shoe. "She knows I hate the Montgomerys. With my luck, she'd believe you."

"So?"

"So that better not happen."

Why? Allie wondered. Because then she'd cut him off financially? Probably. He couldn't survive without his parents' support.

Allie was finally beginning to understand. But, as much as she didn't want to admit it, she got the impression Joe might be telling the truth, at least about his involvement in the shooting. "If you didn't hire Hendricks, who did?" she asked skeptically.

"Think about it," he replied. "Who wants you to find Barker's killer even more than I do?"

"No one!"

He put a hand in front of her, ostensibly to lean against the post that supported the cabin's small overhang. But he managed to pen her in at the same time. "Wrong. Check my bank accounts, if you want to. I haven't paid Hendricks a dime. Why would I? We've got Clay by the balls already."

Allie shook her head. "Come on, Joe. The trial hasn't even started."

"We have another search warrant." His teeth flashed again. "This one's for the entire property—the house, the barn and outbuildings, the land. We won't leave a single inch of dirt unturned."

Allie went cold inside. Jed had just told her the Montgomerys had buried the reverend behind the barn, but his remains weren't there when the police searched before. Where had they been moved? She guessed what was left of Barker was still somewhere on the property. As bleak as the Montgomerys' outlook seemed, they had a better chance if the police couldn't prove beyond a reasonable doubt that there'd even been a murder.

"You didn't have the warrant a month ago," she pointed out. "And it bothered you that I wouldn't go after Clay, although I didn't have the evidence to justify it."

"It didn't bother me enough to waste two grand."

"Is that how much Hendricks was paid?"

"I'm guessing it was about that much."

Enough for a down payment, like her father said... "Still, whoever—" Suddenly, Allie fell silent. A snippet of conversation had popped into her mind: *I'll bet fifty, too. I'm expecting a big tax refund.*

Enough to spare two thousand dollars?

And then another snippet, from a different time and place: *Has the reward you posted for information on the shooting turned up any leads?...No...None?...Not one.*

True or merely self-preserving?

Could it have been Madeline? No! Clay's stepsister wouldn't do anything to make Clay look guilty. She defended him constantly.

But it was entirely possible that Madeline hadn't seen hiring Hendricks as a risk to her stepbrother. Clay had told no one he was coming to the cabin. After his call that Thursday night, even Allie hadn't been expecting him. Maybe Madeline had believed a mysterious scare would simply increase Allie's determination to prove Clay *wasn't* guilty.

Allie remembered the way Madeline had acted about the shooting. She'd been so upset, she'd called Allie almost daily that first week.

Because she was afraid it might happen again, as she'd said? Or because she felt responsible?

Do you know who did it yet, Allie?

"Oh, boy," Allie muttered.

"Now you're catching on," Joe said.

"You think it was Madeline."

"It *was* Madeline."

"Hendricks told you that?"

"I got it out of him eventually. He came to me, saying he was afraid you thought he'd shot Clay, that because of the rumors Cindy's spreading about seeing your gun in my house, you thought it was *both* of us. I bet he was hoping I'd solve the problem by making sure you wouldn't be able to tell anyone else."

Allie felt a shiver of fear. They were completely alone. It wouldn't be hard for Joe to do just that.

"He acted as if he'd done me some kind of favor, planting Jed's hat up here," Joe went on. "As if I *owed* him for dropping that cap in the woods."

"Why would Cindy say she saw my gun at your house if it wasn't true?"

"Because she hates me."

Covering her mouth, she mumbled through her fingers. "I can't believe Maddy did it."

"Call her and see for yourself. Tell her you've got proof it was Hendricks and that he's claiming it was her. See what she says."

Allie's phone was inside. She hesitated, because she didn't want to risk being cornered, but he handed her his.

She stared down at it for a moment, then dialed Madeline.

"Hello?"

"Maddy, it's Allie."

"Hi, Allie. What's going on?"

She glanced up at Joe. "I'm at my father's cabin with Joe Vincelli."

"Joe?"

"He says you hired Hendricks to scare me the night Clay was shot. Is that true?"

Silence. Allie waited, but there was only more silence.

"Maddy, is that true?" she repeated. But she knew from Madeline's lack of response that it was.

"I didn't mean for Clay to get hurt," she said, tears in her voice. "I didn't even know he'd be up there. He—he's always in town or at the farm."

Closing her eyes, Allie shook her head. "What were you trying to do?"

"I just—I was afraid you were giving up. I wanted you to keep looking. You're the only one who might be able to find my father, Allie. But…it was a mistake."

"You nearly cost Clay his life!"

She was sobbing openly now. "I feel so bad. I—I'm actually glad you know. I was going to tell you myself, but…I was so afraid Clay wouldn't love me anymore."

"Maddy, he'll always love you."

"I've lost too many people. And Hendricks! He's such an idiot. He thought Clay had spotted him, but even if Clay *did* see him I would never have agreed with firing that gun! Clay's my *brother*."

Allie didn't know what to say. Madeline, in all her denial and confusion and desperation, had hired Hendricks to motivate Allie to solve the case. And Hendricks had shot Clay on his own, out of fear of discovery. "Joe's still here. I'll call you later, okay?"

Madeline didn't answer. She was crying too hard.

"See?" Joe said as she handed him his phone.

Allie ignored him. Lee Barker's life—and death—had affected so many people.

"So you're going to quit trying to pin it on me, right? Forget that bullshit of Cindy's and keep me out of it."

She was still collecting her thoughts when he said, "Because if you don't, you'll be damn sorry."

"Is that a threat?" she asked.

"What do *you* think?"

"Madeline knows I'm here with you."

"So? Accidents happen. It'd be a real shame if your car was found in the bottom of a gully, wouldn't it? But these roads twist and turn something awful."

Joe's character had never been much to admire, but the disappointments and challenges of his life had turned him into a darker version of what he could've been. She knew Grace was sincerely afraid of him, that he'd probably given her reason to be.

"The truth is out," she said. "Why risk that kind of trouble?"

"Because I don't like anyone getting in my way."

He still saw her as an impediment to his revenge against the Montgomerys.

"And they wouldn't be able to prove anything," he added. "I'd make sure of that."

"You're not stupid enough to land yourself in jail when you already have the search warrant you've always wanted. If Clay killed your uncle, that should be enough, shouldn't it?"

He chewed, spat and chewed again. "You're right. The body's there, and I'm going to find it."

The sudden lightening of his tone released the tension between them. He didn't intend to hurt her. He didn't need to. He had the D.A. pressing charges against Clay and a search warrant that would most likely turn up the proof they were lacking—while she had nothing.

"You look sad." Joe bent his lanky body to make sure she could see his taunting smile. "Don't tell me you finally realize that the man you've been protecting is really going to prison."

"Clay's innocent," she said stubbornly.

Joe laughed. "Face it, Allie. You lose." Grabbing her chin, he held it fast while he delivered a revoltingly wet, tobacco-tasting kiss.

"Get back!" She shoved him away, then grimaced as she wiped his saliva from her lips and cheek.

"How touching," he said, his hand over his heart. "You're saving yourself for Clay. You care so much about him. But if you think he cares about you, you're wrong. He's using you, babe. Pure and simple. Beth Ann says he doesn't have a heart. Just a big dick."

Still laughing, he got in his truck and drove off.

As Allie watched him go, depression settled in, as deep as the surrounding darkness. She'd been wrong. The shooting wasn't connected to the Vincellis. Nothing she'd been chasing could help Clay.

Face it, Allie. You lose. And so did the man she loved.

23

When Clay passed Joe on the winding road that led to the cabin, he didn't recognize him at first. It was too dark. But Joe's was the only vehicle he'd seen since leaving the highway, and the make and model soon registered, turning the unease Clay had been feeling into all-out panic. What was Joe doing up here?

Again, Clay wished he had a cell phone. He'd never seen a need for one in the past. He hadn't been interested in making himself accessible to people; he was usually at the farm, anyway. But today he was handicapped without one. He'd been able to call Allie only once since he'd left his house—at a pay phone along the way. She hadn't picked up and he hadn't wanted to waste any more time. Something was wrong. He could feel it. And the sight of Joe's Explorer confirmed it.

"I'll kill him," he muttered. If anything could turn him into the kind of man everyone already thought he was, it'd be finding Allie hurt—or worse.

Tree branches slapped the windshield and scratched the sides of his truck as he barreled through the woods, indifferent to the potholes and rocks. He kept imagining Allie shot as he'd been shot, bleeding....

But when he reached the cabin, his headlights showed

her sitting on the front step, staring at the ground. A light gleamed behind her.

She looked up as he got out, but didn't move.

"What happened?" Clay asked. "Why was Joe here?"

"They have another search warrant," she replied. Then she stared past him into the darkness, and he saw the sheen of tears in her eyes.

So the Vincellis and their friends had been able to discredit her father's handling of the investigation, just as Clay had feared.

Clay should've been used to such setbacks, numb to them. He'd battled the Vincellis since he was sixteen years old. But the news cut him so deeply, he knew he wasn't the same unfeeling man he'd been before Allie came back to town. Going to prison didn't just mean going to prison anymore. He finally had something to live for, something to hope for, someone to care about.

And they were going to take that away from him.

He didn't know what to say, how to express the emotions that were twisting his stomach and clogging his throat. "It'll be okay," he said, trying to convince her. The only thing worse than his own suffering was the thought that she was hurting, too.

"It's not going to be okay! You didn't do it."

He could tell by the conviction in her voice that something had changed. "How do you know?"

"Jed told me. He saw everything."

Jed. Clay had always wondered. "Why hasn't he told the police?" he asked.

"He was friends with Eliza. He thinks—" she paused to take a breath, "—he thinks Barker might have killed her."

He said nothing.

"That doesn't surprise you?"

"No. Nothing surprises me where he's concerned."

"I guess she was beginning to figure out what he really was. Jed's convinced he did it to shut her up."

"It'll break Maddy's heart if she ever learns."

"Barker's dead. I don't see why she has to."

Reaching up, she pulled him down beside her, and they sat there together. After a few seconds, she said, "Where are they?"

"Where are what?" he replied.

"Barker's remains."

He'd never told another living soul where he'd moved them. Not even his sisters. And he couldn't tell Allie. She meant too much to him. "I can't say."

"If they're at the farm, move them," she said. "Tonight."

The fact that she was still so ready to stand by him made Clay wish he could take care of her the way she deserved. But it was too late for that. It was too late for a lot of things. "It won't make any difference," he said.

"I won't give up."

Leaning forward, he wiped away the tears sliding down her cheeks. "Don't cry."

"It's not fair," she said. "That…that *sick* bastard."

He didn't have to ask who she was talking about. "I want you to step back from this and reconcile with your parents. Or move somewhere else. Find a new life entirely."

"You want me to leave you to face this alone? *Why?*"

Clay felt so weak and exposed, it made him angry. "Because I can't do anything to protect you from what's about to happen, dammit! Don't you understand that?"

"I'm not asking you to protect me!" she shouted back.

He jumped to his feet. "It'll be harder on you this way."

"So you want to forget about what we *feel?* Walk away and let them win?"

"What's our alternative?" he asked. "Do you want to marry a man who's going to prison? Do you want to waste fifteen or twenty years waiting for me to get out? What kind of life would that be?"

She stood. "The life I want, if it means we can be together in the end."

The fight suddenly drained out of Clay. "Allie—"

"I just need to know one thing," she interrupted. "And it had better be the most honest thing you've ever said to me."

"What is it?"

"Do you feel the same? Are you willing to hang on regardless of what happens?"

When he didn't answer, her voice dropped. "Do you love me, Clay?"

He knew the unselfish answer would be to say no. Then she'd move on; she'd have to. She'd eventually get over the grief, fall in love with someone else, find a better life.

"Clay?"

Wrestling with himself, Clay let his forehead touch hers. He could smell her perfume, feel her breath on his face—and knew he wasn't strong enough to lie to her. "Yes," he said. And then he carried her into the cabin, where they were both crying and kissing and pulling off their clothes, as if this was the only moment that mattered.

Allie lay with her head on Clay's chest. He was so still she might have assumed he'd gone to sleep. But she knew he hadn't. The depth of feeling they'd experienced while making love had left them more than a little awed. She knew she'd never given so much of herself to another human being and doubted Clay had, either.

"How long will we have?" he asked.

"Together?"

He nodded. "Weeks? Months?"

"I don't know. It depends on too many factors. The court battles. The judge."

He didn't respond immediately, but then he said, "You can have the farm. It'll give you and Whitney a place to live. Or you can sell it and use the money to live somewhere else."

He was still worried about her, still trying to protect and provide for her. She smiled as she pressed a kiss to his warm neck. "If they get a conviction, we'll see where they send you."

He smoothed the hair off her forehead. "I like the way you make love," he said.

"Yeah, well, you could use some practice."

He returned her teasing smile as his fingers brushed the side of her breast. "As long as I can practice on you."

She sobered. "I'm going to hate it if they take you away from me."

"We'll be too old to have children by the time I get out," he said.

She rested her chin on her hands, thinking about the future. "We could get pregnant now."

"No," he said, as if he wouldn't even consider it.

"Why not?"

"I won't leave you with two children to take care of."

She touched the end of his nose with her finger. "Have a little confidence in me. I can do it."

It was too hot for the sheet tangled around their feet. He gently shifted her as he kicked it to the bottom of the bed. "And what will my kids think of having a convict for a dad?"

She could hear the grimace in his voice and leaned up on her elbows so she could look into his face. "They'll know the truth, Clay."

"And what's the truth?"

"That you're the best man I've ever known."

He stared at her for a long moment, then removed the medallion he wore around his neck and slipped it over her head.

She felt the satisfying warmth of the medal as it settled between her breasts. "Are you sure you don't want to keep this with you?" she asked, deeply touched by the gesture.

He tucked her hair behind her ear. "I'm sure. If there really is a saint who watches over people, I want him to look after you. Especially if I can't."

He'd given her the one thing that meant the most to him, that represented the family he'd once had but lost.

She ran a finger lightly over his lips, then kissed him, and soon they were making love again. When it came time for Clay to put on a condom, Allie tried to stop him, and she could tell he was tempted to let her. But, ultimately, he followed through.

"I'd worry too much about you," he explained when they were resting in each other's arms again. "We have enough going on already."

She put her head on his shoulder, wishing they could remain as they were—forever. But soon the tree frogs seemed to grow louder, reminding Allie that she should be getting home. She'd been gone more than usual lately and wanted to see her daughter. But she was reluctant to bring her time with Clay to an end. Every moment seemed so fleeting and precious.

"Are you going back to the gas station to search for Hendricks's blood?" he asked.

"Yes."

"What if you don't find it?"

"I'll bluff and say I did in hopes of getting a confession."

"Do you think he'll tell us who hired him?"

Allie knew that once Hendricks was busted, he'd have no reason to keep it a secret. So she told Clay about Madeline.

When she was finished, he sighed. "She's a victim in this, too," he said. "I can't blame her."

"I know."

"What do you think will happen to her?" he asked.

"Not much. She didn't mean for anyone to be hurt. She merely wanted to get my attention focused where she thought it should be. The fact that she'd sacrifice the money from her tax return tells you how much her father's disappearance is still bothering her."

"She broke into Jed's auto shop last year, hoping to find some evidence that he was involved."

"Poor thing."

He ran his fingers lightly over her skin while they lay in companionable silence. Allie was about to make herself get up, when he spoke again.

"How'd you know?" he asked.

"Know what?"

"The kind of man Barker was."

"Grace didn't tell you about the package I received from Reverend Portenski?"

Clay made her look at him. "You received a package from Portenski?"

"He didn't let me know it was from him, but Grace guessed and Jed Fowler saw him put it in my mailbox."

"What was in it?"

"Polaroids."

She felt Clay stiffen. "Of Grace?"

She nodded.

"Portenski figures I killed Barker. Why'd he give them to you instead of taking them to the police?"

"I think he believes you deserve a second chance."

He didn't respond right away, leaving her to wonder what he made of her comment. "Where are they now?"

"Grace had me burn them."

He relaxed. "That's good."

"I'm not so sure," she said.

"I don't need the prosecution producing those as my motive."

"But they could've been helpful in your defense. Especially if the police dig up Barker's remains. If we had the pictures, at least we could provide a sympathetic reason for what happened."

"I don't care," Clay said. "I would never let the abuse she suffered be dragged into public view. And think about what it would do to Madeline to find out that the father she's always loved wasn't worth the air he breathed. His reputation as a good man has been the only thing she's had to cling to. That, and us. But considering the circumstances, we've been as much a curse as a blessing. Bad as the situation is for her now, it would be much worse if those pictures came out."

"But what about *you?*"

"Allie, people in this area worshipped Barker. They wouldn't be happy to discover he wasn't the man they thought he was. Human nature being what it is, I certainly don't think they'd go easier on me because I proved they'd all been taken for fools."

Allie knew that was true. But considering what the

police were likely to find when they searched the farm, it might be worth the risk. Especially if—

She sat up.

"What?" Clay asked.

"Nothing," she replied, because she was positive he'd never let her do it if he knew. "It's late. I have to get back to Whitney."

The next morning, Allie perched on the edge of an old-fashioned wingback chair, breathing in the scent of lemon furniture polish while facing Elaine, Roger and Joe Vincelli in the elder Vincellis' living room. When she'd called to ask for this meeting, Mrs. Vincelli had reluctantly complied. But now that Allie had arrived, she could sense their curiosity.

"Marcus, get in here!" Elaine called.

Her husband had been on the phone ever since Allie was ushered into the house. He'd glanced up as she passed by the kitchen, but he hadn't so much as nodded a greeting. Neither had he bothered to cut his conversation short. They'd all been doing their level best to prove that she wasn't a priority, that they wouldn't allow her to disrupt their schedules or cause them the slightest inconvenience.

But she felt fairly certain they were about to change their minds.

"Can we get started?" Elaine asked.

Allie straightened her white blouse. "When your husband joins us."

"I already told you, I had nothing to do with it," Joe muttered, scowling heavily when she met his questioning gaze.

"I know," she replied politely and continued to wait.

Finally, Elaine seemed to lose patience. She hurried from the room and, a minute or two later, came back with her husband in tow.

"What is it?" he asked as he took a seat next to Elaine on their rose-colored sofa. "What could you possibly want with us?"

Allie didn't bother to reply. Instead, she withdrew a folder from the book bag on her shoulder, opened it and passed around copies she'd scanned and printed on her computer—copies of four of the pictures Portenski had delivered to her mailbox. One showed a young girl with her legs tied apart and Barker forcing a dildo inside her, his face pressed low on her belly so he could get into his own picture. It was a straightforward case of child rape. Another showed a man wearing Barker's distinctive ring forcing his penis inside the mouth of an even younger girl.

Elaine Vincelli's gasp told Allie that what she saw shocked her as badly as Allie had expected it to. But shock wasn't capitulation and did nothing to ease Allie's nerves. This meeting was her last hope.

"That's Rose! And Kate Swanson!" Elaine exclaimed.

"Where did you get these?" Marcus demanded, jumping to his feet, instantly furious.

"Does it matter?" Allie responded. She was quaking inside. She had so much riding on the next few minutes. But she tried to appear calm and collected.

"Yes, it matters!" he shouted.

Again she replied in a civil voice. "Someone put them in my mailbox."

"Who? Who would pass around this…this filth!"

"There was no return address," she said.

Joe and Roger both looked as if they'd been struck dumb.

Joe managed to find his voice first. "This can't be real," he muttered. "This can't be—"

"Your uncle?" Allie filled in. "I assure you it is. If it's necessary to convince you, the authenticity of the actual photographs can be verified."

The color had drained from Elaine's face, and her hands were shaking. "Marcus, my brother would never do this. Especially not to children. Not to Rose and Katie. My brother was a preacher. He…"

Elaine couldn't seem to continue.

"I don't know what to say," Marcus said, obviously just as stunned. "I can't—he was our pastor. If we'd had a daughter, we would've sent her to his church."

"Surely he would never harm…*family*."

Judging by the expressions on their faces, they weren't so sure. They could see that, contrary to Elaine's assertion, he had hurt *children*.

"He always seemed so…good," Elaine said helplessly.

Allie almost felt guilty for the tears welling up in the other woman's eyes. She wished Barker was around to see the pain and disgust he'd caused. But she doubted he'd care about anything except the destruction of his all-important reputation.

"Why are you showing us these?" Joe demanded. "What do you hope to gain?"

Feeling Clay's medallion around her neck, Allie kept her focus on the elder Vincellis. They were most likely to consider all the ramifications of these pictures. "Me? I'm here to point out how unfortunate it would be if I had to present these in court," she said.

"In *court?*" Elaine repeated, her tears spilling over.

"For *everyone* to see," Allie emphasized. "I'm sure all the major newspapers would pick up the story. A sexual sadist, a pedophile, using his position as a man of God to sexually torture young women in a small Mississippi town where that kind of crime is virtually unheard of. It would cause quite a scandal."

"He'll become a hiss and a byword," Elaine whispered, quoting the Bible.

"Why be connected with something like that?" Allie murmured earnestly. "Especially when everyone thinks so highly of your family." She paused for maximum effect, then continued. "Wouldn't it be better to leave things as they are? He's gone. The truth doesn't *have* to come out. If only…"

"If only *what?*" Joe said, his eyes narrowing.

Allie took a deep breath and faced him. "If only you make sure that the case against Clay Montgomery is dropped. No search. No charges. *If* he killed your uncle, you now know why. Isn't that enough?" she asked, turning back to Elaine.

Mrs. Vincelli looked as if she was on the verge of passing out. "I've always been so…*proud* of Lee."

She broke into sobs and Allie waited patiently for Marcus to comfort her. Joe and Roger had gathered up all the copies and were busy tearing them into bits too small to be recognized. "That's what I think of these," Joe said.

Allie didn't reply. She didn't care what happened to the copies. She only cared about what the Vincellis would decide.

"She won't do it, Mom," Joe said. "Clay won't let her. Think about it. These pictures will hurt Maddy more than us."

"Maddy!" his mother wailed, apprently just realizing that Barker's daughter would be crushed, too.

"Don't you think it's a shame that Clay's more concerned about Maddy than you are?" Allie asked Joe.

"Go to hell!" he replied. "You're not going to pull these out at the last minute. Clay won't let you."

Panic coursed through Allie. Evidently, Joe knew Clay better than she'd given him credit for. "This isn't up to Clay," she said. "It's up to me. And I'm going to do everything I can to see that he doesn't go to prison."

"You'd hurt Maddy?" Roger asked.

Praying that she'd sound convincing, Allie turned to meet his gaze. "I'd reveal the truth in a heartbeat," she said without flinching. "One way or another, people are going to be hurt by this trial. That's what I'm here to stop."

Joe stepped in front of his parents. "She's lying."

Roger joined him. "He's right. She's bluffing."

Elaine lifted tear-filled eyes. "Did Lee do this to…Clay's sisters?"

"What do you think?" she asked.

"It doesn't matter," Joe insisted. "We've got Clay this time. We're not going to let him get away."

Allie held her breath as she waited to see how the older Vincellis would respond. Finally, Marcus turned to his sons. "If a man did this to my sister, I'd kill him, too."

"We're talking about *murder*," Joe said. "Clay can't take the law into his own hands."

"He was only sixteen," Elaine murmured.

"That's true." Allie reached out to take her hand. "And it was an accident."

Joe stabbed a finger in her direction. "She admitted it! Did you hear her? She knows what happened. *She just admitted it!*"

Elaine stood up. Her husband had to help her because she was more than a little shaky, but she managed to gather her composure. "I didn't hear her say anything of the sort, Joseph."

Joe and Roger both gaped at her. *"What?"*

"It's a shame that we've made the mistake of accusing an innocent man. I'll talk to Mayor Nibley and the district attorney tomorrow and make sure we set the record straight."

Allie stared up at her in disbelief. She'd been banking on the Vincelli pride. But it was a woman's compassion that would save Clay.

Her throat constricted. "Thank you," she murmured. "Clay's a good man. I promise you that."

"He couldn't be any worse than my brother," she echoed sadly, staring at the bits of paper covering the floor. Then her husband led her out.

Joe leaned close and lowered his voice. "This ain't over," he said furiously. But his father heard him and turned back.

"Yes, it is. You do or say anything to Clay or anyone connected to him, and we'll disown you, do you understand? This is family business, and you'll respect our wishes. Or you'll be on your own."

Joe's eyes flicked from Allie to Roger and back. He opened his mouth to make a retort, but his father spoke again.

"From now on, we won't mention your uncle Lee. Ever. What he did is in the past. It's over, and we're going to leave it as dead and buried as he probably is. For Madeline's sake, if no one else's."

A vein stood out on Joe's forehead. "That's *it?*"

"That's it," Marcus replied. "Surely we can be as good as Clay Montgomery." Then he disappeared down the hall with his wife, and Allie kissed Clay's medallion as she let herself out.

Clay could hardly believe that it was all over, that he'd be able to remain on the farm where he belonged. It'd been only twenty-four hours since Allie had called him after leaving the Vincellis' house but, sure enough, the district attorney had already dropped the charges.

He found it especially ironic that without Portenski's involvement, the situation would've been much different. "The Lord giveth, and the Lord taketh away," he muttered. Only he'd done it in reverse order. Still, maybe God was more forgiving than Clay had assumed.

The doorbell rang, and Clay's heart hammered against his chest. He'd invited Allie over for dinner—and she was bringing Whitney.

The moment he opened the door, he wanted to pull Allie into his arms. But, in deference to her daughter's presence, he kept his distance.

"Hi," he said.

Whitney stared up at him, her pretty, brown eyes so much like her mother's. "Hi!" she replied brightly.

He chuckled at her enthusiastic response.

"Whitney, this is Clay. Mommy's…friend," Allie said.

"You're *really* big!" Whitney breathed.

He arched an eyebrow at her. "And you're a half-pint like your mother."

She wrinkled her nose. "A what?"

He shifted his focus back to Allie. "You're just right."

He held the door open, and Allie smiled as she led her daughter into the living room. "Where's Molly?"

Clay felt his own smile disappear. "She went over to my mom's."

"What's wrong?" she said.

He rubbed his neck. "My dad'll be there."

"He didn't go back to Alaska?"

Clay had mentioned Lucas's visit when they'd talked on the phone yesterday. But at the time, he'd thought Lucas had gone home. "No."

"How come he's going to your mother's house?"

"He called and asked to see her."

"I can't believe she agreed."

"Nothing she does surprises me anymore."

"What about Grace?"

"She won't see him."

"Do you mind, about Molly and your mother?"

"No. If they can forgive him, I suppose it's a good thing," he said, but he wasn't sure he really felt that positive about it. He resented the way his father seemed to think he could just waltz back into their lives.

"They're probably more curious than anything else," Allie said.

"Who knows?"

She slid her hand down his forearm and entwined her fingers with his. "What about you?" she asked. "Will you ever be able to forgive him?"

He watched Whitney drift off, examining the unfamiliar room. "I don't know. Definitely not right now."

She didn't tell him he should try. She didn't pass any judgments on him at all. "You'll know when you're ready."

He nodded toward Whitney. "She's pretty, like you."

"I'm proud of her."

"How's your mom?" he asked.

"She's going out with my father tonight. For the first time since The Big Event."

He brought her into the kitchen, where he had a salad, baked potatoes and garlic bread waiting for dinner. The steaks were on the grill outside. "You think they'll be able to patch up their marriage?"

"They're going to try." She set her purse on the counter. He liked seeing it there. It showed that she was starting to feel at home in his house. "It'll take time, but...maybe."

Suddenly, Whitney let out a squeal and clapped her hands. "Look, Mommy! Outside! There's a *puppy!*"

"Puppy" came out as if there could be no better thing in the entire world. Clay's surprise had just given itself away, but in the face of Whitney's excitement, he didn't care that the pup had announced his presence a little too soon.

"Can he come in?" she asked, looking up at him with such earnest hope he couldn't have refused even if he'd wanted to.

"Sure." Clay could see the three-month-old Labrador retriever he'd bought jumping up against the house, trying to reach the humans he'd spotted through the window. "It appears he likes you, too."

"Is he yours?" Whitney asked. "He has a bow around his neck."

Clay moved to the door. "That's because he's a present."

Allie glanced over at him, but it was Whitney who asked, "For who?"

"For you." He let the puppy in and she squealed in delight. Amid the licks and yelps and giggles of their mutual admiration, she managed to calm down enough to turn to her mother. "Can I have him, Mommy? Can I have him, *please?* Huh, Mommy? *Please, oh, please, oh please!*"

"I'm sorry, honey," Allie said gently. "But we can't have a dog at the rental house. The landlord won't allow it."

Clay bent down to Whitney's level and petted the puppy while he talked. "See, that's the thing," he said. "You can have him, but you and your mom would have to move in here with me so you could help take care of him."

"We would?" she asked, suddenly leery. "What about Boppo?"

"Boppo?"

"Grandma McCormick," Allie supplied.

"She'd probably stay at the rental house," Clay said.

"By herself?"

He offered Allie a hopeful smile. "Unless she moves back with your grandpa."

Whitney kept her eye on the wriggling puppy as if she feared he might disappear. "But Boppo wouldn't like it if me and Mommy moved in with you, would she?"

"Not at first," he agreed. "But she'd get used to it, and she wouldn't mind nearly as much if your mommy and I got married."

"Married?" Whitney breathed.

This was where Clay feared he'd run into opposition. "How do you feel about that?"

"You'd be my new *daddy?"*

"You wouldn't have to think of me that way unless you wanted to," he said. "We could be friends, until we get to know each other better."

"So we'd live here and be friends and then I could have the puppy?"

Allie was far too quiet. But he'd plunged in wholeheartedly, and it was too late to back out. "That's right," he said. But he knew Whitney would have much more than that. She'd have everything he could give her.

"Okay!" She made the decision that easily, and it wasn't a moment later that she was rolling around with the puppy, squealing as he licked her face. "He likes me!"

"You could've warned me," Allie murmured, looking a little shocked. "I sort of expected us to take things a bit slower."

"Why? I already know what I want." He ran his thumb along her jawline. "Don't you?"

She met his gaze. "Yes, but—"

He slipped his arms around her and nuzzled her neck, hoping to encourage her to forgive him. "I'll be a good dad."

She seemed more exasperated than upset. "I *know* you will, but…you bribed her!"

"I have a bribe for you," he promised.

She pulled back to stare into his face. "A wedding ring?"

He grinned. "That, too."

Epilogue

Clay held Whitney's hand as they strolled behind Allie, who was pushing their cart, in the Piggly Wiggly. He'd felt Beth Ann's eyes following them since they'd walked through the door, could almost hear her whispering when she turned to speak to Polly, who worked in the deli section right next to the bakery. He had no idea what she might be saying—what was there to say? He'd been married to Allie for six months, and they were the best six months of his life. Although they saw Beth Ann at church each Sunday, he hadn't spoken to her, didn't miss her in the least. But she always reacted to their presence.

"Daddy, can I have a doughnut?"

Clay looked down at the little girl who'd brought him to his knees in the first few weeks of their acquaintance. Although he'd wanted a child, he'd never expected to love one this much.

"I don't think so, babe," he said. "You had ice cream earlier. And it's almost time for dinner."

"What if I only eat half of it?" she asked. "Or save it for tomorrow?"

He knew he should say no. But she was giving him the dimpled smile he couldn't resist. "Please, Daddy?"

She probably thought "please" was the magic word. But it was the "Daddy" that got him.

"Listen to your father," Allie said, preoccupied with her shopping. But Clay had spoken at the same time—and already succumbed. "Okay. If you save it."

Stopping, grocery list still in hand, his wife turned to face him. "You're giving in to her just like that?"

"Don't I always?" he said with a grin.

Shaking her head, Allie chuckled. "Who would ever have thought you'd be such a pushover?"

"You?" Pulling her to him, he stole a kiss. He knew she wasn't really annoyed; she loved the way he treated Whitney. She was ready for another child, especially since she'd decided to be a stay-at-home mom for a while. But he was the one who'd chosen to wait, so that Whitney could have a solid year, at least, alone with them.

"You've got to stop spoiling her," Allie said, halfheartedly.

"You get the milk and eggs, and we'll meet you at the checkout," he said so she wouldn't have to go to the bakery with them.

Frowning, Allie glanced Beth Ann's way, confirming the fact that she was more opposed to the other woman's proximity than to Whitney's eating a doughnut. "Okay, but don't let Beth Ann poison it," she muttered for his ears alone.

He squeezed her arm, then led Whitney toward the display case that held the cakes and doughnuts.

When Beth Ann saw them coming, she stopped whispering and straightened to her full height. She'd also unbuttoned the top two buttons of her uniform—as if it was so hot in the store she simply couldn't keep her clothes on. Even though it was the dead of winter…

Clay had no trouble ignoring her cleavage. He squatted in front of the glass, more interested in enjoying Whitney's excitement over her treat. "Which one do you want, half-pint?" he asked.

"The long one. The one with brown frosting."

"We'll have a maple bar," he said to Beth Ann, rising.

Beth Ann reached into the case, pulled out a maple bar and put it in a sack. But when he tried to take it from her, she wouldn't let go. "How've you been?" she asked, her eyes hungry enough to make him pity her.

"Fine," he said. "You?"

"Good."

She offered him a brief smile. "I hear Allie's parents are living in Jackson."

"That's right."

"I'm glad they were able to reconcile."

"So are we."

She licked her lips nervously. "What's Chief McCormick doing now?"

Finally getting hold of the sack, Clay handed it to Whitney. "He's been hired to handle security for a big company there. He likes it."

"And her mother?"

"She's teaching piano lessons."

"That sounds ideal."

"It seems to be working." He started to move on, but she spoke again, giving him the impression she couldn't bear to see him go.

"How's your own mother?"

Irene was doing surprisingly well, considering the heartbreak she'd suffered when Allie's father reconciled with his wife and relocated. "She's keeping busy."

"I run into her every once in a while. At the dress shop." Beth Ann smiled prettily at him again. "Anyway, it's good to see you."

"Take care." He turned away, but he and Whitney hadn't gone two feet before Allie came rushing back to meet them. He could tell by the look on her face that something was wrong.

"What is it?" he asked.

She drew him farther away from Beth Ann and lowered her voice. "Grace just called."

"What did she say?"

She stared down at her cell phone for a moment, then met his gaze, her eyes filled with worry. "They just found Barker's car in the quarry."

* * * * *

So, the Reverend Barker's car has now been found.
What does that mean for Grace, Clay—and especially
Madeline? Will the truth finally emerge?
Turn the page to read an excerpt from
DEAD RIGHT, the third book in Brenda Novak's
outstanding Stillwater trilogy.

The first condition of human goodness is something to love; the second something to reverence.
—George Eliot (Mary Ann Evans) English novelist, 1819–80

Was his body inside?

Hunched against the freezing January rain, Madeline Barker felt her fingernails cut into her palms. Along with her stepbrother, stepsister and stepmother, she watched the police and several volunteers attempt to pull her father's car out of the abandoned water-filled rock quarry. Her head pounded from lack of sleep, and her chest was so tight she almost couldn't breathe, yet she stood perfectly still…waiting. After twenty years, she might finally have some answers about her father's disappearance.

Toby Pontiff, Stillwater, Mississippi's police chief, knelt at the lip of the yawning hole. "Careful, careful there, Rex," he called above the high-pitched whine of the winch attached to a massive tow truck.

Joe Vincelli and his brother, Roger, Madeline's first cousins, hovered on the other side of the quarry, their faces betraying their eager anticipation. They spoke animatedly to each other, but Madeline couldn't hear them above the noise. She was fairly sure she didn't want to. What they had to say would only upset her. They'd long blamed her father's disappearance on her stepfamily— Irene, Grace and Clay—who were gathered around her now. Unfortunately, the fact that the Cadillac had been found in the quarry five miles outside of town would only convince them they'd been right all along. It would certainly prove that her father hadn't driven off into the sunset.

The black seal-like heads of two divers who'd gone down a few minutes earlier popped up and, with a gasp, Madeline realized that she could see the front grille of her dad's car through the murky water. Experiencing a sudden rush of tears, she instinctively moved closer to her stepbrother, Clay, who remained as dark and silent as the surrounding rocks.

The car didn't break the surface. Rex hit a button that stopped the clamoring winch, halting its progress. The sudden silence made Madeline's ears ring.

Her stepmother, a short buxom woman with hair like Loretta Lynn's, whimpered at the sight of the barely visible car. Grace shifted to try and comfort her. But Clay didn't move. Madeline glanced up at him, wondering what was going on behind his intense blue eyes.

As usual, it was difficult to tell. His expression mirrored the gray, overcast sky. Maybe he wasn't thinking. Maybe, like her, he was simply surviving the cataclysm of emotions.

It'll be over soon. No matter what happens, knowing is better than not knowing. She hoped…

"This is starting to make me nervous," Rex complained. Short and wiry with the tattoo of a woman partly visible on his neck, he frowned as he joined Chief Pontiff. "What if we clip the edges of the rocks? The car could get hung up."

"It's not gonna get hung up," a police officer by the name of Radcliffe said.

The tow truck driver ignored the unsolicited input, keeping his focus on the man in charge. "I don't think this is gonna work," he insisted. "I say we get a crane in here, Toby, before someone gets hurt or we ruin my truck."

Toby, a slight blond man with a neatly trimmed mustache, had become Chief Pontiff only six months earlier and was a friend of Madeline's. They'd grown up together; she'd been close to his future wife all through high school. He shot Madeline a sympathetic glance; then, lowering his voice, he turned away from her.

Still, she could make out his words. "That'll take another day or two. Look at that group over there. See the woman in the middle? The one who's white as a ghost? Her mother killed herself when she was ten years old. Her father went missing when she was sixteen. And she's been standing here since dawn, getting soaked. I'm not going to send her home until I get her father's car out of this damn quarry. We need to see if his remains are inside. It's already taken me a week to arrange it."

"If she's waited that long, what's another two or three days?" Rex asked.

"It's another two or three days!" Toby nearly shouted. "And she's not the only one with an interest in what's happening here, as you can tell."

Obviously, he was talking about the Vincellis, who'd been impatient with the police for being unable to discover what, exactly, had happened to their beloved uncle. No doubt Pontiff didn't want them going over his head to the mayor again, as they'd done with the previous police chief.

"My entire town is sitting on pins and needles," Toby continued, his voice growing calmer. "I'm going to catch more grief than you can imagine if I don't put an end to it. Soon."

The man called Rex scowled and shoved his hands in the pockets of his heavy coat. Madeline had never met him before. A distant relation of Toby's, he'd been called in from a neighboring town when their local tow-truck owner said his truck wasn't capable of getting the job done. "I'm sorry," Rex said. "But with all this water and silt, combined with the weight of the car, I don't wanna risk burning out the engine of my—"

"If we wanted to wait, we would've waited," Toby interrupted. "We wouldn't be standing out here in the cold, freezing our asses off. But we called you, and you said you could do it. So can we please get this damn thing out of the water? Your truck's powerful enough to tow a semi, for cryin' out loud!"

Madeline flinched, her nerves too raw to cope with the anxiety and frustration swirling around her. It had been an emotional seven days. A week ago, a group of teenagers had come here to party, a girl had fallen into the water and had been too drunk to climb out. She'd slipped under the surface before anyone could reach her and the resulting search for her body, which police located as darkness set in almost twenty-four hours later, had finally turned up the Cadillac missing since Lee Barker disappeared.

As the owner, editor and major contributing writer of

the *Stillwater Independent*, Madeline had followed the tragedy of the girl's death since the first frantic call. But she'd never dreamed that it would lead to this. Had her father's car been here, so close, all this time? Since she was sixteen? That was the question she'd been asking herself for seven interminable days, while the town dealt with the immediate tragedy of losing Rachel Simmons.

Rex spat on the ground. "Toby, the divers don't know what the hell they're doin'. With the color of this water, they can hardly see down there, even with a light. I can't be sure we won't break a tow cable and send that car crashing right back to the bottom."

Clay spoke up for the first time. "The divers said they found the windows down, right?"

Toby and Rex turned to face him. "What does that have to do with anything?" Rex asked.

"If the windows were down, they were able to get the cables through. You're going to be fine. Just pull it out."

Clay was respected for his physical power and mental acuity, but he'd also endured enough suspicion where her father was concerned to give him a pretty big stake in all of this. Madeline knew the chief of police had to be thinking of that as he considered the stubborn set of Clay's jaw. She could almost read Toby's thoughts: *Are you trying to help because you don't know what's in that car? Or are you trying to cover the fact that you do?*

Madeline wanted to scream, for the millionth time, that her stepbrother didn't have anything to do with whatever had happened to her father.

"Let me handle this, Clay," Toby said, but there was no real edge to his voice, and his hazel eyes returned to the water-filled quarry before his words could be taken as any sort of challenge. Even the chief of police was careful around Clay. At six-foot-four and two hundred and forty pounds of lean muscle, Clay certainly looked formidable. But it was his manner more than anything that made folks uneasy. He was so self-contained, so emotionally aloof, some people had convinced themselves he was capable of murder.

"Rex," Chief Pontiff prodded. "Let's get this done."

Rex indulged in a particularly colorful string of curses but finally stalked to his truck. The winch started again, slowly pulling the car from the water.

Madeline caught her breath. *God, this is it.*

"Watch those divers," Rex called.

Chief Pontiff had already motioned them away. "Let the winch do the work, boys," he shouted. "Stay back."

The scrape of metal against rock made Madeline shudder. It was an awful sound—almost as awful as watching the dark, dirty water seep out of the car that had belonged to her parents when she was a child. Why was the Cadillac in the quarry? Who had driven it there? And—the question that had plagued her for twenty years—what had happened to her father? Would she finally know?

As the tow truck driver had predicted, the car got caught on a large, sharp rock. "I told you!" he yelled, cursing again. But before he could shut down the winch, the rusty rear axle broke and the Cadillac continued to emerge, groaning as it climbed out of its watery grave.

Madeline's nails cut more deeply into her palms. The familiarity of that vehicle threw her back to her child-hood—as if someone had yanked her up by the shoulders and deposited her in the front seat. At age five or six she used to sit beside her mother while Eliza drove around town, visiting various members of her father's congregation, bringing food and comfort to the sick and needy.

Madeline had believed, back then, that her mother was an angel.

Squeezing her eyes shut, she pressed a hand to her forehead, trying to stave off the memories. She rarely allowed herself to think about Eliza. Her mother had been a gentle soul—she'd represented everything good to Madeline. But, as Madeline's father had pointed out so often after Eliza's suicide, she was also weak and fragile. Lee had had little that was positive to say about his first wife, but Madeline had never blamed him. She hadn't been able to forgive Eliza, either.

Clay's arm went around her shoulders, and she turned into his coat. She wasn't sure she could watch what was coming next.

"It's okay, Maddy," he murmured.

She took what comfort she could from his warm strength. He was capable of surviving anything. Secretly, she wished she was as tough. She also wished Kirk was here with her. They'd dated for nearly five years, but she'd broken off the relationship just a few weeks ago.

"That's it." Pontiff waved the divers out of the water as Rex towed the Cadillac onto stable ground.

This time when Rex stopped the winch, he turned off the truck's engine, too. Madeline felt Clay tense, so she forced herself to look and saw her cousins hurrying to the car.

Chief Pontiff sent her an anxious glance, adjusted the hat that was keeping the rain out of his face and intercepted them. "Give us some room," he said, barring them from getting too close.

Madeline was glad that Irene, Clay and Grace stayed put, or she would've been standing there alone. She didn't want to move any closer to that car. She had no idea what she might see and feared it would only fuel her nightmares. Every few weeks, she dreamed that her father was knocking on her front door in the middle of the night. He was always wearing a heavy coat that, when she answered, parted to reveal a skeleton.

Grace, a more refined, elegant version of Clay, took her hand and Irene edged closer. Clay stepped in front, but he seemed even more reserved than usual. No doubt he was thinking of his new wife and stepdaughter and how this might affect them. Since marrying Allie, he was happy at last. But for how long? The police were always quick to point a finger at him. Last summer they'd nearly put him on trial for her father's murder—without a body, without an eyewitness, without any forensic evidence at all. Unless there was something in the car that proved Clay *wasn't* involved, this could put him at risk again.

"Door's rusted shut," Pontiff said. "Get a crowbar."

Radcliffe, who was in his early twenties, returned to one of the police cars and produced the crowbar, which he carried to his chief.

As Pontiff began to pry open the door, the car complained loudly, ratcheting up the tension that made Madeline's muscles ache. Her heart lurched as the metal gave way and the water from inside came pouring out over everyone's shoes.

Pontiff didn't seem to notice. No one did. They were

all busy staring at the gush of water as if they expected parts of her father to come floating out along with it.

How could this be happening? she wondered. How could she have lost her mother *and* her father—in two separate incidents?

She didn't see anything, so she inched a little closer, straining her eyes for the smallest bit of clothing or—she grimaced—bone. At least, if her father's remains were in the car, she'd know he hadn't meant to leave her. She'd never been able to accept that he'd walked out on her. As the town's beloved pastor, he was a God-fearing man, always ready to help out in an emergency, always a leader. He would never abandon his flock, his farm, his family.

Which meant someone must have killed him. But who?

As the water seeped over the ground to the lip of the quarry, mixing with the runoff from the rain, Madeline clenched her jaw. Nothing macabre. Yet.

They were opening the trunk. The Cadillac's keys had been left dangling in the ignition, but the locks were corroded, so they were using the crowbar again.

Bile rose in Madeline's throat as the minutes stretched on. She tried to keep her mind busy. But what did one think about at a time like this? The teenage girl they'd buried on Wednesday? The miserable weather? The years she'd lived without her father?

Pontiff lifted something with one hand. "You recognize this?"

Belatedly, Madeline realized he was speaking to her and nodded. It was the Polaroid camera she'd seen her father use on various occasions. Seeing it, she felt a chill crawl down her spine. Finding his camera made him seem so close, but it didn't *tell* her anything.

"Is that all?" she asked around the lump in her throat.

The police chief pulled out some jumper cables, a couple of quarts of oil, a sopping blanket. Familiar items that could be found in any trunk.

He'll find something that'll finally reveal the truth. Madeline was praying so hard she almost couldn't believe it when she heard him say, "That's it."

"What?" she cried. "There's nothing that tells us where he went?"

Pontiff shrugged uncomfortably. "I'm afraid not."

She didn't move—felt absolutely rooted to the spot—as Clay wiped her tears with his thumb. "I'm sorry, Maddy."

Sorry didn't have any meaning. She'd been expecting so much more. It couldn't be over. If so, she was right back where she'd been before they discovered the car. Where she'd been all along—faced with the nagging mystery and the prospect that she might never know.

"There…" Her teeth chattered from her reaction to the situation as much as the cold. "There h-has to be…something else here," she said. "You'll…look, won't you? You'll…let the car dry out and…and go over it inch by inch?"

Chief Pontiff nodded, but she could tell he wasn't optimistic.

"Will you let Allie take a look?" Her sister-in-law had been a cold case detective in Chicago. Surely she'd find something.

With a grudging glance at Joe and Roger, Pontiff scowled. "You know I can't do that."

"Don't let the Vincellis dictate how you handle this," Madeline said. "She's the most…qu-qualified person around here."

"She's also married to the man who did it!" Joe shouted.

The cleft in Joe's chin was a little too deep to be attractive. Or maybe it was his close-set eyes that gave him a shifty air. He stood six feet tall and was almost as muscular as Clay, but Madeline had never found him good-looking. "Stop it," she murmured, but he talked right over her.

"Give me a break! Will you listen to yourself? Maddy, if you want to know what happened to your father, ask that man right there!"

He pointed at Clay, but wilted when Clay pinned him with a steely gaze. Not many men could stand up to Clay, and Joe was no exception. He shuffled back, muttering, "Tell 'em, Roger."

Joe's brother was even less handsome. His teeth were straighter, but he was thinner, a full three inches shorter, and had a severely receding hairline and a furtive gaze. Although he was the older brother, he typically remained in Joe's shadow. "It's true," he said weakly, as if he didn't really want to incite Clay.

Chief Pontiff ignored them both. He was well aware of the suspicions and accusations of the past. He'd been on the force when Clay's wife had first returned to town and begun following up on the Barker case. He'd been around when her father, the former chief of police, charged Clay with murder and put him in jail last summer. He'd also been around when they let Clay go because there wasn't, and never had been, any real evidence linking him to the crime.

"This car has been submerged for more than half our lives," Pontiff said, his attention on Madeline. "Look at it. Even the metal's begun to corrode. Much as I hate to say it, the Caddy might not tell us what we want to know. You need to prepare yourself, just in case."

"No!" She hugged herself to stop the shaking. "There could be a...a tooth, or a comb stuck way down between the seats. *Some* evidence, *s-s-ome* lead." She watched those forensics shows religiously, recorded them if she wasn't going to be home. She'd seen dozens of cases solved with the tiniest piece of evidence.

"We'll check, like I said, but..." His words dwindled away.

"Oh, Maddy," Grace said softly.

Madeline didn't respond to her stepsister. She wanted to calm down, for her family's sake. They didn't need the added angst of having her flip out. They'd been through a lot, too. At least no one had blamed *her* for her father's disappearance. But she couldn't seem to keep it together. Not this time. "Don't create an excuse before you even try," she said. "Find something. I want to know what happened. I *need* to know what happened." She grabbed Chief Pontiff's arm. *"Do your job!"*

Pontiff blinked in surprise, and Clay quickly pulled her into his arms. "Maddy, stop," he murmured against her hair.

If anyone else had asked her, she wouldn't have— *couldn't* have—gained control of her wayward emotions. But regardless of the turmoil inside her, she had too much respect for Clay to ignore his wishes or embarrass him further. Burying her face in his chest, she started to cry as she hadn't cried since she was a child, with big racking sobs that shook her whole body.

He hugged her close. "It's okay," he murmured. "It's okay."

"You're hugging the man who killed him," Joe whispered.

"Shut up, Joe," she snapped. Her stepbrother had been the one to keep their family safe through the dark years after her father was gone. At times, he'd been the only thing standing between them and absolute destitution.

"I'm sorry," she told Clay. She didn't want to draw attention to him. She knew he simply wanted to go on with his life and forget. She wished *she* could forget. But it was impossible. She'd tried.

"You have nothing to be sorry about," he said.

With a sniff, she pulled away and dashed a hand across her cheeks. "I'm going home."

"I'll call you if we find anything," Pontiff said.

Joe and his brother were still there, but one look from Clay kept them shuffling around the perimeter of the group like jackals attracted to a carcass. They obviously wanted to come closer, to say more, but were afraid to risk the consequences.

Madeline turned away. The police always said they'd keep digging, keep asking questions, go back through the files, whatever. But they never found anything solid. They didn't really care about the truth. They just wanted to pin it on the Montgomerys to satisfy the Vincellis, who carried political power in this town. Maybe Pontiff was a friend of sorts, but he was subject to the same political pressures as his predecessors and would probably follow in their footsteps. Nothing would change.

But Madeline couldn't accept "nothing" any longer.

She had to take more aggressive action, do something that would finally provide answers.

She was pretty sure what that something had to be. But her stepfamily wouldn't like it. And there was no guarantee it would work.